# Praise for *The Doomscroller's Companion*

"A vivid, sometimes lyrical portrayal of people finding that nature can rudely show us the difference between what we perceive to be important and what really matters. Dark and detailed with a note of hope for us all."
—Christopher Moore, *New York Times* best-selling author of *Lamb*

"If the end times are nigh, it's nice to have a writer as smart, funny, and trenchant as our guide. A terrific book by an unforgettable new writer."
—Dan Chaon, author of *One of Us*

"Wimmer has created a beautiful patchwork quilt of narrative modes to tell a layered story of what it means to be human in a time of species collapse—our own. Both harrowing and heartfelt."
—Lori Rader-Day, *USA Today* best-selling author of *Wreck Your Heart*

# THE DOOMSCROLLER'S COMPANION

WENDY WIMMER

THE UNIVERSITY OF WISCONSIN PRESS

Publication of this book has been made possible, in part,
through support from the Brittingham Trust.

The University of Wisconsin Press
728 State Street, Suite 443
Madison, Wisconsin 53706
uwpress.wisc.edu



Printed in the United States of America
This book may be available in a digital edition.

Library of Congress Cataloging-in-Publication Data

Names: Wimmer, Wendy, author
Title: The doomscroller's companion / Wendy Wimmer.
Description: Madison : The University of Wisconsin Press, 2026.
Identifiers: LCCN 2026026178 | ISBN 9780299360245 (paperback)
Subjects: LCGFT: Novels | Fiction
Classification: LCC PS3623.I5887 D66 2026
LC record available at https://lccn.loc.gov/2026026178

For Steven,
my very favorite person.

Also, for those who stay. The world is better with you in it.

# THE DOOMSCROLLER'S COMPANION

# Day 1

**Cosmoballiton**
**@CosmoNoFilter**

I don't want to party like it's 1999. I like my smartphone. I like having Netflix. For god's sake, Prince, why do you hate technology?

♡ 42 4 13

**Gemma**
**@Gemma1989**

I wish I were as thin as the first time I thought I was fat.

♡ 102 2 3

**WBAY**
**@wbaynews**

A new H3N2 outbreak in Africa could start spreading rapidly if not contained
http://read.bi/Zow2e

♡ 1.5K 97 182

**DB Cooper**
**@DBmm**

I woke 15 minutes early today and treated it like 2 extra hours and now I'm late for work.

♡ 41 💬 0 🔁 1

**Jesus Don't Live Here**
**@karl1952**

Breaking news: First confirmed US case of H3N2. bit.ly/rhWmW Been nice knowing you, folks.

♡ 6.3K 💬 41 🔁 506

**Wolf News WNBS** ✓
**@WNBSNews**

Explosion charges through Indiana mall food court, 9 confirmed dead, mass casualties

♡ 3.2K 💬 165 🔁 905

**Mychelle**
**@MightyMych**

Apparently, there's an H3N2 outbreak in South Korea now. If anyone needs me, I'll be spending the next few days on WebMD.

♡ 14 💬 7 🔁 1

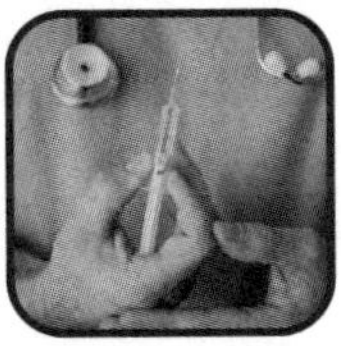

**World Medical News**
**@worldmednow**

Evidence suggests new H3N2 pathogen may have prion component—links to dementia and chronic insomnia

♡ 1.5K 💬 11 ⟳ 374

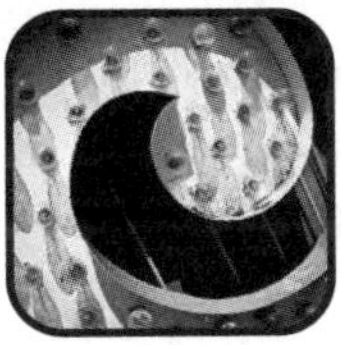

**Jane** ✓
**@erejane**

The joy of working remotely is taking a shower midday. The agony is realizing yes, you have to put the bra back on.

♡ 65 💬 23 ⟳ 43

## Jane

I know too much of wanting and the emptiness of not having, but there's something especially mortifying about seeing how little importance you have when measured in charts, graphs, and Google search rankings.

The world is losing interest in me. I can't really blame it.

My blog's August website traffic was in the toilet. September is already worse. No one reads anymore. My followers are after better serotonin bursts, thirty-second videos of tube biscuit recipes or lip-syncing, slick nineteen-year-old dancers with thigh gaps and insane flexibility, or moms wearing Chewbacca masks. Three affiliate programs dropped the site for underperformance, and judging by the raw traffic numbers in Q4, more deactivations will come. I've tried being in front of the camera already and if anything, it exacerbated the exodus from my intellectual property. No one wants to see a middle-aged face with marionette lines, begging the audience for likes, follows, shares, and comments.

Maybe the viewers sensed that I didn't love them. I only loved *for* them.

The magic influencer money lasted a lot longer than I would have thought. My stupid stories about my bizarre early dot-com job sustained my twenties.

People loved it. Then I quit the weird tech job and wrote about my adventures as an aging single girl, kind of a *Sex and the City* for less attractive people blended with the bizarre things I was trying out for new careers. People loved it more, hearing my witty rejoinders about working in a crematorium, inseminating a cow, spelunking in sewers. The time I job shadowed a dominatrix, the blog earned $100,000 in just a single week, just from everyone clicking on vibrator and stealth bondage gear affiliate links. Mad insane money.

But now? Posts that lured a million new monthly hits years ago only bring a few thousand. The game changes. My tricks to outrun it are running out. New search algorithms, new keyword phrases, new YouTube channels with billions of views on ten-second hilarious clips. Shiny young faces, invisible pores, symmetrical features, size 00, and strong vlogging game. So many things that I am not, could not, will never be.

In my hundreds of unread emails, I stop short and click. I almost miss it. It's the dream job I applied for but was declined months ago.

> From: Aaliyah.Jefferson@fws.gov
> Sent: Wednesday, Oct 01, 20xx 1:13 PM
> To: Jane@janeere.com
> Subject: Bloggers in the Field program
>
> Dear Jane Solveig,
>
> Happy news! You've been chosen for the Department of the Interior's Media Ambassadorship. This fifteen-month fellowship begins immediately and offers five two- or four-week residencies in a variety of United States Wildlife Refuges, with additional duties and smaller projects as available. Currently, this DOI grant offers $125,294 annual stipend, paid biweekly, as well as health, vision, and dental insurance; travel reimbursement, per diem; and potential for additional grant funding. It will be subject to next year's annual DOI budget for increase and renewal.
>
> This is extremely short notice, but your Ambassadorship depends on your ability to join us on the first leg of the program, beginning in three days at the Farallon Islands National Wildlife Refuge, as animal migration is happening there now. Future residencies have more flexibility . . .

Even reading through the requirements, my eyes flick back to the pay. The traffic estimator for the .gov websites estimates millions of pageviews. All that could feed into my own little blog. Traffic like crazy. First page on the Google searches for practically every post on the blog. I pick up the phone.

The Fish and Wildlife lady whoops after I say that I'll do it, I'm in, whatever. The vlogger originally slated for Ambassador has tested positive for that viral encephalitis going around so I'm second choice. Fine. I'm barely listening to her reassurances about medical precautions and bird flu. I give my TSA Known Traveler details and hang up. Then I open a chat window and ping Brian.

> JaneWithAWhy: Hey, looks like I'm getting that government gig after all! First project is a shark island! Cue the Jaws soundtrack.

Yikes. In two days, I'll be with a bunch of strangers, living with them, sharing kitchen facilities and bathrooms. Four weeks. I bite my lip. Meeting new people is always the same, a sensation of falling, the rigid impossibility of sleeping in a room next to a stranger, the way even the air in the rooms smells too much like otherness. This is something I've spent my entire life doing and undoing.

But I'm good at this. I've learned to adapt, pick up their unspoken social cues, sense private jokes lurking, slot myself into the pecking order. My survival has depended upon blending in, going all the way back to the first time that social worker dropped me off at *your new family, honey* with a black Hefty bag containing a few outgrown pieces of clothing and only one sock. After that, and the next one, and the next one after, blending, I became them. I had to. I still must.

They outnumber me.

It's so natural now that I barely notice how my voice modifies, slides into lower or higher registers, saying words differently than I did before, how my face bends itself to match microexpressions. Today is nothing different. This Is Your New Family Honey, only I've opted in, a professional foster adult.

I know how to do this, but it doesn't mean I have to like it.

The activity monitor says Brian's online, but he's not responding. I wait, chewing the corner of my thumb. His reaction will be worth it. It doesn't come fast enough, so I climb over a laundry basket, two boxes marked "Important," and a broken floor fan, all things Aunt Heidi has shoved into my room over the summer months, when I hide away at my seasonal cottage up the Bayshore. At least my room is no longer a third cat box location.

"Hey?" I knock on Heidi's door, which is open. I always make a big show of respecting privacy, hoping she'll pick up a clue.

Photographs are spread on her bed. The beaming faces of my dead grandmother and dead mother shine up from the glossy photos, upside down, looking like gargoyles. Heidi loves these old photos, as though she can believe the iconography of happy birthday parties and loving holidays. *Smile for the camera*, I can still hear my mother slur, *smile, goddamnit, or I'll give you something to frown about* and a click and then the draw of a cigarette from my grandmother's side of the table, followed by the wet sound she'd make whenever her daughters displeased her.

How does Heidi stand it? And does she know that her own face, in certain angles, captures essences of her dead mother and her sister—my dead mother—like brief superimposed nightmares? My grandmother's nose announcing that it could smell lies, my mother's eyebrow arch, an early warning that I should run and hide. It must be why Heidi's house contains only a single mirror, part of a sparse vintage medicine cabinet that hangs above the bathroom sink.

When she sits like this, it's like she's the teenager I remember looking up to as a child, instead of the menopausal maiden aunt she has turned into, with cheater glasses and a thicket of frown lines. Heidi looks up and smiles. "Oh, Jane, do you remember this day? We went to that park over by the Bay. Remember that? Playing at the beach? Look at you in your little hat!"

I remember it. My mom and her boyfriend smelling sour, swearing. I remember my sunburn turned into blisters. I remember being slapped for crying when it hurt, and the blisters popping that night in bed, leaving wet gluey sheets, and an accusation that I peed myself and being slapped again, right on the burned skin. *Remember that.*

I nod. "Yes, that was a fun day." Heidi needs me to say it and I do. She gets to reframe her own memories of our history.

She nods and smiles, dark hair falling over her face. Her expression changes briefly, as though she's snagged a memory, and then she tucks it back away. "You loved playing in the water."

"Speaking of that," I say, changing the subject. "It looks like I'm going to need to go to California in a few days. There's a thing with a wildlife refuge. Pacific Ocean stuff."

She stops stacking photos and looks up. "Er, do you think you should be traveling? The flu thing?"

"That's in Ukraine." The first case was confirmed two days ago in the US, but Heidi doesn't follow the news very closely.

Heidi returns a skeptical look. "Mary across the street is sick too. And her son and his wife. Says she hasn't slept in a week. She's probably exaggerating."

"I'll wash my hands a lot in the airports. I'm careful when I travel. I have hand sanitizer. I pee with my female urinal thing. Besides, the government is paying the bill for this one, plus they're going to link to my own page. So, you know, traffic."

She whirls a finger in the air. "Yes, traffic. Hit counts. Clicks. I still don't understand how that works, but if they're going to give you a job, I guess it's a good idea? Will you get insurance from this one?" She purses her mouth sideways, a gesture I also do. Did she get it from me, or did I get it from her? Or did we both get it from one of our dead family members?

"Not exactly a job right now." Is it even worth explaining? Yet I can't stop myself from wheedling. "It's a contract, they're paying me for it and there's a lot of balls in the air that will help my site, but it sounds like it will lead to bigger things. Someone bailed so they called me, plus there's another thing coming up with NBC in December that I *think* is still on, which should really help because that's my big month for affiliate link revenues. All that SEO work pays off. And there's a bigger Department of the Interior project coming up. They passed that big DNR bill last year and there's all sorts of public relations money about to open in January. They said this is essentially an audition for that. And that means?"

"Health insurance?"

"Yup, health insurance, retirement, pension, trips to DC, and probably lots of national parks and wildlife refuges too. First, it's California, and then after that, Florida in December, and then Louisiana right before Mardi Gras. A bit of security. Adult stuff. So, you know, big deal. Lots riding on this. Besides, every time I go anywhere, my site traffic, like, quintuples, boom."

That was true. But five times not much still wasn't much. With cross-listed blog posts between the US government sites, the blog's search authority ranking would go through the roof. It would also be a relief to get out of Heidi's house.

In my heart, hope. In my head, a ringing peal from one of the comments left on the blog: "How long is this bitch going to play dress-up in other occupations? Shouldn't she have figured her shit out by now?"

From my bedroom, the IM window pings. The comfort of the laptop tugs me from Heidi's haphazard mentoring attempts, mostly gleaned from

’70s sitcoms after school rather than from example. Heidi’s eleven years older than me. She liked to say that she and I were Whoops Babies—on opposite ends of the spectrum, her sister too young and her mother too old. Whoops, accidental children. Whoops, they forgot what to do with them. Whoops!

“Too bad, you only just got settled again. I never meet any of your friends. What about Tabitha and two-name girl? Mary-Ashley? Too bad you don’t have any friends around here.”

“Brian. He’s from around here.” I hate thinking about Tabby and Ash. Two sides of the same coin. The laptop pings again, as though he knows I’m talking about him.

“That pottery guy in Appleton?”

“Brian Arden. He’s on the road a lot. I’ll be in San Francisco after the island thing and Brian has an art opening there, so we’re probably going to meet up.”

It will never happen. It’s an easy lie that will never be caught.

“When can I meet that guy?” She thinks we’re more than friends.

“I don’t know. Soon. We’ve both got busy schedules. We mostly have an e-lationship, although he hates that term. That’s him right now, though. That ding. I better get that.”

Let her think Brian’s my boyfriend. It’s better than the weird reality. I slink out of her doorway and climb over the barricade of her domestic castoffs, back onto the calm island of my pink quilt, inside a dark tiny burrow of the worst bedroom in the house, one meant for the youngest child with the least leverage, appropriate in my case.

Small spaces feel safe, forgotten. They feel right.

The IM window is blinking with responses from Brian.

OTTERYRIDE: Your quest to reenact the “Part of Your World” song from The Little Mermaid is one step closer to realization.

OTTERYRIDE: Did you know that the mechanical shark from Jaws didn’t work right, so it forced Spielberg to shoot around it and be creative?

OTTERYRIDE: Meanwhile, can you imagine if you saw this stupid gimmicky shark in the beginning?

OTTERYRIDE: It would have made Godzilla movies look like SFX feats of wonder. What a lucky break.

OTTERYRIDE: Actually, I hate that guy.

OTTERYRIDE: Fuck that guy.

I should tell him about our overlap in San Francisco, but I don't. It's too much pressure. Too much stress. Too much everything. To be in actual physical space with him at the same time after so long.

No one could live up to the persona I've created. Jane 'Ere is a goofy best friend that millions of people Like and Share. People rarely Like the real me.

Tabby taught me that. I learned it again with Ash. With Knox. With Patrick. Disappointment flickering on Brian's face after so many years. He'd try to hide it, but I'd see.

I depend upon his foggy memory, a girl in San Francisco so long ago, a stranger who didn't matter. Instead, I volley, using the language Brian loves best.

JaneWithAWhy: 

Three dots as he writes, pauses, writes, pauses, and writes again. Then his reply.

OtteryRide: Well done, mademoiselle, well done.

OtteryRide: See, it really does work better if you hide the shark until later.

# Day 2

**Renob**
**@renobgib**

Today I heard the edgy music I used to play to piss off my mom playing as background music at Target.

39 7 9

**Susie**
**@SuzeeeeQ**

You know you have bad insomnia when even the show on Discovery about how they make cheese doesn't put you to sleep.

170 8 6

**Xi**
**@sXlilate**

I donned a scarf in effort to feel jaunty or dare I say more like Audrey Hepburn. Instead, it has made me sweaty

86 12 2

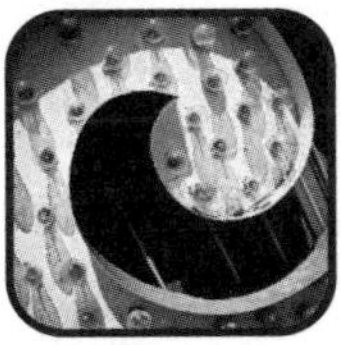

**Jane**
**@erejane**

Light is hitting your body right now at over 100K miles per second and it doesn't even tickle. We are super humans.

75.5K 19 6.4K

# Day 3

### Jane

This will be easy. First, I get on a boat. Then I contemplate my life. What could it take, the slipping overboard, the cold, the dark, the loneliest little starfish at the bottom of the shipping lane. I think about how I'll describe this boat, the best value for Google's appetite, the best boost to organic search traffic, what gets the most eyes, the most unique readers, the most most. It's never been about me.

When the DOI thing came up, shark attacks attracted me the most. Blood. Gore. Carnage. Click click click. I never thought I'd get in, never thought I'd be *lucky* enough to land such a plum opportunity. Lucky. Now I see the islands—SEFI is the one I'll be staying on, short for Southeast Farallon Island—and I wonder about my luck. The islands are godforsaken in that God himself forsook this place. It's hell on a slice of ocean, sitting above a nuclear waste facility, surrounded by twenty-five-foot-long sharks, deadly jellyfish, and decay.

The guy is wearing a $200 windbreaker and has a $40 water bottle. The walking sports model is there to ferry me from the first boat to the godforsaken island where I will plant my flag, devise blog fodder for its best and most captivating narrative, take roughly 3,020 photos to load into a $2,700 software program to make ultra-bright, ultra-rich, ultra-sharp, ultra-saturated, and ultra-beautiful, until I'm not even sure I witnessed this through a flat glass eye, was I even here, did I even see these things?

It doesn't matter. The readers matter. Or their browser sessions matter, clicks, views, endless hunger for new content to appease the site-indexing angry gods. I should grab the camera and snap action shots, sexy sporty Omar with his REI wardrobe as he positions the little boat under the crane, where the sea bit a large crevice into the rock, creating a narrow peninsula, beautiful, framing it.

This is what I do, this is what I do now, this is who I am. A tape recorder made of meat and bone and anxiety.

He smiles at me, not meaning it. "Ready to take a ride up in the swing?"

"Oh, we're going up? I didn't realize it went up too." I say this as though I'm smart. I want to be friendly, so I say things that make me sound stupid. This is how it works. This is who I am.

"This is shitsville for boaters. No dock survives the pounding out here. See those jagged cliffs? Not exactly beach material, you know? Not that any fucker would be crazy enough to dip a toe in these waters. Get it bitten off."

Omar's hair is a mop of dark curls, but the hairs on his forearms and knuckles are bleached blond. He looks older, his skin pebbled and showing signs of age, but chances are that he thought sunscreen was for pussies. He'd be the type to use that term—*pussies*—as though nothing worse than aligning with female genitalia. I shoot myself a mental punch. Snap judgments aren't fair to Omar, who is beautiful, and you're supposed to be nicer to beautiful people, it's a rule everyone understands. That is also how it works. He has been told to welcome and suck up to the new girl, the blogger who is supposed to make people care about conservation, people who weren't already granola-hugging tree crunchers. However, he thinks I'm an imbecile, that I might get myself killed by doing something girly and inane.

And I might.

"Yeah, white sharks, I know."

His spine stiffens, shoulders square, preparing to do a lecture. Lecturizing. Lecturium. I've seen the posture a million times and this observation is a fulfilled prophecy. So sayeth me.

"Sure, white sharks. Blue sharks. Mako sharks. Tiger sharks. All sorts of tropical sharks even though this water is usually a lot colder. Saw a hammerhead shark a few months ago, and usually they only hang out in places you'd go on vacation. Global warming means this is Sharkville and the Farallones are their twenty-four-hour buffet. Whites are only here about eight weeks, if that, but the rest of the tribe? All year. Of course, the basking shark is one of the most beautiful, but it doesn't exactly get Discovery Channel press, so who cares? Hey, hand me those cables there?"

The cables are heavy, clogged, and tangled with all manner of ocean muck, dried and scaly, filthy, and smelling of fish and grease and ancient mariner rimes. Typing and laptop toting hasn't prepared my fingers for the abuse of the next four weeks; already the cable scrapes across the left knuckles turn rosy, shredding skin.

The waves crash against the limestone ledge, shoving the inflatable boat closer to the cliff. I catch myself on a box of groceries, partially crushing it in the process. Probably killed the expensive blackberries they'd had me procure the day before. Omar adjusts his balance, sneaks a look back, and moves his mouth tighter as though my unease has confirmed his suspicion. *Worthless. Crap. Outsider.* In my brain, my dead mother's voice. He hums as he clips each cable to a central rigging and snaps it into place on the crane's hook.

"OK, so the obvious thing here is that this isn't *dangerous*." He stresses the last word, his eyebrows rising over the rims of his $230 polarized adventure man sunglasses. "BUT! It's not super safe either. He can't drop us or anything, and even if he did, it's OK because we're *already in a boat*!" Omar flashes impressively white teeth, as though we're both in on the joke. Omar's personal grooming routines fill my brain like an old-school MTV video—he seems the type to slap cologne on his ass cheeks and buy moisturizers from mall kiosks. Again, I'm being unkind and instantly regret it. *Live a better life, Jane*, I think, drowning out my mother's voice. *Embrace kindness.*

"The most dangerous things are the cables. Don't get your hands anywhere near this cable. It doesn't look sharp, but it's an asshole. The fibers'll cut you. Also, it likes to grab hair and shirts and stuff like that, so don't grab on. It's the thing pulling us up but resist that urge and grab onto one of the action boxes or the side of the boat or the seat or me, whatever. OK? And don't move around. You can pitch over the side. It's not obvious right now, but we're in a little bit of water covering rocks, so you'd, like, land on sharp rocks. That wouldn't be good."

A fly lands on Omar's face. He doesn't bother waving it away. The tough-guy routine, impressive. The boat starts swinging sideways, and I do reach to grab the cables but stop, motivated by the revulsion of proving Omar right.

The crane operator sets the boat down gently on land and Omar grabs a plastic grocery crate and hops out of the boat. The ground feels alive, moving, and unstable, a rejection of my weight on the stones after so many hours on water. My legs quiver. I lunge forward but steady myself on the side of a rock, crumbly with bird shit. It's almost volcanic, punctuated with little bits of greenery here and there. A wave of pure ammonia hits my nostrils with new fervor, as though my poor life decisions have unfolded and taken gaseous form, tendrils uncurling for a quiet embrace.

"Jane? Hey, I'm Rick." The crane operator ambles over, extending a hand, and takes off his sunglasses to make eye contact. His eyes are the piercing vibrant green of a Reduce Reuse Recycle logo. His jaw paired with the cheekbones are the formula for a classic character actor, the kind who is young as a story of the week on *Love Boat* reruns and then looks distinct but less romantic in the story of the week during the *Law & Order* marathon. "I'm a DNR staffer. Good to meet you. Trip good?"

I think he means my fall out of the boat, but he doesn't, he means the ride from the mainland.

"Uh, it was great! Good, I guess, I mean. It's a gorgeous trip." I'm being sarcastic but change my facial expression to earnest, probably a little too late. Flies hover everywhere. I flag one away, only to have a second one land on my hand. I jerk and it flies off, but another one settles on my arm. *Don't insult their home, idiot, don't insult their home.*

He gives my hand a perfunctory one-two pump, without doing that little girl handshake that guys sometimes give women. I like that already. Rick looks back at the island landscape—the sheer horror movie set full of foreboding—and smiles. "Yeah, we like it too."

His teeth are unnaturally white, even whiter than Omar's teeth. Is there something in the water here? Off the shore, my ride heads back to the city. *Come back, don't leave me here.*

Rick bounces on the tips of his toes, his eyes never leaving the water line. "Your partner got sick. Bad flu, huh?"

This is small talk. I don't have a partner—love partner, work partner, or otherwise. I'm a solo act. This is small talk, but I oblige. "Yeah, I mean, I didn't know him, or her, I guess. But the office said they got sick, and their partner is sick. I'm sure it's bad timing."

My small talk is too small.

"Hey, I'm sure the program office covered this, but are you a vegan?"

"Nope. Is that OK? I mean, I'm happy to eat vegetarian. I eat pretty much anything. Vegan's OK, I mean. Vegan's great." *Stop talking. Stop talking.*

Rick leans back and claps his hands, the sound muffles against the crashing of a particularly large group of waves below us. "Thank God. The other blogger was a vegan." He shouts to be heard over a big swell crashing and smashing against the rocky cliffs.

"You didn't want a vegan?" My voice is stupid. Small talk shouldn't be shouted. Inanity at loud decibels seems even more stupid. My voice even sounds unnatural. *Vegan.* Did I pronounce that word right? It comes out of my mouth almost too scientific a word, like trying to say an exotic name and not being sure I heard correctly. *Veeegn.* Does it rhyme with *begin* or *begging*? I've said this word a million times but now I'm not sure.

"I don't give a shit if you eat nothing but apricots." Rick claps my shoulder, his gaze jumping back and forth in the general vicinity of my face and then back out to sea. I smile and he winks. A large black fly settles on his face.

"Oh, you have a fly." I reach up to brush it off his cheek, awkward for taking such casualness. "Sorry, I didn't mean to touch you, I didn't think you'd want a fly on you." I shove the guilty hand into the front pocket of my jeans. *Begin. Begging. Begin begging.*

"Man, newbies are so cute. You're adorable." Rick laughs and chucks me under the chin like I'm four years old. "Well, that's not going to last." He nods toward the freshly stacked food crates, already speckled with dozens of black flies.

"They don't bite. They crawl all over you and have sex on you and disgust you, but they don't bite," Omar offers. Two flies dance on his fancy sunglass lenses.

"You'll soon learn that we have no delicacy when it comes to biological functions. But he's right. They don't bite. And they are everywhere," Rick says to the ocean.

A man and a woman approach along a concrete walkway, struggling with a battered clattery metal cart.

"Liz, Patty, I'd like you to meet Jane. She's going to be with us for four weeks helping with the Farallonathon."

*Help*, he says. Like what I do will be *helping*. I'm eyeballs. I'm just a megaphone. I'm bait for an audience that wouldn't otherwise care about dirty smelly islands and weird, not-especially-photogenic seabirds, an audience more concerned with their eight-dollar cold brew sustainably collected free-trade coffee because it says so on the cardboard sleeve, held so that the brand faces out into the world.

I'm not sure which one is Liz or Patty so I shake the woman's hand and mumble, "Hi. Hi." Her hand is soft, damp, an uncooked boneless chicken breast.

"Four weeks!? Shucks, that's nothing." The lady has colored her hair at one point, but three inches of gray-and-mousey-brown roots don't match the auburn rest of her hair. Her face is jowly and her bra is no match for the pendulous breasts that rest atop her belly. Her giant glasses combined with her short round torso give her the appearance of a large daytime owl. *How many licks to get to the center of a Tootsie Pop*, I want to ask her. As though she anticipates this joke, she smiles with crooked yellow teeth. I press my own lips together closed in a tight smile. How long have I not been thinking about my teeth? How could I not ever be thinking about my teeth?

The guy clears his throat. "Nice to meet you." His hand is massive and hot, the tips of his fingertips brush the inside of my wrist, leaving an impression, a zither of energy that burrows down into my wristbones. He's tall and solid, the kind guarding a door at a nightclub. He doesn't wear sunglasses. His hazel eyes look kind and don't match what I presume about tall beefy guys. He then hefts two boxes at once—each one weighing no less than sixty pounds.

Rick struggles with the antique cart. Hipsters on the mainland would pay top dollar for it to showcase their flatscreen TVs and vinyl record collections, even with the bird shit. I make a mental note to photograph it, macro lens. Maybe in black and white with lots of vignette-ing. Find dupes, simulacrum, at West Elm and Room & Board, for affiliate links so I make money off each click and hate the constant cash register that runs inside my brain.

Survival. If I wanna eat I gotta work. Just like these birds. Just like those sharks. Without my income, the family fishing cottage gets scrapped and replaced by a fourth garage stall for the rich Chicago weekenders next door. If the ancient seawall doesn't get fixed soon, the winter storms will wash our little relic into Lake Michigan. It's not much, but that's our only family history left.

And I need health insurance.

Aunt Heidi needs the help too, even though she'd never admit it. She can't keep her house on unemployment checks alone, and those will run out soon enough. She's willing to take my coin because she doesn't believe blogging is real, like I've unlocked cosmic trickery. The truth is worse, an incantation I whisper into the internet, a selling of my soul to an algorithm devil tucked inside HTML.

"Liz, give her the rules and a quick tour?" Rick says from behind the beautiful behemoth.

The woman takes a sharp intake of breath. "A tour? Sure, but let's hit the rules first, since that's the most important."

Ah, she's Liz then. Patty must be short for Patrick. I wince thinking of my Patrick. Except he's not *my* Patrick anymore.

"First—this one is important—only walk on a path. I'm sure the Fish and Wildlife folks explained during orientation, but we can't destroy nesting sites." She waves her hands elaborately toward the verge, shiny and damp, scattered with twigs, shells, and bones.

"I didn't really get much of an orientation. I only flew in yesterday."

"She's a replacement," Rick reminds her. *A replacement.* Yes. That's what I always have been. Replacing. He speaks the truth.

"Oh yes, that's right, I knew that. The other blogger came down with flu? Their loss is our gain! If I remember right, you're a big deal."

Not me. Me the URL. Never me. But I appreciate that she has boiled down my value within seconds of meeting. My shoes are wet through to the socks, toes cold. When did my shoes get wet?

"I know the program office wants you to cover the shark program, but there's other great things happening on the island year-round. Our birds. Pelagic studies. Amphibians. Lots of great exciting predation other than sharks. Unusual species here right now." Liz smiles briefly with lips pressed together, breathing hard through her nostrils.

"That's good!" I think of breaking news, exclusive blog content.

Liz presses her lips together. "Not good, no. We're in the middle of a bird population shift. It started about fifty years ago, but since 2011 or thereabouts the birds started really declining. Well, changing. Anyway, there's a magnitude of loss in certain bird populations, while birds like raptors and Canada geese are in population explosion. Anyway, lots of exciting changes to observe here in birds on the Farallones."

"Are birds nesting in October? I thought that's a spring or summer thing?"

"Oh, it is, but birds still sleep in nests without chicks. Plus, the migrant birds come back to the same nests year to year. Even if you can't see the nest, you might be walking on one. Birds are burrowers. As you see, the island's rocks aren't exactly the most stable surface in the world and you'll cave in a burrow if you step off the path."

"Easy to break an ankle that way, if anything," Omar says, piping up from the rear of the cart.

"Right. That's really the main thing," Liz continues. "We can't rush anyone to the emergency room here, so it's better to only stick to places where other people have walked before. Anything paved is fair game, of course. This big field, by the way, is where we collect our water."

She points at a cement strip, caked with white bird shit, and dotted with nests and both dead and live birds, gray-and-black fluff bumps. The living ones swivel their heads and focus on me, the obvious replacement and odd man out.

"It's stored in those tanks over there, piped to the houses." Liz motions to an unobtrusive pipe that runs along the side of the raised walkway. "Don't kick it or anything. This is a corrosive environment. Metal doesn't do well."

"That died recently." I point to a pile of feathers lying next to the pipe. The bird's beak is as yellow as a school bus, frozen open in a silent rebuttal, a tiny bit of blood leaking out of its mouth. Its dull eyeball is set off amid a snowy field of white feathers. More blood is spattered across the pavement, as though it has suffered a drive-by shooting over a turf war between two avian gang lords.

"We got that one already. This morning." The beefer named Patty passes by, carrying my backpack, laptop bag, and duffel bag. Chivalry!

"OK, good! You're already catching on!" Liz claps her hands. "Yes. We monitor and log every dead bird that we find on the island, noting the species, presumed cause of death, and location. And age, if you know how to do that, but until then, find Patty or Omar and make sure they know about it." She nudges the body out of its ossuary against the pipe. Its head pitches. The gray feathers are so dark they're almost blue, the color of midnight, of old-fashioned chalkboards. The body shifts, revealing two reedy pink legs with tiny claws at each toe, impossibly small and delicate.

"See how this one has the feathers cut? Someone logged it. That's how you tell if you need to care about it or not."

She toes at the wing and the entire body responds to the insult, lolling. Liz should be teaching kindergarten. *Class, see the dead bird? Can you say "dead bird"?*

I nod because I'm supposed to nod. "If a dead bird's feathers aren't cut, I let one of you know, check."

"In the beginning, yup," Rick says, "but after a few days, we'll teach you how to log them too. It's not as tough as it sounds. You'll get used to it . . . or you won't." Rick shrugs and jerks the cart harder. The cart squeals in response.

"Keep a pair of good gloves whenever outside." Liz turns around and waggles a broad backside, a pair of dirty men's leather gloves waving hello from her back pocket, then eyes the carcass. "PIH, Patty?" She calls out to the muscly guy, already halfway to the house.

"Yup, PIH, probably a gull," he shouts back over his shoulder.

“What’s PIH?”

“Pecked in head.”

I smile at this joke, but no one smiles back.

“Pecked in head,” I repeat. My voice still sounds weird. Liz kicks the tern off the path and continues up the way, the gloves in her back pocket fingering me as an imposter and a fraud. *Begin. Begin. Begin.*

# Day 3

**Mychelle**
**@MightyMych**

I've stopped arguing with people who say we're overreacting about this outbreak. COVID was once in a lifetime, they say. They're going to figure out in a month or so that it's serious.

♡ 45 15 2

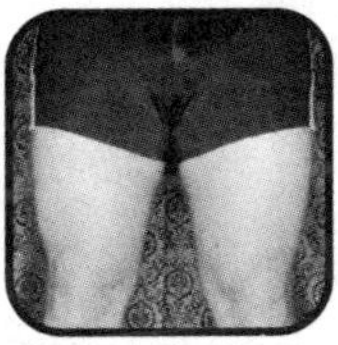

**JeSsBieU**
**@Jessbieu**

Attention pumpkin lovers—hie thee to Trader Joe's and pick up its Pumpkin Spice pancake and waffle mix. It makes the world's best pancakes and also, pumpkin-y!

♡ 1.9K 0 253

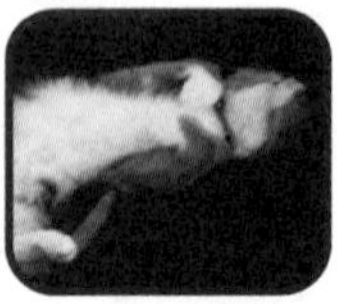

**Go To Sleep**
**@Insomnia**

Sleep deprivation will kill you more quickly than food deprivation.

♡ 387 2.3K 11.8K

**DB Cooper**
**@DBmm**

You know what would be cool? If my anxiety about getting sick would stop actually impairing my ability to do the things I need to do so that I don't get sick. That would be great.

♡ 102 8 3

**Xi**
**@sXlilate**

How can I already have had two lattes this morning? It feels exactly like I had zero lattes. Did not sleep well at all last night.

♡ 219 3 40

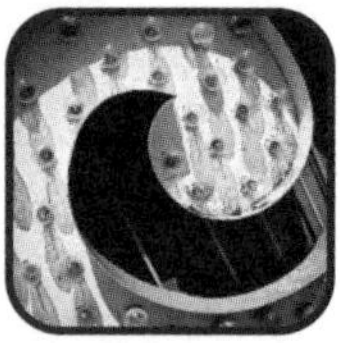

**Jane**
**@erejane**

Sometimes I envy whales, for I too occasionally open my mouth and am all "bloooooop blorp blooooeeeeee?" but they make it sound beautiful.

♡ 16K 85 1.5K

# Day 3

JANE

More bird bodies in various stages of decay. My eyeballs try to make sense of the bird shape in a jumbled jigsaw puzzle. A twig looks like a foot, a foot looks like a twig, a wing without a body, a beak disguised as a leaf, shattered into splinters, tiny bones and skeletons, complicated and intricate, like antique lace the color of dust.

Liz keeps reciting island facts, using the same language I've already read in the handbook. Her voice drones like a foghorn over the heckling seagulls.

"That building over by Maintop? Our power building. It's got solar cells. We're almost completely off the grid here, thanks to those solar panels, and inside, there are a bunch of batteries storing the power for watching TV. The guano renders the solar less efficient." She turns around and grins. "Elbow grease. They run on sun and elbow grease." Her smile holds a wicked sense of pleasure behind it, as though she's delighted by the Victorian-ness of the island.

Two weathered houses, the paint chipping and peeling, the silver wood almost the same color as the dirty white. Identical diptychs from the 1890s looking out of place, Dorothy's house dropped into Oz on top of a wicked witch, standing side by side, accusing the flat ocean, an audience of two.

"That's the Coast Guard house. It's theirs when they're here, which is pretty rare, but otherwise, we use it as overflow. Even though they're DNR, Rick and Pedro moved over to free up space in our house so you wouldn't get stuck over there by yourself as the fresh blood on the island. That's where the best TV is, though, and all the movies are over there, so we congregate there on light duty days."

Ahead on the crumbly weed-covered field lies a shiny speed bump. Brown and speckled, it bleats loud guttural moans, the skin flexing and sending off a flurry of black flies.

"And THAT is our other rule." Liz continues unabated, wiping a sweaty flop of bangs out of her eyes. "That is an elephant seal bull. Best to stay away. They won't hurt you most of the time, but it's mating season right now, so they get weird. The cows, though, you go right up to them unless they have a pup, which they won't for a few months."

Liz kicks another bird corpse. A fluff of agony, for an instant frozen in relief, appearing to give flight, temporarily reanimated, but then gravity. Fucking gravity.

"Pacific golden-plover!" Patty grunts over his shoulder.

"Mark it, Liz?" Rick says, putting his weight into the creaking cart.

Liz flexes her neck and turns short, reaching back for her gloves. "We should have her do it while we're all here to show her." She holds out her gloves. Before I decide how to take them, how I'll apologize to this bird, with a thin teardrop-shaped head and a scattered speckled white plumage, its tiny dark beak and fashion model legs stuck up in rigor mortis, Rick stops the cart and turns to give Liz a warning glance. "Let the kid unpack first, eh?" Without waiting for Liz's reply, Rick pushes the cart, grunting.

Liz gloves up and grasps the legs like handles, like chicken drumsticks. They ARE bird drumsticks. Perhaps I'll never be hungry again. The wings fall forward, the takeoff in flight, what was not and will never be again.

"Plover, right. Can't see anything obvious here." She sets it down, gingerly this time.

"Then bring 'er back to the house and I'll take a look as soon as this cart and Jane are settled?" Rick phrases it like a question, but it's not a question.

Liz exhales through her nose, picks up the stiff little creature by its twiggy legs, then toe-steps through the rocks back onto the path. The elephant seal toots a loud wet sound akin to a Marx brothers fart joke. *BLAT!*

The cart stops at the second house and Omar clips on the front brakes. "You like this cart? It's, like, sixty years old. We have a newer one, but this one is the shit." Omar pats the old metal.

"And this is your new home for the next twenty-eight days!" Liz says brightly from behind. Her dead bird glares with one black eye. "This is the program house. Four bedrooms, two baths, and one of the best-stocked kitchens this side of San Francisco!"

Rick and Omar say in unison, "It's the ONLY kitchen this side of San Francisco!" They all look expectant, so I smile obediently. Unlike "pecked in head," this is a joke they must find funny, the dad joke of the island. Through the front door is a small vestibule, filled with cubicles and coatracks.

"OK, another rule," Liz says, continuing her lecture. "Outside shoes stop here. Shoes must be always worn on the ground floors, so do you have another pair in your bags?"

I nod. I paid attention. I'm no rule breaker. I've brought many shoes. I've done well. My wet shoes are even more squeaky in the vestibule.

"Great, put them on and then go inside." Liz kicks off her boots and slips into a gray, well-beaten pair of hard-soled house slippers, the dead plover swinging from her gloved hand like a handbell. I dig through my pack and slip on a pair of gym shoes I envisioned using for morning jogs on the island seashore, which, judging by the habitat, is pointless.

Liz grabs a plastic bin off a bookshelf, causing a small avalanche of notes and receipts to drift to the floor. She regards the drift of paper and leaves it, placing the bird into a makeshift coffin and throwing it toward another desk, a tumbleweed of work in progress. She leads down the hall, weaving past long-handled fishing nets on shaker pegs to a modern kitchen with a beautiful restaurant-quality gas stove that seems out of place, gleaming and cold stainless steel, the last beacon of civilization.

The dad joke pays off.

The men finish swapping shoes, some of them into identical but clean pairs of work boots. Liz assigns me the job of uncrating and placing groceries on the table. It seems like a task you'd give a small child, but I don't know where anything goes, so I'm less valuable than a small child. Omar is conscripted into grocery service by Liz as well. He studies each item, reading the labels thoughtfully, while Liz chatters on, her voice rising and falling in nonsensical patterns. She's not matching her inflection with what she's saying, making it difficult to follow. I'm not sure if she's talking to me or Omar or no one.

She flips from island mechanics to editorializing in the same breath. "So, the thing about SEFI is we don't have creature comforts. I mean, don't get me wrong, we could be out here in tents battling fifty-knot winds, but the reality drains. Food keeps us grounded. Plus, so much sea air! You're not going to believe how much you eat out here."

"You're the island chef?" The kitchen is well stocked. On a high shelf, scores of cookbooks, some with disintegrated spines.

"We take turns. Whoever cooks gets off for their afternoon duties. That's how serious it is. And tonight? I'm making stuffed peppers, dolma, and berry crisp for dessert." It seems criminal to waste the fancy Petaluma market blackberries on a crisp, their beautiful drupelets bursting in the oven. I want to tell her how British folklore warns blackberries shouldn't be picked after Michaelmas Day, two weeks prior, because the old wives' tale believes the devil spit on them. Except it's probably *Botrytis*, the same fungus that makes the best dessert wines, a fact gleaned from a Life List project in Burgundy during harvest season. An interesting bit of trivia, but perhaps not interesting to anyone but me, and she'll think I'm dissuading her from using blackberries, she'll think I'm being contrary or showing off. I say nothing, like Omar, who views each box with wonder and scholarly reflection.

After we've unpacked, Liz goes quiet, her brows furrowed. Omar nudges me and tilts his head toward the door. "OK, put your stuff upstairs. You're in the Jane room, which is second door on the left. Why don't you get settled and changed into appropriate field gear. You brought a good jacket and a hat, right?"

I did bring a good jacket—or what I thought was good, but now, after seeing the elements of the Farallones, I'm not sure my gear is good enough—everyone here is prepped to climb Mount Everest.

At the top of the stairs is an open lounge space used as a sleeping area cordoned off by a blanket over a clothesline, behind it a twin bed, unmade, and a slew of bird identification books and dirty clothes. Down the hall, the first door on the left is closed. The second door on the left is mine.

I'm pleased they have named my room "Jane," but I find two twin beds, one obviously occupied by another woman, judging by the hairbrush and lip gloss sitting on the bedside table. With some dread, I consider sharing a room with Liz for four weeks. However, the pair of dirty jeans thrown across a rocking chair are too small for Liz's solid round self. The room's closet contains two purple storage bins stacked on the floor and no clothing. I stow three pairs of jeans and two pairs of yoga pants in a dresser drawer, removing small gray feathers from the margins, then open another drawer, containing another wispy feather, and lay a big woolly sweater and ten pairs of underpants inside. I leave two dresses in my bag. I don't want anyone to think I'd hoped for cocktail hour or fancy dinner parties on SEFI.

The boat ride settled a fine film of grit and salt into my pores, so I wash until I'm scoured, Lord Nelson returning from afar. Back in my bedroom, a thin blonde girl, much younger than me, sits on the opposite bed. The owner of the lip gloss.

"Hi! Jane?" She stretches out a clean hand. She's lightly tan with rosy cheeks and bright green eyes. Her blonde hair was originally dark blonde or light chestnut but has been bleached by the sun, a lustrous halo effect combined with a sprinkle of freckles across her cheeks. "I'm Kylie. Looks like we're roommates for a little while?"

I shake her hand and smile—it's not Liz. God is good, the voice of my camp counselor from childhood filters into my brain, a sanctimonious Bible type with physical and attitudinal similarities to Kylie.

"Awesome. Hi! I'm so happy to meet you?" Kylie's nervous energy unsettles. Her eyes run along my body, lingering along my shirt, pants, shoes, back up to my stomach and soft middle. "So, all unpacked? Sorry I didn't greet you before. I was clear on the other side of Lighthouse Hill, so they let me stay put and took care of the unload? Now I'm free, though, Pedro asked me to give you a tour of the island?" She upturns almost every sentence with a little flip of her voice, as though everything is a question. Perhaps everything is.

"Pedro. I didn't meet Pedro. How many people on this island?"

Kylie laughs. "There's six of us? I'm not sure who you met, but there's Liz, Omar, Patty, Pedro, Rick, and me. And now you?" She crinkles her nose and chuckles, flirty. "So, I guess there's a lucky seven of us now! And a whoooooole lot of pinnipeds. That's seals? Sorry, we tend to use family and genus names for the species on this island, since 'seal' is too generic a term, but I don't expect you to know that."

"I did know that. Pinnipeds, weirdly related to weasels."

"Yup, and there's a HUGE difference between the attitudes of, like, a fur seal versus an elephant seal versus a harbor seal," she continues, unimpressed by my Wikipedia memorization. "Not to mention a couple thousand pounds in some cases. But pinnipeds are the family of flippery marine mammals? Walruses too, although we don't have any walruses around here. Man, cool though, walruses. OK, so do you want to go get the, you know, lay of the land and stuff?"

"Are my jeans OK? And I'm guessing I need a hat and a jacket?" Her upturn question/statements are contagious and now I do it too.

Kylie smiles. "Oh, you don't NEED those things, but when a gull, like, shits on your head, you'll wish you had a hat? It's miserable to get out of your hair and sadly? I know from experience."

The orientation PDF said to bring a hat I didn't care about. My fourteen-year-old pink baseball cap now seems especially twee considering the reality of these surroundings. It advertises a sorority car wash.

"I like your hat?" she says, walking out the door. The compliment doesn't reach her eyes. Once we swap house shoes for the outside shoes, we're hit smack in the face with the smell of organic misery.

"I'm jealous! You don't seem to even notice that . . . the smell." My voice sounds weird again, like I'm mispronouncing words. I sound out the phrase inside my brain. It morphs into another language, something forgotten perhaps in the dark neurochemical corners, the verb tenses for the language of flowers, the rhetoric of wind.

"Oh, the smell out here? This is nothing. Wait until I show you Garbage Gulch or Mirounga Bay. The seals are literally methane machines, but they also secrete a musk from, like, their butt glands? It must be smelled to be believed?"

"Worse than whale breath?" I'm eager to show her I'm hip to the wonders of the Farallones. A gray whale had surfaced on the cruise out, giving a close and personal view of its barnacled snout, speckled like an eighteenth-century tombstone, an eerily intelligent mammalian eye, and then a hot fecal olfactory nightmare came from baleen plates hanging like a fringed curtain from its jaws. The white of its eye rolled, spotting me, focusing, then it exhaled a spray of rot and decay hearkening from my distant future grave.

She contemplates the comment. "Hmm. I wouldn't say worse, but definitely different? Whale breath has got that, like, fishiness to it, the concentrated brine smell, plus it dissipates literally as soon as the whale goes under. It's like wasabi: It slaps you and then it's pretty much gone after a minute. Seal farts, though? That smell keeps giving and the only way to escape is some distance? You know not to step off the path, right? So, like, this green stuff is called the marine terrace? It used to be the ocean floor, and it kind of looks like it, doesn't it? There was some, like, seismic activity literally hundreds and hundreds of years ago, and this is probably due to some tectonic shifting—watch your step, dead gull—so, like, this part of the island? Is where the big boys like to chill out and get some sun." She nods to the snoozing elephant seal. The exposed skull of a dead seagull grins nearby, the eye socket repressing a crusty mess of bird brains.

"Unfortunately, the bulls, like, destroy bird habitats along the way and cause cave-ins for the Cassin's auklet burrow there. Sucks to be a Cassin when, like, a bull elephant seal decides he needs his shut-eye."

It's difficult keeping up with Kylie as she steps off the cement path. "OK, so, you definitely have to, like, be careful, because there are nest sites, like, literally on top of the path in some places? You must avoid them. Right, so here is where they collect the water in the winter months." She nods over to the giant white cement pad.

"That's water for laundry and stuff?" Hopefully she isn't going to say drinking water.

"Yup, laundry, washing your hair, boiling pasta, mixed drinks. We eat it, drink it, wash in it, and literally everything. It looks pretty gross right now, but that's because we only collect during the winter months, so it's been getting crapped on almost a year at this point? When the rains start next month or so, then whoever gets sent goes out with giant brooms and literally waits for it to fill with water, then scrubs like crazy, drains it, then, like, waits for it to fill with water again, scrubs like crazy, drains it, and does it all over again? They, like, literally do it four times total, to get all the bird poop and carcass detritus off of there, then it goes through seven filters inside the containment, plus another one inside each of the houses. In theory, it's cleaner than the stuff we drink in San Francisco, but . . ."

"But?"

"I still taste minerality? I'm not sure. It doesn't smell bad, necessarily, but it's certainly nothing you'd buy at Whole Foods. It's, like, rainwater with a hint of guano?"

I smile without intending to because Kylie seeks a reaction.

"Did you have a roommate before I got here today?"

She turns, studying my face. "Sort of? There's supposedly a ghost, so probably? The cool thing about this is we're literally almost entirely off the grid." She continues her fresh, outdoors-person pace up the narrow path that trails up into a steep vertical. I don't have time to react to the ghost comment because I'm audibly panting and gasping for breath. How can she keep talking conversationally?

"We get our electricity from solar. The only generator runs the East Landing crane. That's the blue one. The other one we use in, like, emergencies is over on the other side? I'll show you in a bit. That one, though, works completely by hand and it's literally MISERABLE to work. I don't know how anyone cranks a boat full of stuff, like we do with East Landing? I don't think even Patty's strong enough to do it."

The ground is hard, compacted by thousands of tiny feet, but here and there angry rock, an exposed nerve of a tooth. Almost every footstep slips under my shoes. The hill doesn't want people to climb it.

"Of course, it's not so bad right now. During seabird season, like in the winter? Forget about walking this plane. Gulls attack so bad we'd literally have to be wearing hard hats." She stops and looks back at me for effect. "I am serious. Hard hats."

"Because they peck you in the head," I say. Ghosts. Kamikaze birds. Everyone seems to need me to be scared.

"Yes, because of the pecking." Kylie's mouth turns. I've stolen something from her, like beating her to the punch line. "We still have lots of birds here right now, of course, but they are smaller ones? It's songbird season right now, but we still have to preserve the nesting sites. Just not, you know, like such a huge deal?" Over the hill, more landscape. Two caves gape like surprised mouths, the waves make a choir-of-angels-singing kind of sound. The entire island says *Awwwww awwww awwww.*

"Drat." Kylie purses her mouth. "You could see the Golden Gate Bridge this morning when I came this way, but now, not really? That little hut is the murre blind, where the scientists monitor murres and auklets during breeding and fledge seasons. That," she says, cocking a thumb at the big rock jutting out into the ocean, "is Shubrick Point. It's, like, a major landmark on the island. Think of it as three o'clock, with the lighthouse up there being the center point. Sugarloaf is its own little island and sits at midnight. Saddle Rock, over thataway, that's six o'clock. And West End, which we can't see right now, is nine o'clock. The bays are all slightly off the main points of the clock. Maintop is eleven o'clock, Fisherman's Bay is one o'clock, and Mirounga Bay is seven o'clock. That's how I remember where everything is? And the Golden Gate Bridge is two o'clock. Did that make sense?"

"Crystal clear," I lie. The rocks are nuggety and uncaring, as incognito as Fate.

"Just remember the clock, but they look like teeth, right? Devil's teeth, that's what Farallones means." She clucks and tilts like a grackle, looking sideways. We round the hill, the footing more precarious. I stumble against the loose gravel. Kylie pauses in her recitation of the types of birds that aren't here right now and then resumes. Finally, we're rewarded with a view of more rocks looking exactly like the last rocks, only without a cool singing cave.

"See, that's Sugarloaf? And it's sitting in Fisherman's Bay. Noon and one o'clock," she says, more to herself than anything. Her little code game is alternately enchanting and irritating.

"OK, do you want to go up to see the lighthouse? Great view." She gestures to a practically vertical hill, topped by a concrete shack that does not look like a lighthouse. A crumbly path doubles back and forth on itself up the hill. It even has a hand railing at the top, where it transitions from insane to impossible. Up top, a man scans the horizon with a giant pair of binoculars.

"Can we see the flat parts first? I'm still kind of wiped from getting up so early."

"Oh, of course, duh! Sorry! I don't know why I thought you'd want to climb a 350-foot hill after all that."

She plays it off out of politeness, but too tired for a hill has never occurred to her. Maybe it's a test. I'm ashamed.

We backtrack onto the cart path and continue the tour. Kylie chatters about her past on the island during various seasons and describes in detail each season's perils.

"I'm a SEFI addict. It will happen to you too."

"So most of the scientists have been here multiple times?" I swat the supposedly harmless kelp flies, which have done their damnedest to land on the wet parts of my eyeballs.

Kylie laughs. "You called me a scientist! Thank you!" She says this with a hint of ruefulness. "Omar and I are interns, although this is my fourth rotation and Omar's fifth. We've always overlapped somehow. We track nights spent here, so my SEFI number is currently . . . ah, fifty-nine, I think? Yeah, something like that. Omar's probably hitting 110 right now. Almost half a year for the man. Patty's with Fish and Wildlife. I think he's done like four hundred nights or something? He's here during songbird season because that's his game. Liz is literally a bureaucrat. She keeps us in line, does the data entry stuff, fundraising, that kind of thing. I don't even know if she keeps track of her SEFI nights. But the real islanders are Rick and Pedro. Rick's put in like a couple of thousand nights, and Pedro's been here off and on since the early '80s, hasn't missed a shark season yet. He must have something like ten thousand nights out here or something. Crazy." She rolls her eyes and tucks a gold tendril curl under her hat. Her tanned face is without a blemish or a wrinkle. She belongs on the cover of a rock-climbing magazine.

The island is a hellscape. How could so many people be banking on ways to get here? Even the flat parts are difficult, in this apparently hospitable time of year for leisurely strolls. Nothing currently pecks my head.

Across the marine terrace, Rick and Omar jog toward the big blue crane, where Patty stands at the controls. They hop into the boat, which immediately launches up into the air, setting into the swirling waters.

"Ooooh, there must be an attack in progress." Kylie nods. "You'll catch the next one. That's one of the great things about SEFI. Never a dull moment."

It would have made for a great blog post. I stupidly don't have my camera with me, though. There have already been four or five missed opportunities for header shots. Next time.

Kylie chatters while crossing the loose scree, the stones chatter back.

"That area over there is off-limits. Even though this is a so-called national wilderness, and we have permission to be on the grounds, there are still areas literally protected even from the biologists. That's one of them, on the other side of North Landing over there."

In the cove, four sea lions play with a long strand of kelp. Then the kelp slithers across the water.

"Holy crap, that's a snake! They have a snake!"

"Huh, yeah, they do. Good job! You identified a sea snake!" She frowns and pulls out a tiny notebook and an even smaller pencil from one of the many pockets on her field jacket and writes in girly script:

*sea snake, mirounga bay, 5 ft*

She lifts the pencil up to her mouth in thought and then adds,

*(Blogger)*

"So, this is the fun part of being on SEFI. It's kind of like a scavenger hunt every day. We track all the species we see, where we see them, you know, and then at night someone inputs it into our database. By using lots of other stuff like water temp, sea conditions, air temp, junk like that, they do predictive analysis and understand how species act."

"Are there lots of sea snake studies?"

She casts a stern glance. "You'd be surprised." Then her face brightens as though a switch has been flipped. "OK, come on! I'll show you the stuff I've been doing!"

I scuttle after her, feet slipping against the rocks, an acrid punch of ammonia in every burst of disturbed dust and puff of feathers. A fly lands on my upper lip and attempts a nostril intrusion. I swat but instead punch my nose. In the breaking waves of pain, I realize I now have the comedic opening to my blog post. It's worth blinking away the tears.

Ahead, Mirounga Bay opens up, along with a long-pointed finger of island. Kylie explains that West End is only reachable by a zip line combined with a series of rope ladders. She's disappointed they don't get to cross more often. Kylie probably does zip lines for fun. The shallow chasm filled with swirly ocean water is a situation begging my fall onto the rocks, cracking my skull so I'm permanently paralyzed and then swept out to sea before the biologists save me, only to find a sad end when a white shark chomps my body in two and spits me back out, declaring my ass not worth her time. And the biologists will shrug and have some laconic commentary about the circle of life.

"Well, that concludes our tour, except, of course, the lighthouse. But you don't want to do that. But we have plenty of time to climb after you've had a chance to rest!" she says brightly. Her face is once again Biology Cheerleader. "Are you hungry? Because I'm FAMISHED! We have an hour before dinner, but let's go see if there's anything to scavenge in the kitchen. Did they bring the cheese curls?"

"I did. I got cheese curls."

"You're the BEST! You're so sweet! Those are my favorite, bestie!" she exclaims. It's hollow praise. I followed the grocery list the program office had given me, not as a personal favor for Kylie. I didn't even know Kylie then.

"I try!" There's no other answer.

The house is a shipwreck pulled from the deep and set here haphazardly, weathered and worn, a mirror image to its twin across the yard. Each feels haunted, an antiquated face about to sit in the dark window, undiluted by years of cross-pollination, an organically German or Dutch or Hessian face. Or Russian. Or Aleutian.

Inside, the food smells different from the constant Farallon stench outside—but also not entirely appetizing. It's acrid and smoky and somehow insect-like, as though involving mysticism, larvae hatching. In the kitchen, Liz bashes some onions into pulp with haphazard cleaver chops. In the sink, a blackened pot of something unholy sputters. Kylie reads the situation without saying a word, grabs four bananas off the hook near the door, and backs out.

I obediently trail her to the living room, where she plops into the thrift store couch. Kylie sets three bananas on her lap while peeling one. "Want some?" she says as an afterthought, shoving a pointed white end into her mouth. I take one. Kylie had obviously grabbed all for herself. She makes determined work of the fruit, gathers the peels, and shoves them into a pocket.

"Come on, let's ditch these out in the compost pile and find out what the guys saw."

Outside, the elephant seal waddles off toward the Mirounga Bay cove, slowly but with great conviction, a reluctant stately process.

"It's going to take him all day to get over there," I mutter, because otherwise I have nothing to say.

"Oh, Busta Rhymes? Don't let that fool you. He moves surprisingly fast if he wants to. Like, as fast as you run. Maybe faster." In one breath, her expression resembles the sunny teenage actress shilling orange juice, and in the other, she goes dull in the eyes, studies my face with the detached interest of a higher being. One of those versions of Kylie is real and the other is for show. I'm not sure which is which.

By the landing, Rick and Omar work on the inflatable boat.

"How's it going, guys?" Kylie says, her expression morphing back to Cheerful Kylie, lover of exercise, bananas, and calling strangers "bestie."

"It was brutal!" Omar extends his arms big and wide; his eyebrows disappear underneath a bird shit-splotched SF Giants baseball cap. "We saw a partial breach, and after she chomped a Stellar's sea lion, she actually tried to go after a brown pelican that was hanging out fifty feet away."

"Whoa!" Kylie says. She glances at me. I'm the morning obligation that has kept her from joining the fray. I kick at a stone that turns out to be a bird skull. It crumbles into dust and a beak.

Rick slaps me on the back, a little harder than I expect. "So, Kylie's given you the tour. How's that view, eh?" He nods to the lighthouse.

"Oh, we haven't been up yet," Kylie says. Something flashes between Kylie and Rick.

"Sorry, it was my fault. I wanted to see the seals," I say.

"Yeah, she was excited to meet Busta and his harem." Kylie exhales through her nose at the untruth.

"Ah, got it. Well, Pedro's looking forward to meeting you, so you girls relieve him for dinner."

Kylie beams as though she has won a prize. I'm resigned to being a girl now. My calf muscles ache, a pulling kind of tired that will crescendo into muscle cramps by morning.

Back at the house, Liz's culinary chaos has devolved into some level of anarchy. New pots smoke in the sink and the discarded hulls of three lemons weep juice onto the floor. Liz throws up her hands when Kylie tells her we're going up to the lighthouse during dinner, as though we've destroyed her careful orchestrations.

When Liz's back is turned, Kylie palms an apple, so I do too. Liz notices my inept sleight of hand and scowls. I smile in apology and follow Kylie out the door.

As we scale up in the gloaming, Kylie explains the proper hill itself is called Tower Hill, but the Lighthouse Hill has, no duh, a lighthouse on it. The actual lighthouse dates to the 1860s, but only the stub is left after the giant Fresnel lens was dismantled and sent back to the mainland, where it now sits in a San Francisco museum. Solar-powered batteries, sucking juice off the giant solar panel on top of the little shack, now run the work lights there.

*Fresnel. Fresnel* is a cool word. *Fresnel* lens. Lensel frenz. Looking up at the tiny structure—resting impossibly on the steep and crumbly hill—makes me dizzy. Even certain balcony seats give me vertigo, severely limiting my theater seasons in London and New York. Each step shifts and moves beneath my shoes, the panic building, the pecking of a thousand bird ghosts. The path gets steeper on the first cross back and the second cross back is worse.

"The flies. They sure are . . . everywhere." I blow a mating pair off my lips and pull something still alive out of my hair. It buzzes like a small firecracker and then flies off.

"Yeah, there's literally only one place on the island with no kelp flies at all." Kylie has yet to breathe hard during the aggressive climb.

"Can we go there?" I'm joking, although Kylie misses or ignores it.

"We'll have to get permission. It's a cave? Rabbit Cave. It's kind of small and weird to enter it, but once you get inside, it's huge. There are a lot of murre sites and rhinos in there."

"Rhinos?"

"Oh Jane, they are the COOLEST birds. Rhinoceros auklets. I hope you get to see one. They have this horn thing sticking out of their beak that helps them filter seawater to drink. It's SO so so so cool. Plus, their mouths are bright red." Kylie's enthusiasm is boundless. "I'm sure they'll show you Great Murre Cave, though, because that's where they found the skeleton."

Under my feet, hundreds of bird skeletons, wing bones, and skulls stare up, mouths open, astonished. "Not a bird, I'm guessing?"

"Nope. A lady?" She looks over her shoulder, checking my reaction.

"Did she die. Trying to climb. This hill?"

"You're so funny? I see why you're a writer," she says flatly, as though doing a mathematical formula in her head. A biologist has classified me.

My beak is appropriate for gathering humor at sea. My nest is a burrow with a fantastic Wi-Fi connection.

From this height, the sea is smaller and somehow larger at the same time. A man paces the balcony of the squat building, a giant pair of binoculars in his hands.

"Pedro! I'm here to relieve you! And also, this is Jane the blogger!" Kylie bounces up the final apex as though she's moving downhill rather than up. Any hope that the lighthouse would be cool—an evil genius hidden lair—is dashed. It's a small room filled with more dead bird detritus and feathers and bird excrement, but it does have a few cool scientific-looking electronics.

"Howdy, Jane-the-blogger." He might be thirty or fifty, but his skin has a leathered Clint Eastwood patina from spending an entire lifetime outdoors. However, his trim goatee and mop of amber hair don't show a trace of gray.

"Hi there." It will be at least five minutes before I can talk. I want to bend over and pant but I won't give Kylie the satisfaction.

"Hey, thanks for relieving me for supper, guys. I'd better get down there." With that, he hands the binoculars to Kylie, who immediately presses them to her petite face and scans the horizon. He touches my sleeve as he passes by: "Hey, do me a favor and keep an eye out past Saddle Rock. I have a sharky feeling in that direction, OK?" And with that, he tromps down the hill as though it is a flat runway, whistling a tuneless melody.

Kylie fiddles with the radio, then clips it to her belt, all without taking her eyes off the waterline.

"So, what are we looking for exactly? A dorsal fin?" Spotting a *Jaws* shark fin amid chopping water and waves seems less likely than being able to read a street sign from atop a thirty-story building.

"Nope, look for a water disturbance, a blood slick, or a big cloud of gulls dive-bombing the surface."

"OK." The extra pair of binoculars are the second-string players in this venture—they are weaker and less impressive than the mega pair Kylie hefts. I lift them anyway, but, after trying to focus on one of the jagged rocky outcroppings, give up and just shade my eyebrows with a hand.

"Dolphins. Risso's, I'm guessing." Kylie points out a bit of white foam.

"Oh my god, seriously? This day has been so amazing. I saw a gray whale this morning and now dolphins!" I try to match Kylie's excitement for nature, the world, bananas, Fresnel lenses.

"Just another day on the Farallones! Best job in the world!" She smiles and sits.

"You, uh, sat on a dead bird."

"Yeah, I did." She gets up and knocks the half-rotten bird carcass off the poop-spattered chair. "Wouldn't be the first time. I probably knocked it off the roof when I was scrubbing yesterday, so it's my own fault. Ugh, that one had maggots. God, I hate it when they're still juicy."

My throat clenches. Don't let it show. *Remember you're strong. Remember this.* Instead, I amble around the walkway, breathing through my mouth. It isn't as scary as it seemed. It isn't sheer death on the other side of the rail but rather a gradual rocky descent with opportunities to grab pointlessly at boulders and bird nests before falling to my death of a broken neck and subsequently having my broken corpse ripped apart by various oceanic scavengers.

Far offshore, three gulls are joined by a fourth and fifth, interested in something in the water. "Hey, Kylie, is this what you're talking about? The birds?"

She's about to say I'm wrong, but then she spots it too. Into the walkie, she sings, "House, there's predation in progress at 6:30, southeast of Saddle Rock. Over."

"On it," mumbles the voice on the other end. Rick, identifiable by his bright orange jacket, and two others run, scanning the direction of the giant rock. One of them points, and they run even faster. Rick and another guy jump into the orange boat, while the third climbs the crane's controls to launch the boat into the water. And then the boat takes off, but already the birds are dispersing, a cruel trick they have played on the scientists.

"Yeah, bird activity has decreased. Might have been fishing. Over."

"Roger that," says the radio voice. The orange boat trolls around the big cove for hours, hoping for another hunt. Across the grand expanse of the Pacific headwaters, the Golden Gate's sentinel guide lights come on, and the city of San Francisco casts an aura in the darkness.

As the moon rises, a creepy sound, like the cry of elves, banshees, demons. Kylie laughs and says, "Welcome to the Farallon lullaby. It's the auklets, singing themselves to sleep."

"Just up here, though?" The noise grows, as though the entire hill was a giant harmonica.

"Oh no, all over the island."

"When do they stop?"

"When they leave the burrows to hunt before sunrise." She dances in and out of the benevolent lamplight circle. "You learn to sleep through it. When I go home, it takes me a few days to be able to sleep without it, actually."

The sound is a roller coaster, a thousand frogs suffering from laryngitis, the soundtrack to countless nightmares. It's the welcome song for here. I'm here now. *Remember this.*

# Ten Years Ago

Sometimes it's easy to imagine yourself as someone else. Someone who doesn't say ridiculous things, someone who doesn't perpetually lose her phone and get tangled in laptop cords and leave the Bluetooth headset running so that it drains every battery on every device she owns. Someone who dresses better, someone who stays out late and who laughs in a charming way rather than in a way that is a bit too loud or a bit like a donkey with bronchitis. ~~Someone who doesn't get dumped by her boyfriend over text message, someone who actually tells the strumpet who cheated with him to go take a hike (instead of this simpering "Let's all stay friends, OK?" business that has been bandied about with a little too much freedom, can we all agree right now that this is bullshit?)~~

Under the Golden Gate Bridge, for a second, I was that someone.

I flew over a bike path at ridiculous, unsafe speeds on a borrowed fixed-gear bike. It felt good to use my legs for something other than trudging up and down Potrero Hill, almost missing the bus. For perhaps the first time in my entire adult life, I was exercising and had not turned into a sweaty, red-faced monster. (You have no idea what kind of accomplishment that is. Tick one more thing off my bucket list. Next stop: Learn how to cry pretty.)

A giant warship sat in the Bay. I expected a bald eagle to soar by holding an American flag in its beak, and perhaps the Oscar Mayer Wienermobile to make an appearance, driven by an actual hot dog, because it was that kind of afternoon. The bridge over my shoulder looked majestic. The city off to my left and ahead of me in the harbor, everything was majestic. And for a minute, I felt fucking ***majestic***.

Normally, whenever I'm under the Golden Gate Bridge, I can't help thinking about the suicides that occur there, how people who jump facing the city and are saved usually never try again, but people who jump facing away from civilization usually try again if they're rescued. And they usually succeed. It's a predictor, this turning a back to the city.

I didn't know how anyone could turn from this glorious place, where everything sparkles and everything feels like magic.

The sun had found its way through the shoreline fog and Sutro Tower threw rock-and-roll devil hands while the tourists clustered in confused schools at the Golden Gate Vista Point across the Bay. And for one brief instant, while flying along this perfect bike path, I felt like I could peddle that way forever, making concentric circles around the peninsula, using hills and gravity to propel me into perpetual motion, like an executive desk toy. *Click clack click clack* I would never ever stop.

It was a glorious moment.

And then I wiped out.

It was, in retrospect, a beautiful and comical pratfall of a landing. You would have enjoyed it if it had been filmed on YouTube.

(Oh God, please let it not be on YouTube.)

I hurdled the handlebars like a track star, a Cirque du Soleil gymnast, or, more likely, a sack of damp laundry thrown from the back of a truck. There was the sensation of flying, my arms and legs flinging out to catch something, anything, the feeling of a carnival ride fluttering in my pelvis.

And then the ground disabused me of any notions that I could ever be graceful, that I could ever engage in flight. The path and the grit and the grass met my face with a sad, tragic finality.

You know that minute when you fall and you think, *Am I dead? I might actually be dead.* A beautiful stillness happens, somewhere between realizing that you're not in fact dead and when the first thing starts to hurt.

I summoned up my bravado to shake off the concerned bystanders undoubtedly rushing over to see if I died. Perhaps there would be a handsome man. Certainly, a young mother wearing yoga pants, pushing a stroller that cost more than my exorbitant rent, at the least. "I'm OK!" I tried to muster up a laugh, as though I do a double pike over vintage bicycle handlebars every blessed day of my life.

Footsteps approached; dozens of people in the park enjoyed the aerialist in her finest hour.

I propped myself up on my elbow so that I could turn down the proffered extended hands and show that I could stand on my own. "I'm fine!" I said again.

No one rushed over. The footsteps I had heard belonged to a jogger, sidestepping to avoid my feet. He kept running, not even altering his stride. The young mothers whose children played not forty feet away had returned to their magazines and bored gazes. The jocks playing catch on the verge hadn't even noticed. Then I had an epiphany.

**This was not my beautiful life.**

This was the universe telling me that San Francisco and I would never, not ever become BFFs.

It was, as they say, a defining moment.

A guy in a speed bike shouted, "On the left!" and sped past, his wheels of fury barely missing my foot. I hiked myself up with whatever dignity I could (I suspect I drew strength from future dignity, which I will have to pay back with interest over the next several months), made sure that my boobs hadn't fallen out of my shirt (because that would make sense, right?), and pulled up the ridiculously heavy bike.

The chain dangled unnaturally loose around the gear mechanism thingy. Whether the chain came off the track in the fall or whether it caused the fall is unclear, but I was left with a broken craptastic super expensive hipster bike.

I fixed the chain—or so I thought—got on the bike and went about twenty feet before it fell off again. Thank you, San Francisco, for your warm embrace. Jane is out. I am done with this town. It's not you, San Francisco, it's—well, it IS you. You and your ridiculous overpriced lattes. You and your weird rideshare rules. You and your four-thousand-dollar basement studios that are just closets, murder holes, or BDSM dungeons. You and your impossibly insufficient infrastructure, your refusal to build cell towers, which results in hollows of dead air and five bars, no one bar, no four bars, no zero bars when you move an inch to the left. You and your three-toed pigeons, artisanal urinal cakes, and piss-smelling neighborhoods. You and your carpeted Muni buses, why would you put carpeting on surfaces so frequently vomited upon, for the love of God? You and your eucalyptus trees that smell so perfect, like a fancy spa or like the collarbone of a gorgeous boy. You and your beautiful men of the Castro who loudly critique my outfits and boobs and who once celebrated me walking convincingly in five-inch heels while shouting, "From the hips, sweetie!" while they themselves wore assless chaps and who so earnestly invested in making me a better person and even now would kindly say, "Oh honey, all chaps are assless."

Oh, I lost my phone in the entire mishap, adding insult to injury. Luckily a Good Samaritan picked it up and contacted me. It should surprise no one that he's from Wisconsin. It doesn't surprise this girl Jedi anyway.

Xoxo,
Jane

# Day 3

## JANE

The moon hides behind low cloud cover, and the air feels heavy. The darkness makes everything risky, every step fraught with invisible scuttling, chittering, and struggling away of tiny creatures—mice, perhaps, terrestrial birds, amphibians, or imagined—under step.

Omar and Patty are ahead, too far to hear our conversation, but Kylie lingers back to keep me company, her red lantern turned off, despite my request to turn it on. She murmurs something about the auklets and then launches into a monologue about the island that is a repetition of stuff she's already said, some of it verbatim, earlier in the day.

"You know, the darkness tonight is going to fuck up the songbird counts in the morning," she says. The tone of her voice blames me, my request for the light adding insult to injury.

"That's too bad. Do you use the lighthouse then?"

"We never use the lighthouse, Jane. The lens is in San Francisco." Her words bob somewhere to the left, even though her form is directly ahead. The island plays tricks, echoes bouncing off unseen hollows, auklet burrows amplifying and resounding like Wayland Flowers, Kylie's creaky voice young and old at once, ending each sentence with a croak, a frog princess.

"We would never use the lighthouse," she repeats softly, as though speaking to an unknown third companion, as though she can't fathom the nerve of this suggestion.

Again, she switches, as though some entity has control of the Kylie steering wheel. Now she discusses bird migrations with her chipper voice, a bird itself. With low-hanging cloud cover, seabirds can't see the island. I could be a little canary or tiny little sparrow, flapping forever and ever without the bursts of wind and the benefit of giant wingspreads like pelicans or albatross, and flapping until I literally fall into the ocean, exhausted, a cold embrace that has been patiently waiting the entire trip. Songbirds are badass.

After being in the well-lit kitchen, I find the dark island takes on a sinister cast—an even more sinister cast. *Sinisterer.* The ocean is the inside of a conch shell, dark movement and waves, but Saddle Rock, the jutting rock formation off the little bay, is the absence of anything, like a black hole or an open grave. A yawning mouth stifling a groan.

Several soft crunches—dead birds—I trip, falling forward, and catch myself, hands on the ground into something feathery. Sinistererer.

No maggots, no maggots, no maggots, I push away dark thoughts, push them, drown them in the archive of bad feelings to be unpacked at a later, safer date while wearing white cotton gloves, preferably by a historian or not-yet-born archaeologist.

"Ready to play Farallon volleyball?" In the miserly glow of Patty's red headlamp, Omar's all-American grin gleams white like the Cheshire cat. Only Omar is close enough to hear Kylie's soft commentary.

Patty strings gossamer fabric—mist net—across poles. Then we all crouch flat, Kylie and Omar on one side of the net, Patty and me on the other, opposing badminton teams.

Minutes after I settle into the crouch, the Cassin's auklets' nightly dirge, an announcement they are leaving their subterranean nests for the dark sea to hunt krill and other zooplankton. In the air above, movement through the night. We're perched on the edge of a harmonica as these maniacal little birds pray to Poseidon.

The net shudders, alive. Patty turns on the red light and extends a giant paw into the net. "I'm going to show you how to handle the birds. Come here," he whispers to me. The chickadee struggles in his massive palm, its little head swiveling and its eyes bright as emeralds in the red light. "See how you never touch the wings or the legs? Then carefully . . . carefully . . . untangle their feet. Sometimes they get caught in there bad and we must snip them."

"Snip their legs off?" I choke.

"No, snip the netting. See the ragged spot right there?" He points to a shaggy bit of mist net six inches away, a snarl in an otherwise perfect bridal veil. "Had a bad one knotted up in there. Then we need to identify them, do a wingspan, and do the band, then we let them go. Got that?"

"Uh . . . you want me to band it?" The little bird's breast thrums, its needle beak opens and closes. My heart breaks for all of it, a tiny miracle flying until exhausted and falling into the sea, the meal for predators, the undignified pile of fluff, bones, and maggots that will be its final landing spot.

Patty's brow furrows. "No, sorry, I'll do the banding. I should do that. Yeah. So I want you to get them out of the net and then do the recording of the data. Or record. You record at first, until you get the hang of this?"

The battered notebook has spatters of bird poop and looks psychedelic in the red headlamp—a murder journal. It's difficult to record in the dark. I write in the brief headlamp bursts when Patty happens to turn this direction. If I had my own headlamp, it would be easier, but of course I don't. I have nothing. I'm a terrible scientist.

Omar and Kylie band and grab birds left and right, nattering softly between themselves in a kind of shorthand, mostly initials—while Patty barks full names of songbirds and wingspans faster than I write in the dark. Bird names and measurements are written over the same spot on the paper, so I flip the page and start a new one. *Be more careful.*

Between lulls, the three of them gossip about the other staffers, past and present. Any tiny community, even one of only seven people, thrives on gossip as much as on dolma and berry crisps. Omar tells us how Liz and Rick had been arguing about something big almost as soon as they finished with dessert. Liz had left the room to check her email. Omar speculates he heard Liz crying, but Patty dismisses him, simply by saying "Pfft" and turning his head and the lamplight away. Omar clears his throat and changes the subject.

"So, Jane, sounds like you got a taste of Pedro's shark sense?" Omar says from the other side of the net.

I'm not sure how to answer for a second. "Oh right, the shark attack. He did say he had a feeling about that area and that's right where it happened."

"Or it's right where you were looking because he suggested it."

Kylie pipes up, a bodiless voice from the dark. "No, she was over on my side before that? She wasn't looking in any area in particular? Jane, did you even know what Saddle Rock was?"

Kylie had certainly mentioned it during the tour, as I recall the name, but there are so many colorfully named rocks and ledges on the island, Sugarloaf, Indian Head, Saddle Rock, Emperor's Bathtub, the Saddle, so many to pinpoint all in a half-hour walk. It's a little insulting she'd imply I've forgotten in the space of an hour. Truth is, I don't know if I remembered or not.

"No, I don't think I did." It feels weird to disagree with her, oddly impolite.

"See? A true blind study."

Patty coughs. "The only true blind study would be if Pedro had his creepy shark sixth sense, said nothing about it, and hid up here on the lighthouse, having written his prediction on a sealed envelope in the house. Like Carnac."

"What is Carnac?" Omar asks.

"I forget you're a tiny baby. It was on a show back in the day. You were in your Batman footie pajamas fast asleep by then."

"I'll bet Omar wasn't even born then," I say softly. "He's pre–Johnny Carson and Ed McMahon." We share a laugh.

"Hey, are you too old to get warbler up there or do I have to come around and do it myself?" Omar calls out.

"Crap, that's us." Patty jumps up to untangle the bird.

"Stay on your toes, old man. Stay on your toes," Omar says from the safety of a dark ridge.

"Lucky there's a net between us." Patty fakes a growl.

Dark shapes shoal in the midnight sky, twitters and wings strumming. A bigger shape, large as a cow, flies ten feet above our heads, but the others say nothing so I must be seeing things, something closer is throwing off my senses, a trick of perspective. The wings create mini breezes, tiny hand fans in the cool briny mist, wafting the strong ammonia smell away for microseconds. The wings beat and the wings beat and the auklets dally and dance and beat and fly and fly, screeching a broken calliope of sound to celebrate the hunt.

Then, an unwanted memory, called forth by the mention of Johnny Carson, staccato rhythms, and children's pajamas. When I was small, my mother brought me to an afternoon parade. It couldn't have been a morning parade; she would have still been sleeping off the night's excess. The wind was hot, an approaching thunderstorm still hours away. The pompom girls were my favorite, mesmerizing swirls, red and white and blue fronds shaking, rustling like terrestrial anemones. Then people in glittering spangled coats in the July heat, long white fringes, horses with long shining manes and tails, their hooves striking the city pavement. Then a marching band, regimental, raising their instruments, their shoes striking in time, the drumsticks hovering. On cue, they all bleated the first note, the bass drum thrumming, the horns spanking the air.

I started to cry. The big cotton-covered drum mallets rearranged my heartbeat, touching inside my rib cage, stealing my breath. The tubas, their big open mouths inhaling like monsters. I could disappear down those chord slides, be consumed by this noise. Drums and drums and beats and breath and blasts and booms. I cried harder.

My mother hissed, "What's the matter with you why are you embarrassing me," and then slapped my face. I sat on the curb as the band approached and understood it was a moment when I could be taken, the threat I'd heard so many times from teachers and my mother and the news, those strangers who wanted to steal me, the strangers there now, the strangers blew their horns, they had organized, they all moved as one, they were here, their drums signaled their intention to want and covet and abscond.

Cheek hot from the slap, I cried harder, terrified.

A hand ripped me up off the curb away from the street.

I shrieked. The moment had come.

It was my mother's hand. I was taken as I'd known taking would occur, taken to a spanking, another slap on the same cheek and then a night of thunder and rage and torrential rain and blame, ass cheeks prickling red-hot from a second episode, with a leather strap, once I had returned to the tiny rental house we both lived in, or where we each lived, separate organisms, the act of dutiful correction hidden from the public spectacle where she might have been recognized.

I'm here now. On an island. *Come back. Come back.* I'm safe. I don't know why I remember this now. These moments come back uninvited. Must be the birds. *Remember this.*

At 1 a.m., we stagger back to the house. Kylie chatters across the dark room about the different ghosts on the islands. She doesn't believe in ghosts, she says, and then tells stories about the lighthouse keepers' children who died of diphtheria, probably in this room, and the skeleton of the woman found in Great Murre Cave, positioned as though she might be sleeping, and the Egg Wars when people shot each other to put murre eggs on San Francisco's Victorian breakfast tables, and then more deaths, and more, and isn't it a hoot, she giggles, ghosts, and I'm falling asleep to her stories, responding "mmhmm" and "mmhmm" and "mmhmmm" until I don't.

# Day 4

**DB Cooper**
**@DBmm**

25 confirmed cases in my county—that's it, I'm not going out. We learned this lesson once with COVID. The mayor needs to declare a shelter in place or something. All those people outside acting like this is a normal Tuesday WTF.

♡ 78 💬 5 ⟳ 0

**Julie Mons**
**@monsjul**

Nothing like an awkward bump into a toxic family member at the grocery store. Hi, Evil. Run out of daggers, did we? Try Aisle 7.

♡ 586 💬 10 ⟳ 145

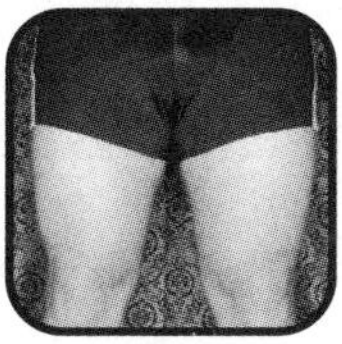

**JeSsBieU**
**@Jessbieu**

Have had religious experience while eating a Wallace pear while the sun rose over Ferry bldg. Seriously, amazing pear!

45 5 1

**Xi**
**@sXlilate**

Loving the first authentic blustery chilly day of fall. Bring on the argyle sweaters, acid-yellow birch leaves and the smell of neighbors' bonfires!

198 12 14

**Jesus Don't Live Here**
**@karl1952**

If the president had controlled our borders and closed them in September when this thing first broke in Asia, people would have called him a dictator. Now where are we? #invisibleenemy

785K 5.6K 9.5K

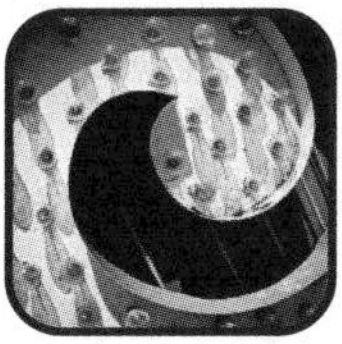

**Jane**
**@erejane**

Putting myself on an island in the Pacific for 30 days right when the rest of the city ends up having to stop going outside is absolutely Peak Jane.

15.4K 154 3.5K

# Fourteen Years Ago

CHIHUAHUA, MEXICO—Large crystals containing bacteria and other microorganisms have been discovered living inside a large mine outside of Chihuahua, Mexico. The organisms were kept in stasis for 60,000 years inside enormous gypsum crystals.

NASA's astrobiology arm has discovered that the extremophiles contained tiny bugs in a state of "geolatency," in which living organisms are frozen in rocks or fossils for long periods of time. Much like a scene out of the Michael Crichton novel *Jurassic Park*, the living organisms were viable for reanimation.

About 1,900 different organisms have been identified and are estimated to have been suspended in animation for anywhere between 10,000 and 90,000 years.

"Our team has already been able to resuscitate several of these organisms, although roughly 75 percent are not viable. However, the scientific breakthroughs that could come from these preserved specimens won't be fully understood for decades," said Janis Hopkins, head of public relations for NASA's astrophysics and biology teams.

# Day 4

From: Jane
To: Brian
Sent: Saturday, Oct 04, 20xx 12:54 PM
Subject: The subject line is without recourse.

When I first landed, I never thought it would be like this. What you need to understand about the Farallones is the smell. The smell, Brian. The smell of rot and seal shit and whale breath and seagull guano. There's a candle store in a hipster little street near my house back in Green Bay that has "Pacific Island Breezes" as one of the scents. That particular candle is a peachy pink and there's a faint smoky palm tree in the back of the label. Perhaps I can interest the Ginger Birch Candle Company in a Farallon Sunset candle. The candle would be layered with ammonia, bracken, and elephant seal musk, and when you burned down the wax, it would gradually unveil a rotten bird carcass. A real one. Note to self: Approach them with slick marketing strategy. Step three: Profit!

The kelp flies are constant. The hipsters of mainland San Francisco don't know what they're missing a short thirty miles offshore. These unholy demons don't bite, don't sting, and what's more, they don't seem to die—they play pretend dead when you swat them but then about five minutes later, they get back up, shake their tiny little brains, and start all over again, like a video game character getting a second life. I had two flies fucking between my temple and my sunglasses yesterday. There is a fly defense station, like an airlock for terrible flying vermin: When you go into the house, you stand still and do a shake, then you kill all the flies. There are fly swatters pretty much within arm's reach of every seat in the house. I have gotten used to the smell (oh God, I can't believe it but it's true), but I don't think I'll ever get used to the flies.

Next, there's the noise. When you think about islands in the Pacific, you think of soft waves lapping against golden warm sandy shores, but on the Farallones, there's a bare minimum of twenty feet of craggy rock walls. There are blowholes where the waves roll up into hidden crevices and make snorts and wuffles, all day and all night long, like a randy buffalo. Then there's the seals and sea lions. The males with their giant proboscis noses fighting for territory. The little seals, with their pretty dappled flesh and their puppy dog eyes, they honk about any chance they get. And let us not forget the gulls. They'll slap you in the face faster than an angry nun in catechism. I'm lying. I'm Lutheran. The only thing I know about catechism is from movies set usually in the '60s.

The Farallon team takes these things in stride. They don't even notice the flies anymore, they tell me, nor the smell (bless them, they are liars to a man), because they know how these are the least of your discomforts here. The reality of bird lice doesn't set in until day six or seven, when you can't stop scratching. The lice are so infinitesimally small. It's like trying to notice a flake of pepper on your shirt, only it's even smaller than most table pepper. Bird lice are micropepper. Fancy French ultrafine pepper. Great, I'm never going to eat pepper again.

The biologists inform me that the bird lice won't survive for long without an avian host, meaning that unlike human lice, I won't have to worry about taking these creepy little parasites home with me, but this is little comfort because I'm sitting in the middle of approximately 58,438,395,848 birds. There are nests everywhere, discarded or active. And dead bird bodies everywhere you look. I'm probably sitting on one right now. (Actually, I'm writing this from inside the house so God help me if there's a dead bird inside the couch cushions.) (True fact: There are right now three dead birds in the kitchen freezer, right next to the ice cream. So tell me, my dear artiste, what would YOU do for a Klondike bar?) Even if the lice that are biting my tender bits decide to give up on my decidedly not-avian blood, there are probably a million bored little bird lice within ten feet of my body at this minute, ready to jump on and try some Brand Jane. So you scratch and you try to forget about it and then you go out looking for sharks, with or without your lice companions.

I've named my current cadre of lice Millicent, Torvald, and Bruce. If I believe there are only three, it keeps me from losing my mind. Three is a manageable number.

You're getting itchy right now, aren't you? Go ahead and scratch. I'll be right here waiting for you when you get done.

I lied.

Go with God,
Jane

PS. I saw your name in the San Francisco paper for an upcoming show. Forgive me, but I think I got a little starry-eyed. I know, of course, that you're fancy, but I forget sometimes how fancy! You never tell me about these things, so I usually find out after the fact. Consider me dazzled, Mr. Fancy. OK, not so dazzled that I'd refrain from regaling you with tales of my bird lice.

PPS. I'm afraid I'll be long gone from our shared former haunting grounds by the time your show starts. My tour of duty ends but four days before your show opening. Unless you're going to be here early, and our plans overlap? Shall we break the rules of our e-lationship?

PPPS. That probably won't work out, I'm guessing, and unfortunately, it's not possible for me to extend my visit here, as I'm due in New York on Oct 28th for my next *Jane 'Ere* Life List thing—working behind the scenes of a Broadway show. So, I propose that the next time we meet will be at the top of the Empire State Building on New Year's Eve. Sound good to you? I'll bring the lice shampoo and you bring two solid sterling silver backscratchers from Tiffany's. We'll toast the new year and then escape in a hansom cab driven by a man named Artemis (and the horse will be Daisy). Artemis, as it will turn out, is an eccentric billionaire and asks us to help him catalog the city's old buildings. We have nothing better to do, so we agree, if we stop at the occasional hipster coffee shop for organic Chemex drip coffee for you and a salted caramel hot cocoa for me. Artemis, or Artie as we will call him, has an itchy back, so we hand him a Tiffany backscratcher. He's so delighted and declares that for the first time, he's found true happiness. After a magical evening, he reveals that he tragically has only two hours left to live but we've made him happy, so he writes an impromptu will, giving us his share of stock in about every major company in the US and EMEA. We spend the remainder of the year digging through his vast collection of porcelain dog figurines, rock-and-roll memorabilia and antique birth control devices. Daisy goes to live in a petting zoo where only polite children with clean hands are allowed admittance. And a good time was had by all.

From: Brian
To: Jane
Sent: Saturday, Oct 04, 20xx 3:43 PM
Subject: Missives from a dull bastard

Ah yes, flies. God's little proof that we're never going to win the war against pestilence. Isn't that the sign of the end times, by the way? Good luck with that. My best to Millicent, Torvald, and especially Bruce. Bruce and I go way back. We were in a fraternity together, or perhaps I'm confusing him with a particularly virulent strain of pubic lice that was going around the Greek row. You should be honored, however, as only the finest aristocracy are normally graced with bird lice. In fact, I hear the Japanese are shipping them in for the sex clubs. No one trusts a geisha who isn't subtly scratching.

I'm humbled that you saw the art thing. However, once again, the universe has conspired to prevent our meeting, as the art thing is in the process of being an un-thing. The rules of our e-lationship remain unsullied. The art world pretends to be important, but we cannot live up to the fanciness of dung flies and dead bird ice cream. Speaking of which, I think I saw a dead bird ice cream in an art show in New York. You may want to save a few, as I believe you could get at least $10K per little, tiny corpse. Much less if the dead bird's lice have moved on to greener pastures (or fluffier down feathers), though. Even the art world has its deal-breakers.

Cheers,
Brian

PS. Do you like how I've gone ahead and made this all about me? You were warned, vis-à-vis the dull bastard thing.

PPS. Alas, Tiffany's has discontinued the sterling silver backscratcher. I have set up an alert on eBay, however I did research and found some *silver-plated* backscratchers. I think we both know that would never do.

# Day 5

Official SEFI Blog

—Guest blogger Jane 'Ere

On the Farallones, you're not the most important species. Humans take precedence over just about everything on the mainland, even endangered species, like sea turtles or banana slugs or Sierra Nevada red foxes. If it were a question of putting an elementary school in the same place as a grove of the last remaining grey-headed chickadee in North America, people would earnestly fight for urban development. Here, there is no debate.

Mostly I've been doing errands for the naturalists. I'm less than an intern because I don't have the 1,220 college credits of biology and environmental sciences to understand the difference between a common murre and a thick-billed murre. I see jellyfish and think, "Whoa, cool jellyfish." They think, "That's a lion's mane jellyfish and its presence on this day and time supports proof of global warming."

And then there are the sharks. Humans aren't even the alpha predator on this island, because of sharks and their great blind eyes rolling over as they strike and kill mammals four times the size of your average hippy dude. The animals come first here, whether they're mating or defending their turf or plain annoying the shit out of you. You don't fuck with nature. Period.

Nature has full reign to fuck with you.

"Obviously, if it came down to you or a seal, we'd kill the seal," Pedro Muñoz, head conservation and island super guru here on SEFI, said bluntly, but I'm not entirely convinced.

But today, we're doing the boat thing. I was ready for blood and gore, but now, looking into the giant limpid pools of adorableness of the harbor seals' eyes, I sentimentalize their cuteness.

"Sharks got to eat. Seals got to eat. If the seal didn't need to eat, it wouldn't risk getting eaten by the shark," says Muñoz. "The seal is carnivorous too, don't forget that."

Seals eat fish. Fish eat other smaller fish. Smaller fish eat smaller organisms like plankton and larvae from the bigger fish. So yeah, everyone's a predator.

The harbor seals are ridiculously cute though.

The sharks target cow-sized elephant seals, full of blubber and nutrients worth the caloric effort of stunning, kill striking. It's the human equivalent of being starving and either ordering a giant juicy hamburger and a side of fries or getting one perfect tiny raw oyster. The shark wants the most calories for the least amount of effort.

Kylie Gilmore is an intern on the island, on her fourth rotation here. "My specialty are puffins and pelagic, so I'm a bit out of season right now, but you know how it goes," she says conspiratorially, as though I know how it goes. I don't know how anything went, goes, has, does, etc. I'm the new kid.

She's my roommate in the Jane Fonda room, so-called because there used to be a poster of Jane Fonda on the door. They say it's haunted by one of the lighthouse keepers' kids who died of diphtheria in the 1910s. Which one, no one seems to agree upon, because three different kids died of diphtheria during one particularly bad outbreak. At night, they mention rasping high-pitched breaths of a tiny ghost child. I take the left bunk; Kylie takes the right. Her garb's sealed in bright purple Rubbermaid containers. I assumed it was because she was worried about her stuff getting wet when it got hauled up on the crane at North Landing, but she has ignored the dressers and keeps her stuff sealed. After two days, when I find my stash of protein bars and Hershey's Kisses completely pillaged by mice, I understand. Then I envy her purple bins.

Mice are invaders on this island, just like people. Centuries ago, mice stowed away on a Russian ship during fur seal hunting parties and liked it so much, they decided to call it home. The burrowing owls love the mice as much, if not more, than the mice loved our energy bars.

Today, Kylie compiled her stuff into one purple bin and gave me the other one. This is the stuff of true friendship. While on lighthouse duty, I made Kylie a bracelet, but then I was too weirded out to give it to her, because is thirty mumblesomething too old for friendship bracelets? Yes, it's too old. But she hasn't taken it off.

I'm home. Or so I tell myself.

So much of my life on SEFI reminds me of going to summer camp: we sleep in barely habitable rooms, socialize only during meals, and the rest of the time is spent getting so much fresh air you feel drunk on it. Now if only something repelled kelp flies the way bug juice worked at Camp Twakamonga.

Kylie loaned me a pair of hiking boots; I gave her a headband for her gorgeous naturally curly blonde hair. Kylie's skin is perfect. Meanwhile, without constant toning and French grape facial washes every night, I'm congestion city. Between the sun and the windburn and the slightly damp sheets, I have a colony of blackheads across the bridge of my nose that now resembles a small moon. This is to say nothing of the giant cystic bump on my chin. I suspect it might have been a gull laying an egg there. Liz Summers tells me about how she and her husband were one of a slew of island romances back in the day. It must be true love, when you smell like an outhouse and are constantly scratching your bird lice bites. People still manage to latch on and get under one another's skin in such a way, but already, I suspect I'll ask Kylie to be my maid of honor in some distant future wedding to a yet-to-be-named groom. When she tells me my breath smells worse than seal shit, I say her armpit hair is thicker than Farallon weed. Then we laugh. Our besties status is sealed.

In the movies, sharks are gray and white, almost the color of kittens. In real life, sharks are the color of mountains, the soulless basalt black of statuary. They are so big it doesn't seem like they should be able to move, much less knock you out of the water and stun you before you even realize your legs have been bisected from your body. Or your flippers, in the case of elephant seals.

You look for shadows under a murky depth of churning water. Later, Muñoz explains to me they often don't see the sharks so much as feel them, sensing the danger with our lizard brains, and then our eyes look for the shapes causing the sensation, the prickling at the base of our skulls. What you're hoping for is a sense to run away. That's what you should be listening to, your instinct to hide.

There's nowhere to hide in a tiny rubber boat.

"What if a shark capsized this boat?" I eep out, over the squalls of seabirds on the island.

"Won't happen," one of the naturalists, Richard Chernowski, assures me.

"Won't happen? Or couldn't?" I want *couldn't happen*. Couldn't. Couldn't. *Couldn't.*

"Never happens," says Chernowski, but instead of shaking his head, he's nodding. "It probably could but hasn't. Won't happen. Nah." He pauses for a bit, looking at the decoy. "Don't put your hands over the side, though."

Sigh.

"Your job is to look for boils. You know what a boil is?"

I want to say I do, of course I know what a boil is, doesn't everyone know what a boil is? I have no idea what a boil is. The biologists constantly slow their game to explain things to me, dumbing things down so I understand it without my 10,000 hours of field research everyone else seems to have under their belt. I almost never know the answers when they ask me questions, so I take a stab.

"When there are lots of bubbles? Like a boiling pot?"

"You'd think, but no. The opposite. Smooth water. Bubbles happen, but it's under the water. The surface water flattens out. It spreads in a circle and indicates there's something large flashing its tail. Or it could mean there's a bunch of sea lions swimming under there. But either way, we want to see it, because sharks are interested in sea lions too."

"Boils don't happen naturally?"

"You mean, not an animal? Sure, but then they don't move, they stay in one spot, like if there's a land feature or something. We're looking for boils where there wasn't a boil a minute ago."

"Why do they do that?" I gesture to the seals, flipping in clusters. It seems like the most obvious way to lure a shark to their presence, all movement and white water, exactly what the Discovery Channel told you NOT to do if you fell into the kill zone (KILL ZONE . . . usually said with its own theme song during Shark Week).

"Ah, the weaving and bobbing?"

I nod and brush a pair of fucking flies (that is, flies who fuck) out from under my sunglasses.

"It's called porpoising. Like dolphins."

"Oh, sharks and dolphins are enemies, so the seals have learned they fake out the sh—"

Muñoz is shaking his head. "A little of that, but think about the seal's perspective. If they are swimming in a straight line, the shark has a reasonable understanding of where the seal's going. Every shark in the world needs Lasik surgery. They can't see for shit. A seal hops up and down like that, the shark sees flashes of shapes. Light, dark, light, dark. It's selfish herd theory. If you're in a group of ten, and that group gets hit by a shark, there's only a 10 percent chance the shark is after you, but if you're by yourself and a shark comes after you, then it's all you, baby."

"Isn't a big group easier to see for the shark, though? There's more churning of the water, there's noise and vibration."

"Ayeah. That's what Pedro's going to prove. Or disprove."

"Couldn't it be a case of training the sharks to look for behavior?"

"I believe our little blogger is catching on." Muñoz tosses six seal silhouettes into the water, each attached to sensors.

"Each has photorealistic cells and electrodes to make them flip from light to dark, simulating movement. The white is invisible to the shark, while the dark allows the shark to see the shadows. We watch to see if the shark attacks on white or black."

The fake seals flicker in the water. A real seal comes over to check it out, the little whiskers quivering, eyes big and sensitive like a bulldog puppy, but it loses interest and swims off. Chernowski regales us with tales of past grisly shark predation, about how he's seen seals bisected, or disembodied seal parts floating in Mirounga Bay, much to the delight of the SEFI gulls, eager little omnivores with a strong sense of entitlement.

While we wait, we listen to KQED's reports of four different new strains of the $H_3N_2$ flu and the rush for a vaccine and Muñoz and Chernowski discuss antibiotic-resistant bugs as casually as you or I might talk about the latest Taylor Swift album. Avian flus, as you might imagine, are kind of a big deal on SEFI. The naturalists have had a growing distaste for the intervention of man in the natural order. Chernowski plays devil's advocate, suggesting that if man hadn't created penicillin, the bugs wouldn't be quite so adept at killing us like Raid kills cockroaches, but Muñoz points out that the Spanish flu pandemic of 1918 predated penicillin by ten years.

So there's that. That's all I got until next time.

Jane

# Day 5

**DB Cooper**
**@DBmm**

The governor is closing all schools for at least two weeks due to five confirmed cases? I mean . . . okay, sure, but how am I supposed to work if my kid can't go to school and the daycares are all closed too?

♡ 32 💬 7 ⟳ 9

**Jesus Don't Live Here**
**@karl1952**

WHO blew it. Funded by the US taxpayers but for some reason focused on Asia and Mexicant countries. #americafirst #invisibleenemy #liberalmedia

♡ 16.3K 💬 41 ⟳ 506

**Gemma**
**@Gemma1989**

If mosquitos sucked fat instead of blood, there would be mosquito rooms at Planet Fitness.

♡ 36 💬 1 🔁 1

**Cosmoballiton**
**@CosmoNoFilter**

The older I get the more I identify with Emily Gilmore. Lorelai IS a terrible daughter. Rory DOES need to network with better people!

♡ 147 💬 3 🔁 17

**World Health Organization** ✔
**@WHO**

Simple ways to prevent the spread of illness in your workplace: Brief your employees, contractors and customers that anyone with a mild cough, fever, headache, or insomnia lasting more than three days needs to stay home. #h3n2

♡ 1K 💬 147 🔁 618

# Day 6

## BRIAN

The first time I went into a fugue state, I was a kid. My mom had scraped up money to send me to a weeklong camp in northern Wisconsin after my dad walked out on us. She thought I needed more male role models. The camp counselor was a college freshman named Ryan. I instantly disliked him, like I disliked all Ryans due to frequently mishearing their name as my own.

On arrival, we toured the camp, a cluster of eight preteen boys and our collective prepubescent funk cloud of armpit, peanut butter, and blooming testosterone.

We passed an insect-filled buzzing fetid pool more algae than liquid, and a bullfrog croaked. I did a spot-on impression of the bullfrog saying "Fart," which made everyone laugh, even the counselor.

Then, without warning, this big kid named Randolph shot his left arm out and knocked me off balance, straight into the brackish water.

The green light glimmered through the duckweed and watermeal, speckled at the surface, while fronds of coontail and bladderwort caught in my grasping fingers. I tried to push off the bottom, but my feet sunk into the ooze. The water clouded; the light was gone— "up" was an impossibility. My mouth filled with slime, grassy and sulfur-tasting, cool and hot at the same time.

A hand pulled me up out of the water, sputtering, covered in a slick of cadmium green *Microcystis*. Ryan patted me on the back while I choked and sobbed, revulsion and humiliation competing for first billing inside my brain, while the other kids roared, elbowing each other.

When Ryan was satisfied that I wasn't going to die, he tried to make peace. "Randy, don't you think you should apologize to Brian, buddy?"

The Antichrist of Camp Waubanoosa looked at me through baleful pinpricks and said, "My name is Randolph. Not Randy. I'm not a hoooooorrrrrny gaylord like Brian."

The other six boys erupted into laughter, and then all raced to come up with similar jokes at my expense, landing immediately in the vicinity of green M&M'S making you horny.

What the fuck. This demon child—Randolph—had already marked me as a target for the entire time at camp after, what, eighteen minutes?

Ryan turned to me and whispered, "OK, Brian, why don't you go back, take a shower, and meet us out by the archery field." He clapped me on my shoulder again—I would later learn that Ryan's shoulder clap was the only tool in his toolbox for mentoring adolescent boys—and off they went, still snickering like gibbons, shoving each other, Randolph leading the way.

Along the way, I passed a gaggle of teenage girls who sneered at the tears burning my cheeks. In the shower, I peeled off the putrid stinking pair of shorts and what I had thought was a cool polo shirt, a selkie shedding its coat. I didn't bother to shower with my bathing suit, unheard of at '90s preteen camps where death was preferable to appearing even slightly homosexual. Under the hot water, my skin turned bright pink, bare-assed, my young wiener for all the world to see. Word got around. The caste was set.

But showers became my safe space. Stay underwater until it all runs away, buddy. Down the drain, buddy. Let it wash away, buddy.

And so even now, every morning, my reward for keeping my heart rate above 150 for at least forty-five minutes is the most luxurious shower I can afford. There is no bad side to this, no gambling habit burning through my 401(k), no white delight snorted up a nose, just a bottle of nice-smelling body wash.

I had taken a scalding, aggressive everything shower last night after the news, the terrifying new virus, a megaflu that was keeping people up at night . . . literally, not figuratively. Who needs a therapist when you have incredible water pressure?

Practically everyone on my social media streams was down with the H3N2 thing—most of them known hypochondriacs. We each hold tiny blue suns up to our faces and then are surprised when our primate selves can't get a decent moment's rest. H3N2 was the new thing. Gwynnie had it, purportedly. Taylor. One of the Disney kids. It would probably cull a few oldsters from the herd—which terrifies the baby boomers and sends them into a scurry of pearl clutching.

How much worrying about not falling asleep causes you to be unable to fall asleep?

New social media influencers—apocalypse crazies—had brewed up and trended too. What was it with the apocalypse? You didn't hear about the end of the world in the '80s and '90s, other than that movie where a passing comet turns everyone into red dust. Between the Mayan calendar and the drug that caused people to lose their minds and eat people's faces off, everyone's favorite fantasy is one where the world is coming to an end but they're the rugged last few survivors.

The thing that killed the dinosaurs wasn't a comet or a dust cloud but the assumption when the end came for most of the population, somehow, they'd be one of the few dinosaurs left unscathed.

I scraped up the last of my breakfast—a cold mess of groats that was starting to taste more annoyingly healthy by the moment—rinsed it in the sink, then checked out the weather at the window. Like a hard brown pit inside a juicy peach, my industrial loft sits on South Island, a weird industrial no-man's-land sheltered by steep-cut banks on either side of the Fox River, the entirety of Appleton cradling it on either side. A conglomerate of Victorian houses along the riverbanks sits audience to this little blighted pimple in the river, and high behind them, Craftsman bungalows and pale cream bricked businesses comprise the bulk of downtown.

Despite the worrisome headlines, there was nothing awry out there—the same old trees, the same old staid church-going Midwesterners in their various and sundry pursuits of happiness. The sun glinted off the river below, while a semitrailer full of beer lumbered across South Bridge.

Summer was so fast here in Wisconsin. When I had originally purchased the flour mill and started prepping it for a full-time studio and business, Californian friends were incensed. "You know it snows there, right? Say goodbye to your balls, son. You won't see them for six months!"

They would never have had such concerns about New York or even Boston. Californians like to think they have weather drama, but they have nothing over the resigned complacency of the Midwest. Snow—*actual snow!*—would begin to fall out of the sky any day now. And while this holy miracle was occurring, the Wisconsin natives, unlike the divas in New York and Boston, will continue their grocery shopping and trundle off to church on Sunday mornings all the same, without much of a sniff toward the impractical juxtaposition of their plans and the inconvenience of the weather.

The snow, it is. The seasons, they just are. The people, they just will. After three years, I still found the quickness of the seasons charming. I never appreciated it when I grew up here—not until I had lived in California for a decade did I realize this was the glimmer of Zen that I'd been searching for, a dedication to forging onward, the unending reminder that time was passing.

Somewhere upstream, the Fox started its descent from Lake Winnebago at least a hundred feet higher. Where once there had been angry rapids, man's instinct to triumph over nature in the nineteenth century involved a series of twenty-two gull wing canals, elevators for boats. A boat goes into the lock, a door shuts behind it, and the boat lowers as water drains out slowly until the boat reaches the water level below. A reverse operation raises the boat to the height above the rapids. The locks began as a way to transport goods to and from Winnebago all the way up to Green Bay and then into Lake Michigan, and presumably the world. One such lock sat to the west of South Island, creating a fast-moving channel of water that dead-ended at two formidable concrete sluices, then diverted off through an iron screen that kept any lost swimmers from shooting down twenty-six feet to the rocks below. The navigation channel skirted up against South Island for its length and often hosted pelicans, Canada geese and their goslings, and the occasional South Island hobo. His name was Bob.

And even though everything looked entirely normal, on either side of this island, contagious people were walking around like assholes with all manner of fauna and germs and bugs that wanted nothing better than to settle into your sinuses, lungs, bowels, or groin region.

Unlike the dinosaurs and their hubris, I fully expected to be slammed by each and every new horror. It was only a matter of time. Every cold and flu I'd had could be traced to plane trips or handshakes at various Chicago and New York art galleries—or that dreaded European double-cheek kiss Midwesterners confused with actual lip contact. I was in the thick of it. Cold and flu season. *Abandon all hope, ye who enter here.* Y2K and 9/11, $H_3N_2$ and whatever other initialed horror was going to take us all out next, let it all come. Come take me home.

When did I become so ambivalent about the Grim Reaper?

When my mother died in her terrible apartment above a bakery in Wrigleyville, after the funeral, after being found by her hospice worker while I was at work, after all the meaningless litanies of her friends patting me on the hand and pulling me into embraces that I neither wanted nor deserved, I had a "bad moment."

I never knew someone who died. I didn't have a family other than her. I was unfamiliar with the solid press of dense matter that settled into my chest cavity like I was the damsel in that Fuseli painting, pressing against my sternum and making human interactions nearly impossible. Her friends—fuzzy-headed, asterisks for mouths, lipstick bleeding into deep vertical wrinkles from decades of smoke breaks—infuriated me. *Why aren't you dead instead of her? Why aren't all of you dead?* The entire room reeked of too much L'Air du Temps and the caustic ripples of poorly chosen words.

After the service—as though someone had done me a "service" by burying my mother, as though the incubus sitting on my chest awaited some "service" in kind—I didn't know what to do with myself. I'd told my boss that I'd be out for the rest of the week, but the black suit I wore propelled me like a marionette onto my commuter train and up through the station, into the building and then up to my desk in my cubicle high above the Loop. Everyone avoided my gaze. At least they didn't try. *Why weren't they dead?*

My desk was on the seventeenth floor, in the outer part of a series of identical cubicles. My stanchion had a half wall that looked out onto another high-rise office complex. People often mistook me for a receptionist and informed me that the copier was running low on toner. When the sun hit right, you could see the reflection of the top half of the Hancock building. There was a signal that it was coming, the reflection serving as a flashpoint, so I'd hold up an empty file folder to shield my eyes for three minutes until it traced over my shoulder. Approximately four minutes after that, the reflection faded and the Hancock building reflection was perfect, a crystalline beacon to man's surge toward Heaven.

But it didn't make sense: The Hancock building was west, and it shouldn't reflect from the east. A mystery every day. How did it happen? It felt like a gift from God, a real-life Easter egg.

My mother was in a coffin, her remains bald and scorched by radiation, poisoning her grave for future decades, and I would have nothing but this cubicle with its half wall and its eight-minute mystery reflection.

It was, until then, my crowning achievement.

That afternoon, after that funeral, the *service*, I stared at my inbox, not clicking on anything, the unread emails coming one approximately every forty-three seconds. I could not be of service any longer. I needed servicing. I was a copier, out of toner, drained, unserviceable.

I waited for the reflection, but instead of my normal eight-minute break to enjoy the high-definition crispness of the Hancock's steel girders, I rose the moment the light struck my eyes. I wrote "I quit" on the file folder I normally used to shield my eyes and taped it to the window. It hung crooked, and I resisted the urge to adjust it. As I left, my coworkers looked downward, afraid of my contagious grief.

Outside, I turned and faced the building, scanning until I finally spotted the file folder askew on the seventeenth-floor window. The damp clung to the sidewalk, the slightest dense tang of fish water rising from Lake Michigan. The sheer glass building across the street still had the mysterious reflection, as did the building to the left. And another building, a matte glass monster that seemed to absorb light, was, at that moment, lit up like New Year's Eve in the setting sun.

It was a mirror trick, a fata morgana. The blue glass acted like a movie projector, and Hancock reflected and refracted over and over again, first to my building and then bouncing across the street. The people there had an even better view than I had, for those brief eight minutes. As soon as it crested past a water tower, the light show was over and the blue building was dull once again.

I went back to my mother's beige-and-cream apartment, grabbed our family photos, her wedding ring, and the sweater she had worn the last time we went to tea at the Drake together—light blue with white snowflakes, a terrible acrylic thing, pilled at the elbows. I had been so ashamed with her, sitting there among the old grand dames and little rich girls dining with their dolls on Michigan Avenue, but I had said nothing. If I had, my mother certainly would have said, "Oh, Brian, get over yourself," and changed the subject to her latest crafting extravaganza.

I made the grievous mistake of bringing her sweater close to my face and caught her scent—a punch to the gut that I was neither expecting nor worthy of withstanding. That moment, everything solidified—I was done. Done with here. Done with this. I crammed the thing into a too-small plastic zip bag. I could huff it like a junkie in a quiet moment, bring it out for Christmas and drape it over a chair as though she had stepped out of the room and might return at any minute.

Then I got into my car and drove. I wanted away from Lake Michigan. Its color was too bright. Too much like her sweater. The easiest direction to go was west—away. Just away. I thought I'd drive for a few hours and then turn around and come back, but instead I drove for three days, resting my eyes in truck stops and stopping at twenty-four-hour drugstores to purchase things like a toothbrush, pit stick, and a giant bottle of aspirin, along with fancifully colored sodas and gummy candies.

Eventually I ran out of land at the Golden Gate Bridge. As I drove across, I unrolled the windows and smelled the salty air, like the taste of a fresh oyster. Mist rolled over the hills. I thought about taking a picture to send to my mother. For a moment, I had forgotten she was dead. Then I hated myself for remembering.

This would be good. This was a sign that I could outrun it, the pain incubus that wanted to crawl inside the hole where my heart once had been. This was a sign that if I stayed far enough away, she was still there, in Chicago, sitting in her stifling hot box of an apartment, crocheting afghans and making counted cross-stitch Christmas ornaments.

In Petaluma, my eyes and initiative gave up, momentum ending, a ball rocking in an executive desk toy that was swinging in shorter and shorter ellipses toward an inevitable stillness. When I woke twenty-one hours later in a hotel, I sent my funeral suit out to be cleaned and then spent the next day waiting for it to come back, sitting in my boxer shorts with a Do Not Disturb sign hanging on the door. Between episodes of *Teen Mom* and *Dance Moms* and *I Didn't Know I Was Pregnant*, I arranged to have my mother's and my furniture sold in a double estate sale back in Chicago. It was excruciating and took six hours to fax back and forth from the business center in the lobby, where I was unapologetic about my boxer briefs.

And so it was in Petaluma that I gave in to the fugue state—I blew through dozens of stiff hotel towels during two weeks of seven to eight showers a day.

Eventually, for lack of anything better to do, I had to rebuild my "estate," as the lawyer called it. I would distract myself, create a new moiré pattern to focus on instead of the heavy weight that pressed on my sternum and made every intake and release of breath a refrain of *She's gone. You're alone. She's dead. You're alone.* Wearing my freshly pressed funeral suit out of necessity more than any need to impress, I went to Heath Ceramics to buy some plates. Four was a non-sad number, hopeful, optimistic I would meet someone to have dinner with eventually. Three other someones.

A sign in the window—Now Hiring.

This was the first time Other Brian—a false cheerful charming bastard—appropriated my body and forced the right words out of my face. Other Brian impressed the factory manager with my knowledge of Big Ten football, my few ceramics electives in college, and the famed Midwestern politeness. Other Brian kept his shit together. I was grateful. Other Brian became my best friend and most trusted ally, ready to do difficult interactions. Other Brian took that Heath job and asked for better pay.

And wouldn't you know, the asshole got it.

I lost myself in pottery. Six days a week, I refined the rims of expensive dinner plates. Circle after perfect circle, boring grunt work typically given to underpaid migrant workers, had Sausalito not been such a cradle for nouveau riche and had Heath Ceramics been unable to command idiots with MFAs for slave wages. After work, another four to six hours making my own wares in the factory, for lack of anything better to do. The porcelain felt good. It was control. The weight on my chest was pushed forward to the hump on the wheel, spinning round and round, fighting against my left hand to create symmetry and fluid vessels.

Out of lumps, I made mounds, out of mounds, I raised mountains, out of mountains, a hole, a well, a deep longing and yearning for form.

Using the studio for your own work was the only perk of the job. Well, that and telling beautiful young ladies about Heath, and your personal indie cachet rose three notches in a millisecond. Pottery whores, my co-potters called them. I was never so crass. Besides, a gentleman never treats his lady callers with anything but respect, but yes, after rounds of Pabst Blue Ribbon in the parking lot of the No Name Bar there was a lot of gratuitous oral sex.

But one day off, it was one of those perfect San Francisco days that made Tony Bennett insist that his heart had been left behind. After more than a year of staring at the famous skyline from the Marin side of the Bay, I had the irrepressible urge to stare back at Marin. So I jumped on the Sausalito ferry and made a day of it.

It was starting to be less painful, enjoying myself. On the boat, I practiced the phrase in my head: *My mother is dead. My father has no idea what I even look like. Everyone I ever loved has left me.* It was benign, a matter-of-fact statement, one that didn't pull Other Brian from his hole and into action. I kept trying it, like a hot stove you want to touch. You are a lone. You are. A. Lone. A new magic trick.

I started at the ferry building and meandered along the water, past Fisherman's Wharf until I hit Fort Mason and onward to Crissy Field, where a silver phone lay in the duckweed. Ahead, a girl fought with her bike chain on her fixie.

"Hey, you drop this?"

She looked up at me and squinted in a moment of pure brilliant sunlight. In a movie, she would have been some kind of perfect beauty, an impossible mixture of Audrey Hepburn and Goldie Hawn and Julia Roberts, ready with a giant smile or a flutter of four-inch eyelashes—except she was perfectly ordinary, perfectly forgettable. Brown hair, brown eyes, turned-up nose that might have been cute ten years ago but would become more snout-like as she aged. Almost the same height as me, but long in torso, thick but with an appreciable sturdy quality to her. She wasn't even a girl next door. She was a girl from the block, one whose name you don't bother to learn.

*Your mother is dead. Your father doesn't know you. You're alone.*

The fixie girl checked the pockets of her capri pants, which had the unfortunate quality of making her legs look short and stubby. She patted her ass and groaned. Her forehead had a dirt smudge on it and one shin was bleeding.

"Oh my god, I'm such a wreck. Yes, it's mine. Thank you thank you thank you!" Her words rushed and breathless, like a staccato fire of a machine gun. Her voice was raspy, the voice of an animatronic badger.

Her fingernails were a bright blue underneath the oily bicycle grease, and I wanted to absorb that combination. The colors together, the bright blue and black oil. It was a touch brighter than the cobalt glaze I'd been experimenting with, and the secret with the black was that it was all the colors at once, shimmering with the greens of the grass and the blue and white of the sky, a camera obscura capturing the hot pink of the fixie girl's truly awful choice in capri pants.

"You're totally welcome." I handed her the phone and continued a few steps. Then guilt got the better of me.

"Hey, are you OK? You got things?" Other Brian took over, did a little head tilt as though to say, "I'm not hitting on you, I'm a nice guy, promise." Both things were true. Or so I allowed myself to believe.

"Uh . . . yeah. Yeah, I got this. Boy, do I totally have this." She crinkled her forehead. It was clear that she did not in fact have it. The heavy bike wobbled as she wrenched the chain, edging it up over the teeth of the stubborn chain mechanism. I took one more step away, then stopped and turned to watch.

"I'm OK, I said. I'm fine. I can do this." She knocked back a piece of hair from her forehead, leaving a black grease smudge across a cheek.

"I see that." I leaned against a garbage bin, making it clear that I wasn't going anywhere.

"Then . . . why don't you . . . there!" The chain snapped over the mechanism into place. "See? I had it."

"That wasn't in question. I wanted to see how it was done. I've been thinking about buying a ridiculously overpriced vintage bicycle myself. Would you know someone who wanted to, say, unload one?" Other Brian smiled warmly. Or I smiled. It felt real. It hit my eyes. Maybe Other Brian sank back into his warren and let me take the wheel. *You are alone. Your mother is dead.*

She took a breath and then looked back at the bike with skepticism. "I couldn't part with this one, of course. It's my Zen koan."

"The grease under the nails is part of the humility?"

"Part of the fun!" She knew exactly how ridiculous the entire endeavor was but smiled anyway. She pumped the pedal to get some momentum, but the chain threw again and the pedal flew around, nailing her in the back of the calf.

"BALL SACK!" She winced in pain, dismounting the bike with a triple hop. She was light on her feet for such a sturdy girl.

"Nailed the dismount. I mean, the Russian judge only gave you a 4."

"The Russian judge is still bitter the French judge didn't laugh at her joke."

"The German judge thinks they're all weak." I said it before I could stop myself, but she smirked.

"You know what?" She blew a chunk of hair up out of her face as she kneeled, again taking grasp of the chain and trying to work it up over the teeth. "This isn't even my bike. I borrowed it from the girl who is sleeping with my boyfriend. My ex-boyfriend, I mean."

You had to consider your next move carefully. Girls bringing up ex-boyfriends were either looking to hook up/trigger the jealousy response, unfiltered and socially awkward, or batshit crazy. You don't stick your dick in crazy, as my sort-of roommate Taylor liked to say. This girl would be Taylor's type. Probably.

"Did she say, 'No take backsies?' Because even if the guy is a loser, he's probably a more reliable mode of transportation than this thing. I mean if he has a strong back." I winced even as it came out of my idiotic face.

She pressed her mouth into a tight line. "Something like that."

I pretended I hadn't knocked her to her knees with my stupid comment. "Well then, I say you give it to that crackhead over there." I nodded to a shabby individual sitting on a park bench, menacing some seagulls. "He probably needs a ride back to the Tenderloin."

She snorted in response and slipped the chain back over the teeth. The pedals whirred like a roulette wheel, and for a moment I imagined a ball popping and popping, pushed by the hand of Fate to land on 00.

Satisfied that the chain would hold, she threw her leg gracefully over the bike and tried the pedals again. "Thanks again for my phone. I better get going before the crackhead gets ideas."

"Well, keep passing the open windows." I turned, pleased at having had a brush with a Bay Area hipster that I could relate back to the other guys at the pottery factory.

The bike wheezed, clattering up behind me. She was back. "Wait, what did you say?" She stuck a foot out to the pavement to steady herself.

The bike's frame was too big. The ex-boyfriend stealer must have been significantly taller, or possibly set the seat high on purpose. It's what I would have done. Perhaps I wasn't a nice guy after all.

"That sounds like you've got some more enlightenment coming. I like a koan that has its own alarm system." The high-pitched whining of the gears tricked some Ultimate Frisbee dorks into checking their phones.

"Did you say 'Keep passing the open windows'?"

I paused. She dragged her rough hemp sneakers along the path, stopping the bike like a Flintstone.

"I did. It's a line from a book." What a dick. Explaining it like a literate snob. The book was from the '80s, and not exactly *On the Road.* I liked my little references, the way it kept people at a distance while also putting them off-kilter.

"*Hotel New Hampshire*. Yeah. I know it."

"Pretty corny." I tried the self-deprecation angle to shut her down. As much as I didn't want to explain it, it unnerved me that she got the reference. I stuck my hands into my jean pockets and looked off into the distance, scanning a pair of bouncing Marina Girl asses in tiny yoga shorts. She followed my gaze and squinched the corner of her mouth.

"Yeah, well, thanks again for my phone back." She stood on the pedal and passed by in a clatter of chains, widgets, and bike springs. Her slow departure gave ample time to consider her uninspiring ass.

*You are alone, buddy. Everyone you've ever loved is gone.*

Then, a distinct silver cell phone lying in the grass. There was a smudge of black grease on the side.

She had known the line from *The Hotel New Hampshire*. One of my favorite books in the entire world. It was schmaltzy and sordid and a little indulgent. I had a weakness for maudlin, it seemed. Her fixie was nowhere to be seen. What would John Irving do? I pocketed it and headed home.

That night, I spent an hour texting every contact and searching the internet. It was a welcome respite from my post-factory downtime, four guys crammed into a one-bedroom apartment in Mill Valley, two futons in what should have been a living room, a refrigerator dedicated to Belgian ales and Cowgirl Creamery cheeses. She was the "chief storyteller" (one of the owner's phrases), worked for a start-up in the city. She wasn't unimportant but wasn't important either.

Jane. Her name was Jane.

What made me take the phone?

*Alone. You are alone. Alone.*

Something familiar in the curve of her nose, the spatter of freckles across her cheeks, and the way she looked uncomfortable against that backdrop of famous hills and eucalyptus trees. She was the first person I'd met who wasn't judging me for being there, like she wasn't waiting for me to trip up or be cool or ironic or entertaining.

It was one of the fanciest phones I'd ever seen—of course, now it would seem practically prehistoric, like trying to communicate with two seashells. After some monkeying around, I logged into her email—something that wasn't even a thing with phones back then. After I noted the email address (JaneWithAWhy@aol.com), I logged out of the network so I wouldn't be tempted to read her emails. Normally, I would have happily snooped through a stranger's email. Perhaps even popped popcorn and settled in. Somehow this one felt different, as though it would damage something already made permanent in the future.

She lived in the Castro, in one of those skinny apartments with four electrical outlets shared between six rooms. The email address was a riddle, a brief intelligence test to see who listens closely. I already liked her.

Dear Mademoiselle—

It seems while you keep passing the open windows, I keep passing a familiar phone on various bike paths in the city. Proof of life attached.

Best, Brian

I used my roommate's digital camera to snap a photo of her phone next to that day's issue of the *San Francisco Chronicle* and attached it to the email.

An hour later, there was a reply.

Dear Sir,

It's not often a gentleman comes to my rescue twice in one day. Are you perhaps a pickpocket with a guilty conscience? Or perhaps my phone is trying to make its escape and find a better home. I promise if you trust me with this phone once more, I'll stop beating it when it misbehaves.

Cheers, Jane

PS. Where can I pick up my phone? And what's your favorite guilty pleasure? Guilty pickpockets should be rewarded for coming clean.

Dear Mademoiselle Jane—

Virtue is its own reward, and I would not be a gentleman if I didn't offer to return your little silver phone. It cries at night without its owner. I tried singing it to sleep but I fear I have a tin ear and only know bawdy sea shanties. One too many songs about swimming with bowlegged women and your delicate little piece of technology is unlikely to stray from your hand again, I suspect.

Best, Brian

PS. Also, I live in the wilds of Marin County, where the city folk are loathe to pause unless on their way to Healdsburg for expensive libations. I'm making a delivery into the city next Monday. I'll drop it off.

Dear kind sir,

Do not let outer appearances fool you, sir, as my phone has heard far worse cussing and dirty conjecture from my own mouth, I'm afraid. This Wisconsin girl unfortunately picked up a trucker's vocabulary along with her pasty white complexion and love of dairy products.

> Cheers, Jane
>
> PS. Can I buy you a coffee or lunch or a Krugerrand for the return of my phone?

My fair Mademoiselle,

This Wisconsin-born guy is well-versed in the mother tongue and would suspect, however, what serves as cussing in the Hinterland pales in comparison to the salty, colorful phrasing of the Golden Coast. This is a melting pot, full of the hard consonants of the Slavic lands mixed with the trilled R's and lilting clicks of the Hispanic and Asian communities. I have but to look at the reaction of your fancy little phone to know you could do your worst, fine lady, and it wouldn't even shock me. I do remember a fair lady filling the delicate flora of Crissy Field with the battle cry of "Ball sack!" Also, I live with three guys, so . . . yeah.

> Best, Brian
>
> PS. We'll do the exchange over coffee. I'll wear a blaze-orange hunting cap and a pair of red long johns. Actually, I have neither of those things, but I guess you already know what I look like, so look for a guy that looks exactly like that guy. 10 a.m.?

Good kind Sir,

Wisconsin, you say? I should have known. Your honesty should have tipped me off, like a cow is tipped in the cold autumn nights of homecoming. I work in the Mission, but parking is a bitch there, so there's a little lunch counter in Potrero Hill that has ample parking and a decent cup of coffee. They don't do slow drip or espresso or anything like that—it's diner stuff tasting kind of alkaline and smelling like cat piss, but it's cheap and they have donuts, one of which is filled with a peanut butter banana buttercream, which means they also have my heart. I will be there at 10 a.m. with bells on.

Cheers, Jane

PS. I blew my PS wad in the body of the email, it seems, so I will tell you this: The drummer from Def Leppard only has one arm.

As I read her email, I heard a surprising sound.

Laughter. Not Other Brian's smarmy chuckle. My own actual laugh.

A guilty invocation, as though my throat had forgotten it was supposed to be sad. I clamped my hand over my mouth. The sound still hung in the air, but the apartment was still.

Unabated, I turned back to my computer. Our emails grew longer and more intricate, with flurries of small observations. She volleyed my pop culture references into elaborate puns and turns of phrase that I admired for their compact wit.

She was *everything* I wished I could be.

At work the next day, I developed a complex system of plastic wrap around my laptop keyboard at the pottery factory, earning the nickname the Keyboard Condom from my fellow Heathens. Each key strike left a dusty hieroglyphic on the plastic until the entire surface was covered in my porcelain slip fingerprints.

That Monday I rose early, loaded up the Heath delivery van with two yards of tiles bound for the city, and tucked Jane's phone into my flannel shirt pocket, where it bounced against my nipple.

At 9:49 a.m. in the diner, I picked a stool where I could look casual while also seeing both doors—without giving the appearance of watching for her.

"Are you Brian?" The waitress poured me a cup of standard-issue black coffee.

"Yeah." Was I being set up? Had my last email ventured out of audacity into some convivial gray area that should never have been breached? In an instant, I worried I'd never get another email from her, about the physical withdrawal I sometimes felt when she took more than three hours to respond, the way it felt a little bit like hunger and a little bit like being horny and a little bit like the first minute of bewilderment upon waking up in a new place.

The waitress dug behind the straws in her apron and extracted a small envelope with "Brian" scrawled across the entirety of the front of the envelope. Inside, a gift card to the diner and a nice letterpress stationery note engraved with JMS on the top, and straightforward, almost masculine printed black ink on the note itself:

> Brian—Sorry, meetings! No excuse, I suck. I didn't want you to wait around. I appreciate your bringing the phone, so can you please leave it with Suzy (waitress) and I'll pick it up later? Have coffee and a donut on me! Have a steak if you want (actually, don't, you might get food poisoning, but the donuts are perfectly safe. Believe me, I'd be deathly ill if they weren't).—Jane

I handed the phone to the waitress. "You'll give this to Jane? The girl who gave you this note?"

"Yeah, she stops in here for coffee. She's got a tab with us."

"Great. Can you put this credit on her tab?" Jane would never notice the five or ten dollars in her pool of coffee debt, and it would be my little joke to myself, a shallow victory.

I wouldn't find out what she had worn to work that day. Probably not the terrible capri pants. Not seeing her felt like a much bigger disappointment than it should have been.

Already I was forgetting exactly what her face looked like.

Days later, when I put on the jeans fresh out of the dryer, I found her note, semi-disintegrated. It had taken on the soft sleepiness of a child's comfort blanket. Pulling the clinging paper apart, I hoped against hope the message had remained. Most had faded into whispers, only "wait around" and "leave" and "poisoning" and "deathly" were strong enough to read. I could almost make out "donuts are safe" if I squinted.

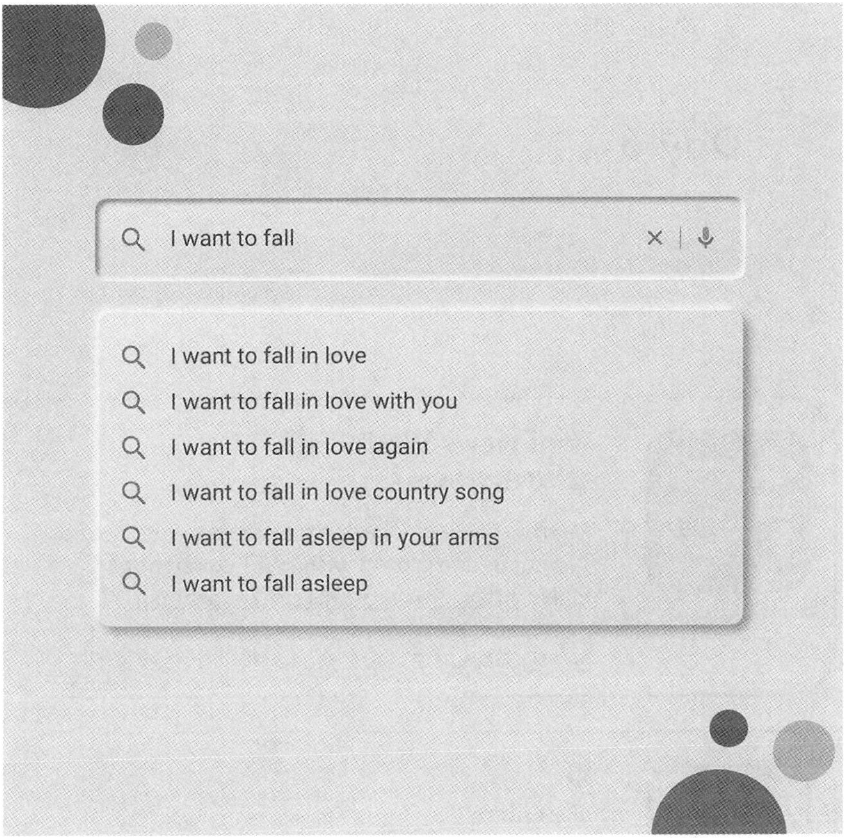
I want to fall
I want to fall in love
I want to fall in love with you
I want to fall in love again
I want to fall in love country song
I want to fall asleep in your arms
I want to fall asleep

## Day 6

**Wolf News WNBS**
**@WNBSNews**

Miami mayor declares state of emergency after 15 people confirmed with nSFI covalent of $H3N2$ http://www.bit.ly.com/miaminsfi

♡ 19.8K 💬 4.1K ⟲ 5.7K

**Xi**
**@sXlilate**

It's been lovely to meet you. Some of you less so. I don't want to be on this earth anymore. All I've ever wanted was for people to be helped and happy.

♡ 1.1K 💬 118 ⟲ 3

**Mychelle**
**@MightyMych**

My anxiety is off the hook. I got a spontaneous nosebleed and of course it means nothing but it's so damn ominous.

♡ 302 ◯ 17 ⟳ 39

**DB Cooper**
**@DBmm**

The recorder. The child's teacher has mailed us a recorder for distance learning. A. Recorder. Move over, H3N2, I have a new enemy.

♡ 187 ◯ 7 ⟳ 9

# Day 7

## H3N2 Live Updates: What It Is and What It Isn't

There's always something new happening in the microbial world. Scientists find an average of one new pathogen every year and this year has already broken virality records. On top of numerous continued mutations of known viruses, an H3N2 flu virus has recently emerged, an especially virulent strain that kicked off the traditional northern hemisphere flu season with a bang, followed by the identification of a new form of fatal insomnia prion disease that seems to be riding alongside or taking advantage of newly weakened immune responses to the standard seasonal flu.

The rising strain of respiratory influenza is nothing new—doctors gamble every year on which strain will most likely be most prevalent by packaging and designing flu shots around those gambles. Influenza typically kills around 250,000 to 500,000 people around the world annually, according to recent World Health Organization estimates, but a recent study showed an increase in mortality burden to another 200,000 deaths from lower respiratory tract infections and other outlying causes linked directly to influenza. H3N2 is on course for a more virulent influenza outbreak, impacting primarily those with heightened immune risks and preexisting immunocompromised conditions like asthma, diabetes, and cancer as well as geriatric patients.

While H3N2 and the emerging strain of virulent fatal insomnia prion disease are both transmitted from person to person, the level of Ro, or contagiousness, is still being determined. H3N2 tracks marginally more fatal than a common flu outbreak, but those with the prionic complication have a serious condition that may be mitigated by early detection and medical treatment. However, for those who go untreated, the prognosis is not reassuring—no one has spontaneously improved or eliminated an integrated prion infection to date.

For most people, H3N2 and the growing transmission of novel sporadic fatal insomnia (nSFI) share similar symptoms—problems with muscle coordination, slight personality changes, headaches, insomnia, and mild to severe depression. Individuals with H3N2 can expect their symptoms to alleviate as the body's own immune system fights off the virus. Individuals with nSFI must be diagnosed through spinal lumbar puncture or electroencephalography (EEG) which records the brain's electrical patterns. Advanced cases of the disease can also be diagnosed using a standard MRI, which is noninvasive.

**DB Cooper**
**@DBmm**

How can we stay home if we're infected with H3N2 if there are no tests available to check if we're infected with H3N2? It's not like the WHO didn't have warning that a super contagious thing was coming.

♡ 956 💬 45 ⟳ 17

**First World Facts**
**@firstworldfacts**

Cell phone radiation causes insomnia. People who use their phone before bed sleep less.

♡ 1.1K 💬 17 ⟳ 110

**World Medical News**
**@worldmednow**

Supreme Court debating states' powers during pandemic, while Germany institutes full mandatory lockdown to reduce viral spread

♡ 1.8K 💬 11 ⟳ 374

**DB Cooper**
**@DBmm**

It takes the confirmed cases to climb to 324 before the idiots in city hall will admit there's a problem here? SHELTER IN PLACE. STAY THE FUCK HOME. If no one goes out, no one catches the virus, and it gives people who have it time to get better. This is simple science.

♡ 1.5K 💬 17 ⟳ 19

**Jesus Don't Live Here**
**@karl1952**

What happened in Korea is the beginning—what happens when you take our guns. #takeamericaback

♡ 28K 💬 78 ⟳ 9.5K

**Gemma**
**@Gemma1989**

Big sign at work—if we're sick, we have to find someone to cover our shifts or we lose our jobs. No sick pay, shitty health care, and hardcore guilt about taking off—why do I work here again?

2 0 3

**Wolf News WNBS**
**@WNBSNews**

New York facing significant increase in public suicides, as many as 200 per day off the Brooklyn Bridge alone. Counselors have been stationed on critical zones.

934 40 62

**Wolf News WNBS**
**@WNBSNews**

Machete attack at popular park in Eureka, Missouri, claims 11 lives, some children. Attacker has taken own life in the jungle gym after failed negotiations with police.

301 61 24

**Xi**
**@sXlilate**

As someone with immunocompromised everything, would sure appreciate not having to go to the office but the boss has sworn we must be in the office or life as we know it will cease. Sure. Cool.

♡ 17 💬 2 ⟳ 1

**Julie Mons**
**@monsjul**

Young 'uns, I am here to be the bearer of sad news: You will still have zits in your forties.

♡ 45 💬 4 ⟳ 0

**Tiffany Ziese**
**@tbangerzbanger**

Best way to kill a zombie: Reduce infection. Hefty claw hammer (use the claw side, stupid). Gunshot to the head (double tap) from at least 20 feet away. Molatov cocktails (only viable if you're not going to create a running flaming zombie who will burn your city down before it stops twitching). A katana or another well-made Japanese sword. A pissed off badger (Be careful with this, as a zombie badger would be worse than the original zombie)

♡ 345 💬 80 ⟳ 56

# December 1898

# DIPHTHERIA ON THE FARALLONES.

## Lighthouse-Keeper's Young Son Dies—Two of the Other Ten Children on the Islands Stricken.

GEORGE EDWIN CAIN, 9 years old, son of the head keeper of the Farallon lighthouse, died last Thursday of diphtheria and the Madrono will go to the island this morning to bring the remains here for burial. Permission to land the body has been given by the Board of Health, provided the usual regulation is complied with by providing a sealed casket.

Mrs. Nellie Cain, mother of the boy who has just died, is in this city attending another son who is in the hospital, and is heartbroken that she could not be at the bedside of George to comfort his last hours. "I did not know that my boy was sick until they sent for a doctor, and even then I had no idea that it was so serious and the next thing I heard he was dead," she said yesterday evening.

Mrs. Cain is worn with her troubles. "Three years ago last October my boy Cecil fell from the north landing of the lighthouse and was drowned," she said. "Now my Georgie is gone, and Harold is sick in the hospital. We want to bring Georgie here for burial with his brother."

Still another child met death at the Farallon lighthouse within the last three years. The one before this was little Royal Beeman, son of William and Minnie Beeman. Mrs. Beeman is a sister-in-law of Mrs. Cain. The boy died from the result of internal injuries, and the storm that was prevailing at the time lasted so long that all vessels kept clear of the islands. The anxious parents became impatient, and, resolving to wait no longer, attempted to reach the mainland by bringing the body to this city in the large lifeboat called "the black boat," belonging to the lighthouse. It was a perilous effort, considering the weather, but Mr. and Mrs. Beeman could wait no longer. After hours of struggling with the waves they reached the entrance to the Golden Gate just about dark, and were dismayed to find the tide running so strong against them that they could make no headway with their oars. The prospect of having to pass the night in the open sea beyond the mouth of the harbor threatened, but at that moment a pilot-boat swept past them. By great efforts they managed to make themselves heard and were picked up and brought to the city in safety.

Mrs. Cain says that she and all who have investigated the circumstances have been unable to explain the origin of diphtheria on the islands. Three children were attacked, and their condition grew to be so bad that Dr. Frank Gray was sent out to do what was possible for the sufferers. He arrived too late to help the Cain boy, who was first stricken, but the others he has saved, and by isolating them he hopes to prevent the spreading of the disease to the remaining ten children on the islands.

Application has been made to the Federal authorities at Washington to remove the little patients from the lighthouse to the Quarantine station at Angel Island, where they may have the advantages of hospital treatment. If permission is given the transfer will be made to-day by the Madrono at the same time that the body of the Cain child is borne hither for burial.

| | | | | | | |
|---|---|---|---|---|---|---|
| Thur | 22 | East | " | " | | worked at Signal Oil to Tower. |
| Fri. | 23 | " | Strong | " | | Repaired East Furnace Sloop Mabel called. |
| Sat | 24 | N. E | fresh | hazy | | Recd Quarterly Ration Pot & Onions Schooner ... Keeper arrived 3.30 a.m Mr Cashin went in on |
| Sun | 25 | N. W | " | " | | Merry Xmas Keepers son taken sick. |
| Mon | 26 | " | " | " | | — |
| Tues | 27 | " | " | " | | Keepers Son very sick nothing in sight. |
| Wed | 28 | " | Gale | Clear | | " worse " " " |
| Thur | 29 | " | Strong | " | | Mr Beeman Wife Son & Daughter & Mr Engelbrekt went to City on the Black boat 12-10 pm. |
| Fri | 30 | " | | " | | Mr Engelbrekt returned from City with Black Boat & Mr Beeman Son very sick. |
| Sat | 31 | South | light | Cloudy | Odd jobs | on Pilot at 11 very rough in the landing. |

C. J. Cain
Asst Keeper

# Day 5

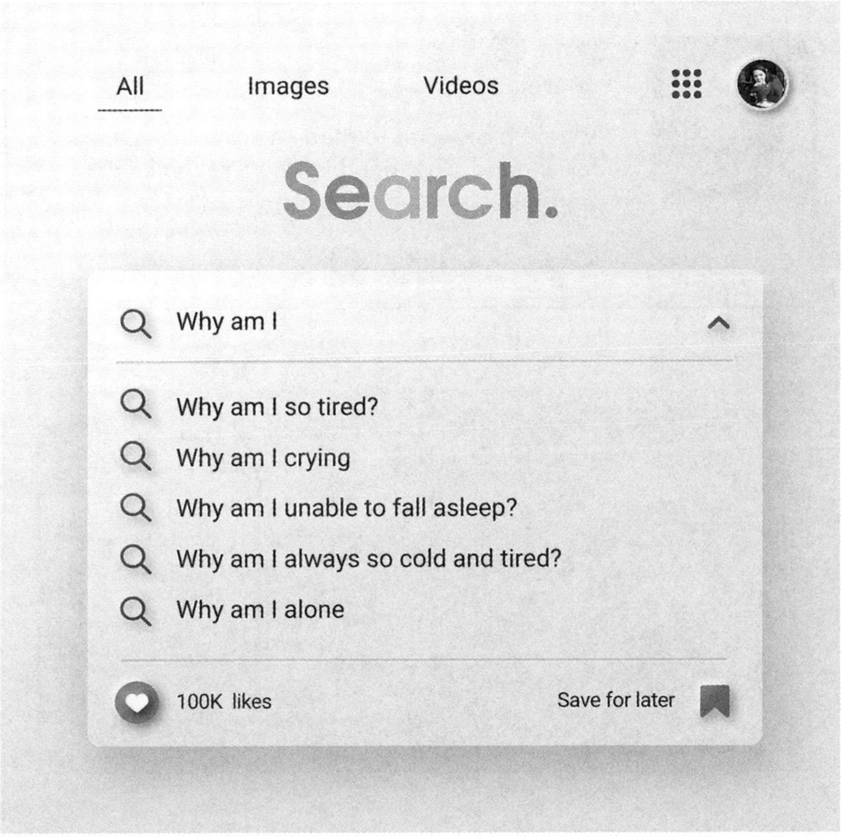
All
Images
Videos
Search.
Why am I
Why am I so tired?
Why am I crying
Why am I unable to fall asleep?
Why am I always so cold and tired?
Why am I alone
100K likes
Save for later

# Day 7

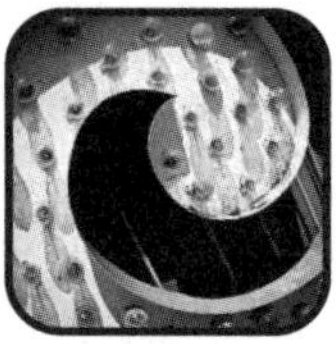

**Jane**
**@erejane**

Would it be weird to marry a seagull? Asking for a friend. The friend is also a seagull, fair warning.

♡ 654 💬 83 ⟳ 4

Obviously, living on an island surrounded by millions of birds, everyone talks bird flu situations. Rick and Pedro have been talking of nothing more than this insomnia virus. Rick did a hardcore rotation in England during the mad cow thing, so he's got a brain chock-full of the horrors of biology, of how proteins cause the body to turn back on itself, basically start devouring itself. Pedro researched chronic wasting disease. He's got theories about sharks being the key to everything.

Sharks seem not to sleep. In reality, Dear Reader, this is a myth (I did not know this myself), and they zone out, taking mini naps while in gliding patterns so water is still moving over their gills (allowing them to take in oxygen). There's also an underwater cave with such high levels of oxygen in the water that biologists have witnessed sharks there actually sitting still and hanging out, all lazy, because they didn't have to move. So, the more you know.

Being scientists, they kindly dumb down a lot of the talk for me. I think they enjoy an attentive pupil. Patty said the interns are all so eager to prove they belong on SEFI that they come off sounding like know-it-alls. I, on the other hand, don't know my ass from a hole in the ground. Dumb is refreshing for them. Here's the video and transcript recorded while on the boat—hear me scrambling to keep up from behind the camera:

RICK: Nah, it's the spillover theory.
ME: (*because I don't ever know a damned thing*) You mean, when the disease travels from animals to humans.

PEDRO: Or vice versa. Really, though, it doesn't travel. I mean, it does travel, but it travels as itself. The big thing is a virus replicates itself in a host cell. It's like a lock and a key. Most of the time, that key doesn't fit the lock and the new host rejects it, but sometimes, the virus is able to either be a key to fit that same lock, or it happens to mutate into a new, different key, working for that lock.

ME: So, at some point, the theory is this H3N2 virus was in birds, the way that COVID was in pangolins maybe?

RICK: Well, jury is out on that, but H3N2, birds, yes, seals, you name it. Avian flu is always bad mojo but the source virus is something else entirely. The SEFI project was working with the government, what was it, Pedro, fifteen years ago?

PEDRO: Something like that. Before my time here.

RICK: Right, before our time, but the CDC often has us collecting samples, fecal, embryonic, all sorts of data gathering.

ME: What did you find?

RICK: The same thing we always find. Things will fucking kill humanity.

ME: That's comforting.

RICK: Ah, you know, everything is ready to take out any species. There are something like 24,394 different organisms on the island right this minute that will take you out in less than a week. Bubonic plague is hiding in your grandma's vegetable garden. It's a matter of the tipping point. Each of those pandemic-type situations can happen at any moment, it's the case of conditions being perfect. Kind of a once-in-a-blue-moon situation within a nested series of once in a blue moon. Like, the odds are ridiculous.

RICK: About as ridiculous as the one sperm needs to connect to the egg inside your mother's womb to create the set of instructions for the special snowflake Jane, I suppose. Look at COVID. Or look at HIV.

PEDRO: What about it?

ME: It went viral in the late '70s or early '80s, but it goes back to the '60s, right?

PEDRO: Further back than that.

ME: I thought they had proof it was in the '60s?

PEDRO: That they do, but the actual spillover, they think happened in 1908.

ME: Seriously? Someone had sex with that infected monkey in 1908.

PEDRO: So, first, it is unlikely someone had sex with a monkey. That's a mixture of racist and homophobic propaganda floating around in the '80s. I'm surprised that people are still thinking that's true.

RICK: People are jackasses.

PEDRO: That IS true. People ARE jackasses. However, no, there are two hypotheses. One is a hunter was butchering an infected monkey and the hunter cut himself, creating a blood-to-blood contact for the spillover.

RICK: That's the one I subscribe to, by the way, but I didn't think it went back to 1908. Imagine all those old asshole men, the ones who insist things were better in the '40s and '50s because *we ain't got no homosexuals with the AIDS back then*. And it turns out HIV was floating around the gene pool before Prohibition, even before the *Titanic* even hit the iceberg.

PEDRO: So, the other one, supported by the '60s cases, is polio vaccines.

RICK: (*clunking on the tape—he's loading a fresh battery into a seal decoy flasher thing*) That's the monkey cell growth one, right?

PEDRO: (*scanning the horizon constantly, sounds distracted*) Yeah, exactly.

ME: Monkey cell growth?

PEDRO: When you get flu shots, they ask if you're allergic to eggs? Because flu shots are grown inside fertilized chicken eggs. They grow vaccines in animal cells, and for some polio vaccines, they used monkey kidney cells in the '50s, end scene, HIV-o-rama.

(*A splash I wasn't fast enough to catch on film—Rick tossing the seal decoy flotilla back into the water. That's him grunting with satisfaction as the faux animals bob in the waves, mimicking the undulation of the real animals.*)

ME: Oh right. I hadn't thought about growing the antibodies. It makes sense. People think they introduced the spillover through polio vaccines.

RICK: (*back up onto the binoculars, scanning the horizon*) A very special polio vaccine, given as a test, to millions in Rwanda, Burundi and the Democratic Republic of Congo .

PEDRO: The only problem, of course, we have samples of HIV-infected human tissue predating the vaccine, so . . . (*Pedro trails off, his eyes fixated on one specific spot off the coast.*)

RICK: See something?

PEDRO: Nah. A shadow.

Rɪᴄᴋ: We'll send them over.

(*As if on cue, a jet-black V-shaped shark fin cuts through the wave, cresting through the water and then back down, right where Pedro had targeted.*)

Mᴇ: That's fucking eerie.

Rɪᴄᴋ: Oooh, she says fuck. (*starting the motor*) Hold on.

The video cuts out here because I ran out of storage space on my video card. Then, a shark—eighteen-footer, easy—struck four times on the seal panels. All chatter ended. The next four hours felt like forty minutes. Soon, the sun had dipped down behind Sugarloaf and we could see the lights on in the kitchen of the program house. Dinner was on its way. I was salty and sore.

I could tell Pedro didn't want to leave, but a wordless discussion seemed to happen between Rick and Pedro, one even I couldn't miss, dense as I was. Rick prevailed, as Pedro gave a tremendous sigh of acceptance and pulled the seal decoys back into the boat.

"Ready?" He stowed his hat inside one of his vest pockets.

"Hit 'er." Rick nodded. In a spray, we headed back to the island.

# Day 8

REDDIT—R/ASKCHICAGO—IT'S COMPLETELY OUT OF CONTROL!

This is serious. The government is rounding up people from the streets, people who are healthy and fine and people who are obviously sick. They're putting them into the same vehicles, which means they don't care about the safety of those healthy people. This is worse than the Gestapo. We don't know where they were taken, just that they were taken. There are rumors of internment camps out of the country. We're trying to find out more information. My friend and his family are missing now and I can't find anyone. His phone is turned off. His pets are alone in his apartment—I can hear his dog whining behind the door. If someone asks you to take any culture tests, don't. Just . . . don't.

**Wolf News WNBS**
**@WNBSNews**

All public schools in northern Illinois, northwest Indiana and southern Wisconsin are closed for the next two weeks to allow for cleaning, reduction in contagion.
http://www.bit.ly.com/schoolclosing

♡ 6.9K 453 33K

**Xi**
**@sXlilate**

I just found myself contemplating the purchase of a Bedazzler. Send help (and rhinestones).

♡ 54 💬 2 🔁 2

**Julie Mons**
**@monsjul**

I spent most of the morning obsessing over warm winter boots the way some people obsess over the SI swimsuit issue.

♡ 78 💬 1 🔁 2

**Mychelle**
**@MightyMych**

A guy removed his mask, licked his fingers, and then rubbed it all over the grab bar on the bus. If this isn't proof demons walk among us, I have no idea what is.

♡ 1.8K 💬 45 🔁 84

**DB Cooper**
**@DBmm**

Thinking about my ex and how terrible this time would be to be stuck in a house with him, his fists, alcohol, nothing to do, nowhere to go, and a child sleeping in the next room.

♡ 2.5K 💬 95 🔁 17

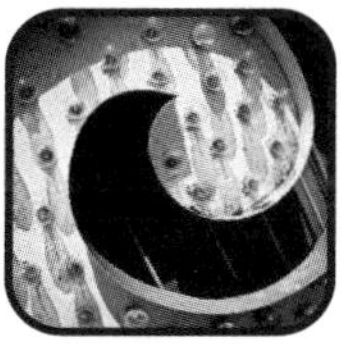

**Jane**

**@erejane**

"We're coming for you" and "no one is coming for you" are both equally terrifying threats.

♡ 3.1K 💬 185 ⟳ 483

# Day 8

OFFICIAL SEFI BLOG

—Guest Blogger Jane 'Ere

Today, a shark attack. A flurry of birds clued in Omar, the naturalist, and if he hadn't elbowed me and then pointed, I wouldn't have noticed the slight bit of action. You'd think from the lighthouse's vantage point, it would be so easy to spot something as dramatic as a three-ton fish devouring a one-ton elephant seal, but you'd be so wrong. Everything looks like rice grains on the floor. The sea is churning all the time. Your eyes go crazy with so much movement, you focus on nothing.

They tell me sometimes the sharks hit in a particularly deep section off SEFI, and they get momentum to breach out of the water during the stun strike. First, the shark takes a small bite—it's more for shock than anything. Then the prey is mostly incapacitated, and the shark makes the killing blow. It seems like they're playing with their food, but the shark thinks about protection. It knows it can't get a clean kill on the first hit when the prey is in motion, so it goes blunt and forceful. If it didn't kill this way, it might get hurt. The seal could bite back, tear into the shark's sensitive nose area, or even get away. The shark minimizes the calories spent earning new calories. By hitting with a stun, it can be a bit more selective, grapple around the head and give it a violent crunch. That's why surfers usually survive shark attacks if they can staunch the blood: When the shark realizes a surfer isn't a juicy fat seal, they know it's not worth their calories and energy to take out some bong-sucking hippy.

Sharks: smarter than you think.

That belongs on a bumper sticker.

The shark ate, tearing and bumping through the seal. Certainly, none of the violence they'd like you to see on Shark Week. I wouldn't say I was disappointed . . . OK, I was a little disappointed. After all, I came all this way to watch the evisceration of adorable elephant seals and I wanted to see some gore.

Pedro has promised to bring me out in the shark boat tomorrow. Technically, it's a whaler, but whatever. Shark boat! I expect it has its own theme music. *Na na na NAAAH nanana Shark BOAAATTT!*

I perhaps also have unreasonable expectations based upon shark documentaries. Until tomorrow, SEFI readers!

Your new friend,

Jane

## Day 9

**Mychelle**
**@MightyMych**

All schools closed at least three weeks. All nonessential stores, restaurants and bars, and services closed or have minimal hours. What is going on? This is like the Twilight Zone!

♡ 15 💬 0 🔁 0

**Cosmoballiton**
**@CosmoNoFilter**

I'm less concerned about H3N2 and more concerned everyone seems to have only now cared about washing their hands.

♡ 27 💬 2 🔁 1

**Xi**
**@sXlilate**

My confinement would be so much nicer if I also had a quiver of beautiful dancing British boys at my beck and call, for spontaneous montages and occasional well-choreographed light housekeeping duties.

♡ 14 💬 12 ⟳ 0

**Wolf News WNBS** ✓
**@WNBSNews**

1 year later, Allentown mosque attacks alter many lives <u>www.wnbs.com/PAmosque492</u>

♡ 285 💬 425 ⟳ 15

**Jesus Don't Live Here**
**@karl1952**

Sure, vaccines are coming. Sure, we'll all line up like sheep to get 'em. Invent the problem and sell the solution. #thegreatawakening #fulldisclosurenow

♡ 33.6K 💬 4.5K ⟳ 9.1K

# Day 6

### Brian

If my mom were alive, I might have gone to her house. Now I allowed the ache of her absence to flow for a moment and then clenched it once again. She had been so permanent in my life, a quiet presence. So quiet that, even a decade after she passed, I sometimes dialed her old number without thinking, only to break down when the automaton's voice informed me the number I was trying to reach was not in service and to please check and try again. And without fail, I would.

I had lots of oatmeal and beans, plenty of canned goods in the pantry already. I could last for four weeks alone. Whenever there's a virus running rampant, I lay low and avoid all human contact, even though it's a weird thing I don't want anyone to know I'm doing. It's kind of like how I refuse to touch the handles of public restroom doors once I wash my hands—I wait so no one sees me being crazy.

I know these fears aren't right or rational, they just are. Some therapists might break it all down to spending weeks and months in hospital corridors with my mother, breathing sanitizer fumes and watching cascading failures while she dwindled. Without anyone to answer to, I could tuck into my nice solitary loft and wait this virus out. Sure, it won't be fun living on two-year-old cans of beans, but I'd been meaning to clean out the pantry anyway.

The water cooler burped. The bottle was half full, with four empties sitting next to it. I'd been putting off a trip to the store because, well, the clay was already a huge pain in the ass to haul up to the studio and I didn't want to add twenty gallons of water to the mix. The tap water, of course, would do in a pinch. The old copper and lead pipes in the former factory were fine for washing, but the thought of drinking that water made me queasy. It was enough to knock me briefly off the smug mountain I'd been enjoying.

I checked the local art group forum—it's one part craft and one part gossip and northeastern Wisconsin news board. Message after message detailed people who had come down with H3N2. The Heenie, they are calling it. There were testimonials of potter friends who were fighting the infernal headaches, and at least four of them said they were making the best art of their lives after forty-eight hours with no sleep.

Posters who had never made a spelling error or typo in the entire time on the message forum now had posts riddled with homonym confusion and incomplete sentences and phrases. *Hear* for *here* and *their/they're/there* mistakes. As I scrolled down, at least two of the most recent posts from H3N2-infected had devolved into meaningless word salad, all capital letters and exclamation points.

Outside my back door was a giant, fast-moving freshwater river, water enough for years if I got into trouble. Of course, a century of paper mill sewage dumping had ensured it was full of CFCs, PCBs, and a host of little nasty fish-killing nitrates, not to mention cryptosporidium from the cow pastures upstream. A few years ago, an acquaintance had gotten a mouthful of the stuff while waterskiing and spent an entire week puking and shitting out his guts. I'd rather have the headaches. Which reminded me, the loft was low on toilet paper.

I was getting carried away, my internal monster kicking in. A racing monkey powered my brain, Other Brian, yearning to sort everything into ones and zeroes, dirty and clean.

After working up the courage to be That Guy with a fucking mental anxiety disorder, I took neat little pills when life got too much, mostly before plane trips and gallery openings. The drugs made my brain feel fuzzy. I hated being dull. I didn't trust the disconnect. Artists have always been escape artists first and foremost. While it played well in Manhattan, the whole "eclectic artistic freak" thing didn't do so well with my demographic—the art aficionado in Chicago or Boise who didn't trust the Coasters but secretly wanted to be accepted by them. Be approachable but still aloof. I couldn't argue. The brilliantly shy cool potter thing earned a decent amount of indie hipster tail.

I talked myself out of going out again. How silly I had been. Another thing I blew out of proportion, letting the hourglass of anxiety cascade into my skull until the sand had completely buried any ember of rationality. It was disgusting, a weakness, terrible. If I became sick, no one would take care of me and I'd fall in the bathroom, perhaps in the shower, and then lie there in my own filth and if that happened, I deserved it. Maybe I deserved worse.

My tension was rising. Then, an ambulance siren in the distance.

It was probably nothing. Well, not nothing, a fire or a car accident, another shooting, enough to chafe my brain.

I couldn't stand it.

I grabbed my keys and clay-speckled boots, flipped on a dusty T-shirt, and took the elevator down, so I could use it for the supplies when I got home.

The city was weirdly normal. How could we face another pandemic on a perfect day like this? People on bikes, taking dogs for walks, all healthy activities. I even passed a cute family pushing a stroller. In some secret twisted place inside my psyche, I truly believe the universe doesn't want to be second-guessed, so it throws the worst possible scenario at you when you swore it couldn't happen. The *Hindenburg*, the *Titanic*, everything everyone had said could never happen: It was inviting Fate to pull that string. My fevered imaginations were nothing if not a prayer against calamity. And they kept me sane. The first time I get on a plane and don't envision it plummeting to everyone's bloody, fiery death will be the time it happens, of course.

I went to a warehouse store, stopping first for water. I normally nabbed three five-gallon carboys, which was good for at least four weeks, but when I found the racks almost empty, I took as many as I could fit in my cart, seven in all.

Shit.

You don't think about your fear until it kicks you in the stomach. I wanted to hide, to lock down again. If this was going to be bigger than COVID, cool logic trickled forward like ice water. I was either infected right now or I wasn't. Pulling out now wasn't going to change that, and if I was about to get sick, then I absolutely would need some supplies, not to mention some hefty megavitamins to stave off any dents in my immune system. As I passed the cashiers, they glared at me, and two raised their hands to their temples and winced.

I hustled through the acres of shelves, nabbing some calorie-dense, satisfying food like oatmeal, canned tuna, pineapple chunks in juice, and two massive jars of peanut butter. I hit the pasta aisle and snagged a case of tomato sauce and ten boxes of angel hair pasta for good measure. Me and carbs, it was better than Valium. On my way to the toilet paper aisle, I grabbed three boxes of Twinkies, because the little nuclear disaster cakes are fantastic when you're sick. Then, thinking twice, I picked up twenty-four rolls of toilet paper and a case of canned chicken broth. Worst-case scenario, I'd have nonperishables for the next year, to go with the stash of cold medicine I'd hoarded right before they started carding everyone under suspicion of making meth.

In the health and beauty section, I came face-to-face with an entire aisle of almost empty shelves. Every pain remedy was gone. Every single one. Every bottle of aspirin, every cough syrup, every child's remedy, everything. A sign saying they were restocking. The shelves were scourged from top to bottom, the luxury brands and the generics gone. Like locusts or a product recall. Even the Aspercreme. All gone.

Dead. Mother in the hospital. A nurse patting my hand. Dropping my bike in the garage after school and my mother sobbing from somewhere inside the house. Death. It was coming.

*Christ, Brian, get a hold of yourself.*

The cart was loaded. It felt like pushing a Buick up to the checkout. Then I remembered Bob and grabbed him a pack of Morleys and a gallon of drinking water. Then I grabbed a package of peanut butter crackers. It made me feel slightly less like a freak, and if the cashier asked, I could have earnestly said I was feeding the unhoused, but the cashier was busy complaining to another customer. I thought better of it and went to the self-checkout, which was normally used by people buying single bottles of malt liquor and tired parents buying formula and diapers. Today, lots of other shoppers were loading up with what I thought of as survival gear—dozens of packs of AA batteries, bandages, paper towels, neon rubber dishwashing gloves. I got a free lane and rolled through my purchases quickly.

In my car, I gripped the steering wheel. *Think of the V&A, animal crackers, relax you fuckwit* until my chest tightness abated. On the way home, a few weirdos on street corners. One took off her shoes and left them in the gutter, walking across the cold damp sidewalk pavement, perfect bright pink toenails vulnerable to the slick autumn leaves stuck to the ground. A block later, an older man wearing a uniform of some sort, an insignia above the left breast pocket. He was also shoeless but otherwise walking with intent.

Crossing the street, a woman pushed an empty baby carriage in yoga pants and a crisp blue workout jacket but with two mismatched socks, both muddy and torn. She must live around here. She looked like every middle-class mom-aged woman in the area, toting the outlet version of a high-end purse fallen ever-so-slightly out of style.

I rolled down the window. "Miss, do you need help?" The empty baby carriage, upon closer inspection, looked dusty and forgotten, as though recovered from storage. Where was the kid?

"Miss? Are you OK?" I said, hoping she'd wave me off, offer an explanation. Instead, she didn't react or even seem to hear me, the wheels squeaking as she pushed the stroller over a lawn and then back to the sidewalk. She stopped, checking the buggy as though she were checking the infant, seemed satisfied, and kept walking.

"Miss?" I said again, but she squared her shoulders, ignoring my call. The wind bit my face. I called 911 but the line was busy.

Across the street, an older woman spotted her and went off in pursuit—eyes fixed, running faster than seemed advisable for someone of her age. The older woman was probably the woman's mother or perhaps aunt and would escort her home. I felt absolved of responsibility. As I turned the corner, however, in my rearview mirror, I caught sight of the older woman's feet. She also wasn't wearing shoes and had torn her nylon socks. By then I had turned the corner and it seemed unwise to turn back. If anything, what could I do? What would anyone think about a man trying to convince an attractive young woman to come with him when she was obviously suffering delusions? The authorities would have to handle it.

I dialed 911 repeatedly as I drove, but it was busy each time. The farther I got, the less likely it would be I could even find the two women again, much less help. I tried to put them out of my mind but even still wondered if the older woman was pursuing with the intent to help or something else.

Back at the flour mill, I needed the handcart and utility elevator for all the water—but there were several hundred pounds of clay on the handcart for the studio. Normally I would have taken the clay up in the freight elevator and then brought the cart back down, but my heart was racing. I wouldn't feel better until I locked the doors and took a shower.

By working quickly and dumping most of the heavy boxes of damp moldy porcelain inside the factory's front entrance, I got everything on the cart and into the elevator in a little under ten minutes. My biceps ached. Even more surprising was the fact that eighteen cans of marinara sauce felt heavier than one hundred pounds of deadweight porcelain.

Once up to my loft, I left the grocery-laden cart on the elevator like a coward. I couldn't take it anymore. I ditched my clothes on the front stoop and ran naked into the bathroom to douse my hands and face with antibacterial lotion. Then I made a strong saline neti pot, which burned like a son of a bitch, followed with a shower, probably too hot.

Pink and steaming, I thought about the cashiers with their headaches. What had I done? Why did I brave the store? This was going to be the death of me.

I sat at my laptop, popped open the email browser, and wrote an email to Jane, telling her about the grocery trip. Even as I typed, I thought back to the last time she had reached out to see me. I was genuinely sorry for going with my dick instead of honoring my pretend internet friend, as I thought of her back then. In truth, I had forgotten what she looked like—my memory of Crissy Field, a woman wrestling a bike chain, the top of her head bobbing in frustration was solid, had been revisited so many times, polluted by thoughts of other women, pop culture references. The precise arrangement of her features, the exact shade of her eyes—were they blue? brown? green? I had no way of remembering. It felt cheap to ask her now—and she rarely posted clear images of herself on her blog. She showed only parts of herself, a smirking mouth, the curve of a shoulder. When she left California, I could no longer play the little game inside my head whenever I went into the city for pottery deliveries, spotting slightly wide girls wearing unfortunate capris. *Is that her? Is that?* I had picked up the habit again after I moved to Wisconsin, every time I went out and saw a woman in the distance with the right build, the right stance, wearing capri pants. Jane? Could it be her?

In fact, I suspected my critical nature was why she was reluctant to meet now that we had both moved back to the same general geographical area. In our emails, we often bashed on pop culture icons, other artists, other figures in the tech world. We invented fictional conversations between dead Leonard Nimoy and dead Steve Jobs, concocted an elaborate fantasy in which we sent famous potters into a secret Illuminati-like cavern under the city of Denver, where they set about crafting the perfect pink glaze.

Why pink? Because it was a practically impossible glaze for high firing, as I had explained in chat one night in perhaps far too much detail. Of course, it could be done through a complex chemical reaction, but true potters eschewed anything requiring technology younger than 1,000 years. She wouldn't let me send her anything—she was holding out for a custom Brian Arden set of bone china, glazed in a pink somewhere between Barbie and Hello Kitty.

Maybe I would have considered Jane a suitable girlfriend in our San Francisco heydays, but now she had become ultra-Dot Com Zinternet Winnerest Blog Maven. She was, as they say, famous on the internet. Her kooky Life List had been picked up by the *New York Times* and featured in national magazines, her crinkly eyes peering over a laptop, half-hidden from view on glossy pages right next to the gym-wrought abs of the latest hunk in swim trunks. Jane was a Thing. Everyone posted his or her Life Lists on her big Facebook page. When she flew to a small fishing village in Nova Scotia to go diving for sea urchins, she found a small coterie of fans waiting for her dockside, digital cameras in hand. I had even picked up a fair amount of Janeling traffic—as I snidely referred to her fans, perhaps in reference to define myself from them—from a link on her blog's sidebar, and sales on my little pottery webpage spiked whenever she deigned to throw me some linkage.

I often told her not to link to my sad online store. I didn't want her to think I was only participating in the e-lationship (a term so awful and unaware it came right back around into charming) because it benefited my floundering independent pottery career. "Oh, Brian, your worries are adorable," she instant messaged me one evening, late for her, and then, of course, she linked to my site in spite the next day. It was a way of asserting power, I suspected, and so I let her have the guise of control. She seemed to need it.

She also seemed to need the presumption that we were destined to be connected, kindred spirits, platonic life partners, but we always happened to be dating someone else.

Jane had gone through a series of "nothing" relationships (her words). I tried to retain my distance, but I knew what games these guys were playing, I knew that possession came with the desire to control and consume a mate. These assholes pulled the same tricks I did when things got too close. Jane refrained from commenting on the more egregious antics of the less-stable-but-fuckable women I entertained. The last one, an art student from the local college, Gemma, was impossibly gorgeous in that West Coast trust fund kind of way, but eventually my misanthropy and hatred of anything social outweighed the perks of being with a Heathen, so she dumped me. I waited probably too long to mention it to Jane, afraid of what it would mean, or what our converging availability wouldn't mean.

When Jane mentioned Gemma six months later in a late-night chat session, asking if Gemma was bothered by my typing from bed, I confessed that she had moved out. Gemma may have had excellent taste in art: She eventually clocked that my personality wasn't as special as my work.

Jane had paused, typed, paused again, typed again, a quivering flash of the three-dot bubble. It was unexpectedly affecting, wondering how she was editing herself, what devastating rejoinder would drip from her digital pen.

Then she said "gtg bye."

We never mentioned romantic partners again. Which was fine, because I hadn't had one since.

I needed more psychic space for my own side business. Working at Heath paid the rent, but sales of my own wares had been increasing to the point I had to start thinking about it more seriously. I had rented a small storage closet in San Leandro for the stuff I was making after hours in the Heath studios. After a debacle giving a roommate money to buy what turned out to be a massive decaying sailboat, I stashed my pottery cash in a mutual fund, minus the cost of materials and storage space.

It was about that same time that Jane started hawking my stuff to the general internet and things got a little crazy. I could barely keep up with the orders doing it part time. I'd put eight hours in at Heath, eat a sandwich in the courtyard for dinner, and then go back in and center a twenty-pound wedge of porcelain to start churning out vases with that distinct peaky little lip. The Brian Arden Pottery business began in earnest. Quickly, I amassed enough capital to put a down payment on a more permanent location and was ready to jump to self-employment. But space in the Bay Area kept hitting new highs. If I was going to make it, it had to be somewhere cheaper. Then COVID hit and no one had to be anywhere important anymore, so it made zero sense to keep paying NorCal rent.

I investigated several locations, close enough to be a three-hour-or-less drive to major hub airports, but far enough away so industrial space wasn't a premium. And I hadn't cracked the numbers, but I was pretty sure I would only be able to do it because of Jane's continued online support, so I sought her advice.

Jane had settled into a derelict 1940s three-season cabin on the south shore of Green Bay. "The OTHER city by the Bay," she said, inserting an eye-rolling emoticon. After years of scrapping along in northern California, the cost of living she detailed seemed like pennies. Waterfront property for less than half a million dollars? It was like going back in time, and her maiden aunt was happy to have extra income for Jane crashing during the winter while everyone was getting furloughed. Jane sent me photos of salmon spawning outside her back deck. She referred to it as #theotherbay. Pelicans ate cheese curds from her hand. She saw Bigfoot riding the Loch Ness monster to a Packers game.

It was enough to give me pause, especially when she coaxed me even closer.

# Day 11

REDDIT—R/ENDTIMES—BIG PHARMA HAS CREATED HUMAN COLONY COLLAPSE

We've been reading about the bees dying for years, and now it's our turn. Bees and humans are essentially the same type of animals—we live in "colonies" and have worker bees that rely on a vast network of traveling and pollination routes. We even travel over the same pathways (highways and cars) and use communication to indicate when there's a different food source available (the internet). Big Pharma introduced a major insecticide years ago, which has decimated the honeybee population and caused colony collapse disorder. With much of our food source threatened, our instinctive biological mechanisms are orchestrating a herd kill. You can see this in the wild: When herds of animals have a threatened food source, they will start doing mass suicides to ensure at least some of the members of the herd are able to survive on what rare food source is left. This is also mentioned in the Bible. Our herd immunity is backfiring on us, and thank Big Pharma, flu shots, and every childhood immunization. Also, the Democrats.

Encourage your friends and loved ones to end it sooner rather than later. It's either ours to die a slow and miserable death or else to take matters into our own hands and die as we lived . . . free. Hopefully with enough of the herd removed, we can prevent any additional loss of human life. So sayeth the Lord.

# Seventeen Years Ago

(Reuters) TAMPA—Research facilities with some of the deadliest biological agents in the world are currently at risk in rising floodwaters from Hurricane Carla.

The facilities—Neuronal Morpho Sciences (NMS) and the University of South Florida's BiomedCon—are located within 1,000 yards of each other. Both sit in extreme flooding zones and have been evacuated.

USF researches pathogens such as HIV, tuberculosis, malaria, influenza, MRSA, Ebola, and smallpox. NMS studies and houses contagions of the brain, such as viral encephalitis, chronic wasting disease (CWD), and Creutzfeldt-Jakob disease (CJD). Each facility has passed the federal requirements for housing virulent agents and is certified as environmentally sound.

As of 9 p.m. locally on Tuesday, floodwaters were estimated from a helicopter to be approximately four feet deep at each facility. In each lab, the containment fields are in basement or sublevel floors.

"We've been tracking this storm for weeks and are confident that the measures we put into place with our emergency management processes will more than triple hold the biological agents," said Arlo T. Huntsman, dean of USF's Morsani College of Medicine.

This is not the first time in recent history hurricane-related floods have impacted biomedical facilities, such as the 20xx incident in Houston's Texas Medical Center and a breach in Atlanta's CDC headquarters when flooding from Supercell Daria devastated the region in 20xx, each resulting in fatalities from infections that were however ultimately controlled by quarantine efforts.

The Hurricane Carla damage in Tampa and the Gulf coastline is estimated to reach $175 billion, according to J.P. Morgan analysts, and is almost certain to be classified as the worst storm in US history, surpassing Katrina, Andrew, and Ike.

# Day 11

## Jane

"I have to leave." Kylie is sitting on the edge of her bed, the threadbare rug between us a vast continent, frayed and faded, strings surrounding it in an aurora of tentacles. Two squat mouse turds lurk beside it, a reminder of our unseen roommates.

"Seriously?"

"I'm pregnant."

"Oh. Oh my gosh." My hand flies up to my mouth as though I'm a shocked maiden aunt. Maybe I am. Is this a happy or a sad thing? It seems like a sad thing, given what I know about Kylie, given what I know about the world. Could she have contracted something from the birds? The dusty feather imprints on the backs of her gloves, all those birds. I scratch my scalp, scratching the creatures making a living off their host, off me.

"What are you going to do now? I mean . . . now with this going on?"

"The program doesn't know? I wouldn't have been able to come if they knew. God knows I'm not the first pregnant resident of SEFI and I'm sure I won't be the last, but officially, you can't be here if you're pregnant. There's too much possible . . . risk."

With her big hazel eyes, she's every popular girl I knew back in high school. She should be cheering for boys to win football scholarships.

She shrugs, the spell broken, and she's Kylie once again, hoarder of secrets, whisperer behind backs. "Everyone's lawsuit-crazy these days, don't you know. I mean, I'm not worried about the fetus's health. There's nothing I can catch on this island I haven't caught already. You know? My blood is probably 1 percent bird shit at this point."

Her mouth is a grimace approximating a smile. It never reaches her eyes. Microexpressions, something I learned while part of a Stanford psychological experiment. Tiny frozen bursts of smiles, frowns, and other in-between faces that happen so fast you barely notice it. It's how to recognize liars—their brains fight with their muscles until they turn into gargoyles. Kylie smiles when she's supposed to be frowning. The words never match her face. This time maybe she's truly scared.

Kylie has never mentioned a boyfriend. She doesn't even talk about the last guy she dated. Just like her expressions, the conversations I've had with her are never deep; she sidesteps every question—she redirects. She didn't have her own place, she'd said days before, waving her hand about couch surfing between internships. When she was desperate, she went back to Kansas to stay with her mother and stepdad, but mostly, she liked to keep her life confined to two purple Rubbermaid containers.

"But then Pedro and Rick were talking about the Spanish flu pandemic when you guys got back. Do you know who the number one casualty for the Spanish flu was? It wasn't old people. It was pregnant women. If they survived the flu, they lost the baby, but most of the pregnant women died. Something like 70 percent fatality for pregnant women." Kylie stubs a bit of fluff on the floor with her toe. Her stomach looks flat and perfect, her eyes bright.

"So. You're going to keep the baby?"

"That's a gooooood question?" She turns away. So no, then. It has to be no. This is all for some other reason. It's one of those moments where I've learned not to pry, to stay quiet, because to speak is to shut down everything. Her shoulders rise and drop slowly, like an exaggerated shrug. There, in the Jane Fonda room, Kylie's trying on possible futures the same way we've tried on each other's clothes. The same sense of incompletion hangs between us, loose, too snug, never right.

"I mean, things are not looking good for it? But we'll see? We'll see."

Is the ghost child in the Jane Room listening right now? Does it want me to make a case one way or the other? It is a bad place to die, this island. This room, with the cold seeping in through the slats. The plaster cracks migrate with new earthquakes, and, much worse, powerful nor'easters are coming soon in November. We're on an island more like the surface of the moon, surrounded by water dotted with nuclear waste. Do you bring a baby you want to keep to a place like this?

In the room, tiny little gasps for air. Is it the ghost child? Has Kylie started crying? It's too dark to see her face and it feels wrong to turn on the lamp.

"Well, whatever you decide, I'm sure it will be the right decision." Do I believe this? It seems like the appropriate thing to say. How do you support a friend when you want to shake her and say, *What the hell are you thinking?*

Kylie turns and smiles. The ghost child runs away to wherever it hides when I can't feel it in the room. Things are normal again. We have another secret.

"I think so too? But I need to get the flu shot? No matter what . . . what happens." She absent-mindedly places her palm flat against the snap of her cargo pants, her stomach still taut, although now there's a fullness in her hips I hadn't noticed before, a blossoming to her stance.

"How far are you?"

"Two months—ish? I haven't been to the doctor? I didn't want to—I don't want to SEE it, you know? I figured if I see an ultrasound, then it's all over. No more SEFI, no more career, like, Pampers and *Sesame Street* and a minivan."

Everyone was an individual before they started having babies. My mother never ceased reminding me of the woman I had killed when I myself decided to become a constellation of cells, a pink line on a pregnancy test. It's impossible to see Kylie ever schlepping a gaggle of second graders to dance classes, but then again, maybe not. Kylie could easily turn into one of those moms who sew Halloween costumes and make cupcakes look like ice cream cones.

"Two months. Wow." Sometimes when I can't think of what to say, "wow" is a good alternative.

"I know. Wow. Fucking wow."

"So . . . you're leaving then."

"Yeah. I'm going to leave. For the fetus's health, it's for the best."

She keeps saying fetus. It might be because she's scientific, a biology student who has dissected the fetuses of various species, intimately connected to the functions by which cells replicate, the magic of life creation—or it might be the reality of her condition, the fact sinking in: She's not driving her life path any longer.

"So . . . here I go!" She smiles brightly, freckles across her nose squinching up.

Will the baby have her upturned nose? Or will the mystery father's DNA pop out and remind her of him at odd times? Will she ever tell the baby it was once on SEFI, chasing great white sharks, listening to her heart race faster with every kill strike? Even as I contemplate this, it feels like it doesn't matter. The baby is a non-baby. The ghost child knows this and whispers it to the room, to Kylie, to me, to all the unbabies who ever hoped to be. You will be glad to be saved from being an unwanted, I think to it, a clump of cells, a curd of an idea erasing itself.

She bounds out the door. I can't hear what she says as she whispers to Omar behind his sad dingy blanket, the miscellaneous blue noise of voices dampened.

I pop open the laptop and work on the website, uploading and color correcting the white balance on the 1,859 photos taken with my sad little prosumer DSLR. Approximately 1,700 of them are simply ocean waves. I'd been trying to catch boils, to validate four hours of fruitless observation, but flat spots are impossible to spot in a photo. A few action shots of Pedro and Rick, and over a dozen mostly identical photos of the light-changing cells on Pedro's fake elephant seals. Flipping files, I spot a distinct shark fin point. No one had seen it. Rick and Pedro would have said something, noted it in their field journals.

My first up-close shark experience and I fucking missed it, despite looking right through the camera lens. I haul my laptop downstairs. Omar and Kylie are gone. Rick and Pedro are at the kitchen table, the battle-ax laptop open to CNN, where the video is stuttering and buffering on the pathetic internet connection. Flu epidemic and hospital overcrowding, the most recent mass shootings.

"Check this out," I say. Pedro and Rick both glance over at my laptop.

"Yup, look at that. Stumpy, looks like." Pedro returns to the news site.

Rick stands up, finished. "Liz is going back with the supply boat."

"She is too? Is that . . . supposed to happen?"

"No, not in the middle of October. She's not slated to go back until November eighth, when you leave, but Liz's mom is sick and she's elderly and alone. The DNR heads of state are all coming down with it, so she'll remote work to help headquarters while she's in—where was it she said?"

"Omaha."

"Right. Omaha."

"Boat's due in the next hour or so." Patty peers at the dueling laptops. I hadn't heard him come in. Patty's talent is appearing and disappearing in places without a sound.

"I think Kylie's leaving too." The words come out of my mouth before I even realize what I'm doing, already betraying Kylie's trust to be as in the know as Pedro, Rick, and Patty. All stop and look at me, Rick and Pedro exchange a glance I can't decipher. Patty snorts and stomps out, letting the door to the fly station slam behind him, the first time he's ever made noise while exiting a room. We all listen to him grunting into his outside shoes. The squeaky door slams.

I want to take back Kylie's secret.

When Kylie comes in, she says nothing and heads upstairs. Pedro heads upstairs too, and his voice drifts down, asking Kylie if she needs help carrying stuff. After twelve days that seemed like the longest days of my life, things are now happening so fast. I drift back upstairs, passing Pedro toting one of Kylie's bins.

Kylie sits on her bunk, filing her nails. "What did Liz say?" I slump down onto my bed. Maybe I should have sat next to her, in solidarity. She looks small by herself, young and tiny, almost prepubescent.

"Oh, nothing." Kylie exhales, not looking up. "She said everyone makes the choice and she knew it was hard and she wished I had known sooner."

Kylie has presented the situation as though she hadn't known she was pregnant. It doesn't gel with what she told me earlier. Already the story crosses over itself, the lines overlay and erase. She either believes this new version or she doesn't want to acknowledge the previous facts. Kylie might not even be pregnant. She is both pregnant and not pregnant at the same time.

I don't address the fiction. "I heard Liz is leaving with you?"

"News travels fast on SEFI, huh?" she says sharply, and I flush with guilt for having told the guys. I'm irritated she thinks I told them. Even though I did tell them.

"Are you going home when you get to Berkeley? What's happening?" We've talked about everything under the sun, but I really don't *know* Kylie. We're like strangers trapped in an elevator together, only instead we're trapped on a haunted island.

"I'll call one of my friends. I haven't been able to reach anyone on the satellite phones yet, but you know how that goes." I didn't even know how to work the satellite phones, so I didn't know how it went, but I just nod.

"Right. Well, send me an email letting me know where you go, OK? I'd like to keep in touch with you. Kansas isn't far from Wisconsin, and I want to see pictures of the baby!" I smile, implying baby showers and first teeth and Johnson's shampoo smell.

She scrunches up her face in confusion for the briefest of seconds but nods. "Of course." She hands over a notebook and I scrawl an email address and then write (***SEFI blogger***) next to it, in case she can't remember.

"Of course, I'll be following the blog? Keeping up on what I'm going to miss and stuff?"

"Of course." An awkward silence while we both try not to look each other in the eye. "Do you want help carrying down?"

"No, Pedro said I could leave my stuff at the top of the stairs and he'd hump it down."

"Pedro's a good guy."

"The best guy." She has such earnestness; I almost believe she isn't the girl who the day before called Patty "Rain Man" because of his affinity for specific ropes.

"OK, well, I got to get back down to show Rick . . . some photos from our launch today." How ridiculous it sounds. There aren't timeframes on SEFI, there's never a rush. It's not like Rick is going somewhere. I'll regret not staying with her longer, absorbing every bit of her sunshine. She's a friend, at least on the surface, maybe there was even a best friendship in progress, as though something indelible had been interrupted by events outside our control. Is surface all there ever is to friendships? Maybe it's all there ever is. I think about Brian—are we even friends? Would I even recognize him in real life again?

After she leaves, it will be me and the ghost child up there in the Jane Room.

Rick sends me out to finish Kylie's bird tagging and promises he'll give a shout when it's time to say goodbye.

I'm not feeling especially optimistic about spending the afternoon with Patty, who hasn't said a word to me since that night helping him with the mist netting. He seems annoyed to have me instead of Kylie, but my job is dead simple: Write things down while Patty grabs the birds, takes measurements, and softly says what to write in the weathered, bird-poop-smeared notebook. In the first thirty minutes, I knock over his water bottle, drop the can of alcohol wipes halfway down the hill, and lose the pencil between rocks and nest holes at least six times, all while a gull has decided that I am its personal Antichrist and continues to launch poop attacks closer and closer to my perch.

Patty is a strange juxtaposition. He can hold and identify the sex of birds that don't even weigh two ounces, using hands more appropriate on a professional wrestler, his fingers large enough to spread a wing without needing a second finger. Tiny fragile beating breasts look like jewels against his rough, torn skin, a scabbed gash on his thumb in contrast to the spidery feathers.

I screw up the measurements repeatedly, asking "what?" and "can you repeat please" until Patty asks me to repeat what I've written, correcting me when I make mistakes.

"That female probably wants you to shave an ounce off the weight anyway," I whisper to myself. Patty stops what he was doing and looks up. It is the first time I've seen his eyes, a striking shade of hazel with dark, long lashes right at home on a mascara commercial. It was such a lame joke, I think about apologizing again and assuring him I'm taking this seriously, but he smiles and nods, holding my gaze for an uncomfortably long time. I look back. He does have very nice eyes. Then he reaches up into the mist net and carefully extracts a bird from its lacings.

"Black-throated blue warbler. Male. Wingspan 7.1."

And just like that, we're back in rhythm. Write. Measure. Sex. Age. Write.

"You know about the Farallon sacrifice, right?"

"You sacrifice something here?" Perhaps they throw a canned ham over North Landing to the sharks, or perhaps dump a bunch of shrimps into Seal Hollow. Or maybe he was talking about the ghost child, although I'd never be able to ask him about such foolishness.

"No. The island does. When someone's been on the islands for a long time, like Liz? The day they leave, a good bird shows up. Liz's been here seventy-two days this stretch. The way I figure it, we're due for a pretty good bird today."

"Like what? A bald eagle? An albatross?"

"Eh, bald eagles here all the time. Albatross would be good. Black-footed albatross are here enough, but maybe a short-tailed albatross. There hasn't been a short-tailed here in over a century. They breed in Japan, so, you know . . . tough haul."

"You know, Patty," I say, taking a chance. "I think your goal for a short-tailed Japanese albatross is a good one, but we need a stretch goal. I would like to see a dodo bird."

He squints, his mouth twitching, ready to say dodo birds are extinct, but then the joke sinks in.

"Or a passenger pigeon?" He raises an eyebrow.

"Maybe a pterodactyl. That would be cool."

"A pterodactyl. I like how you think, blog girl. I like how you think." He clips a yellow band to the bird's left leg and releases it. For a moment, it nests there in his giant hands and looks up with beady black eyes, shiny as jewels. Then the little bundle takes flight with a whisper of feathers.

"Ready to move?" He smiles this time and waits for me to put together the tools.

In biologist terms, this is what we call "an event."

Patty leads, pointing out hidden crevices perfect for trapping a boot and snapping an ankle. He explains why today will be slow, SEFI sacrifice notwithstanding. The marine layer, a dense blanket of fog, plays a huge part in whether the migrating birds spot the island or the mainland first. The fog gets so thick and inland birds fly so high that the winds push them farther and they don't realize they are flying over the ocean. They hit the Farallones to recharge their energy stores, eat some calories, and if the mainland is visible, then they turn back. If the biologists didn't happen by on a twice-daily sweep of SEFI, they'd never know those temporary travelers had rested their wings on its hallowed grounds. There are so many other islands—each desolate and jagged, each a potential resting point, most never walked upon. It's impossible to know which birds were resting on them, which rare visitors happened by. Patty frowns at those far-reaching dots of forsaken rocks in the distance.

So close and yet so far.

When we crest the hill, he points out the marine layer. One of the spires on the Golden Gate Bridge is visible, the telltale orange barely a dark shadow against the mist. It looks small, like a part of an erector set. The night before I met the volunteer boat in the Berkeley Marina, I did another Google search for the Farallones and found a photo someone had shot from the Marin headlands on an unusually clear day. There was Lighthouse Hill in clear relief against the glimmering Pacific at sunset. Most of the residents of San Francisco never even realize this place is here. Now, looking to a lone sentinel, orange and majestic, I don't know whether it's the north or the south part of the bridge. I think again about the people who commit suicide off the bridge. I'm always thinking about them and how if they jump off the side facing the Pacific—and the Farallones—then they try to commit suicide again. One might be falling right now. One, two, three, how would I know? Look at me, see me. *I'm here. I care.* I won't share this observation with Patty. Like most things, if anyone knew what was in my head, they wouldn't care for me much longer.

*I'm here. I believe in you.*

Patty teaches me how to identify the gender by looking at which band he clips on each tiny leg. I find a Chestnut-sided Warbler, which Patty is excited about, and makes me excited too, as though perhaps I have spotted a rock star at the deli. Patty might be making up the rarity and I would be none the wiser.

Together, shoulder to shoulder, we work quickly. Patty nods at a long sailboat aimed for North Landing.

"Shouldn't we go help with the landing?" I say. There's another hour of birding, with two more sections of the grid to count and catalog.

Patty glances down the hill. "Pedro's got it under control. They won't leave without saying goodbye. Remember, today's a Boat Day. We're going to find us a unicorn today, I can feel it."

Together we tag and photograph and measure and sex. Patty works with the diligence of a surgeon but still takes moments to wonder at each species, to point out special feathers, tiny white stars, small spirals and notches, subcutaneous fat deposits that show a bird's ready for nesting, how he can tell the age by its skull ossification. Ossification, I think in my own skull, which has ossified undoubtedly, ossify, ossifood, ossifull, ossi-fucked. He points to other birds fishing, using terms I don't know. Alula. Zugunruhe. Booby. When he handles a less common songbird, he says its name with reverence, a benediction. Sometimes he rattles off the genus and species in Latin. The scientific names are so pretty, *Passeridae*, *Mimidae*, like Hollywood baby names. He shows off a lean little bird, spreads apart the legs, and says, "Look, see, this one has a good cloacal protuberance. Females would have a brood patch right here, but he's a big guy."

"Patty," I say, "are you showing me this bird's penis?"

His face flushes. "Well, I—uh." He releases the bird, which shuffles off quickly in a burst of wings and feathers. "I guess so." Then he takes a sharp intake of breath, reaches out quickly into the netting, and cups a small vibrating emerald bird.

"Ow, easy there." He cages his hands. "You'll have to come to me, I can't risk squashing the little guy. I can't believe he made it this far." I crawl forward, slowly, and then peek between his giant fingers.

Inside his palm, an acid green hummingbird with a bright fuchsia head. Its body is no bigger than a kumquat, a goldfish, an exhale. Tiny bright alien eyes peer out from between Patty's knuckles while the needle beak pecks angrily at his inside thumb crease. It is every color at once, green and purple and magenta and orange, somehow a living breathing metallic robot crossed with a dragonfly. A soft sound comes from beneath Patty's whiskers, and he lifts the captive bird closer to his face. It pauses for a moment, contemplating him and me, looking for microscopic weaknesses in our fragile human bodies to plunge its stylus beak into, the corners of our eyes, perhaps, or maybe the trachea. Patty opens his hand and the tiny deity rises like a Harrier jet, not taking off but taking UP from his creased calloused dirty palm. It zips off, avoiding the mist netting by millimeters, and shoots out toward the Coast Guard shack, where I lose sight of it in the distance.

"We weren't going to tag it?"

"No, no tags small enough or light enough, not here. Too big a tag will interfere with the bird's flight. Anna's hummingbird, male from the coloring. That might have been our unicorn. They never make it this far from the mainland. The wind is perfect, blowing this way from San Francisco. Neat little bird. So bright. Note it. Trochilidae Calypte."

I dutifully scrawl the name and location in the spiral notebook, reducing everything to numbers and taxonomy. The pencil nub presses harder into the page, indenting the paper. *Make this matter. Remember this. Remember it.* Already it is fading.

Patty points out a tableau unfolding about fifteen yards away. The same gull haranguing me with guano and flapping behavior is now stalking a puffin.

"Are we going to try to save it?"

"No. You don't interfere. Ever."

"That seems . . . I don't know, wrong somehow."

"Biologists can't get attached. That's something to remember, Jane, while you're on this island. These are animals, not pets. Remember. Not pets. We aren't here to save every animal on this island."

"Except . . . you are."

"No, we want to save the *species*. There's a difference. Take the gulls. One chick survives for every three nests, and those nests contain anywhere from one to three eggs. That's a poor chance of survival if you're that chick. But if we save all the chicks from their inevitable failures to thrive, then we've got a population explosion, which would then eliminate the resources and those populations go extinct, at least in that biome. The gulls' food supply would be wiped out, and then we'd have a gull population crash, then everything predating on gulls will have a population crash, and then anything else those predators normally eat will have a population surge in response, and so on. That gull over there is one chick out of maybe six to survive. If we stop him from making his living, then he starves and the things that that puffin eats will also respond, and the animals eating those things, and so on. It's a complex food chain, and one we shouldn't even pretend to understand."

These are cold hard truths. I'm not a fan of the gulls, but the seals have giant trusting eyes, like puppies or toddlers. One of them will be the next shark meal. For there to be seals at all, there must be seal casualties. Seal bodies. Seal babies. Seal after seal after seal after seal.

Patty grunts and snaps the leg band case closed, tucks it into the pocket on his field jacket, then puts his gloves back on.

"Well," he says after a moment. "Let's go see if they need some help." By the time I shut the notebook and cap the pencil, Patty is already fifty feet down the path, and I scrabble across degrading hillside alone.

I've disappointed someone again.

At the landing, Liz and Pedro console Omar. He's unusually affected. Actual tears are on his cheeks—it doesn't fit my mental picture of Omar, this crying. Patty and Rick ignore the emotion—they focus on securing the last of the pallets.

Kylie stands near her purple bins. "Going out with the trash. Just the same way I came in?" She giggles, but Liz shoots her a baleful look.

No one responds. Liz wrings her hands and chews on her lip. What's the story with her sick parents? Is it the H3N2 thing or something else more serious, something terminal, nSFI? I consider taking Liz aside and sharing that I understand how hard this is, that I had to give up so many things for my grandmother in her final days battling cancer, and, in the end, that I was so grateful to spend that time, to get a glimpse of my grandmother as a mortal. Did Liz want to hear pithy Hallmark sentiments from some greenhorn blogger she'd never see again? She probably would want to punch the person in the face. That's what I'd want to do. But I only guess at what everyone else thinks, feels, and considers regular and earnest behavior. What should I be doing with my hands right now? I clasp them behind my back, but then I just seem useless. With them in front, I feel like a child in *Sound of Music*, about to burst into song about deer and rays of golden sun. I let my hands drop and choose to look concerned with eyebrows knitting together. Concerned human face.

Pedro clears his throat, and they all quickly say "good luck" and "be well" and "stay safe" and then Liz, Pedro, and Kylie jump onto the swinging Zodiac and hunker down.

I sniffle a bit, and Omar gives me a quick hug. "Be well." He jumps into the Zodiac and motions for Rick to lower them down.

Confused, always a step behind, always missing critical information. "Omar's leaving too?"

"Yeah." Rick spits. A kelp fly buzzes off his mouth and lands on his sunglasses. Is this disdain meant for Omar or the kelp fly? "Wants to do right by Kylie."

Even when I'm the first to know, I'm the last to know.

The elegant sailboat is incongruous with the slimy rocks and grimy shoreline. When Kylie stands to leap from the dinghy, Omar puts his hand on the small of her back, a protective gesture I've envied before. A gesture the recipient rarely ever notices or even feels, a naked traitor of intent, entirely for the benefit of the hand owner, not for the owner of the back. How many other subtle gestures transpired before my eyes?

"Did you know it was Omar?"

"Eh, two good-looking heterosexual kids trapped on an island with lousy TV reception? This place, it is both the slowest place on earth and automatic fast-forward. It's not the first time there's been a secret love affair, you know." He stares at me flatly. I'm again missing something, but I'll never catch it. All the its. There are too many its.

My mind drifts to the old lighthouse keepers, the emergency departures. Little Royal Beeman rushed in a rowboat by his parents, paddled by hand, his mother still nursing a two-month-old infant, in an eight-hour storm surge, only to watch him die in San Francisco. Little Georgie Cain. His little four-year-old brother, never named in the newspaper articles, but surely he had a name. Maybe he's the ghost in the Jane Fonda room, willing someone to remember him, remember them. *Remember me.*

Patty has again left without anyone noticing. How could a guy with so much physical girth be so stealthy? The sun bounces off Sugarloaf and the water surface sparkles like sequins. It's the golden hour, perfect for taking photos for the blog. Once again, I don't have a camera and feel guilty. Rick lands the Zodiac and together Pedro and Rick secure it for the next shark event, working in short bursts without speaking.

Without Patty giving me instructions, no one cares what I do, so I climb the crumbling slope to North Landing, watching the boat make its way around Great Murre Cave and Fisherman's Bay. A wave of abandonment settles into my belly, followed by a whole-body urge to burst into tears.

The Farallon desolation feels like an animal itself, lurking in its burrow, in crevices, on precipices. Every nautical knot of separation makes that animal hungrier. It feels like Kylie or Liz or someone sees me wave, but then they spot something in open water, and all turn their heads away from SEFI, away from me. *Goodbye goodbye goodbye goodbye.*

The entire cooking schedule needs to be reorganized. The duties will shift. Maybe I'll take more showers.

Upstairs, my stuff, which had formerly been tucked inside one of Kylie's purple bins, is now nicely laid out on Kylie's bed. Her former bed. The underpants have already been chewed through at the crotch by the resident mice.

I sit on Kylie's bunk and the little wooden chair gives its familiar *sigh* in response, this same sound I've heard in the dim hours. Without Kylie, I'll be alone with that creak. It's a ghost. Even though it's not a ghost and there are no such things as ghosts and of course, I'd never tell the guys about this ghost, I know it's a ghost, and more specifically a young ghost. An earnest ghost. It's a floorboard easing pressure on the chair whenever someone moves on the beds. Except it's a ghost at the same time. I take a breath and stand. The rocking chair shifts again in response. I stash the chair in the hallway. Maybe Patty wants it. Maybe Patty would let me sleep in his room, but after the bird penis remark, he'll probably take it the wrong way. Would it be worse for Patty to think I want to sex his cloacal protuberance? Or to think I'm afraid of a child who died of diphtheria in this room one hundred years ago?

It hits me softly: I'm the only woman on this island. Perhaps even within thirty miles in any direction unless a container ship happens to be going by at any moment.

Huh.

Out in the hallway, the rocking chair creaks again. *Not alone. Not alone. Not. A. Lone.*

*Remember me.*

# Day 12

Of SEFI, a US navy chaplain said, "God has done less for it and with it than any other place." Even the wind picks up tiny bits of the granite from the island and pummels surfaces, scratching everything, including exposed skin. The term "godforsaken place" often springs to my mind when I do my little walkabouts up and down the mule path. The crags are full of death. The shores are full of death. There's a gravesite with a poem for a mule that died in 1908, the only grave on this island although not the only death and certainly not the only internment. And despite this massive crisis on the mainland, we remain safe here on SEFI.

Three biologists left SEFI yesterday afternoon, all for reasons pertaining to the H3N2 and nSFI situation. As for the remaining four of us, we're in it for the long haul. The program office will fill those vacancies over the next few days, and I should have a new roommate shortly, if they bring out at least one if not more females. Right now, though, I'm the only girl on the island.

Dear Reader, I can imagine that, years from now, I'll be able to tell my grandchildren (or grand-nieces and nephews) where I was when the $H_3N_2$ epidemic hit the West Coast. I'm sure they won't believe I was on a national wildlife refuge no boats could land on, surrounded by dozens of giant great white sharks. "Sure, Aunt Jane, whatevs," they'll say. I'll bet they'll have something more annoying than "whatevs" by then. "Whatever" will become our generation's "groovy."

Oh, Dear Reader, what a sad legacy we leave.

Signing off from shark central. Peace be with you. Stay safe out there, you guys.

Jane

## Comments (43)

Niel
Be glad you're in a safe zone, Jane. Unless the seals are carriers, you shouldn't have to worry about contagion.

Monica
How can I volunteer to be an intern? I was a biology major and live not too far away from San Francisco (I'm in Orange County, about a seven-hour drive, not a big deal) and would love to come out and keep you company.

Shannon
Jane, please call home. Your cousin hasn't been able to get ahold of your aunt. I don't want to scare you but maybe you know where she might be? Shannon

# Day 13

HACKERS USING H3N2 CONCERNS TO TRICK US, CYBERSECURITY PROS WARN

Hackers and cybercriminals have long leveraged the hype and fear around fast-moving world threats as a tool to steal passwords and data—and H3N2 and nSFI are no different.

Domain registrations themed around the quickly spreading H3N2 flu and nSFI prion contagion are 90 percent more likely to be from malicious actors, according to a recent study. Cybersecurity blogger Vincent Stewart reported on Thursday that the interactive pandemic tracking map maintained by Cornell University has been targeted by hackers who are selling malware claiming to compromise the map and infect users.

Just as distancing and handwashing are the best defenses against these pathogens, technology professionals stress that computer and mobile device users need to be more wary of what they click. Experts recommend never downloading an email attachment from an unknown source.

**Cosmoballiton**
**@CosmoNoFilter**

Do you think shoes miss us?

♡ 29 ○ 10 ⟲ 3

**Wolf News WNBS**
**@WNBSNews**

Silver Alert for missing Elgin man
http://www.bit.ly.com/silveralert584

♡ 4.4K 🗨 34 ⟳ 1.8K

**DB Cooper**
**@DBmm**

As we all are accustomed to wearing personal safety medical masks, this is going to be the end of facial recognition software until it gets good enough to recognize retina patterns from distance (and that can be fucked by wearing sunglasses)

♡ 9.1K 🗨 7 ⟳ 13

**Xi**
**@sXlilate**

Found a dismembered human ear in the front yard, except it's a piece of the dog's chicken jerky, rehydrated by the rain. I should probably stop watching old CSI episodes.

♡ 95 🗨 12 ⟳ 0

# Day 12

BRIAN

I lubed my hands up with women's cold cream. It was the same brand my mother had used. I liked the smell. It was the memory of bedtimes, of late nights after the divorce with hot bowls of buttered popcorn and *Saturday Night Live* sketches. I was afraid of the Land Shark, but I couldn't let on or she wouldn't let me stay up late to watch the show with her. After the chemo had taken everything she had to give, I didn't let myself dwell too much on her, but the cold cream was a nice soft memory that didn't get too much in my face.

As moisturizers went, however, it wasn't the first or even the tenth choice for most potters. The best hand lubes were usually imported from Canada or Greenland. As much as I liked the cream's smell, sometimes in the morning, while it was still cold, it felt like congealed fat.

Sometimes I thought of disgusting images intentionally, to shock my inner fussbudget into surrender. It hadn't worked quite yet, but I was pretty sure I was desensitizing myself. Someday I'd manage to man up and be the tough guy I pretend to be. Fake it until you make it, they say.

Yep, faking the faked fakery like a faker. *Fake off, buddy.*

When did my hands turn into my father's hands? How'd that happen without my noticing it? My knuckles looked burled and knotty. I poked my skin, wiggling the loose parentheses apart. Each hand had four blinking eyeballs over the big knuckles. He was thirty-five when he walked out on us. I'm about to turn fifty.

The cold cream needs five minutes to soak in, so I used the time to start a pot of coffee and then checked my email on my studio laptop—an old laptop, the keyboard wrapped in regular old kitchen plastic wrap. Once upon a time, I had enjoyed email, mostly my electronic dalliances with Jane.

Now pain and badness and all manner of annoyances came through the ether and landed in my inbox.

There was a fresh order from a wholesaler in Houston, forty-eight units, mixed vases and tiles. I was pretty sure I had enough tiles to fill the order in the warehouse downstairs, but I'd have to check on the vases. It was probably time to do a decent inventory anyway.

I cracked open a new box of kaolin clay. Black mold spotted the bottom of both twenty-pound bags, puffs of black rising from the seams of the cardboard. The skin on my back crawled with imaginary vermin, and inside my stupid crazy brain, I felt the panic start to rise. *Breathe. Breathe.* I had a secret crazy person trapped inside my brain. I kept him occupied most of the time by having a song stuck in my head, and, of course, keeping busy while repeating mantras to myself.

*"We clean. We clean but dirt is natural and good. Dirt is clay. Clay is clean. Clay is antibiotic. Dirt makes us stronger."*

It was pathetic but it worked.

Sometimes it wasn't enough. I could feel my inner nutcase trying to get out, so I pulled out the next best thing: creative visualization technique. It was kooky, like something you might find in a 1970s self-help book, but it worked for me.

This time, I imagined the Medieval and Renaissance wing of the Victoria and Albert Museum in London. Before the happy drugs for the art shows, a therapist (or as I liked to refer to him, The Rapist) had taught me cognitive therapy, using re-created mental imagery as a form of self-hypnosis.

It was a recollection back to one of my more dramatic fugues, back when I was twenty-four or twenty-five. As I earnestly took notes in my MBA program, I knew I'd never actually do the homework being assigned, and the textbook was the last thing in the world I'd read. The next day, I withdrew myself from the classes. Then I went outside and hyperventilated, wondering what the fuck I had done, what was I doing, quitting grad school after less than two weeks?

My mother—smart woman that she was—knew the signs and had been waiting for my call. She encouraged me to get my head clear, and besides, I could go back to school later. I took off to the first place that popped into my brain—the United Kingdom. There, I sat in old churches and stared at the busts on the crypts. These craftsmen were gone and even now these countenances stared out across time. Their work had meaning. Their lives had meaning. I had run my hands across the noses pilgrims had rubbed into nubs centuries before me, pressed my fingertips into eye sockets worn into cracked gouges, like the craftsmen were whispering back to me somehow.

But one day, a Tuesday when I had no specific place to be other than tramping through the V&A, in some weird bit of what might have been synesthesia or perhaps some snake oil brand of religious piety, when I looked up into the luminescent eyes of what might have been my four hundredth crucified Christ figure, I heard the sound of ancient church music, some version of a pipe organ accompanied by a chorus of voices singing in Latin. The hair on my arms had stood on end, and I'd looked around the wing to see if anyone else had heard it, but there was no one.

And on the same day, everything changed . . . again. That afternoon, a television in a pub showed a plane flying into a tower and then another one hitting its twin, and then the footage again, from a different angle, as though it was an endless cascade of planes and towers, more planes more towers, towers and then planes and then fire and then fire and then nothing. Everything that would ever be built could be torn aside, people jumping out windows. We could all fall. Nothing was certain. Plans were prayers against a future we thought we could control. You had to hold on to what mattered. Be the person who could do some good somehow.

I moved to Chicago to be near my mom. Somehow standing amid the steel girders and unbroken glass of a shiny proud city felt like doing something, making a stand for the side of good. Somehow it felt like it mattered to someone. To anyone. Eventually it could matter to me.

As it turned out, it never would.

And now, that magical—perhaps hallucinatory—moment was my own. A Zen koan, as Jane called it. Anytime I felt stressed, I visualized that moment of wonder, the memory of footsteps on the V&A's floor, polished and uneven from millions of feet over the decades, granny boots and spats and penny loafers and Chuck Taylors, tired tourists determined to eke out as much culture as humanly possible. I would make myself be there, remember it all, my new therapy. I would push onward through the rooms, examining each Mary with Child in detail, until the creepy crawlies went away. *Breathe. Breathe.* Until I no longer panicked about mold colonies in my lungs, or worming into hidden nooks and crannies in the studio's old beams.

*Good job. Go back to sleep, fruit loops.*

With my clean hand, I opened a window and tossed the box in the general direction of the studio's dumpster in the parking lot. I'd pick it up later. It was my parking lot, after all.

A second too late, I remembered that South Island's resident homeless guy Bob might be down there. In a way, it was his parking lot too.

"Oh shit! Incoming!" I shouted, sticking my head out the window.

Bob wasn't in the path of the moldy box—luckily, he was on the river piling, taking off his shoes, giving his yellowed old man toes a stretch. A plume of mold spores trailed behind the box as it fell four stories. It missed my dumpster with a wet *thwack*, and Bob looked up but deemed it unworthy of inspection. He stretched out his tramp toes and then leaned back to enjoy the last of the autumnal sun.

I sprayed a diluted bleach water solution on my hand, then on the table and the window handle for good measure.

I felt bad for Bob, and I felt bad about myself.

I always tried to make the careful dance between my middle-class white-guy guilt and my unexpressed feeling that the unhoused were somehow getting away with the best heist imaginable. I did what I could to balance those two opposing forces: Fruit and water were both cheap but heavy to lug home. I rationalized against the purchase often—especially on days when I biked. I couldn't fund Bob's tramp lifestyle entirely.

Maybe Bob resented these small acts of kindness. Perhaps it interfered with Bob's mantra of living from the land. *Did Bob even have a mantra?* I didn't know. I respected Bob's aesthetic, whatever it was—even if his mission statement only involved the quiet and slow descent into alcoholism.

This made me a bad person. After all, I had at my disposal the best rainfall shower that money could buy, fitted with a repurposed copper shower I had polished with a hand grinder while listening to my stash of *This American Life* podcast episodes. Whenever I heard Ira Glass's voice, it triggered a memory of the environmentally friendly epoxy that stopped copper oxidation.

My shower felt like being in the epoch of a sunset. If Bob experienced the luxuries my loft hid behind the rusted door of a nineteenth-century factory, he might resent me more.

Bob didn't seem like a resentful type—we had a nodding acquaintance. Once I had even given him a pair of alpaca slipper socks a gallery owner had sent me for Christmas that were too large for me. I envisioned Bob putting those slipper socks on wherever he went to—wherever Bob went at night. Hell, I wasn't even sure. It might have been a warehouse somewhere nearby, perhaps one with the door cracked open, where a rusty hinge had finally given way. There were plenty of empty buildings around the Fox River locks. Or hell, maybe Bob had himself one of the fancy condos in the old sewing needle factory and spent his golden years collecting my castoffs and selling them on Craigslist and eBay.

Respect. I gave Bob respect. It was respectful to not pity him, allow the man his dignity in his bohemian lifestyle. It was the least I could do.

My wire cutter sliced ten pounds of clay off the knob, cold and hard as chilled butter. If I didn't occupy myself, I'd start spraying everything with sanitizer, thinking about invisible clouds of mold spores. Wedging the clay into submission felt good. It gave me permanence. The ache between my shoulder blades felt real, the way those English and Welsh craftsmen might have felt with their chisels and augers, sculpting and carving what they worshipped and adored.

Solar panels powered the studio's water heater. Wisconsin's winter days weren't long enough to even pay for the panels themselves—and they certainly couldn't power the loft or any of the flour mill's luxuries, like security lights or my delicious shower. It *was* enough to keep honest my claim of running a 100 percent green pottery studio. Part of my "schtick," as a review once called it, a word I had failed to eradicate from my brain. From organic glazes (which made every self-respecting potter I knew snort) to the vintage tools I used, the pottery was from start to finish carbon neutral. Between that and the corn waste packaging material I used to cushion my wares for shipping, the indie artistic community ate it up.

"Whore," I whispered to the clay. The water was marginally hot. Winter was coming.

Did Bob have a place to stay for winter? I could let him stay here. The ABC Afterschool Special sepia fantasy was interrupted by the thought of Bob's undoubted case of lice, genital herpes, warts, or any number of other effluvia tramps carry on their persons. The sanctity of my loft would be undone by one particularly gruesome and contagious hobo penis.

Nope.

We'd all like to believe we're Batman, answering the Bat-Signal when citizens need our aid, but almost no one's able to be a do-gooder. People create the shapes in your life that you mold yourself around. At some point, you stop being malleable.

Jane was my perfect friend, an ideal relationship, held at arm's length behind my phone's smart screen. I was in total control. She only got to see this ideal version of Brian, one I couldn't accidentally fuck up.

I could go to my grave without ever meeting her again. The thought should have scared me, but it didn't. She said she wanted to see me, but I was sure she didn't. After all, we'd been in the same area code for years. God, it felt like only a few years, but COVID had made everything feel compressed and long at the same time. Regardless, she never once asked to meet up, not directly anyway. It was all pretext. We hadn't even talked on the phone, much less on a video call, even though we texted in spurts.

"Wipe your tears with hundred dolla bills, rich boy!" Jane had chided me in an email with the subject line "My pony's diamond shoes are too tight!" after I complained that museums and galleries kept requesting the same damned mid-century throwback vases for their overpriced gift shops. How many times would I create the same vase? Instead of making new wares, I felt the pull of strings on my back, making me throw pottery in a certain, marketable style, over and over repeatedly. Like that rat who made the chef cook in that Disney movie.

My lungs seemed thick. Mold. The fucking mold. The clay was stiff and petulant, like me. Luckily, tiles required clay slabs, which needed drier, stiffer clay than the stuff I used on a wheel. Slab work was clean business: I could have made slabs in a Lagerfeld black suit and no one would be the wiser. I set up a production on the big wooden studio tables, rolling out four master slabs from which I could cut six individual two-by-six tiles. I signed the wet clay and numbered each piece on what would become the backside, flipped it over, smoothed and buffed ninety-six edges, then carved individual designs into each flat. It was fast work in multiples, assembly line style. It was certainly no different from when I made my own tiles, but this push-button response to the gallery cheapened the process.

While flats dried, I got busy throwing the small vases. I queued up a 1940s Lead Belly collection and got into a good throwing trance. When the mood was there, the velvety porcelain contained me for hours. Sometimes I only realized time had passed when the studio was too dark to see the clay. The misshapen vessels were what my unconscious mind would make, if it could only take control. I could throw blind. Buddhist monks threw using the wheel as a meditation, destroying the vessels afterward. Self-awareness came forward, pushing out of nowhere, like reading braille. The true magic was throwing what you THOUGHT you were seeing, the soul of the clay seeping into your mind's eye. Metaphysical nonsense, perhaps.

With a dozen vases planked up, I took a break, washing and greasing my hands with my dead mother's cold cream. The telltale tightness of the porcelain leeching moisture from flesh, clay dust everywhere.

My cell phone buzzed—the house-cleaning service calling.

"Mr. Arden? I'm sorry, but we need to reschedule your clean today. Does tomorrow work?"

"Oh. I work from home, so it's fine."

"Thank you for understanding. Our girls are all out sick. It's this bug that's going around, the headache-y thing."

"Oh, that sounds awful." My usual crew of craggy women—their "girls"—would be more haggard than usual. "Thank you for calling. They shouldn't be working while they're sick."

"You're so nice. Some looked awful yesterday and they're worse today."

"OK then. So, you're going to send a new crew?"

"They'll be better tomorrow and so you'll get your usual crew. With my luck, they gave it to me. I'm all flushed, woke stark up at 3:10 this morning. Isn't that a funny thing, how you always remember the exact time you bolt out of bed, but Lord blessed if I remember any other time of the day. Like dinner time." She chuckled at her own joke.

I checked my pulse while offering a polite laugh. My heartbeat felt normal. I didn't feel warm, but the weird lung thing I had noticed prickled my neck. "You know, if people have some kind of bug, let's put a hold on it this week."

"Oh, we don't have to do that!"

"No trouble. If you're short-staffed today, there's twice as many jobs tomorrow. You might be out too. Might as well hold off for a week."

"You sure?"

"Absolutely. How messy is one lonely guy?" I said, using gender stereotypes to my favor.

We did pleasant Midwest goodbyes, assuring the other to stay healthy, a new mantra in recent weeks. Afterward, I slowly let out the breath I'd been holding in.

This wouldn't do. I pulled up the "Who is Sick" bookmark on my browser. Bubbles of self-reported illness in the 54195 zip code turned the entire map red. What percentage of sick people used this website? Then another three bubbles popped up.

I was starving. It was well past time for lunch. I'd make dinner instead. Normally the UPS guy shocked me out of my throwing stupor, which . . .

Shit. I'd missed the UPS guy.

I pictured Bob the Hobo pawing through my delivery outside. I was expecting some ceramic tools, which were a little too expensive to give to the Bob Foundation—tungsten steel trimming tools tended to shatter if you dropped them on the ground. I bought in multiples to maintain productivity, but I was down to the last of my four favorites and had broken three I needed to trim the vases drying downstairs.

The elevator needed a human in it, so I couldn't call it up to the studio. It was good to shake a little blood into my joints. I had stiffened from holding the throwing position for so long. Jane was right: Getting old wasn't for whiny bitches.

Downstairs, nothing in the entryway. No packages leaning up against the dumpster, nada. My first thought was Bob, but he had never stolen a thing from me, so I don't know why I kept thinking he was a thief. But the packages I had packed the night before were still sitting inside the door, untouched. The UPS guy never came.

On the shipping company's site, my account was still flagged for pickup. The ETA was four hours overdue. I always had loads of shipments going out, so Chuck checked daily for my packages as a courtesy. Chuck was a walking petri dish, given the sheer number of people and sneezes he must meet on a given day.

The moldy clay was still sitting in the lobby where I had left it, growing more mold by the minute. Chuck had delivered the boxes two days earlier, within the incubation period of most viruses.

Maybe Chuck wasn't picking up my packages because he was also sick? And so many of their drivers were out sick they couldn't cover his route? How many sick hands touched all my boxes before they landed in the vestibule?

Bleach water. Time to spray all the cardboard boxes with bleach water.

I took the stairs back up to the studio two at a time, breathing hard by the time I got to the fourth floor. My lungs were congested, like I was coming down with something. I was filling a spray bottle with water when I heard fireworks from somewhere.

Wait. Fireworks? In the middle of the day?

I couldn't see anything out the open window. A car idled on the drawbridge, no driver.

A second series of loud pops. This time the reverb bounced off the old warehouse just thirty yards away from my building.

I ran to the window on the wide side of the river. Someone with a large gun stood on the roof of the old Lutheran association building. Smoke rose from the muzzle and the shooter wore goggles that reflected sunlight. Then they ducked back behind the heating unit.

Jesus. Was someone shooting off the top of the building?

The Lutheran association building was the highest building downtown, plus, it was situated on the highest point overlooking the river. A strategic advantage, as a shooter would have not only a 360-degree panorama but also a clear view through the buildings downtown via two major arteries.

The rifle pointed at the big drawbridge that connected South Island to downtown. A series of puffs rose from the road of the drawbridge before I heard the *poppa poppa poppopopopopop!*

What was he shooting at? The idling car? The driver?

Fuck. What if he was just shooting for the sake of shooting?

I should be panicking, but it didn't seem real. Even as the gunshots happened, I was safe in my beautiful studio, with my dead mother's face cream, with my kiln and my retro vintage coveralls and my entire little peaceful world.

I crouched anyway, feeling stupid. A sniper just could point and shoot in my direction, even accidentally, and blow out my beautiful eleven-foot-tall industrial windows, special-ordered and salvaged from a pre–World War I factory in Montreal. It had taken three months to get the glass on a truck and through customs. The harsh reality of broken windows through December and January. Then I felt ashamed for worrying about bespoke windows when a guy had a gun. A guy had a gun and was shooting! Was this really happening?

The shooter had ducked out of sight. 911 had a busy signal. Then the emergency sirens blared. It wasn't an unusual sound: The municipalities tested them every Wednesday at noon. However, a test lasted only a minute. Now it wailed a terrifying low vibrato, up and down and up and down, *eeeee errrrrrrr eeeeeeeeeeeeee errrrrrrr.*

Would they use sirens for a mass shooting? Yes, of course they would. It was a pretty good way to get everyone's attention, but who could have missed the gunshots? I scuttled over to the radio. A Bee Gees song asked how deep my love was. I crawled to the stairwell and then bounded up to the loft to check the TV for news. I'd be safer upstairs, anyway—if I didn't go into the bedroom, which looked right at the Lutheran building.

It was the junior reporter, she usually did special interest stories, high school playoff games, and holiday parades. She hadn't even taken off her Fox 11 yellow windbreaker. She was calmly reminding everyone about the need to lock down, don't mingle with extended family, and quarantine in place for everyone's safety to contain the spread of illness. Nothing about the shooting.

I tried 911 again. Still busy. A prerecorded and artificially cheerful story on a group of volunteers who were making deliveries of groceries and medical supplies to homebound seniors. Then back to the live desk, the camera catching the newly minted anchor yawning and touching her temple gingerly as she read the weather forecast. No mention of the shooting. Why even have a live news desk if you're not going to alert the public to dangers happening right then?

Something itched inside my brain, the urge to take an hour-long shower, followed by a soak in rubbing alcohol. I unearthed my stash of antianxiety drugs and popped two.

The TV had switched to a local doctor talking with the junior reporter. "First intense headaches, followed by restless leg syndrome and a decreased ability to fall asleep. Finally," the doctor said, stressing her words emphatically, "extreme cases have lapsed into a dissociative catatonia. So, the ill person is mobile but not psychologically present."

The shooting had stopped. I dialed 911 again. Still busy.

Someone online had mentioned something about Chicago being under quarantine. I hadn't thought they were serious.

"Are such infected people dangerous? Either to themselves or others?" the reporter asked.

"No, they're not. They're highly contagious, but even during the times when they've gone several days without sleep, the people who are in the very rare 2 percent of sufferers, they're no more dangerous than your average sleepwalker or narcoleptic. That's what's happening. Their brains cannot instigate tonic immobility—the thing that prevents us from acting out our dreams—and the infected resort to an ambulatory coma."

"That's a frightening term for our viewers, Doctor."

"It's a serious condition."

"But again, as you said, this is for rare cases and is not fatal. How long does the disease run its course?" She gingerly touched the side of her head. Her guest inched back in the chair.

"Expect to stay home from work three to five days for most cases, until you stop sleepwalking or get restful sleep. Some high-risk cases require hospitalization for extra fluids. Sleepwalkers often eat and drink in their ambulatory states. H3N2 stage four sufferers are feeding and drinking when they have thirst and hunger, it would seem, and urinating and defecating, although they have trouble finding toilets. And of course, with additional fluids, rest, and staying warm, the body will recover faster."

"Thank you, Doctor. And again, if you or someone in your home has come down with the H3N2 virus, please contact your family doctor. Next, sports anchor Brian Rastman on staying healthy through handwashing."

Outside, police and ambulance sirens. Flashing red-and-blue lights bounced off the building's cream brick. A calm certainty rolled over me as the news switched to a commercial for a blanket with sleeves.

This was bad. Way bad. Exactly my worst crazy pants scenario coming true.

I swallowed two more antianxiety pills, followed by a giant gulp of water.

Shooters. Mass contagion. Would the water be contaminated? No, now I was being silly. Stay inside. Stay calm. Probably a kook out there with bad aim. The police have it under control.

Aha, I could look at the traffic cameras! The local news website must have been getting hammered and wouldn't load for me. The news anchor still hadn't mentioned anything about gunshots or shootings. I Googled "College Avenue Appleton web cam" and found even more cameras than I thought. Each showed the same story: College Avenue—normally a constant stream of traffic—deserted except for police cruisers, some parked, some trolling the streets.

The tornado siren had stopped, although when, I wasn't sure. I crawled on hands and knees into my bedroom and cautiously peered over the windowsill to see if the shooter was still there. The rooftop was empty, not even any police.

Just to be safe, I crawled back to the living room and dashed off an email under the guise of giving Jane a heads up about the shooter and that I was safe. I hoped for a fast response since Jane was never far from her smartphone and was an obsessive email checker. Nothing.

Finally, I got onto the local news website, but it was more of the same babbling about public health officials. A call for medically trained individuals, including paramedics and veterinarians, to report to their nearest high school or civic center, where makeshift triage centers had been set up to deal with the influx of H3N2 victims.

The island was quiet. It was disturbing. *Understatement of the year.* Then I giggled, the sound slapping the air in hiccups and guffs in such a way that I creeped myself out and stopped immediately.

## Day 13

**Mychelle**
**@MightyMych**

Well, the world is going up in flames, but my dog still loves me, and they can't get $H_3N_2$ or the fatal insomnia thing, so I guess that's good?

♡ 290 💬 19 ⟳ 31

**Xi**
**@sXlilate**

This feels like shock and awe without missiles being fired. I saw armored vehicles in Dupont Circle neighborhood today.

♡ 929 💬 89 ⟳ 45

**DB Cooper**
**@DBmm**

Gonna start a support group called Adult Children of Boomer Parents During $H_3N_2$ Pandemic Anonymous or ACBPDH2N2PA, which is pretty catchy, honestly.

♡ 4.5K 💬 158 ⟳ 89

**Jesus Don't Live Here**
**@karl1952**

Immigration without assimilation and rules is invasion. Why are we allowing an invasion with open arms? #americafirst

♡ 11.1K 💬 485 ⟳ 3.8K

**World Health Organization**
**@WHO**

Active field epidemiological investigation on #H3N2 in South Korea is to ensure appropriate measures taken ASAP to interrupt transmission.

♡ 18.4K 💬 87 ⟳ 14.4K

**DB Cooper**
**@DBmm**

Is anyone else constantly nervous to turn on the news in fear of seeing a shooting happening right now in their community?

♡ 5.4K 💬 542 ⟳ 1.9K

**The Raw Story**
**@rawstory**

WHO: H3N2 outbreak "out of control"
http://www.imgur.com/h47t

♡ 78K 💬 874 ⟳ 32.6K

**Amy**
**@AmyBedeliaBrown**

I can't sleep and I can't eat. Other than that, it's a beautiful sunny day and things are going my way.

25 4 7

**Gemma**
**@Gemma1989**

I wish guys got their body hair waxed. They are hairy and gross plus it hurts like a fucker and they are assholes and deserve their nethers ripped clean.

22 3 1

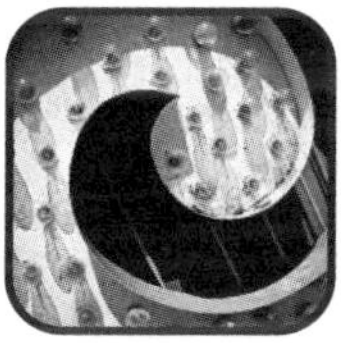

**Jane**
**@erejane**

Me before the Farallones: Ugh my room is the grossest, tear this place down! Me after the Farallones: Should I submit this place to Homes & Gardens?

11.5K 43 584

**Jesus Don't Live Here**
**@karl1952**

Word to the wise: You know the globalist shills are losing the argument when they trot out immunizations to convince us we are bad people for wanting #americafirst #liberalmedia

11.9K 84 4.5K

**Wolf News WNBS**
**@WNBSNews**

Breaking news: 19 killed, 48 wounded in Harvard-Westlake shooting in Studio City, Calif. Alleged shooter is son of Bullets to Heaven star

48.3K 1.8K 27.9K

**Cosmoballiton**
**@CosmoNoFilter**

7 am: Avoided donut. 8 am: Avoided donut. 11 am: Ate salad. 2 pm: Avoided donut.
2:12 pm: Ate donut and pie and chips and four packets of Taco Bell hot sauce. Am now fitness influencer.

46 2 0

**DB Cooper**
**@DBmm**

Sleep is "peels" backward.

875 4 15

**Jesus Don't Live Here**
**@karl1952**

We the people are facing H3N2 with an untrustworthy FBI and DOC, a batshit crazy speaker of the house and lying NY Times. #americafirst #liberalmedia

18.5K 542 4.4K

**Doctors Without Borders**
**@drwoborders**

The H3N2 epidemic appears to have been successfully contained in Malawi; we've concluded our emergency response.

8.7K 78 1.3K

**Sharky**
**@CmdrSharkington**

It's stunning all these high school shootings keep happening, after all we've done nothing to fix the problem.

1.5K 18 65

**Wolf News WNBS**
**@WNBSNews**

Alex Simons, father of accused Plano shooter, says 15-year-old son was a "good boy" who had been "mistreated at school," suffered from H3N2

1.6K 45 894

**Susie**
**@SuzeeeeQ**

Seriously. Srsly. Sleep nao.

11 0 0

**Wolf News WNBS**
**@WNBSNews**

Studio City shooting death toll rises, Bullets to Heaven star's son in custody

♡ 1.1K 💬 187 ⟳ 671

**Susie**
**@SuzeeeeQ**

Tony has it too now.

♡ 3 💬 1 ⟳ 0

# Day 13

BRIAN

The shooter was in custody. Not dead, because he was a white asshole, but I still wasn't going anywhere. News crews, emergency vehicles, and ominous black SUVs were everywhere. I stayed in and pretended to work but mostly watched the news, now all about the shooting, interspersed with the weather and events canceled due to the shooting. A list of companies now closed temporarily—an astonishing number I could see directly from the loft, including the paper pulp mill that occupied half of South Island, as well as the big restaurant in the old trolley station on the far end. All closed due to the incident. The yellow-jacketed junior field reporter interviewed the shooter's neighbor while standing in his driveway at a cautious distance, and he said the shooter was fixated on zombies and the biblical Armageddon. Back at the studio, the two anchors made an awkward joke about a zombie apocalypse, then went back to reading the teleprompter.

The air pressed out of my chest, a weight on my rib cage. It was the Encyclopedia Britannica description of a garden-variety panic attack.

From my eastern window, the little tavern looked open, a Coors Light neon sign hanging in the back window, a few cars parked outside. It was an odd little joint, close enough that I sometimes heard live music through open windows.

Sometimes I even thought about going in.

I never went in.

Where was Bob sleeping tonight? It was supposed to get cold. If people were under quarantine, where would Bob be quarantined? There must be homeless shelters somewhere. I'd investigated them before, worried about Bob during winter.

I'd even asked Bob outright the first winter I had been here, on a day when the wind chill was daring to be what they call a "drunk killer," so named for professional drinkers who get kicked out at 2 a.m., nap in their cars to sober up, and sleep into forever. A few notables manage to drive home and pass out in their own driveways, to be found the next day with liver core temps around fifty degrees.

Bob was in danger of becoming a hobo-sicle.

"Hey man," I had said then. "You staying warm out here?"

"Ya, man, thanks for the gloves." Bob clapped his hands against his chest, as though either celebrating his new gloves or perhaps proving he was entirely solid and without pain. I was lost in male rituals.

"No problem." I could have walked away right then. Bob was giving me the out. He had turned back to scraping the labels off glass bottles rescued from the dumpster behind the tavern. I considered leaving it, but the forecasted windchill nibbled my mind.

"Seriously, buddy, you got a place to sleep tonight? You want me to drive you to one of the—I think they have beds, hot meal, nice warm place to sleep, that kind of thing."

Bob gave me a withering glance. Like an idiot, I kept talking through it, pushing forward, no way out but in.

"They've got, um, coffee. Hot coffee. And games at night. You might even meet some ladies."

I caught myself from launching into a terribly inappropriate pantomime of sex, complete with thrusting of hips—this urge to fill the space between us. By an ounce of foresight, I resisted. Silence always frightened me, an unanswered call. I finally ceded with a pathetic "Yeah."

Bob shook his head. I was selling him something he'd already turned down a dozen times before.

"Nah, I'm good. I'm good." There was an edge to it, the threat of Bob unleashing a flurry of insults or fists and steel-toed kicks upon me.

I took the hint. "OK, see you around." I walked back to my building.

"You too!" Bob returned to the chipper homeless guy demeanor, as though all things were right in the world and *hey man, spare a dime.*

It was my first inkling that Bob resented help. I regretted saying anything. I enjoyed the happy fiction of a resident hobo of South Island. I wanted Bob to be like Otis, the Mayberry drunk from *The Andy Griffith Show*—grateful, subservient, a constant but cheerful reminder that I had a warm, soft bed to sleep in every night. Or perhaps the idea that the world wasn't so scary, that people could sleep out in the open without being dragged off by wild dogs or wolves or bandits or any number of the medieval constructs of terror authorities used to keep everyone in check and in church. Grimm's fairy tale stuff. Bob had gone from Otis the Drunk to the Bad Wolf himself.

I threw on a scarf and warm gloves and hauled down garbage and recyclable bags. I had been leaving my recycling bin unlocked with the lock closed on the eye so I wouldn't lose it. Bob liked to dig through it for containers and aluminum cans and I imagined he appreciated my generously lax security.

Someone had knocked the nib off the Dumpster, cleanly broken it. The broken piece of metal was on the ground, but the lock was missing. Why would someone want a lock for which they had no key?

I swung the recyclables into the bin. The bags in the Dumpster were still neatly tied off, so Bob hadn't been by recently. The smell reached up and smacked me when I opened the lid. The truck should have come by the day before, but this was all old garbage—in fact, there was the moldy porcelain box I had thrown onto the parking lot from the studio's window. Bob must have put it in there.

*Thanks, Bob.*

From the secured area across the river where the shooting had taken place, a man garbled emphatically. Maybe he was on a cell phone? Then he thrust his arms up in the air, pantomiming an elaborate evasion of an aerial assault. He hinged at his waist, dropping forward while his legs stood rigidly. He hung there, his arms limp for a minute, two, his legs still holding him up but making him look like a marionette whose strings had been clipped. Slowly, with impossible muscle rigidity, he rose back from the waist. Was this exercise, a form of yoga? He resumed his frantic arm movements and punctuated them with punches into the air, as though his conversation had continued.

His erratic motions unnerved, but with all the flashing lights from the cop cars across the river, it felt safe here. Like everyone was forgetting about this little secluded spot right in the middle of a small Midwestern town, a popcorn hull lodged in the gumline of the riverbanks.

It was Jane who had told me about this place. Jane, whose memories of the valley always popped up in our correspondence, like she was planting a seed, getting me used to the idea of returning to the same town where my father left us, making it feel normal when nothing in my world ever did.

I went back inside and locked the door firmly, concisely. Was I OK? For how long?

**Mychelle**
**@MightyMych**

I have so many things to say about my various trips to buy toilet paper to eight (8!) different stores, but I think I should go meditate or take a Xanax or something first.

♡ 78 💬 23 ⟳ 1

**World Health Organization**
**@WHO**

To alleviate suffering and save lives, WHO is: supporting countries to prepare and respond; providing accurate information to fight the infodemic; ensuring supplies of medical equipment for #healthworkers; training and mobilizing health workers; accelerating research to cure and create a vaccine #h3n2 #nSFI

♡ 8.7K 💬 69 ⟳ 145

**Xi**
**@sXlilate**

Freaking out at Asian people because you think you're going to catch #H3N2 isn't funny by the way.

♡ 72 💬 23 ⟳ 15

**Jesus Don't Live Here**
**@karl1952**

White men getting lots of hate these days. Not every Black person is a criminal.
Not every woman is crazy. Not every immigrant carries disease. How much do you like gambling? Do you feel lucky? #h3n2 #nSFI #invisibleenemy

♡ 2.8K 💬 122 ⟳ 742

**Wolf News WNBS**
**@WNBSNews**

Noah Galt, son of star Tom Galt, hospitalized, in critical condition. Doctors say advanced case of H3N2 nSFI dementia symptoms

♡ 6.6K 💬 14 ⟳ 125

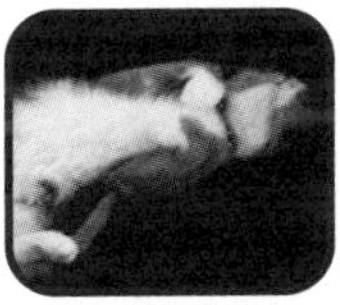

**Go To Sleep**
**@Insomnia**

Fact: people with ADHD/ADD are significantly more likely to suffer from #Insomnia.

♡ 39 💬 2 ⟳ 4

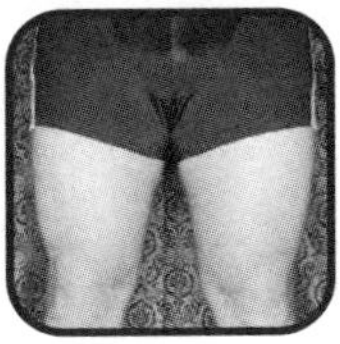

**JeSsBieU**
**@Jessbieu**

It's like my body won't allow me to leave it unprotected while it sleeps, so it stays awake.

♡ 2 💬 2 ⟳ 0

**Wolf News WNBS**
**@WNBSNews**

Cambridge, MA—Active shooter in daycare. Sheriff reports mass casualties taken to area hospitals. 31 confirmed fatalities at this time. Story developing

♡ 42 · 9 · 2

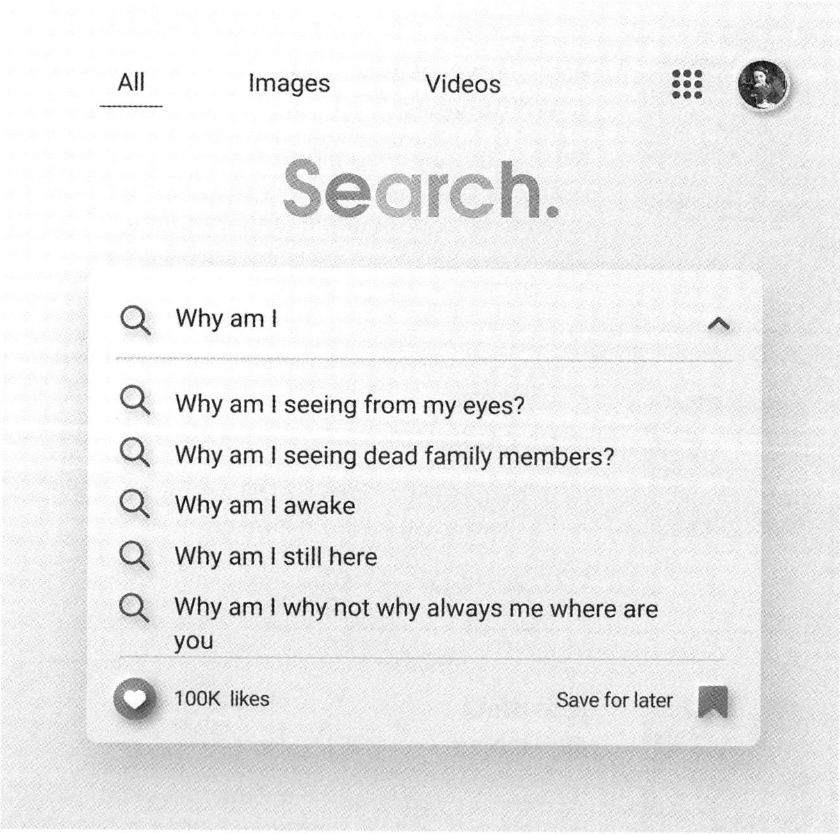

# Eight Years Ago

——Original Message——
From: Jane
Sent: Tuesday, January 08, 20xx 7:14 PM
To: Brian
Subject: Hmmmm x2

I'm very bored tonight.
Very sad and bored.
I wish my scars were sexy.

——Original Message——
From: Brian
Sent: Tuesday, January 08, 20xx 5:18 PM
To: Jane
Subject: RE: Hmmmm x2

Sexy scars are enigmatic fine lines giving distinction and mystery to a body part. Mine don't qualify. I may also be dying. I might already be dead. Or perhaps this is an elaborate fever dream spurred by having taken too much over-the-counter cold medication. I probably shouldn't ever consume something vivid blue anyway.

Why are you sad? Is there anything I can do to help?

——Original Message——
From: Jane
Sent: Tuesday, January 08, 20xx 7:24 PM
To: Brian
Subject: RE: Hmmmm x2

I'd like to think my pinky scar would be sexy because it's so very faint and delicate, but also so very banal in its origin I cringe. My skin is too fair, and every little mark shows up.

Inappropriate confession time: I have unnatural feelings for Donny Osmond . . . I have a picture of him, circa 1975, sitting on my desk right now as I type this. He's with his sister Marie, but I wrote "Bitch" over her face. No. I'm making that up. Not the picture part, but the besmirching of Marie's pretty Mormon face. I could never be so evil.

I'm sorry you have a cold . . . or perhaps are simply taking cold medication for the beneficial med head feeling. If I ruled the world, Ab Fab would be on many channels, pay raises would be based upon the ability to surf the internet, and codeine would be given out like after-dinner mints. Try eating something other than tea and Cheetos. Might I recommend some Fudge Fluffs and Chicken & Stars soup? I like to add Goldfish crackers to my soup . . . they are orange, which means they have vitamin C in them, which is good for colds.

Apropos of nothing, I saw a "Baby On Board" yellow sign today at lunch. I don't know what that means for society, but it was on a minivan with a bumper sticker on it which said, "Ask me about Herbalife."

——Original Message——
From: Brian
Sent: Tuesday, January 08, 20xx 5:53 PM
To: Jane
Subject: RE: Hmmmm x2

They probably own the entire series of animated biblical tales, boycotted Harry Potter because the magic was satanic, and have the Christian Relationship videos. He's probably 5′2″, whisper thin, and balding while she thinks Denny's is high dining, shops at Walmart, and secretly wants to bed an uncircumcised atheist (I don't know where that came from).

Your world sounds nice. I could live in that world. I had soup for lunch, from the coffee shop in Marin. I had the chicken noodle and received scorn from the hot barista who is undoubtedly a raw vegan and won't blow guys who eat dairy because she claims their spunk tastes like death. I think I have strep, which has sent me scuttling like a vile crab man into a pharmacy, begging for a sledgehammer of liquid cold salvation from the pharmacist, who thrust upon me a Smurf-colored bottle of chemicals and told me to chugalug. So I did. Like Wilford Brimley says, it's the right thing to do.

Also, you can't fool me about Marie.

——Original Message——
From: Jane
Sent: Tuesday, January 08, 20xx 8:03 PM
To: Brian
Subject: RE: Hmmmm x2

Dear Sir,

You mean you don't like Denny's Grand Slam whatever it is????

I can't lie to you. You know me too well. But do you also know about the Donny blow-up doll I have stuffed in my back bedroom closet?

Whichever part of my brain (Broca's area? Wernicke's area?) controlling spelling has decayed from too much Diet Coke abuse, I believe. Medicate away, mon ami. I fully support your endeavor.

Sincerely,
Jane

——Original Message——
From: Brian
Sent: Tuesday, January 08, 20xx 11:12 PM
To: Jane
Subject: RE: Hmmmm x2

Dear Jane, I'm not knocking the Denny's, I'm saying it's not fine dining. It's drunk dining. Or OH MY GOD I AM SO HUNGOVER AND IF I DON'T EAT MY BODY WEIGHT IN PORK I WILL DIE. It doesn't say *I love you.*

I did know about the doll. I'm a gentleman.

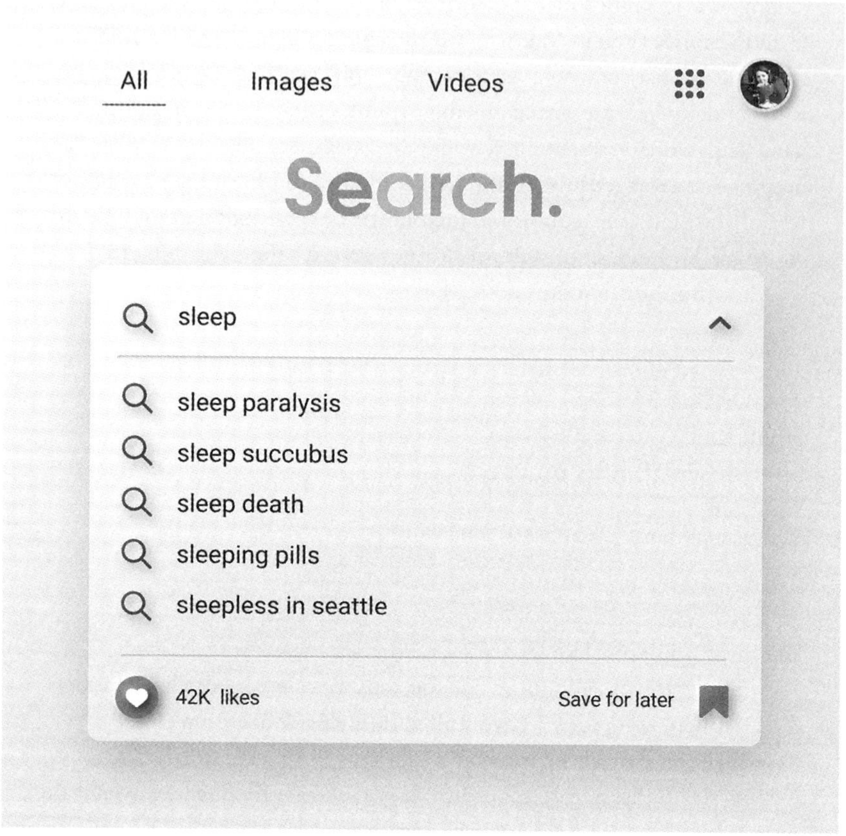
All
Images
Videos
Search.
sleep
sleep paralysis
sleep succubus
sleep death
sleeping pills
sleepless in seattle
42K likes
Save for later

# Day 14

**Mychelle**
**@MightyMych**

We are in a dark timeline right now. Is this a play by Beckett?

25 4 7

**Xi**
**@sXlilate**

Does it seem weird that "fake it till you make it" actually works for falling asleep?

0 0 0

**Wolf News WNBS**
**@WNBSNews**

Boston daycare fatalities now hits 50. Many victims in ICU, critical condition. Community grieving, Mayor to make statement at 3 pm EST

17.8K 2.2K 4.5K

**Wolf News WNBS**
**@WNBSNews**

Boston daycare shooter identified as Ryan Wilson Rummel, 24. Rummel's ex-girlfriend worked at Bouncy Tots Daycare, according to her social media

11.4K 689 3.8K

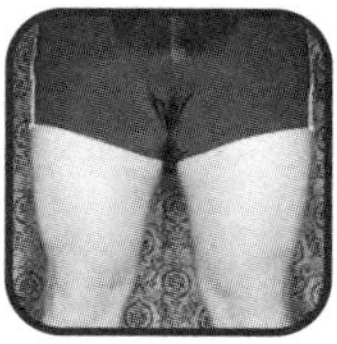

**JeSsBieU**
**@Jessbieu**

Hey, insomniacs have SICK open gym status at night. Miles of treadmills, no one on 'em.

42 4 6

**Julie Mons**
**@monsjul**

When you don't sleep, you end up eating meals 5 and 6. Insomnia is fattening.

39 7 9

**Susie**
**@SuzeeeeQ**

Went to hospital. Back home. No room at hospital.

11 4 0

**World Health Organization**
**@WHO**

We can expect further changes in the #H3N2 numbers in South Korea with new suspect cases being detected, investigated, confirmed, or discarded

♡ 3.3K 💬 59 ⟲ 1.5K

# Day 13

**Gemma**
**@Gemma1989**

Joke's on me—restaurant is closed for #H3N2 because the managers are sick. How am I going to make my rent this month? Too bad, so sad, #sorrynotsorry says the owner.

♡ 23 💬 4 ⟳ 10

**Jesus Don't Live Here**
**@karl1952**

Just like FAG AIDS, this H3N2 is caused by the devil due to the sinfulness of our earthly morals. Cast them out! #invisibleenemy #americafirst #fakenews

♡ 6.3K 💬 41 ⟳ 506

**Xi**
**@sXlilate**

A local business posted their special on their FB page: 15% OFF Ponchos! Come in and mention the deal at checkout! Oh! That's right, it IS poncho season. My ponchos are totally last year. At 15% off, how can I not rush right down? Excuse me, I must dash.

♡ 25 💬 0 ⟳ 3

**Susie**
**@SuzeeeeQ**

I think I'm sleeping in microbursts . . . I keep having mini nightmares but I'm still awake.

♡ 18 💬 7 ⟳ 2

**Wolf News WNBS**
**@WNBSNews**

Shooter in Port St. Lucie, Florida, high school shooting said to be bullied, humiliated by girls. Guns obtained legally

♡ 5.8K 💬 2.5K ⟳ 284

**Mychelle**
**@MightyMych**

is grossed out by the smell of someone's lunch. How can microwaved box lunches be edible when they smell like hot sick?

♡ 2.9K 💬 584 ⟳ 3.1K

**World Medical News**
**@worldmednow**

Emergency gathering of United Nations Pandemic Task Force over teleconference hacked, world leaders are trolled with raunchy photos

♡ 19K 💬 6.5K ⟳ 12.9K

**Xi**
**@sXlilate**

People who are worried about H3N2 and the insomnia flu but won't even get the damned flu or COVID shot?

♡ 425 💬 21 ⟳ 0

# Day 13

Protein Germ Impacts $H_3N_2$ Virus

LONDON—Some $H_3N_2$ sufferers have also been infected by a little-known prion component within the brain which impacts the victim's sleep patterns.

The prion is caused by a damaged type of brain protein—which is a chain of amino acids. Doctors theorize this prionic condition is caused by a relationship with a weakened immune system, triggered by many factors such as lack of sleep, increased cortisol levels, exposure to increased androgen hormones, and severe influenza cases. Scientists in New Zealand have also found the prions in the brains of people who did not show signs of influenza prior to suffering from the infections.

Prions are the cause of diseases such as mad cow disease and Creutzfeldt-Jakob disease and kuru in humans, and in animals, common forms are chronic wasting disease and scrapie.

Researchers of a rare inherited prion disorder called fatal insomnia have been working with infectious disease researchers at King's College London to identify and isolate the cause of the rapidly progressive dementia symptoms. Doctors have observed radical damage to the thalamus of the brain, which is part of the organ that controls the sleep/wake cycle and is known as the "relay center" of the brain because it is also responsible for helping the different parts of the brain communicate.

Typically, prion diseases are slow but progressive. The prions grow into longer threads that accumulate, like the plaques in Alzheimer's patients. "Eventually there's a tipping point," said researcher Dr. Preeti Sankapathy, head of research at Johns Hopkins University. She has joined the team in London for a special emergency epidemiology council organized by the United Nations.

Health-care providers can test for a prion component by conducting an MRI or spinal tap. Prion diseases are usually fatal, but life expectancy can be increased through modern medical treatments and medication.

# Day 13

**Wolf News WNBS**
**@WNBSNews**

Autopsy shows gunman of Memphis Sikh temple had severe effects of nSFI with prionic component in his brain

♡ 17.1K 💬 1.8K 🔄 4.8K

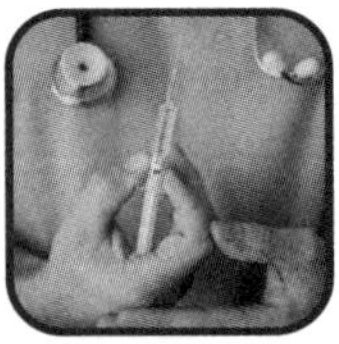

**World Medical News**
**@worldmednow**

Evidence suggests viral contagion passed from food to bloodstream through gum tissue. Experts suggest avoiding raw produce. Viruses cannot survive above 210 degrees F

♡ 11.5K 💬 284 🔄 4.8K

**Jesus Don't Live Here**
**@karl1952**

Muslims, Koreans, Mexicans, Syrians, undocumented immigrants, and you wonder why everyone's sick and dying. #biasedMSM

♡ 38.4K 💬 984 🔁 16.8K

**Gemma**
**@Gemma1989**

It doesn't help people think a four-star restaurant serving Korean/Mexican fusion is somehow related to the outbreak of nSFI and are making zero bookings.
#Mamaneedstoeat

♡ 34 💬 14 🔁 2

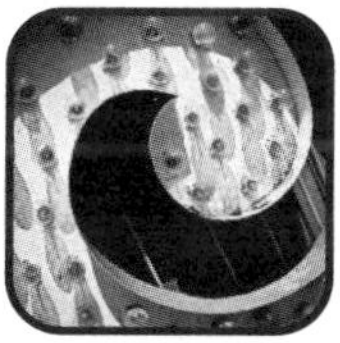

**Jane** ✔
**@erejane**

Anyone who brings home a new pandemic puppy and doesn't name it Meatball, yes, you should know I'm judging you a little bit.

♡ 2.9K 💬 45 🔁 34

# Day 13

Flushing Shooting: Most Violent Week in County's History

FLUSHING, NEW YORK—Seventeen people have been killed and many more remain in critical condition after a mass shooting Wednesday morning that included an elementary school in the community of Flushing, New York, according to assistant sheriff Maria Brandenburg with the Queens County Sheriff's Office.

"It is a sad day for us here in Flushing," said Brandenburg as she addressed the media.

According to Brandenburg, one of the seventeen people killed was the shooter, identified as Brock Jason Davenport. Officials aren't releasing information about the others killed at this time. It's unknown how many of the fatalities were children at the school, which has almost six hundred students, according to Queens County education board data.

Brandenburg added that several agencies are on the ground in Flushing actively investigating over ten different crime scenes, as the shootings spread across many locations including the playground of local elementary school PS 163, two restaurants, and a coffee shop.

Brandenburg said Davenport rammed his vehicle through the school's playground fence and entered the grounds on foot wearing a vest containing semiautomatic ammunition clips.

Witnesses report seeing vehicles marked with the logo of the Centers for Disease Control and Prevention. Several speculate the gunman was infected with H3N2 or a variant.

Davenport's neighbors say he was a quiet person who enjoyed hunting and donated the proceeds to local food pantries. Davenport's address is listed as an apartment on 164th street in Flushing.

Brandenburg said they have no known motive for the shooting and there are no known connections between the suspect and any of the victims or businesses targeted. Brandenburg added there is no threat to the community.

**Cosmoballiton**
**@CosmoNoFilter**

People are taking this insomnia flu thing about as seriously as lactose intolerant people take ordering extra cheese on their pizza.

245 12 45

**WBAY**
**@wbaynews**

Rise in street violence in Congo. Officials report H3N2 testing-related rioting

425 14 17

**Xi**
**@sXlilate**

Coworker's husband showing signs of H3N2 but she's still insisting on coming into work. I left at lunch and then took a sick day, wrote flame email to boss about it.

2 0 0

**Wolf News WNBS**
**@WNBSNews**

Death toll in Plano football rally mass shooting rises to 37, many still in critical care, gunman in custody

5.4K 2.9K 75

**Jesus Don't Live Here**
**@karl1952**

CNN is still trying to avoid the words "gays" and "plague." This is shameful.

6K 85 985

**Mychelle**
**@MightyMych**

In other news, when the challenge is "Given medication rectally in a McDonald's parking lot" in "Never Have I Ever," I now must drink.

68 2 0

**Wolf News WNBS**
**@WNBSNews**

Death toll rising as principal allegedly opens fire on Bergen County, NJ, high school assembly. At least 50 confirmed fatalities, hundreds wounded

5.9K 4.8K 7.1K

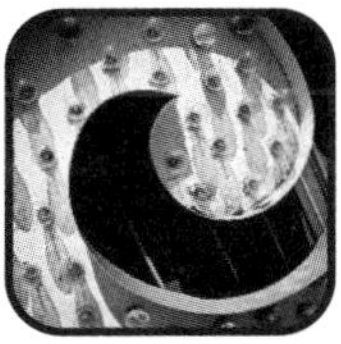

**Jane**
**@erejane**

You know all those scare stories about how doctors misdiagnose female heart attacks all the time because women have different symptoms and also the patriarchy? Basically, now every pain I have, is it a heart attack? Help, my tooth hurts I might be dead in an hour.

1.9K 15 84

# Day 14

Bay Area in Lockdown as More Test Positive for $H_3N_2$ and nSFI Diseases

SACRAMENTO—The governor of California announced on Tuesday a special measure across San Francisco, Marin, Alameda, Sonoma, Santa Clara, San Mateo, and Contra Costa Counties, including travel restrictions and a ban on gatherings, in a bid to stem the spread of $H_3N_2$ and nSFI contagious conditions.

The news comes after the number of confirmed $H_3N_2$ cases skyrocketed over the weekend, with over 1,400 new confirmed tests of $H_3N_2$ within the greater Bay Area collectively in a twenty-four-hour period and an additional 14 nSFI cases confirmed by autopsy. The governor imposed the measures on an area of the country that has seen one of the biggest outbreaks of the viruses. Experts project the actual number of infected is higher but are limited by official test availability.

"We cannot let our guard down," Governor Alvarez said. "Everyone must give up something to protect the herd." The measures include banning all public gatherings and nonessential travel as well as public services such as marriages and funerals.

Given the technology-centered economy of the Bay Area, San Francisco mayor Jill Robison urged companies to embolden workers to work remotely. Mayors of San Francisco, Oakland, Marin, and San Mateo have closed schools, with Berkeley, Richmond, San Jose, and others expected.

Flights in and out of SFO were suspended at midnight, with the order to halt air and seaport traffic.

City officials in nearby cities of Sacramento, Santa Cruz, and Modesto are monitoring the outbreaks but do not plan to lock down.

## Day 14

**World Medical News**
**@worldmednow**

WHO suggests wearing cotton masks and high-filtration fabrics to reduce virus spread

♡ 148 💬 14 ⟳ 27

**Wolf News WNBS** ✓
**@WNBSNews**

Stocks slow, vote of no confidence on government's virus plan

♡ 1.8K 💬 1.2K ⟳ 4.8K

**Happy Toes**
**@HappyNotSad**

Insomnia is the most self-diagnosed disorder.

♡ 4.9K 💬 85 ⟳ 9.6K

**Gemma**
**@Gemma1989**

The dirty secret of the food service industry is waiter and sous chef? They NEVER report their diseases or even go to the doctor when they're sick. It's, like, a thing. We don't get paid time off either!

♡ 956 💬 27 ⟳ 1.5K

**Wolf News WNBS** ✓
**@WNBSNews**

New York City Marathon postponed in wake of fears of viral outbreak #H3N2 #nSFI

♡ 849 💬 92 ⟳ 65

**Xi**
**@sXlilate**

Looks like I got one of the last packs of disposable masks. DC is taking this seriously, and yet I'm the only person wearing them on the street. What is going on?

♡ 20 💬 0 ⟳ 1

# Day 15

## Northwest Suburbs Enforce Stay-at-Home Order

CHICAGO—The epicenter of the H3N2 outbreak in Illinois is located about ten miles northwest of Chicago, where health officials and residents are preparing for a three-week lockdown in a "containment zone" ordered by Gov. William Garbachev.

The governor created the zone on Saturday and mobilized reservists from the National Guard to an area in the northern suburbs that includes Northbrook, Morton Grove, Evanston, and Skokie, where most of the state's H3N2 cases have been centered, along with three confirmed cases of nSFI.

A one-mile radius outside the cities will be maintained as a containment zone, which was recommended to Garbachev by the Illinois health commissioner and the CDC in Atlanta.

"The largest cluster of confirmed H3N2 cases in the Midwest is located in Northbrook," Garbachev said on Saturday. "We needed a strategy to contain it, moving from containment to mitigation."

National Guard troops will distribute meals to homebound residents, but, the governor added, they will not be released to use military or police force unless necessary.

The containment zone comes only a day after the governor announced a statewide ban on gatherings of more than 200 people. The ban is a blow to Chicago's tourism industry. The city's Oktoberfest events will also be postponed until a later date, organizers said. This will be the first time in over 120 years that the German festival has not been held. The parade was part of the musical climax scene of *Ferris Bueller's Day Off*, one of a host of teen movies set in the fictional town of Shermer, Illinois, said to be based on Northbrook, one of the towns involved in the containment.

**Allison Morsette**
posted *Sunday at 4:13 am CST*

Still awake. Freaking the fuck out.

# Nine Years Ago

What's the opposite of being in control?

It's not "out of control," right? Being in control and being out of control both indicate intentionality, some decision-making. Perhaps, Dear Reader, you think "I have everything under control," or perhaps you think "I'm choosing to not care about my set plan right now."

What I am right now is neither of those two things.

Last week, I went to my grandmother's house to take her to chemo. She wasn't outside waiting for me. Odder still, her dog was tied up outside. I let the dog in the house and walked in. Her bare legs were outstretched on her ottoman, feet still in slippers. For a moment, I thought she had passed.

She was sleeping. I woke her and she said she wasn't going to be able to go to the doctor, she couldn't even stand. There was a path of dark staining the carpet, leading to her chair. I called the oncologist, who insisted I call an ambulance if I couldn't get her into my car. Obviously, something was wrong, but I needed a stranger to point it out to me. I called Aunt Heidi, but Grandma perked up enough to start fighting back, like the crotchety old duchess she insists on being. She rationalized that she hadn't eaten and had gotten dehydrated from a bout of the unmentionable. She wouldn't say what had happened, but she hadn't made it to the bathroom and that was the dark terribleness on the carpet. She refused to go to the doctor. Aunt Heidi and I knew that if we called the ambulance, Grandma would dig in more and refuse assistance. She did eventually stand up and walk around and eat something, and Aunt Heidi decided against making her go to the doctor and told me not to call the ambulance, with the promise Grandma would go to the doctor the next day. The next day, Grandma did, after being talked into it by her weekly home care nurse. There they found she was severely anemic, and she would have died had she waited a second day. She then spent five days in the hospital receiving numerous blood transfusions and generally being angry at the world.

Dear Reader, I'm still mad at myself I didn't override her. I know she's stubborn and dismissive of me, as I don't have children nor does my Aunt Heidi, and therefore, in her eyes, my aunt Heidi and I are useless in terms of being caregivers. Heidi caves to her bullying. I'm the only one who will stand up to her. She listens to me because she feels bad about my being the one to find my mother's suicide. It has melted her, made her soft, she says, but at least she listens. It was the one good thing out of my mother's death. I should have stuck to my guns.

During her hospitalization, I'm there daily. The light hitting her face made me want to take a picture, but I knew she'd never let me take her photo in such a state—her hair sticking up in all directions, all weird and fuzzy from her cancer treatments. She waited until Aunt Heidi left the room and then calmly explained to me that her chemo has caused too much blood loss and she's too sick for another session of chemo anyway. I knew all of this already, Dear Reader, but it was much more painful listening to her struggle to find a way to tell me without telling me she was going to die.

As broken as she was, she taught me to love stories. She couldn't say she loved anyone, but she could tell a story, making them the hero who could do no wrong, the person we all cheered for in the end, even if the real person was a violent drunk who neglected and injured those around them. She's a master at show-don't-tell. They sent her home today. She's done with treatment. Now we wait.

As I left the hospital yesterday, the tops of the trees were still lit up with the setting sun. It gets dark so early now. It's an alarming realization, even when you know it's coming.

# Day 15

**Gemma**
**@Gemma1989**

Starbucks won't let me use my refillable coffee cup anymore. They said it's to protect them from the H3N2 virus. Um, sure, and your gross bathrooms are totally fine. #H3N2 #coffee4lyfe

♡ 74 💬 0 🔁 1

**Xi**
**@sXlilate**

We're about a week behind every other country in the world for response to this because why exactly? Other countries are testing? We're evac only in Bay Area and Chicago? I don't get it. DC people are not sleeping.

♡ 345 💬 34 🔁 27

**Mychelle**
**@MightyMych**

My church stopped doing communion and encouraged people to stop shaking hands after the Our Father, my favorite part of mass. Now we hold our hands to our own hearts.

45 0 0

**DB Cooper**
**@DBmm**

Man, if you want to piss off a baby boomer tell them this lockdown is going to last more than two more weeks. My mom literally hung up on me like it was my fault and then called me back to bitch me out for scaring her. Um . . . I didn't invent the pandemic?

578 112 73

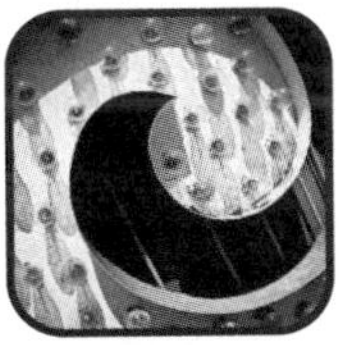

**Jane**
**@erejane**

Typical Sex and the City brunch scene: Samantha, Miranda, or Charlotte: This thing happened that upset me, I was— Carrie: Let me tell you about upset. I stepped in dog shit. S, M, C: Sure, let's talk about your thing, I'll sit here and be supportive.

15.4K 154 3.5K

# Day 15

PRESS RELEASE: ARCHDIOCESE OF CHICAGO

In compliance with the directions of the state and city Departments of Health, all evening church services are suspended. Sunday Mass will be reduced to thirty minutes to decrease the risk of spreading flu virus amid our congregation.

The diocese has taken every precaution in ensuring the safety of our parishioners. Between Masses, the church is to be thoroughly ventilated with high-powered fans. The Ladies Guild will spray and disinfect all surfaces with disinfectants. Special face masks and hand sanitizers will be available for any who desire them. Parishioners who cough, sneeze, or are showing indications of having contracted the flu will be asked to leave.

During this time of healing, the Church blesses and asks its congregation to commend to their prayers our members and pray for the speedy recovery of those upon whom sickness has laid its hand, particularly the children.

May God be with you all.

**Xi**
**@sXlilate**

I love The Commitments (a fake Irish soul band) more than The Replacements (a real alternative band with actual musical talent). Sad.

♡ 48 0 0

**Cosmoballiton**
**@CosmoNoFilter**

I can't stop myself from hoarding irrationally, so now I own more jars of jam than I ever expect to consume in my entire life.

♡ 720 💬 3 ⟳ 48

**Wolf News WNBS**
**@WNBSNews**

Local stores face shortage of household supplies and groceries amid H3N2 and virus fears http://www.bit.ly.com/foodshortages

♡ 3.5K 💬 165 ⟳ 905

# Three Years Ago

Our flights connect at O'Hell. Before the red-eye, we stand outside to catch our breath. The plane's full. We don't sleep. Ever since COVID, I hate everyone around me. I hate everyone. I want to hit them. Everyone. Everyone but Patrick, who is uncomfortable stuffed into the middle seat but perseveres, stoic, determined. In London, today has been replaced by tomorrow and we blink into a hazy gray future.

Our hotel is a former Vanderbilt enclave, but really, it's a twisty mazy series of moldy hallways. Our room, she is tiny. Lilliputian. My gentleman squire Patrick is a large hunk of a man, the type of brawler usually destined to stand near the stage at music festivals, not the kind who wears a hoodie and designs mobile apps. He declares we have arrived in a wee country and our next vacation should be somewhere not so wee. Like Alaska. Or Texas. Fiji, I correct him. We'll go to Fiji, where the population is nee wee. Then, because I'm stupid, I exclaim "Bunch of flowers!" in my best Suzy Izzard, and Patrick reprimands me for being wrong in the head. ~~If he only knew me as well as you do, Dear Reader.~~

The room is hostile to romantic interludes. A mysterious sulfur cloud belches from the bathroom pipes, like living with an unseen flatulent bulldog. Also, the Powers That Be have decided we should have twin beds. Horrible uncomfortable twin beds, like children, like we've been sent to sleep in the nursery. On the first day, I call down and explain to the woman at the desk that we are dating, we are not platonic drinking buddies but Actual Genital Romantic Partners. It is cruel and unusual punishment to be paying this much for a kid's bedroom. They are most apologetic while managing to be not at all apologetic. We soldier through. We keep calm and carry on. *Bunch of flowers*, I grumble myself to sleep at 2 p.m. in the afternoon because jet lag, because sexual frustration, because we are not Carol and Mike Brady or the Newharts, we are Lucy and Ricky Ricardo, or Donna Reed and her TV show husband, whatever his name is. Which perhaps is fine because as you know, Dear Reader, I look damned fine in a shirtdress and pearls.

Our first afternoon-into-night of sleep, bedsprings pierce our tender bits. Patrick invents long detailed histories of our mattresses, involving jail breaks, Sweeney Todd and the Spanish Inquisition. ~~I give up the idea of sex.~~ Sex remains a taboo topic, which is, after all, very British. I admire Patrick's commitment to the charade. At night, we giggle in the darkness ~~like roommates~~, bridging the gap until sleep detangles our fingers.

We take a tour of London from the top of a bus. It weaves through the parks and streets, past J. M. Barrie's house. Across the park, somewhere, the voice tells us, is a statue of one Sir Peter Pan, who appeared in the dark of night. I crane my head but don't catch sight of that playful Boy Who Never Grew Up. Whenever we pass the park, I look for him again but never spot him. At night, in our nursery bedroom, I stare out the window at the rooftops and hope to see a sprite's trail, looking down at the streets below.

What if I fall? But oh darling, what if you fly, I think to myself. What if we both fly?

Together, we wander through museums, shop in food halls amid strange Britannic delicacies, twisting our way through Churchill's war cabinet, climbing up the Bloody Tower, perching in a private box for Shakespeare. After dinners, pubs, sipping pints of dark warm beer and tangy cider, we wander back through rainy streets to our little section of Cromwell Road, trip up the marble steps into a mirrored coffin of a lift, and then fall into our beds, hoping madly we won't be impaled by angry wire coils.

One night I leave Patrick drinking at the pub and go to Evensong at St Paul's. The voices are incredible, threatening to burst through the marble halls and gilded tile ceilings. Midway through the service, I'm overcome by the beauty of the music. I feel ridiculous, eyes welled up, a poseur tourist with religion only for holidays. These voices make swirling patterns in the empty space of God. Basses and tenors pulse along with airy sopranos, each syllable becoming a painting, each note washing color in the current of sound. My program bears inky tear splotches, and even still, I cannot help myself. No matter what I do, I won't be able to explain this to anyone ~~definitely not Patrick~~.

Dear Reader, I think about you. How will I tell you these amazing things I saw and felt and heard, and how can you imagine them? I'll fail to do it justice, not in the face of so much love, of anyone feeling strongly enough to create such beauty. I can't bear it, but I get it, Dear Reader, I finally get it.

At the pub, Patrick has been overserved, coaxed by suited Englishmen enchanted by his beard and his "formal hoodie" ~~and his euphemisms for secretive masturbation~~. That night, while drunk, he says he will never love anyone as much as he loved his first girlfriend. He says I'm unlike any woman he's ever met. He says I'm special, someone he knows will be his best friend forever. Dear Reader, you may have already guessed he says these things out of order.

I teach Patrick to read Tube maps. Our vowels get softer, our accents less pronounced. My brain voice has long *ah*s, short *oh*s, gentle *el*s and *lah*s. Holding hands, we wander through Portobello Road Market, Covent Garden, and Camden Town (which Patrick renames Bong Water Market). Pigeons argue over discarded cigarette butts and the blustery wind blows through our bodies, wishing us to fly. In each candy store, I look for new chocolates to try. Every night, we sit cross-legged on our respective beds, watching weird shows on the four English-speaking non-static channels and using really bad English accents to make up names for new British sitcoms ("Brumbly, Grumbly, and Snout!" "52 Uses for a Cold Pot of

Porridge!" "Cocksmiths!" "That's a town, not a show." "It needs to be a show! It should be a wakka chicka wakka chicka kind of show!") and chomp on many chocolate bars, all of which easily triumph over the flavored sweetened wax we call chocolate back in the colonies.

On our last evening in England, Patrick releases me to go to the theater. He does not like musicals, does not like opera, does not like sitting in wee theater chairs with no leg room. I wander up cobbled streets, through back alleys, down Jermyn and up Haymarket, to sit in the first-row balcony and indulge in one of my guiltiest pleasures. Patrick has recommended taking a black taxi back to the hotel afterward to avoid scary late-night wildness, but I'm trying to soak up every tiny bit of London I can. I walk to the next Tube station, enjoying the water-covered cobble, the smell of wet mackintoshes and the sound of Brits shaking out their brollies. The moon is a fingernail sliver above Piccadilly. In the distance, a low peal of church bells, chiming eleven times through a light fog.

I wander back through Westminster, chasing the shadow of Peter Pan back toward Kensington. I could follow him straight on till morning, without a second thought. What if I fall? What if I never fly? ~~Back at the hotel, Patrick announces we need to talk. We talk. In the end, it's me. In the end, it's always me. In the morning at the airport, he upgrades to first class, an overstuffed armchair which turns into an actual bed. He offers it to me, suggesting this as a favor to me to avoid sitting so close to him, as though we haven't spent an entire trip with a moat of polite distance. I decline. In the gate area at Heathrow, military men with semiautomatic weapons scan the gate. They are looking for someone. *I'm right here*, I think, as Patrick boards with the first-class passengers, off to his own world, his adultness calling him back across the Atlantic.~~ We fly back, fallen along the same trajectory, following the sun which will not set for us, for another twenty hours on the other side of the ocean, and he will go to his connection, and I will go to mine, and it will be as though none of this ever happened.

Maybe I never flew at all.

Xoxo
Jane

## Day 15

**Wolf News WNBS**
**@WNBSNews**

Pepperdine University mass shooting underway. SWAT team on the ground. Students' social media streams reporting fatalities in student union, library, and lecture hall

288 27 1K

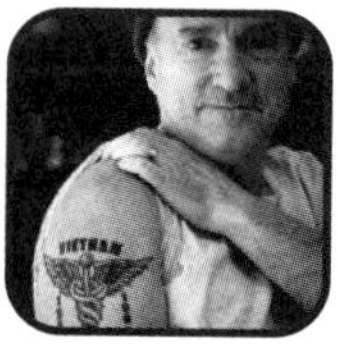

**Senator Bill Watson**
**@watsonsenate**

My thoughts and prayers go out to the Pepperdine University faculty, students, and families.

11.5K 324 5.9K

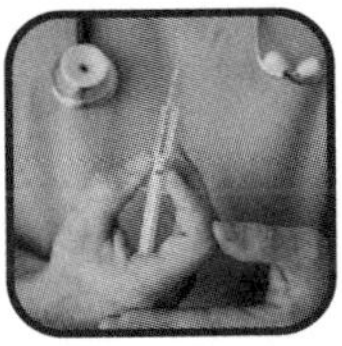

**World Medical News**
**@worldmednow**

Laboratory-confirmed cases in Yemen, Tasmania, Madagascar, New Zealand, and Argentina suggest spread may not be contained despite travel bans

♡ 1.2K 💬 11 ⟳ 374

**Jesus Don't Live Here**
**@karl1952**

The masses keep buying their lies while drinking fluoridated water, which puts aluminum into their brains. Total detox is the only defense now. You gotta get it out of your brain. #nSFI #h3n2 #libtards

♡ 31.9K 💬 875 ⟳ 14.5K

**Shine Beauty**
**@shineyourself**

Got the trademark undereye circles from lack of sleep? We've got the ten greatest concealers! http://www.bit.ly/Ud4bl

♡ 1.6K 💬 5 ⟳ 77

**Wolf News WNBS** ✔
**@WNBSNews**

Pepperdine University mass shooting UPDATE: Gunman in custody. Fatalities reported. Story developing.

♡ 1K 💬 45 ⟳ 1K

**Susie**
**@SuzeeeeQ**

Lady and cops stopped by house. Took samples. Quarantined. Call if need.

♡ 20 💬 0 ⟳ 1

**Jesus Don't Live Here**
**@karl1952**

Men feeling as if they have no purpose is by design. There is honor in duty. Your duty is to protect your family and community. Live with honor. Die with respect.

♡ 9.3K 💬 348 ⟳ 1.4K

**Mychelle**
**@MightyMych**

How is social distancing different than anything else I do as an introvert? Now I guess I can feel good about it, as though my quiet alone time is somehow for the good of humanity? #h3n2 #nosleep

♡ 23 💬 2 ⟳ 0

**Xi**
**@sXlilate**

I witnessed someone getting a parking ticket. How can we be expected to stay inside if we must keep moving cars every two hours?

♡ 34 💬 0 ⟳ 0

## Brian

Without anything to do, I was anxious. Nervous. Maybe even a little jumpy, and one of my tricks was to go back and reread Jane's blog posts and emails, remembering where I was, remembering who I was and who Jane thought I was, a guy who didn't have an overloaded nervous system and a hateful inability to Adult Up on any given day and act like a normal person. Although the shooter, the craziness, I think I could give myself a bit of grace that things weren't exactly fucking normal.

From: Jane
To: Brian
Subject: The subject line is without recourse.

Dear Sir,

It seems I have a larger-than-expected balance on my account at Dottie's Donuts. It also seems as though it's time to undo my rude behavior of six months past—i.e., the inciting incident wherein chivalry returned my lost phone.

My years of no pay on vague causes are now coming to fruition and I find myself with a unique invitation: Myself and a plus-one will be dined and delighted at the Skywalker Ranch by one Mister George Lucas. I don't expect Yoda to be in attendance. If you're free, I have even been given the company Town Car for the evening and can pick you up on Saturday night in Marin. Are you available?

Help me, Obi-Wan Kenobi. You're my only hope.

Best, Jane

I hoarded her missives in a folder marked "E-lationship." When I'd gotten that email, I'd stared at the screen for a long time. It was terrible timing—I had agreed to do a favor for a friend. Taylor wasn't a friend, more of an acquaintance, really, one of the rotating sad-luck cases crashed on the spare futon in the apartment I shared with four other dudes. For weeks he'd look dirty, like if you'd clap him on the back a little cloud of dust and smoke would rise from his clothing, like that kid in *Peanuts*, then he'd swing the other way and kill all the hot water washing everything he could get his hands on. Later, my roommates and I discussed his penchant for mushroom "tea" and mung bean sprouts in rotation on the windowsill, each attributing a strange earthy terroir when combined with his constant bipolar swings between a state of general offal odor and an almost feline cleanliness that made our apartment smell like the back alley of an herbalist. Only long after he had moved away did we learn that we each thought he was the guest of another roommate, and had been too polite or passive-aggressive to press the issue. None of us even knew how he first started living with us.

But that day, Taylor needed my help. Taylor was between his third and fourth stints in rehab for heroin addiction. He'd decided the only way he'd ever stay completely clean was to replace his drug addiction with something completely unrelated, something he could throw himself into completely. As a kid, he'd been part of a Greenpeace sailing crew with his parents and had lived on a 1912 wooden coastal trader sailboat for eleven months protesting nuclear testing in French Polynesia. He said the memories of living on *The Fri* were the only moments he had felt right in the world. Unfortunately, *The Fri* had been scuttled years ago.

He had tracked down a nearly exact twin of *The Fri* in Montecito, badly in need of thousands of dollars of rehab—much like Taylor himself—and Taylor felt a kinship with the boat.

The scab of my own lost childhood still raw and abused, I found myself getting swept along in his excitement, while also hating the fact that he would get something to fill the hole I couldn't quite address in myself. In a moment of complete optimism, I agreed to lend him $10,000 from my freedom fund.

Taylor wasted a year trying to lock down a place large enough to store the massive craft indoors, which tried the seller's patience. If Taylor didn't take the boat immediately, the guy said, he would return Taylor's down payment (minus sixteen months of storage, so Taylor would be lucky to get anything back) so he could sell it to someone else. The idea of Taylor's childhood being disassembled into scrap metal and wooden components seemed to send Taylor into a panic spiral—in the miasma of yearning for and half-owning this boat, he almost felt like this boat was *The Fri*. In his mind, it became his childhood.

To be a less selfish asshole, I agreed to get his boat with the Heath delivery truck Saturday. But even if we left at the crack of dawn, with traffic, there was no way I'd be back in time for dinner with George Lucas.

George Lucas!

I'd have to reschedule the pickup. Taylor would understand.

“’Lo?” Taylor was sluggish.

“Sorry, dude, did I wake you?” It was an odd construct of politeness, to pretend as though you didn’t know you had woken a person. In this case, I didn’t care.

“No, man, s’OK. S’OK.” The sound of him scratching his stoner scruff. “What’s up?”

“Hey, I was wondering if there was any way we can reschedule the trip to Montecito?”

His voice pitch rose immediately. “Um, negative. I’d lose her. I’d lose that fucking boat, man. Negative. Negatory. What’s happening? You can’t get the truck? Did they say no? We can rent a U-Haul or something if that’s the case.”

“No, it’s not that. I’ve got a conflict that night.”

“Seriously? What is it? Work?” The annoying thing about former addicts was they were always fighting their need to be self-involved. Taylor’s twelve-step program had taught him to be concerned with other people, which I respected, but it was so transparent. I fought the urge to shout, “MAN UP! Get over it, you fucking whiner. The rest of us manage it without turning into narcissistic assholes, so there’s no reason you can’t do it too.”

This mental dialogue was part of my problem. In Taylor’s weird cult childhood, narcotic experimentation was not only *not* frowned upon but a rite of passage. Not everyone grew up with my idyllic Midwestern stereotype of Schwinn bikes and the community pool. Not that my own fairy tale had lasted much after my father chose to take that long trip out for a pack of cigs.

“No, it’s not that. I’ve been invited to dinner at George Lucas’s house.” Taylor didn’t need to know I was merely a nameless extra on the invite list—I *was* invited. By Jane. Who was invited by someone who probably knew George Lucas.

Certainly, Taylor would understand. We could get the boat on Sunday. Or the next weekend. Certainly, if the situation were reversed, I’d be happy for my friend, getting a chance to meet the progenitor of every childhood dreamscape from our generation. Hell, I even remembered getting drunk with Taylor and comparing our ideal Star Wars action figure lineup.

But even as the words were leaving my mouth, I remembered how the Star Wars conversation had ended, about how Taylor only had a few of the key figures—Chewbacca, for instance, but only the carbonite diorama; a Han Solo who was forever struck in a single pose. He had C3PO but no

R2D2. Through the haze, I remembered Taylor drunkenly saying, "All I had was that gay fucking robot and the fucking Wookiee." And it had absolutely destroyed us both with drunken laughter.

"Oh, I see," Taylor said in a clipped manner, and then let the silence simmer.

It was another reiteration of Taylor's dysfunctional childhood. I pushed on, hoping I hadn't burned everything. "So, we can go on Sunday?"

"No. We can't. Saturday is the last day."

"Oh. I see. If it has to be Saturday, you could like rent a truck and someone else could drive?"

"Yeah, I know what you meant. I'll call the guy and say screw it, man. No big deal."

Taylor's voice went viper. I'd seen this side of him before but had never been the target. That time, he pissed all over that guy's mattress. I had to proceed cautiously, as he was at that moment sleeping on our couch with my own mattress in the next room.

"No, that's not it. I mean, still do the deal and stuff. I mean, I'll pay for the rental truck if that's it." I had already given away nineteen months of work and scrimping to a guy I barely knew. I couldn't afford it, but if the cost of a rental truck stood between me and a story that I could tell my grandkids about the time I had dinner at George Lucas's house? Here's my credit card number, hook me up.

"Hey, I appreciate that. I do. Except there is no one else. Do you think I'd have asked you again after having to ask you for the loan? Don't you know how difficult it was coming to you with my fucking hat in my fucking hand? That's OK, man, I know how it is. We can't all be rich fucking trust fund assholes. I'm sorry I'm a problem for you to solve with money from your dead mother's will."

It was like he'd punched me in the gut. "I'm not rich, Taylor," I whispered. The specter of my mother's death shut my head down.

One of her favorite sayings was that you needed to be the friend you wanted to have.

It's not like I owed Taylor anything. It was a douche thing to pull out at the last minute because I got a better offer. But Taylor was beyond reasoning, even on a good day. By offering to pay for the van so quickly, I'd loaded the gun now pointing at me. "I'm sorry, I am. There's no one else?"

"Not a fucking commercial driver's license. Not legally driving a vehicle big enough to haul that boat. But sure, I'll ask a homeless guy or something.

I'll post something to goddamned Craigslist. Most people would fall over themselves trying to help an addict recover, but I'm sorry it interferes with your big fucking dinner plans."

A pause hung between us on the receiver. I had expected—or perhaps hoped—Taylor would hang up.

"Taylor?"

"What." His voice was limp and dull, as though all life force had been expelled. Taylor was manipulating me, I knew it, but I couldn't stop myself.

"Let's go get your boat."

My dearest Jane,

You can't imagine how much I want to go to dinner at Skywalker Ranch. You can't imagine how much my heart leaps at the idea of being picked up and whisked away to spout witty bon mots with the man who basically created my childhood experience, the man who rocked me to sleep with the vision of being able to shoot two-meter womp rats on Tatooine and wondering how fast twelve parsecs was. Also, I am blushing to admit to you that being picked up in a black town car by a lovely woman is on my list of things to do before I die. But alas.

I can't believe I'm typing this: I already have unbreakable plans. Not that I didn't try to break them. The plans didn't allow themselves to be broken. Stupid plans.

This leaves you without an escort, and at such short notice too. My deepest apologies. Please forgive me. If it makes you feel any better, I'm not sure I'll ever be able to forgive myself.

Cheers,
B

Dear Sir,

Silly boy. Of course, I forgive you. Since receiving your NSVP I offered the invite to a male colleague, who almost wet himself. I've been anointed queen of the office. There are many jealous glances. I'm sure I'll pay for it at some point, but for right now, I'm enjoying it immensely.

Best,
Jane

The stench of mouse piss was the first indication Taylor hadn't done diligence on this purchase. What's more, the boat—if you could call it that—was in pieces. The seller, a dodgy-looking crusty hippy, mumbled, "'As Is' condition," and then said, "Whaddya expect for a couple grand?" Taylor shrugged and rubbed his hands together, giving me a warning look to not make a fuss. Instead, I was doing the math. When Taylor had borrowed $10,000 from me, he'd said it was the amount he needed to supplement his savings. But Taylor couldn't possibly have contributed a dollar to buy this heap of wood and rotten sails—and if this Jerry Garcia lookalike was to be taken literally, he hadn't even needed ten grand. What had Taylor spent the rest of my money on?

I filed away my indignation for another day. The entire trip, Taylor acted like he was the one doing ME the favor. I had even felt bad about trying to back out, but now? Fuck this. Even if we turned around, my plus-one ticket was in someone else's hands, someone who got to hang out with Jane and George Lucas.

While Taylor finalized the title transfer, I contemplated his new heap of wood and rigging. I dug through the truck and found an old ventilator caked with porcelain dust, which was better than inhaling the effluvia of thousands of generations of Rodentia who had been born, lived, pissed, and died all over a crumpled pile of sail cloth.

Taylor eyed the ventilator with derision. "God, Bri, overreacting much? Nothing a little soap and water can't fix." But as we unfolded the first layer, two desiccated mouse corpses dislodged from a tattered fray of snarls and fell against Taylor's beat-up All Stars. Then the old boat fought back with a stench of raw ammonia. I dry heaved, eyes watering. On another day I might have felt guilty and offered him the mask, but fuck that. *Lucas. George Lucas.* Taylor dug around behind the truck's seat but only came up with an empty In-N-Out Burger bag. He tucked his nose into his sweatshirt, and we set to it with jarring movements and angry yanks, our resentment of the other surging by the minute, like angry siblings told to act nice or face parental consequences.

True to the hippy's word, the trailer had working lights and was street legal, but given the rickety punky hull, I drove slowly the entire way, for fear the Pacific breeze would turn the boat into a flurry of expensive toothpicks. Unfortunately, the reeking sails had to go in the truck's cargo area behind us. I got woozy thinking about taking one of the curves on the PCH wrong and then pitching the boat over the side, still connected to the truck, then having it pull both of us over the edge, my final vision being the smug, insolent asshole seated beside me.

Taylor spent the entire ride back griping that I should have taken the pottery racks out in preparation for hauling the boat. A comment from me about the fact that it was supposed to be all on a trailer anyway, and shouldn't even have needed the cargo space in the truck, seemed to fuel his burn and energize him. I refused to give in and, instead, turned on conservative talk radio in hopes that the right-wing host would redirect his ire. Instead, Taylor and the host seemed to spur each other on, one blustering while the other wheedled, each trying to drill me into guilt or anger, both emotions being equally useless. The boat groaned and creaked while the van struggled with the heavy wooden load. I thought about leaving Taylor on the side of the road, unhooking the boat and telling him to figure it out. I fantasized about kicking him out of the apartment. I composed the tirade I was going to lay on all my roommates about the collective abuse we had suffered under the weight of Taylor's passive-aggressiveness and how whatever slice of rent he was paying wasn't worth it. I fantasized about side-punching him in the mouth every time we passed an off-ramp.

By the time we got to Sausalito, I was gripping the steering wheel with white knuckles. Then Taylor had no idea where his storage guy's phone number was.

At some point, you're so deep into a fucked-up situation, the only way out is through. This was one of those times, so I laughed. Taylor looked at me suspiciously but then relaxed his shoulders.

"Onward!" I said, with a click. We spent another three hours tracking Russ the Storage Guy down, while I coaxed Taylor into remembering more about Russ and his habits.

We found the pot dealer Taylor and Russ had in common. From there, we had to find Russ's girlfriend, who was working at the Pottery Barn Teen. She gave us directions to Russ's house, where we found Russ about to get into the shower, then waited in the truck while Russ took unforgivably long to cleanse himself and then, finally, he led us and the stinking boat to the same self-storage facility we had already passed at least four times. I was so ready to be done and get the truck back to Heath that I didn't even bother to ask Taylor for gas money—not that he offered.

All the while, high above us in the Marin headlands, Jane was being wined and dined by George Lucas at Skywalker Ranch. It was too painful. Jane, I was certain, had had a lovely time.

But we never talked about it. She was so careful with my fragile self, picking up the threads as though my sad lonely whispers were important. She was too kind to bring it up, brushing off my sardonic comments about Taylor's boat fiasco with detached irony.

It might have been in that moment that I could have fallen in love with her. Or with the idea of her. Or perhaps I was a bit in love with the Other Brian who existed somewhere in the empty spaces, hanging in those lost moments between "Send" and "Receive" like a suitor offering his hand for the taking.

The next time Jane invited me to a function, it was in that shielded way you do when you're pretty sure someone's not going to show. "*Well*," she had added to the end of a final email paragraph, "*tonight a bunch of us are going out. Reservations at Foreign Cinema at 7 p.m. All must wear something tidy. Points given for looking like you're trying. Points deducted for hooded sweatshirts.*" It wasn't an invitation, technically. A statement of fact but also a reminder our social transaction was still in arrears. Even if she hadn't invited me to the Lucas dinner, I owed her something, anything. Her emails were the highlight of my days.

After work, I scurried back to my apartment, changed into something I thought she'd like, and then biked down to the Sausalito ferry station. I had missed the ferry and had another hour until the next one, so I pedaled over to Caffe Trieste. It was the kind of Bay Area day that makes everyone forget they live in California, a kind of cold seeping into your bones, a frost demon. I wasn't looking forward to a chilly ride across the water. A nice hot cup of pour-over coffee would gird my loins for the journey plus ensure I wouldn't start yawning like a douchebag at 11 p.m.

Caffe Trieste was slow, but Natalia was behind the counter, my usual barista. She had beguiling lavender eyes and the lengthy white-girl dreadlocks that were almost de rigueur in the North Bay. I stayed away from the manic pixie dream girl types, but Natalia created an itch I couldn't scratch. Other Brian was a bit of a social person since my arrival on the West Coast—I hesitated to use the term "player," although the accusation had certainly been made more than once. I didn't operate under the same principles—like a boy scout, I aimed to leave my trail nicer than I found it. Frequent assignations with new partners felt unsavory, especially with the rampant and blatant overtures of STDs and HIV. The Casual Encounters section of Craigslist was a shopping cart of partners looking for interested parties who matched—or were unconcerned with—their maladies. I was careful.

The idea of barebacking gave me the vapors, and while I liked to think I was a generous soul, I rarely kissed, and I carried my own dental dams like the feminist chauvinist I was.

Even I was surprised at my own behavior when it came to women. Something about nestling into the thighs of a new relationship, a beginning unmarred by my terrible personality and sardonic commentary. It was only a matter of time before they learned I was a horrible person. Everyone was happier if we kept it casual. This was long before those dating apps. I couldn't swipe right and fulfill my romantic leanings. You had to work for it. And back then I *worked it.*

Perhaps it was the way Natalia's guy pants slung low on her hips, twin hollows under her hip bones reminding me of the curve of a bowl, an opposite curve to match the exact strokes of her ass cheeks in the receding view. Proportions, again. I was such a sucker for the call and answer of balanced proportions.

Natalia had the exclusive nature girl thing going on, totally out of my league. Everyone I knew had swung at her and missed. She seemed to only be attracted to the most terribly broken, lackluster gentlemen, the ones who never showered or who made a living selling homemade recycled jewelry on the paths inside Muir Woods.

But that day in Caffe Trieste, Natalia looked up at me and smiled, the kind of invitational look I understood. She was feeling me.

"Hey, you," she said, following the length of my frame with her eyes.

Was it this easy? I only had to put on a nice shirt and a sweater? Seriously? I'd picked a vintage argyle sweater a while back, in honor of one of Jane's rants about how argyle was the thinking girl's tribal arm sleeve or wallet chain, about how all guys had to do to attract a clever girl was dress like Alex P. Keaton. I'd even ended up buying a pair of somewhat matching argyle socks at Banana Republic, which ended up costing more than the sweater, which made me feel both like a douchebag AND a chump, but Jane would notice the socks. She would not only notice them, but she would undoubtedly comment on them, and, on some level, it would be a win. It was a delightful tête-à-tête with her, and I so rarely managed to stump her.

"Hey there. How's it going?" I unpacked my nice Midwestern boy smile for Natalia, feeling power surging from the vintage wool. Natalia shifted forward, her tank top slipping down, giving an extra half inch of her golden cleavage. Bingo! I was in. It was almost a mathematical equation at that point. No matter what the lady looked like, tattooed and eyebrow-pierced or tight-assed Nob Hill socialite, they all responded with the same nonverbal cues and mannerisms. If they knew they were all so similar, they'd probably be shaken to their foundational bedrock.

"What will it be today, pottery guy?" A smirk played at the corners of her mouth, and she touched the long ends of her dreadlocks. Aha, so we'd advanced to the hair-playing stage. This would be too easy.

"Drip coffee, house blend, with room."

"For here?" Her eyebrows raised and she ran a hand over her cheek and neck, as though rubbing the stress out of her day.

"No, to go, actually," I said. I checked my watch, even though I knew the ferry was still on its way toward the city and wouldn't be back for at least another forty minutes.

She pouted. We bantered back and forth. She said I should try the cookies in the oven. I knew I had plenty of time. There was always the next ferry. Or the next ferry after that. I could be a little bit late to the thing at Foreign Cinema. My lateness would keep Jane thinking about me, anticipating my arrival. Every time I made noises about leaving, Natalia got me to stay. A new batch of scones coming out soon. Experimenting with harissa hummus . . . I should try it. I made a comment about how I always thought her dreadlocks would smell bad, so she made me smell her hair. I was cooked, hooked, and booked. Game on.

We went back to her place, someone's pool house in Marin. It felt overly lived-in, like the way hotels feel, like you're walking in someone else's warm shoes. She was a raw vegan, and I told her that must be why she glowed. She nodded, as though it were a fact, a known correlation. I had to fight to not roll my eyes, but by then her hand was caressing my thigh, moving toward my zipper while I desperately hoped she wouldn't notice I was wearing a $140 pair of Theory jeans.

I never made that ferry. Nor the next one. Nor the one after that.

The next morning, I asked Natalia to brunch with me, but she announced she had an exclusive hot yoga class. I pressed for more, but whatever magic I had struck the night before was now gone—her eyes were bored and her answers single-syllabic. I asked for her number, and she said "You have it," and left. I **didn't** have it.

I felt badly about standing up Jane but not about how I spent the evening. I was already making a game plan to get with Natalia long-term. While that would never happen, hope burned in my breast like Gatsby's green light at the end of *The Hotel New Hampshire*. If anything, Jane had probably had a good time with her friends without feeling like she had to explain inside jokes. I hadn't gotten to show off the argyle sweater, but it had served its purpose.

Dear Jane,

I hope your party went well. Alas, I could not make it. Work, traffic, etc., etc., my excuses are paltry. I will make it up to you . . . Shall we schedule a do-over in a month, when the roof of Foreign Cinema won't shower icicle mist onto our heads and the negronis will taste even more enchanting?

Cheers,
-B

Dear B,

This is going to sound terribly vindictive, but I've been given an amazing opportunity to blog full-time. That's right, this chick has officially sold out for some fat dot com cash. OK, the cash isn't so fat . . . It's less Mae West and more Audrey Hepburn. Downside? I can either afford rent in San Francisco or I can afford health care. Hrrrm, tough call, but since I still have my gallbladder, tonsils, appendix, and 100 percent of my top and bottom lady bits, I'm opting for the white coats. As it turns out, my spinster aunt offered up summers in my family's beach cabin on Lake Michigan in Wisconsin's Door Peninsula during the warm months and her spare room in Green Bay when the weather turns inhospitable. Luckily, my new gig involves tons of travel, so I won't spend a great deal of time basking in the odor of feline urine come January (yep, she's a cat lady).

This is terribly dramatic, but I hate maudlin scenes, so I buried the lede and didn't reveal everything until all were well and truly hammered last night. It was a fitting end of an era. But never fear, you can't shake me quite yet. The sirens of SF will undoubtedly beckon from their rocky shores and my escapades should bring my return.

We will, sir, need to postpone that negroni a bit longer, but it will happen. Soon, my fair friend, soon.

Happily yours,
Jane

Dear Miss Goodbye San Francisco,

And so, one lone traveler takes her leave of the Golden State, and the Golden State will be poorer for it. Oh sure, it may not admit it. It may think, "My bicycle paths are free of one more fixie-riding girl on her way to no good. My Mission coffee shops will find their doughnut shortages inexplicably cured." But every night, the Golden State will check its voice mail, perhaps listening to one where you drunk dialed. It will surf your Facebook page and start worrying about what it will do when you say your residence is some other state. It will cry in the bathroom at midnight in some club and all Golden State's friends will assure it that Wisconsin is fat, so fat, and also, it deserves better than some savvy copywriter who will break its heart again and again. And then the Golden State will sign the Dairy State up for a bunch of porn sites. Good times.

Now I feel like an ass for not trying harder to get to your party, but I trust your compadres gave you the sendoff you deserved, nay, your due, miss.

Best, Brian

Dear Sir,

It was a night I'll not soon remember. Let's leave it at that. I'm sorry we didn't get a chance to say goodbye. Perhaps it's for the best. This e-lationship thing is doomed if we ever see each other face-to-face. You'll hate my laugh. You'll hate how I'm incredibly funny and so much smarter than you are, etc., etc.

I'm responding, by the way, from a Denny's. Nothing good ever happens by going to a Denny's. You should remember that.

Best, Jane

Dear Jane,

Thus, you begin the exciting life of the consultant. No more offices! A laptop, an internet connection, and the luxury of working a West Coast shift while living in Central Time. I suspect if I could convince Heath to open a Midwest branch, I might follow your example. Imagine the kind of apartment I could live in—by myself, no less—for what I'm paying to share a loft space with four other dudes and two of their girlfriends, who are de facto roommates who simply don't have to pay rent. Perhaps. Midwesterners like their art like they like their fast food—cheap, mass-produced, easily digestible, and who cares about how many eyesores litter their gaze every day.

B

The size of your typical Midwestern ass is one of the myriad reasons I have decided to move back. Why, I could grow to the size of a small Buick and still be considered svelte by the local stud patrol. The beautiful thing about the Midwest is that plaid flannel, whiskey old-fashioneds, and horn-rimmed glasses never actually went out of style, so now the population finds themselves the envy of both coasts, from Park Slope to Cole Valley. I will, however ,miss my kind friends at the Eighteenth Street Starbucks who appraised my outfits daily and had the good grace to appreciate the cleavage and disregard the cellulite. In the Midwest, alas, my corn-fed milk bags are nothing spectacular, but in SF, among the tiny Californian girls, I was like Venus emerging from the Sutro baths. Pay no mind to the fat ass, sir, and rest your gaze on these glorious sex pillows. Of course, present company excluded, as pale, grumpy potters aren't my type.

J

PS. Confession: Rough trade boys give me special underwear feelings. A well-placed tattoo (NOT A TRIBAL ARMBAND THANK YOU) can do wonders for my appetites.

Dear Jane,

Ah yes, your type. From what you've told me, you enjoy being feted by the burly gays of the Castro, while mothering little emo boys wearing skinny jeans and vintage grandfather sweater-vests. Not that I don't enjoy a sweater-vest from time to time—usually on Sundays, or perhaps during a football game—but it's a look farm boys are typically avoiding. Or so I hear.

B

Dear Artiste,

Your request for information on this gallery's rental space has gone unanswered. We invite you to reinvest yourself in your application and touch base with us again next year.

Sincerely, Jane

Dear Jane,

I love it when you don't know what to say. Cha-Ching! Game point, Brian.

-B

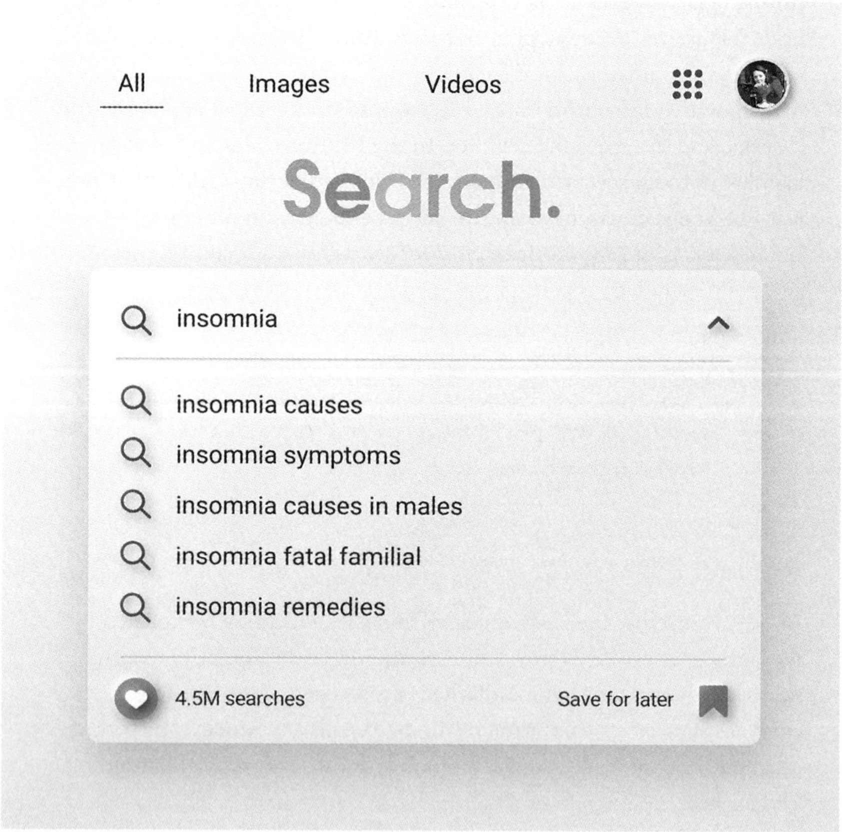

# Day 16

You have one choice, Oakland, starve to death in the apocalypse or eat vegan hot dogs. (Entire city takes a big swig of MD 20/20) "I'll see you in hell."

**Wolf News WNBS**
**@WNBSNews**

The NFL declares that Sunday games will be played in empty stadiums. Tickets refunded to fans, games will still be televised http://www.bit.ly.com/nflsafety

3.2K 165 905

# Day 16

## Jane

Pedro inspects the crane operator station at North Landing. "Have you noticed Patty acting peculiarly by any chance?" He doesn't look at me while saying this, scraping bird shit off nuts and bolts, rubbing his thumb across the flecking blue paint.

"Patty?"

"Yeah."

"No." I'm blank. Patty is always peculiar. What would Not Peculiar Patty be like?

"I think he's got a headache."

The words dangle there between the two of us in the air. Pedro waits for me to understand the implication of a headache. A gull swings low and stabs something in the waves.

"You think he's got H3N2? Or the other one?" I don't want to say it.

"It's a possibility, something we should all think about. We're reliant on the kindness of strangers out here. If one of us gets sick, it's not like he can pop off to the emergency room. If he's got something, I radio for transport because it takes time to wrangle a boat."

"If he's got it, we've all got it." My brain does mental gymnastics. Who would come for us, knowing we're all sick?

"Not necessarily. Kylie and Omar might have taken off at a pretty good time for that baby."

*Fetus,* I think, she called it. *Not baby.*

Pedro grimaces, cleaning bird guano off the controls. It's something for his hands to do, like filling a bucket with an eyedropper.

"What do you do in these situations?"

He snorts softly. "What do we do? We catch whatever we catch, that's what we do. If this bug is determined to take advantage of our herd weakness, we got to build up antibodies one way or another. Just like the birds do it. Just like the sharks. We adapt or go extinct."

The list of extinct birds shuttles through my brain like automated gunfire, like flicking a deck of cards in a magic trick. *Boom ratta tatta boom boom,* see ya wouldn't want to be ya.

Rick clambers up from the seawall.

"Find any?" Pedro stops flicking bird shit and focuses his attention on Rick.

"Mice've been chewing at the wiring, but not through it. Should be good. There are a few new nest sites down there too. Looks like the gulls have been at them, though. They're not mapped on the nesting site schematic."

Rick holds up a hand and Pedro pulls him up over the ledge.

"You talk to her?"

"A little."

They both look at me. I'm a specimen.

"Do you know if Patty slept last night?" Rick says.

"Uh, I think so? I mean, he went to bed. I didn't hear him pacing or anything like that." Patty and I are alone in the first house now that everyone left. Rick and Pedro remain in the Coast Guard house, since a new boat full of naturalist replacements should arrive any day.

I'll leave when the new boat comes too. That's what I'm going to tell them. I've been hearing more ghosts at night in the Jane Fonda room, which is the real reason—there's an unsettling feeling eating at me, like the houses themselves are judging me. I don't like being alone up there, even with Patty across the hall. Either way, I'm a wimp, but I'd rather choose the wimp reason based in biology rather than kook science.

"What time did he get up?"

"I don't know. I heard him go downstairs but I don't know what time. It was still dark outside."

Rick lifts his hat, smoothing his hair back, reseats the cap, then scans the horizon. A megalithic container ship churns the water about a mile out. I know it's as tall as a ten-story building, but the perspective plays tricks with my eyes, the horizon so large, the ship so small. The primary-colored containers are Lego bricks stacked each on the other, the long tail of disturbed ocean serving as a bridal veil as the ship trudges toward the Golden Gate.

"Right. Do me a favor . . . pay attention tonight?" Pedro doesn't look directly at me. Does he feel weird about something?

They were being so weird and unreadable. "Uh, sure. But why don't we, you know, ask him? Say, 'Hey Patty, do you think you're maybe coming down with the H3 business?'"

Rick and Pedro exchange a look.

"Because he'd say he's fine," Pedro says.

I'm the simplest creature in the universe. My face is telling my thoughts again because Rick comes up behind me and pats my shoulder.

"It's a guy thing, Jane. It's OK."

I don't like it when people can read me. *Fresnel lens. Lensel friends. Begin. Begin. Begin.*

"Are you going to call for transport?" I act nonchalant.

"Well, we can certainly do that, but we want to wait until the new boat comes. Rick, Patty, and I are the barest minimum staffing on SEFI. If one of us goes? Then we all go."

"That's silly. Just because one person—"

"It's not silly. It's safety. You can't leave two people on the island."

"I'm a third person."

Rick tilts his head. That's right, I don't count. I'm essentially a tourist, although they're being polite and continuing with the farce that I'm helping somehow. I'm not actually part of the SEFI equation. Besides, I want to leave anyway, although he doesn't know that. I'm offended. I don't matter.

Rick takes a breath. "You haven't been trained," he says, with more sweetness than I expected, more than I deserve. "You're not certified. You're not a lifeguard. You don't know how to use the crane and you can't go out in a boat by yourself. You're not a staff person. The three of us are those things. We can't get down to two because if one of those people get hurt or worse, then the other one isn't able to save them. With two other people, you'd at least have a chance." He's giving a way out, a way to save face. He's read my expression twice with 100 percent accuracy, so I look away.

"It's the crane," continues Pedro, far more pragmatically. "You need two people to work the crane. Simple as that. One person gets hurt, then you have no way of getting on or off the island, short of a helicopter. It's all . . . it's bad, that's all." He licks his lips and stares off toward the continental shelf. "It's bad. What we're doing isn't exactly an essential service. We maintain safety protocol, or we all leave and come back later."

That's why Patty would say he's fine. If he left before the field office sends a new crew, then it would jeopardize the entire shark season, ruining Pedro and Rick's research this year. They'd wait a year to do it over, but their shark grants support the bird research too. Patty won't do that. Patty'd risk everything for the little birds.

Rick points at a cluster of birds off Maintop Bay and reaches to his radio instinctively, even though there's no one in the lighthouse on shark watch.

"That looks promising. Want to hit it?"

Rick squelches up his mouth. "Take it. I'll do the crane."

"Nah, my boots are soaked. You go ahead." Pedro turns with finality. Something has transpired, but I don't know how.

Rick furrows his brow, wavers for a second, and then heads to the Zodiac, prepping the line. "You coming?" he says over his shoulder.

"Hot damn, you better believe I'm coming!"

Finally, I get to see a shark predation. The situation we're in, forgotten for the moment. The boat skids up to a scree of gulls, all interested in something churning the water.

"See that oil slick there? That's blubber." I don't see oil, but I do see blood, clouds and swirls of it in the water, the coppery tang punching my nose. The boat coasts through viscera, making *packel packel* sounds against the Zodiac's orange rubber wale.

Rick hovers in a half stance to get a better look. "Can you try standing to spot it?"

I stand, and now the smell of rancid fat hits. Chunks of flesh and blubber float in the water. The gulls swoop down, snapping smaller bits, then alighting quickly. I point in the direction that seems the most gruesome, off to the left side of the boat. However, in response, the water churns the opposite side of the boat. A tall black triangle fin pokes up and dips under again. Rick sees it too and turns the boat toward it.

All this time, I haven't gotten a good long look at a shark—they've been too quick, a glimpse, a petroglyph against the water. But this time, it's right there, taking its time, allowing us to observe its grandeur.

The shark is immense. The photos and videos during Shark Week haven't prepared me for the fear sinking like a stone through my throat and into my diaphragm, anchoring there, impeding a full deep breath. Without thinking, I step away from the feeding monster and almost topple back into the bloody water. Rich reaches out nonchalantly, his hand on my calf. "Watch it now," he says, never taking his eyes off the monolithic fish shredding the elephant seal.

A rainbow sheen of oil clings to the sides of the boat. The seal's brown skin is confetti in the brackish water, the shark sucks and groans as it pulls and tears at the carcass, and then its nose dips, gone. I feel panic wiggle my brain. It's easily a twenty-foot shark. The boat is fifteen feet away, and only half as big as the shark. The Zodiac is, in essence, an inflatable raft with a motor. Hard rubberized buoyant plastic.

"Oh my God, what if it tips the boat?" One casual swoop of the tail is all it would take. My last adventure as a sad little dog-paddler in the middle of the ocean, kicking pathetically while dozens of great white sharks watch my delicious rump from the bottom of the continental shelf.

"Jane. Sit down."

Ten feet away, the shark surfaces, its eyelid rolled up for protection. The shark's teeth meet the seal's bones, like breaking uncooked spaghetti. This time, its fin pops up again.

"Aha! It's Roger!" Rick snaps a photo with a camera pulled from a pocket on his field jacket.

The gulls mock and scream. One paints the Zodiac's orange wall with a spurt of seagull shit. A mental picture of the shark's giant prehistoric alien eyes popping up next to me, its head almost as wide as the boat, the grin without emotion or feeling. Is this that lizard brain introducing itself? The shark surfaces again, maybe six feet off where I'd imagined it, and grabs a large chunk of seal floating free from the main carcass.

"Is that another one? A feeding frenzy? Are we in the middle of a feeding frenzy?"

"No. That's still Roger. Whites won't interlope on another's kill. They don't want to chance it. If this were a large animal, we're talking blue whale or something, where economy wouldn't interfere, then we'd get a frenzy." Cold hard cash economy, as paid in ounces of seal flesh.

"How big is it . . . how big is Roger?"

"He's maybe fourteen feet, although he's still growing. He's a baby. A teenager, actually."

Bigger sharks out here than Roger. A third again as big. The length of three tall guys plus a suitcase. Roger's girth makes him hard to connect with reality. He's a marine minivan, an elegant elephant, a deepwater dreadnought.

His tough hide bears scars, hieroglyphic nicks, and scratches. What creature would be brave enough to take on Roger? Something from Jules Verne, or perhaps a Kraken, maybe Cthulhu. He flips his pointed tail as he tears meat and sinew from the quickly disappearing seal skeleton. Something wet hits my face, and I wipe it on my sleeve. Is the droplet clear or tinged red, or perhaps the sickly yellow of the blubber slick? As grace would have it, my wardrobe choice of a black sweatshirt this morning takes that question off the table—a dark mark of wet.

"There used to be an abalone fisherman who dove here, in an old-fashioned metal deep-sea helmet. You know, like the ghosts wear on *Scooby-Doo*? He used a hookah hose and went down there like that. He must have had balls the size of cantaloupes."

"Not in a cage?"

Rick clicks his tongue, still snapping photos of the superstar finishing his meal. "No cage. Well, he had a handheld abalone basket, towed behind him. Apparently, it was big enough to hold a man in a pinch, and he'd crawled inside it a few times when the sisters—that's what we call the really big female sharks—menaced him. There's so many nooks and crannies, though, if he kept a rock to his back, not much concern. They're curious more than anything. Kind of like, 'Hey, I've never seen this before' sort of thing. The deep-sea helmet was better because no bubbles. The air is pushed down and back up through the hookah hose. It's dangerous, though; the line gets caught or pinched on something, you're stuck down there, SOL."

S. Oh. Ell. *Shit outta luck.* This seal is shit outta luck too. Roger is the luck collector, luck in arrears.

Rick keeps clicking photos of Roger. "Ayup. One crazy motherfucker. He has cancer now, though, stage four. Probably has absolutely nothing to do with spending twenty years swimming among leaking nuclear waste barrels."

"Leaking?"

*Slurp. Snort. Tear. Suck. Splash.*

"Because they're in fifty-five-gallon drums. Metal. You've seen how well metal does out here, right? Imagine it down there. The newest are more than twenty years old, but most are older than me. Plus, the army shot some of them to make them sink faster, which was some spectacularly idiotic military decision-making."

The entire two-ton seal has taken maybe five minutes to consume. Roger slides back into the deep. A scrum of gulls dive-bombs the water, sniping at pieces of scattered flesh, but they won't light where the shark has been.

"Smart birds," I say.

"Smarter than us, probably," Rick says, snapping the lens on his camera. "While we're out here, let's do a circuit and see if we can figure out where Patty went."

We circle the main island twice, but there's no sign of Patty's familiar yellow field jacket. Rick brings the boat closer to Great Murre Cave and shouts futilely into the constant whisper of waves butting the shoreline. *Oooooh ooooooh ooooh.*

"Well, I'm sure he couldn't have walked over Jordan Channel without getting real wet, but maybe he's stuck over on West End and can't get back. Although that would be a colossally stupid maneuver. Don't ever try this," he says, as though I have ever, even once, driven either of the naturalists' boats. He aims the Zodiac at the narrow gap between SEFI and the off-limits bird territory island, between which a tidal channel surges with angry waves.

Maybe he's trying to impress me with this impossible narrow path. Rick doesn't seem the type to get a rise out of people. I'm below his concern—he doesn't care what I think.

He steers between the jagged sea cliffs, and it feels like we'll get caught, lodged like a grape down a throat, choking on it. The sides scrape against rocks. A noise from Rick, a rising explosion of giggles and hiccups. Up until this moment, it's felt as though Rick wouldn't let anything bad happen to us, but now he's flush with lurching dangerous fun, delighted by his own fear. I'm a passenger, here to witness how unlike this moment is from his serious, safe-and-sound mannerisms and zen observations. If I time it right, I could leap off to safety, the island is right there, but the force and momentum of the engine propel me down into the belly of the boat, the seat pushing between my shoulder blades, pinning me, saving me from my ludicrous notions.

The boat bursts back into the cove. Rick looks back, his unreadable expression morphing back to a regular Rick face, eyebrows pinched together. "That wasn't even a little bit safe," he says, flashing a lusty smile.

I want to scold him, say, "Turn this around right now and take me back." Instead I cover, face blank, and say, "I don't see him. Where should I be looking?"

"Hold on, if he's anywhere, he'd be by Murr Bridge," he says, referring to the giant rock arch on the Maintop hillcrest. "There's murre nest sites up there. He'd know better, but . . ." He doesn't finish. Rick should know better too.

I'm trembling. It's the cold and the damp and the aftereffect of watching and smelling the shark predation, but even as I rationalize it, I know it's just an interlude I've inserted for readers in my future blog post.

We circle West End, but the slopes are barren. Shell Beach is deserted—even the sea lions are gone, out hunting and dodging the great whites with either finesse or failure. Rick points out the small colony of fur seals on Indian Head Beach. More arrive daily, most pregnant, and stay here fishing until pups are born and weaned. Even with a mundane task, Rick turns it into lessons to absorb and write about. Maybe Rick just likes to narrate, but he's back to his usual self. I enjoy time with him and already lose the feeling that he might have crashed the boat.

Lots of birds and seal activity, but no Patty. We circle back over our own wake, and Rick looks at the channel again, glances back, then steers the long way around Fisherman's Cove.

"Fin," he says calmly. He slows, pointing at a vague area off the bow. I squint, a hand up to shade the harsh glare off the water. There's nothing. He waits, stands to scan the water, then sits back down, starts the motor, and we're off again. My eyes aren't quick enough. I'm not.

Back at East Landing, I jump onto land and run up to toss the hook to Rick. I don't know how to work the controls, though, so we wait. Finally, he shouts at the radio. Pedro's terse voice responds, but I can't hear what he says that makes Rick exhale and throws his hands up.

"It'll be a minute," he shouts. We wait. Eventually Pedro appears at the crane controls and hits the lift. They don't say anything to each other and instead say everything to me. These things are meant for them, but I parrot along, a child caught in the middle, a role I play well.

Pedro responds, unintelligible, to which Rick says, "Ayup." Then Rick strides off, followed by Pedro, leaving me at the landing. My usefulness has expired. Over my shoulder, the container ship blonks its horn at nothing. Four short bursts and one long one.

**Mychelle**
**@MightyMych**

If there are elderly residents in our community who are scared or unable to pick up groceries, please let me know. If you order them, I'm happy to pick them up and deliver them to you, no cost.

♡ 200 💬 12 ⟳ 42

**Xi**
**@sXlilate**

My friend was a teacher in a local high school in a low-income area of the city. She's been put into a medically induced coma today in hopes she will be able to come out of it. #H3N2

♡ 39 💬 7 ⟳ 9

**DB Cooper**
**@DBmm**

I have learned from weeks of video conference meetings that everyone wants to see everyone's cat or dog every meeting. Sure, we'll get to the spreadsheets, but first, Linda, we would like an update from Mr. Slippers and his adorable pink nose.

♡ 458 💬 5 ⟳ 68

**Wolf News WNBS**
**@WNBSNews**

Greater Chicago, Miami, and San Francisco areas under lockdown to contain spread of H3N2 http://www.bit.ly.com/prisonprions

♡ 3.5K 💬 165 ⟳ 905

# Ten Years Ago

There's never enough time here. The fog rolls forward, swallowing your best intentions along with the pretty hillsides. The pulse of San Francisco throbs with the waves against the cliffs.

It's the glimpse of the girl I might have been in another lifetime. I came here too late. I'm a Midwest girl through and through. As charming as I find meeting friends for dim sum on lazy Sundays, the land of cheese and cheap rent calls. My SF rent has been increased seven hundo and there are hoodie-wearing tech bros more than willing to pay quadruple. Even if I were to scrape up the extra cash this year, the lay of the land is obvious. It is impossible to be middle class in San Francisco. I can't fight it. I need to jump before I slip even deeper in debt.

It's the right decision. It works. It makes sense. On paper. (So little of my life is on paper, blips and light impulses on recorded magnetic media or floating out in a technological ocean somewhere out there, out where you are, Dear Reader, our relationship only exists in these troubled waters.)

It's still sad. My building sits in the footprint of a ship left behind in the Gold Rush, found when they were retrofitting the area to earthquake-proof it. I dream of waves and seabirds and the rocking of a lifetime spent on water. The Transamerica Pyramid is a giant record needle playing the album of the sky at 33⅓ rpm. In these last days, I take the hills in my car like I'm in the front seat of a roller coaster. At my going-away party, my friends and I laughed on a rooftop bar, huddled around the burning cherry of a single cigarette. They didn't know until the stroke of midnight that it was our last hurrah together, at least in this incarnation. Above our head, a fifty-year-old marquee watched protectively. Everything is a backdrop stolen from a movie set. This is not my beautiful life.

I don't like goodbyes. Who does, I suppose?

I'm sorry, San Francisco, I know I've said the opposite before, but this time it's not you, it's me. I'm too old, I think, and yes, I'm aware of how ridiculous it sounds for a thirtysomething (~~how did I get to be thirtymumblecrumble already? I ask this of you~~) to bemoan the ache and stillness in my joints, the inability to be flexible either physically or mentally. Perhaps I could acclimate by crashing myself enough times against this big beautiful landscape. One of us would be broken by the other and step in line—but I refuse to linger over longing and nostalgia. I should stop this flirtation with the dangerous life not written for me.

I'm not the romantic lead. I'm not a blithe girl slipping across cable car tracks in Pucci-inspired mules with kitten heels. I'm not even her quirky-but-still-fuckable sidekick.

This town has me upended, and I never know which way is up. We never made it to the dance floor that night, instead happening upon a limo looking for a fare. I reclined in the back seat, the spinning happening already. The city flew by in reflection on the ceiling. In the distance, the low thump of jumping cars driving home from the Mission. I think I kept waiting for some notion the city still wanted me, some sign I should have canceled my plans and stay, stay, stay. This city will break your heart, they warned. There's even a song.

This is probably what they meant.

Goodbye, SF, try to forget me.

Xoxo,
Jane

# Day 16

**DB Cooper**
**@DBmm**

It's like my brain forgot how to go to sleep. Ask yourself: Do you have any idea how you do that?

♡ 652 💬 145 ⟳ 24

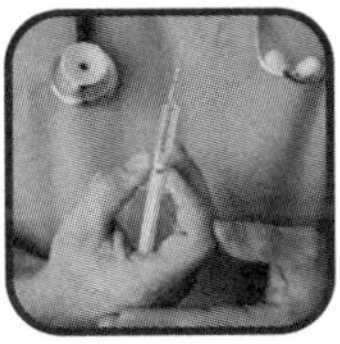

**World Medical News**
**@worldmednow**

H3N2 outbreaks in China, US, India, and Egypt straining local governments. World leaders urge quarantine globally until outbreak runs its course

♡ 5K 💬 27 ⟳ 4.5K

**Susie**
**@SuzeeeeQ**

I want my mom.

♡ 1 💬 0 ⟳ 0

**Susie**
**@SuzeeeeQ**

No

1 0 7

**Xi**
**@sXlilate**

Good grief, I know it's gorgeous outside right now, but did you forget we're supposed to stay home? Where is this traffic coming from? STAY HOME. There are sick people wandering the streets right now.

19 2 5

**Wolf News WNBS**
**@WNBSNews**

Lack of sick leave policies limit options for avoiding seasonal flu
http://www.bit.ly.com/h3n2sickleave

1.6K 165 955

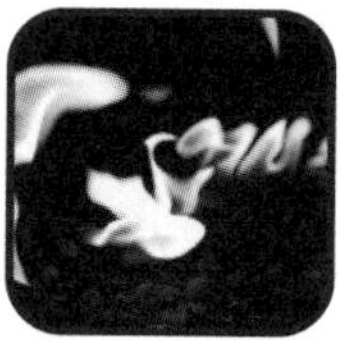

**Shine Beauty**
**@shineyourself**

H3N2 can help shed pounds before your date with Mr. Big http://www.Bit.ly/nosleepdiet

12.9K 498 6.8K

**Wolf News WNBS**
**@WNBSNews**

Bullets to Heaven star Tom Galt says son is victim in shooting as well. Son Noah accused of shooting over 80 people with several military-style assault rifles at LA-area high school

27K 49 5.2K

**Mychelle**
**@MightyMych**

It's okay to mourn the things I was excited about, right? It's okay for you too.

4 0 0

**Cosmoballiton**
**@CosmoNoFilter**

I could be a universal donor because of my blood type, but homophobia doesn't allow for it. I mean, the Red Cross is full of bigots but sure, need blood, I'll be over here.

452 67 3

**Mychelle**
**@MightyMych**

Our local Meals on Wheels is struggling. Volunteers are canceling and the staff needs to get meals out to homebound elderly. If you donate to help them, they might not shut down. I sent some money.

142 2 8

**Xi**
**@sXlilate**

This virus is moving. People move it. I may never be able to leave my house again. I for one welcome my new role as maven of Grey Gardens.

♡ 245 14 3

**Wolf News WNBS**
**@WNBSNews**

Fans of actor Tom Galt have set up a crowdfunding campaign to support Galt's son Noah, who remains in critical condition following gun violence incident at amusement park in LA

♡ 9M 984 47K

**Gemma**
**@Gemma1989**

I enjoy how you can't tell the difference between a hipster and an elder from behind.

♡ 12 0 0

**Xi**
**@sXlilate**

I survived bird flu, mad cow disease, 9/11, a concussion, and swine flu. Bring it on, crazy insomnia plague.

♡ 9K 4 43

**Wolf News WNBS**
**@WNBSNews**

Shooter at large in downtown Appleton, Wisconsin. Authorities tell citizens to avoid the area

♡ 4.1K 💬 85 🔁 2.1K

**Renob**
**@renobgib**

"When was the last time you slept in?" is a question I never thought would leave me feeling so hollow and terrified.

♡ 1.4K 💬 5 🔁 16

**Gemma**
**@Gemma1989**

Holy cow, someone is shooting up downtown where I used to live!

♡ 32 💬 0 🔁 0

**Rachael**
**@miss_rb**

'80s music prepared me for this pandemic: With Or Without You; Sweet Dreams (Are Made of This); Another One Bites the Dust; Don't Stand So Close to Me; Wake Me Up Before You Go-Go; If Only Tonight We Could Sleep; Talking in Your Sleep; No Sleep Till Brooklyn; It's the End of the World As We Know It (And I Feel Fine)

♡ 2.3K 💬 43 🔁 1.1K

**Susie**
**@SuzeeeeQ**

Bigggggggggggggggggggggggggggggg aasp

♡ 0 💬 0 ⟳ 0

# Six Years Ago

OtteryRide: Sometimes I envy Canadians. They seem so much more creative in their spaces.

JaneWithAWhy: Don't be silly. They have longer winters. Move to a place with a longer winter and you'll be creative too.

OtteryRide: You forget, my dear Ms. Solveig, we both come from a place of ice and snow.

JaneWithAWhy: Yes, and we are more creative for it. It's no coincidence we both work in industries fueled by liberal arts programs and NEA grants.

JaneWithAWhy: Well, you are at least—my master of arts is for show on my mental mantel. But certainly both of our creative impulses were implanted by long boring winter breaks and Sunday afternoons spent in children's departments of overheated libraries. This is an elemental thing lacking in the South, in fact (don't look too closely at this logic vis-à-vis Flannery O'Connor, Tennessee Williams, et al.)

JaneWithAWhy: Snow. What we need is snow. Look what it did for the Russians.

OtteryRide: The Russians had better clothing, though. Imagine what we could get done if we all bundled up in furs.

JaneWithAWhy: That's politically incorrect.

OtteryRide: That's not the point. The Canadian government requires a certain percentage of their art, literature, everything to be produced in Canada. You don't get that kind of nationalism with art here. There's a pride. I find it inspiring.

JaneWithAWhy: Perhaps it's because no one can move. They've all eaten far too much poutine and are trapped in booths at Tim Hortons across the land, but everyone is too polite to ask for help.

OtteryRide: LOL right, they're all sitting there saying, "Oooh, sorry about this. I'm all good. Go about your business."

JaneWithAWhy: I read that with a Canadian accent.

OtteryRide: As you should, Jane, as you should.

**Wolf News WNBS**
**@WNBSNews**

Appleton, Wisconsin, shooter detained, 7 injured, no fatalities

♡ 654 💬 27 ⟳ 98

**Cosmoballiton**
**@CosmoNoFilter**

My bitch-ass eight-year-old nephew told me I'm more likely to die from diabetes than H3N2. Beatings are still illegal, right?

♡ 1.5K 💬 32 ⟳ 18

**Wolf News WNBS**
**@WNBSNews**

Visits to federal inmates halted over fears of nSFI spreading after prisoner tests positive for prion-related strains of H3N2 and nSFI http://www.bit.ly.com/prisonprions

♡ 35.2K 💬 437 ⟳ 8.9K

**Xi**
**@sXlilate**

My amazing workplace is paying us full salaries to stay home. If my tiny employer can do that, why can't giant billionaire-run corps do that? Why can't Amazon?

♡ 61 💬 0 ⟳ 3

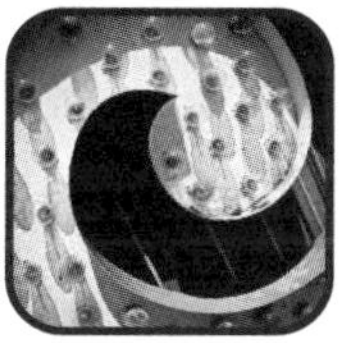

**Jane**
**@erejane**

Humans are inefficient batteries. It takes about 8 hours of charging for 16 hours of use.

♡ 18.5K 💬 486 ⟳ 153

**DB Cooper**
**@DBmm**

Managed to keep it together all day yesterday and then burst into tears about five minutes after walking into work. Fabulous.

♡ 753 💬 0 ⟳ 0

**Gemma**
**@Gemma1989**

The dishwashers touching the dirty and clean dishes with their bare hands? They don't get health insurance. They're kept under 30 hrs per week to skate work laws. They work in many restaurants at the same time.

♡ 53 💬 7 ⟳ 1

**Gemma**
**@Gemma1989**

Also, the average age of a restaurant worker is late 20s. With no health insurance, going to the dr is an INSANE luxury. They literally cannot afford to go to the doctor, period.

98 2 7

**Wolf News WNBS**
**@WNBSNews**

How to clean the bundle of germs on your phone http://www.bit.ly.com/nogerms

1.1M 751 51.8K

**Cosmoballiton**
**@CosmoNoFilter**

How are liquor stores not essential businesses but gun stores are?

9.6K 84 27

**Gemma**
**@Gemma1989**

The US has over 40 million people who work in hourly food service and retail jobs. Most of them live paycheck to paycheck, without insurance. If they don't work their shifts, for any reason, they don't eat.

22 4 10

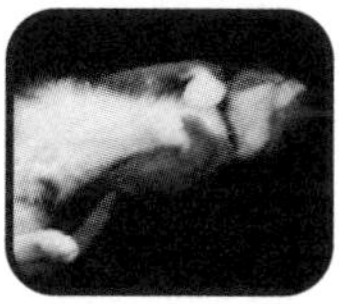

**Go To Sleep**
**@Insomnia**

When you try to sleep in a new location, half of your brain will remain alert and stand guard against potential attack.

♡ 162 💬 1 ⟳ 4

# Four Years Ago

Dear Jane,

I've broken it down to three primary locations, each fitting within my budget and earning projections. They each cost roughly the same amount of money, with heating/cooling needs and industrial tax benefits factored in.

1. An industrial warehouse space in Orange County, California. Benefits: Easy distance to LA, San Diego, and Las Vegas; SoCal; no winter; In-N-Out Burger down the road; Wienerschnitzels a mile in either direction, which would be a welcome change after the Bay Area's wheatgrass and organic crap. Downside: Space is exactly what I need, size-wise, and not an inch more, so potential to grow out of this space in a year or so. It's basically LA's asshole. High crime, area is extremely sketchy, and someone was killed in the parking lot of this particular structure six months ago. Living onsite not a question, would have additional expenses in security cameras, fences, alarms, etc., must deal with environmental inspectors, like at Heath, but without Heath's ability to throw money at the problem. Also, I highly suspect this space was used as a chop shop in the not-so-distant past. It's better than the other thing I suspect, which is that it was used as a meth lab. Chop shop is actually much more of a clean operation, health-wise. I'm hoping it was the chop shop.

2. Former department store in Seymour, Indiana. Benefits: Has a large storefront on a main street in Seymour; Louisville, Indianapolis, Dayton, and Cincinnati are only a few hours' drive in either direction; more major cities less than a day's drive. Downside: I doubt any of the denizens of Seymour would purchase the pottery I sold out of my storefront, but I'd have to hire someone to sit out there and be a clerk, since I'd be working in the studio most of the time. It's culturally an awful city, but they do

have a Chick-fil-A, which I guess is also maybe awful? Also, weirdly, meth is a question here too.

3. Warehouse space attached to a seafood processing plant in Baton Rouge. Benefits: Cheap shrimp. Downside: Hurricanes seem to hate Louisiana; the entire place will smell like rotting seafood; Baton Rouge has horrible crime and poverty; I like Cajun food but it does not like me; summer (see above, re seafood packing plant).

What do you think? I'm leaning toward never moving anywhere and smashing my backstock. What say you?

-B

Dear Dash B,

Of the presented choices, I would lean Indiana. It's near a lot of stuff but not near anything, which I think you might want. It's handy for growing racists and homophobes though, feeling like the center of things but not actually being anywhere. It seems to me your particular brand of loveliness may find a confused audience there.

I did happen upon this space. It doesn't look like much, and of course, it would turn you into one of those insufferable people who return to the land from whence they came but it IS quite the lovely spot with a lot of potential. And that price . . . It's the kind you whistle over, no? Anyway, I know it's much less than what you were planning on spending and far more space than you need, but you might be able to restore some of the space and rent it out to other artists, or perhaps create a beautiful penthouse loft and live the life of refined leisure while surrounded by rapids and water and urban ecology. Bonus: You'd be across the river from an expensive private college, so cheap work-study labor . . . or easy college girls with trust funds, your call.

Best, Jane

Jane,

My brain is rebooting every time I look at financial plans. Even more confusing, I've now been offered a lead position here at Heath. More money, more problems, more freedom, more authority, more of pretty much everything. I love the power. I'm a petty dictator on some level. I have a grand fantasy of drawing up new glazing compounds from a lawn chair out on the marina, hiring fresh-faced interns to run Arnold Palmers out, much to the ire of the other Hairy Potters. I could afford a better apartment. I could kick out Taylor. I could take a shower without worrying whose jizz I was standing in.

And the dream, perhaps it is that. These pipe dreams are there to keep us sharp. Life is what happens, they say, when we are making other plans. I'm thinking about it happening and less about the plans. I need to be ready to jump before the powers that be get frightened and start luring me back with grand schemes and ministrations. I'm a sucker for ministrations, as it turns out. Or maybe I want the luxury of a 401(k) and am willing to sell out to wear a button-down shirt and attend meetings.

Putting the meat in meetings,
-b

Dear Dash B,

If given the choice between the material and the ethereal, pay for your own Banana Republic and imported auto. You have thus far, anyway, and your ability to do so will only increase. Wait. You'll see. It's hard to see when you're entrenched in a situation, but your calling is out there and you'll shine in ways you won't believe. That is what happens when extraordinary people find themselves doing something they love rather than excelling at something they dislike but are good at. Or so I've been told, anyway. Do what you love, everything else will fall into place. Really. Don't deny your creative fulfillment. I had mine squished away into a tiny little place and tried to pretend it didn't exist for the longest time, and I cannot tell you how depressed I was. I certainly couldn't have told you then because I didn't understand the depth of the importance it was to my psyche. Even now I stifle it under the guise of normalcy. It's a plant, you need to nurture it or be haunted forever by the empty place it was supposed to fill.

I'm so bad at moral support. I'm sorry. But yes, practice is the key. If you devote time to your craft, you will be rewarded, personally as well as externally. I'm not saying this so you'll rush to say "but you're not," most of my writing is absolute trash. I have brief moments, yes, things I look back and think, wow, tight and nice, and wow . . . just wow, go me. I reread that viral entry that got so much attention by the big blog roundups and I'm embarrassed. I hate myself for not taking chances with it. I have no grace. I write as I speak, which despite my every effort still means bashing consonants on the head and keening vowels into elegies for the English language. I know no other way and the people who chose applicants for graduate programs recognize this. If given a chance, I'll take the gimmick every time. I allow myself some hubris now and then because of the popularity of my web personality, but it is that, popularity, as much merit and acclaim as McDonald's "99 billion served." It is quite laughable, but usually not in the way I intend. You, dear one, have talent. Not only are you aesthetically gifted, but you also make feelings have dimension and craft moods from colors. You have a natural flow I admire and an ability to twist words into origami. Throw a thousand cranes, Big Poppa. Make them fly.

Best, Jane

**Cosmoballiton**
**@CosmoNoFilter**

I licked some spilled BBQ sauce off the back of my hand and heard my coworker gasp audibly. Bitch, I survived the bathrooms on gay night in the Roxy in the '90s. Don't @ me. #H3N2

♡ 16 12 4

**Rachael**
**@miss_rb**

I've been asked to sign a get-well card for a coworker I don't particularly like suffering from the no sleep flu. What do I write—"Hope you go into a coma, like actually"?

♡ 42 0 0

**Xi**
**@sXlilate**

Artichokes are a weed with amazing PR.

♡ 18 💬 3 ⟳ 16

**DB Cooper**
**@DBmm**

You're an adult when you care more about your parents' health than they do.

♡ 16.5K 💬 27 ⟳ 4.1K

**Wolf News WNBS**
**@WNBSNews**

Local H3N2 patients showing signs of recovery
http://www.bit.ly.com/h3n2prognosis

♡ 58.9K 💬 654 ⟳ 2.5K

**Wolf News WNBS**
**@WNBSNews**

Talking to kids about H3N2 and insomnia?
Experts say to be calm and honest
http://www.bit.ly.com/childrenh3n2

♡ 3.8K 💬 439 ⟳ 895

**Cosmoballiton**
**@CosmoNoFilter**

I went out to buy some beer and peanut butter but not only is everything sold out in the beer aisle, all they had for peanut butter is the healthy stuff with flaxseed and this is the story I will tell about how hard it was during #H3N2

564 3 4

**DB Cooper**
**@DBmm**

I can't sleep!

5 0 0

**Wolf News WNBS**
**@WNBSNews**

US flu death toll rising, hospitalization rates high for children and young adults
http://www.bit.ly.com/fluepidemicrates

14.2K 3.4K 2.3K

**Cosmoballiton**
**@CosmoNoFilter**

Toilet paper also gone. Guess Daddy is getting a bidet for early Christmas!

9 1 0

**Cosmoballiton**
**@CosmoNoFilter**

Day 2 #H3N2 insomnia—have made it through 23 episodes of Law & Order, so almost first of 20 seasons. I'm going to become an LO canonist.

♡ 18.9K 💬 432 ⟳ 12K

**Xi**
**@sXlilate**

A turkey walked into the backyard. A TURKEY! Big like the one in the Macy's Thanksgiving Day Parade! The only way it could have been more awesome is if when the motion sensor spotlight tripped, the turkey broke into a Neil Diamond song.

♡ 23 💬 0 ⟳ 0

**DB Cooper**
**@DBmm**

My 7-year-old child resents homeschooling so much his completed essay is a biography titled "Why I Hate My Mom." Okay then.

♡ 17 💬 0 ⟳ 1

**Xi**
**@sXlilate**

Apparently, my grocery delivery screwed up but I didn't realize until the moment I was making a sandwich that my turkey was actually ham. I don't eat pork. You know what Freud would say? I want a penis.

♡ 745 💬 2 ⟳ 4

**Cosmoballiton**
**@CosmoNoFilter**

At least my dog can't catch this.

♡ 23 💬 4 ⟳ 0

**DB Cooper**
**@DBmm**

My homeschooling teaching pedagogy homework from the child's teacher involves many subcategories of how we need to do this thing and I would like to know where I need to send money so this woman is paid the billions she deserves.

♡ 381 💬 23 ⟳ 2

**Wolf News WNBS** ✓
**@WNBSNews**

DA: SWAT officer's use of deadly force justified in daycare shooting
http://www.bit.ly.com/daycareswat Oct14

♡ 7.8K 💬 1.1K ⟳ 554

# Day 28

BRIAN

Knowing the city was on lockdown, I ached to walk across the bridge and up the hill to a great little coffee shop on College Avenue. Sit in the corner or maybe at one of the tables in the front window bump-outs and listen to conversations. The coffee shop was closed, like every business on College Avenue and most of the city. Students were back to distance learning for the foreseeable future, the news said, but this wasn't anyone's first rodeo. We were all either docile little fools or willfully ignorant deniers.

The bright expanse of the late October sky was painful but alluring. I went downstairs and out the front door with my car keys—the barefoot people were manageable, particularly if I didn't encounter one in a germ-transactional face-to-face manner, and I wanted to get out of the house in a bad way. A large flock of geese settled on the water like a beating thundercloud.

Down the shoreline, across the locks on the far side of the Fox, a man in camouflage stepped out of the brush with a fishing pole. How long had this guy been there waiting to catch a fish, nearly invisible with the fishing line in the water? When everyone had been worrying about canned goods and dehydrated meats, this guy was pulling in his dinner the old-fashioned way.

The rod twisted and wrenched in his grasp; a large fish snagged on the hook. He fought it. The rod looked like it was going to snap. I didn't know much about fishing, but I knew tensile strength, I knew the physics of bending a plane beyond its ability to whip back into place.

For one sick minute, the rod nearly bent in half, but the man changed, a hard jerk rustled the bush he was concealed in, and the fish jumped at the right moment, landing onto the rocky breakwater with a gross jerking splat that traveled even over the rapids. The man crouched out of his hiding spot to walk over to the fish. It flipped once onto a rock, half in and half out of the water. Another twist and it would be lost back to the water, but the man lunged forward, trapping the fish against the rocks. His grunt traveled over the water. At some risk to his own body, he had won the fish.

He slipped his hands up under the gills and hefted it up—it was huge. It had to weigh fifty pounds, although I was no judge of fish, I only imagined it weighing as much as clay, which of course would be ridiculous. It twisted and heaved up again, but the fisherman pulled it back into the hidden enclave of tree branches. The entire operation had taken less than a minute.

There were any number of contaminants in the Fox River, tumorous fish found here only a few years ago. The fishing birds, like pelicans and bald eagles, had returned in the last decade after being nearly decimated by DDT and waste from the paper industry, but everyone should hesitate to eat a Fox River fish.

Seeing someone taking their own life in their hands, I felt the itch to do something too. With everyone gone, it seemed like a good time to gas the car.

Gas seemed like a good preparation. I didn't have a place to go, but oddly the camp where I had stayed as a child popped into my mind, where the gross little turd Randolph had pushed me into the lagoon, souring me on any form of natural flora and ooze for the rest of my days. I had a strange notion that if I could find that place, if it still operated, somehow, I'd also find adult Randolph there, still bullying quiet types, still pushing the unwilling into their worst nightmares.

The gas station was deserted, and the convenience store was closed. However, the pumps were on, and the credit card option was fine with me. Down the block, people were barefoot, some without much clothing on at all. Thankfully none around here.

As though to answer my thought, one of the shamblers emerged from between two badly parked cars.

This one was different.

Unlike the docile, slightly confused people I had seen during my drive home from the grocery store, this one's eyes were wrong—all intelligence had been replaced by something primal and dark. He was operating on rage, an adrenaline-fueled psychosis.

If I hadn't recently seen a video someone shot of a similar person, I would have frozen. That video, called "Guy Chimps Out," had over a million views and culminated with some guy behind the camera shouting "NOW!" and then someone out of frame stepping in and using a cattle prod to shock the infected man into wet convulsions. The victim managed to overcome the tremors and threw himself against the prod guy, bringing him down in a violent shudder. The camera cut away, but according to the comments, prod guy was still in critical condition, with head trauma and facial lacerations from the infected man's biting and gnashing at his cheek. Good. Fuck that guy.

The man in the video was without a doubt an unhoused person—his clothing dirty and stiff from weeks of wear, hair raggedy. This guy at the gas station wore a flawless wool sweater and a button-down oxford shirt, but below his waist he was naked, except for one sock. The ludicrous scene of a half-naked man in bright daylight made the entire surreal moment feel comical. My entertainment-starved brain instantly lit up with delight at the absurdity. Please god, no kiwis and sausage! I couldn't handle it. I stifled a giggle. Thankfully, the tails of his oxford maintained the man's modesty, although any moment, a breeze could inflict me with a glimpse of his zombie unit, a miserable image that would undoubtedly pop into my mind at unexpected moments.

Then I realized it—I knew him. He worked at the Lawton Gallery. What was his name? We had laughed about the last season of *Breaking Bad* and how we could always make meth to support our art. How hard could meth be compared to glaze recipes? He had a nice laugh. Probably drove a Volvo with a Coexist bumper sticker and donated to NPR annually. Probably had a specific fountain pen. I had discarded the idea of being his friend—too fussy, too familiar. Gallery staff were weirdly competitive with artists for some reason. I was sure Josh or Jonathan or whatever his name was would have happily met up for import beers down at the gastro pub or invited me over to eat from his fancy coastal charcuterie board, except Daniel or Kevin or Theodore would use the word "nosh" instead of "eat," and that would be the end.

And now, before I even had the chance to lift the gas hose from its holster, there he was, breaking everything. His fists were bloodied, and one finger cocked out at an odd angle. The bare foot was dirty and scratched.

What I at first thought was a leaf stuck to his bare heel was a flap of skin trailing behind. His foot was bright red and swollen at the ankle, with a definitive crimson line already trailing up his leg.

The gallery guy hadn't noticed me yet, but he was now walking between my car and the driveway out of the gas station. I froze in place, hoping he would move off somewhere else. Instead, he ambled closer to the soda machine. The door of the machine had been removed and was leaning up against the gas station convenience building, while the racks that once contained sodas were empty—maybe looting, or more probably the gas station owner had popped it for supplies after they sold out of other potables.

The man went to the front of the broken, leaning machine and angrily punched buttons, then he leaned back his head and howled. The hairs on the back of my neck rose at his anguish, feral and raw. I opened the car and flung myself back inside. He swiveled his head and charged at my car. I started the engine and cut out of the parking lot, trying to avoid his path despite his erratic movements, disjointed and unpredictable. Even though I was scared for my life, I had decided I wouldn't hit the guy—not that Michael/Kevin/Josh was concerned about being hit. He threw himself at the side of my car without regard for his own safety, smashing against the driver's side with a loud thump, making the entire thing shudder. It happened so fast I was sure I must have driven over his terrible feet. However, in the rearview mirror, Jared/Brock/Winston was still charging after me full steam down Oneida Street, no sign of injury. I drove, back toward the river, probably too fast, swerving to avoid three other people, two of whom were also in stages of undress and one who was completely nude, a young boy beginning to grow chest hair, a fawn on the side of the road, I begged out loud to *stay there, buddy, don't come out into the road.*

The entire time, Josh/Aaron/Jared charged behind, growing smaller and smaller in the rearview mirror, disappearing and reemerging in the fallen leaves kicked up by my tires. I admired his perseverance. There was no logic anymore, no indication or realization he shouldn't keep going.

As I turned the corner, a memory of certainty. His name was Christopher, but he preferred Toph. "Pronounced like the first syllable in tofu," he had said, "not that I can stand the stuff." He had told me he was a fan of yacht rock, and then launched into a five-minute appreciation of "Southern Cross" by Crosby, Stills & Nash. I had said nothing and changed the subject to something pointed, probably in an attempt to build distance in my disdain for him.

How long would Toph chase me? How long after my car disappeared at the turn ahead, how long into the city would he still run, still chasing the memory of me?

My friend would die soon if his foot wasn't treated. Once I got a terrible infection on a hiking trip from a blister on the back of my heel, due to new hiking boots. I tried to be a tough guy, walk through the pain of a popped blister. After two days, it was unbearable. I treated it at home with antibacterial lotions, but by the time I went to the ER, it had become an angry red streak up my thigh that required a three-day hospital stint. Again, a stupid decision that might have killed me. Even when you think you're doing the right thing, you end up almost winning a Darwin Award.

I made it back to the southern drawbridge, back to my island, where I was safe. My heart raced. I needed to take drastic action before the naked shamblers found their way into my own parking lot.

It hit me: South Island was almost a medieval keep, with its own moat and drawbridges. At the end of September, after the last big fishing tournament, the locks were closed for the season. There was no reason to leave the bridge down if no one needed it except for me, right? Well, there might have been Bob. I didn't know if he was around or not, but I also didn't care. I didn't want Toph surprising me outside my building one morning, and that guy wasn't good news for Bob, either.

The bridgetender tower's plain metal door was deadbolted. Ten feet above it, however, a banquet of glass windows. I eased the car onto the bridge's sidewalk until I was parallel with the tower.

Then I climbed up onto the car roof and looked up—I was close enough to break the glass of the window with the tire jack I had in the trunk, but not high up enough to pull myself through, particularly if I had to deal with jagged glass. I jumped back off the roof, noticing with relief that not only had the roof held my weight, but I hadn't dented the top. I had some pottery tools in the backseat, mostly for detail work. Nothing to pick a lock. I sat back in the driver's seat and pulled out my phone to watch videos on picking locks. One showed how to pick a dead bolt with a normal credit card. I watched it three times, glancing in my rearview mirror all the while at the bridge entrance, scanning for Toph or any other infected person who might have gotten interested. The worst thing would be to open the bridge and secure the island but leave a few infected people stuck on the island with me. Using my Wisconsin driver's license seemed like a Freudian way to confess to a crime—how much of a crime was it to play with bridge controls? I wasn't sure—but it was the sturdiest of the cards in my wallet. I got back out of the car again, looked over my shoulder, and set to shoving the card in between the door and the jam. My hands shook. Weird. I didn't feel nervous. I waited for the trembling to stop, but it got worse. My breathing was shallow and tense, even though my brain knew exactly what to do with the card, so I stopped, shook my hands to knock the jiggles out, and, watching the bridge, leaned against the car until my breathing slowed. It was a blind corner and I kept flinching every time wind bristled the tree branches, thinking Toph was coming for me, running at top speed. I would have time to get in the car and lock the door. I patted my pockets—no, the keys were still in the ignition.

Cool.

I took deep slow breaths and tried again, wiggling the card back and forth in the crack of the doorjamb, as the man in the video with the Southern accent had encouraged would-be thieves to do. There was no way this was going to work. What was I even thinking, anyway?

I could stop after three more breaths. One breath. Second breath. Third breath—a soft click.

There was no way that had worked.

The doorknob turned with ease. I waited for an alarm. There was none. If cops showed up, well, what's the worst? A misdemeanor during a state of emergency. Justifiable, in any case. I was taking the shelter-in-place order seriously and securing my residence.

The place smelled like institutional cleanser and mice, reminding me of Taylor and his terrible sailboat. After a few minutes of searching, I spied the service log and the bridgetender handbook.

Press the right levers and press the right buttons. Then the big red lever.

The tower shuddered like a small earthquake as the bridge came to life. Surprised, I jumped back and shouted "Who's there?" and then laughed at myself at how ridiculous that sounded. Such a coward, but adrenaline was a palpable substance in my bloodstream. My pulse hammered against my throat. I pressed another button and then pulled the lever, and the bridge groaned up. Once it was safely into place, I exhaled, gave the big red lever a pat, and left the tower unlocked.

While no one could now get onto the island through the bridges, I was still particularly exposed out on the island's little peninsula. On either side, buildings with dead eyes for windows reached up. Snipers would have gotten me if they'd wanted to take the shot, but it didn't soothe my paranoia. My hands were still shaking, and I couldn't make my breathing normal. My ears felt full of cotton, each heartbeat a speedball staccato.

At my flour mill door, I crafted a barricade, using fifty-pound boxes of porcelain as sandbags. It felt tippy, so I beefed up a second layer, altering the lines, like bricks without mortar, a stable fortress, although it was more like a heavy Jenga tower. It wasn't great, but it was enough to discourage any supply seekers.

At least I'd hear them. The thought gave me a queasy stomach. Toph. Guys like that. Hell, anyone like that.

I locked the elevator shaft, and then bolted the maintenance stairs behind me.

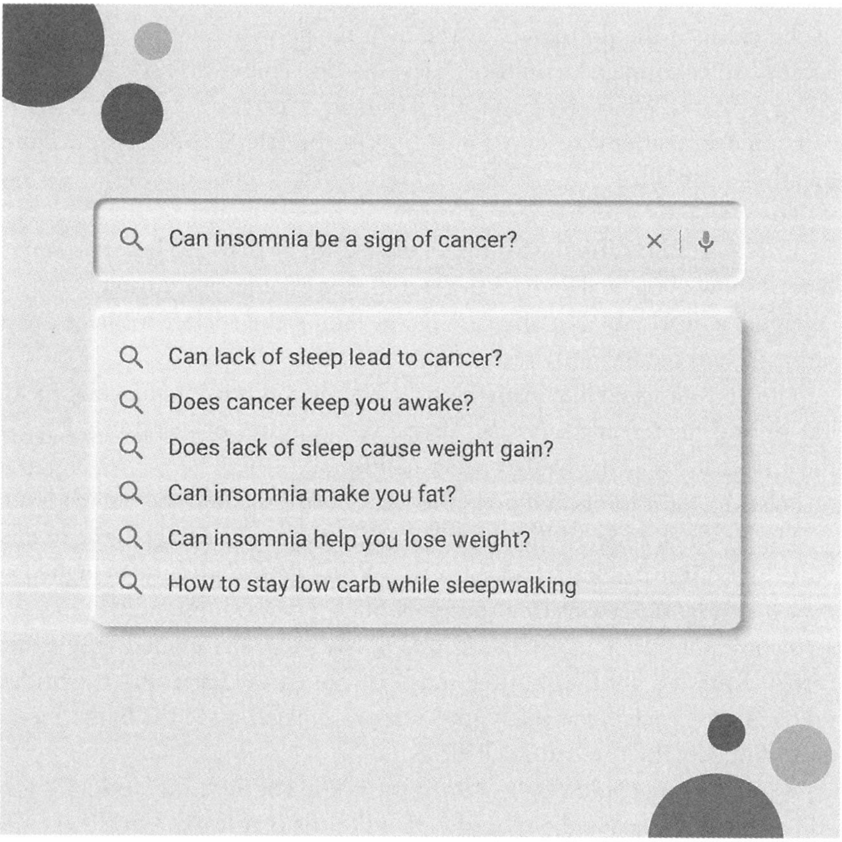

## Day 19

OtteryRide: How old were you in your earliest memory?

JaneWithAWhy: I think two.

OtteryRide: That's rare. Psychologists believe it's impossible for people to remember anything before they were five.

JaneWithAWhy: Maybe it's invented then. Maybe I'm making it up.

OtteryRide: What's the memory?

JaneWithAWhy: I'm in a crib, and it's summer because it's still light outside. It's hot. This was way before air-conditioning and my mother rented dismal little rentals all over the city. None ever had air-conditioning. I'm chewing on the railing of the crib, hoping someone will come and give me a drink of water, but the babysitter is watching TV. I keep calling out, but I hear her talking to someone, telling them to be quiet and I'll fall back asleep eventually.

OtteryRide: That's some sad shit.

JaneWithAWhy: I know, right?

OtteryRide: Did you ever fall asleep, or did they get you a drink of water?

JaneWithAWhy: I don't remember. I remember the sound of the laugh track, though. What's yours?

OtteryRide: Nothing as morose as that. My grandmother had a little pond buried in her backyard. Actually, I think it was one of those metal wash tubs, you know, it was the seventies and people were broke. My aunts were younger than my mom, so they were teenagers or something. They used to go out to the streams off the Bay and catch all kinds of things: little crayfish, minnows, tadpoles, and then set them into the pond so I could watch. I'd spend hours out there. It was a great babysitter, staring into the depths, partially staring back at the reflection of myself.

JaneWithAWhy: That's kind of awesome.

OtteryRide: It's no Norman Lear/ABC Afterschool Special about dehydrating your kid, that's for sure.

JaneWithAWhy: What is your favorite memory of childhood?

OtteryRide: Probably digging through my great-grandfather's war medals in the attic. It was like I had become an archaeologist.

JaneWithAWhy: You kind of were.

OtteryRide: What's yours?

JaneWithAWhy: Sitting on my swing in the backyard, sucking a butterscotch Dum-Dum sucker and watching a garter snake slither through the grass. I was barefoot so I pulled my feet up and then started swinging.

OtteryRide: That's fantastic. Interesting, why is it your favorite?

JaneWithAWhy: I don't know. I think most people would scream, but I was so calm about it. It was like, no big deal, pull up the feet and swing.

OtteryRide: Just swing. That's a good one.

JaneWithAWhy: What was the first date you ever went on?

OtteryRide: I took my little girlfriend to see a nighttime showing of *Starman* with Jeff Bridges.

JaneWithAWhy: Ooh, nighttime! Did you take your bikes?

OtteryRide: No, my mom drove us. I had this whole plan to sit in the back row, under the balcony where it would be extra dark, and we were going to make out. In my seventh-grade mind, pretty much going all the way, you know? End game.

JaneWithAWhy: We were so much smarter in seventh grade. Was it worth it?

OtteryRide: No, because as the first preview started? My art teacher came in and sat next to us.

JaneWithAWhy: You're making that up.

OtteryRide: Hand to God.

JaneWithAWhy: LOL! Seriously, I laughed now. And it was out loud.

OtteryRide: It was pretty pathetic. I think I was too afraid to even hold hands with her.

JaneWithAWhy: With your art teacher? :P

OtteryRide: You're hilarity.

JaneWithAWhy: I try.

OTTERYRIDE: Then when the lights came on, she looked at me like I had caught her doing something. I now realize she was more horrified than I was.

JANEWITHAWHY: Awkward.

OTTERYRIDE: Preteen boner killer.

JANEWITHAWHY: I can imagine. If you and I go to a movie, I do hope your art teacher joins us. I would like to ask her what it was like to befuddle a young art protégé.

OTTERYRIDE: It's true, she was the first teacher to hand me clay. It was a pretty awesome art class, come to think of it. I should write her a letter and thank her. She should be here in Appleton, actually.

JANEWITHAWHY: You should. She'd probably be thrilled.

OTTERYRIDE: She's probably walking around in her nightgown right now.

JANEWITHAWHY: There's that.

OTTERYRIDE: Yeah.

JANEWITHAWHY: This is a weird question, but are you coming down with it too?

OTTERYRIDE: Nope. I got a lungful of mold the other day, but I've basically been holing up in my studio. It will probably take more than a week or two before people get over the infection.

JANEWITHAWHY: If

OTTERYRIDE: They will. Are you sleeping at night?

JANEWITHAWHY: Yes, I am. But we're pretty sure one of the scientists here has it.

OTTERYRIDE: Oh, holy shit.

JANEWITHAWHY: I'm scared, Brian.

OTTERYRIDE: Don't be scared. It's going to be OK.

JANEWITHAWHY: I want to believe you.

OTTERYRIDE: I do too.

# Day 30

BRIAN

Knocking. Something banging somewhere. The sound of metal on metal, like the beginning of an Irish folk song. For a minute, I considered whether it was the UPS guy dropping off the winter glaze materials, but then I remembered: no bridge. Unless the Army Corps of Engineers had been here sometime the day before and I hadn't noticed them, but it seemed like they had other, more important tasks at hand than a little bridge with almost no traffic.

News station reporters and medical officials urged everyone not to drive if they weren't fully rested, and of course, like drunks trying to leave a party, everyone thought they were fine and were driving cars into buildings, pedestrians, other cars.

I crept over to the window and peeked through a gap in the sheer blind. A garbage can was overturned in the paper mill parking lot across the street. It hadn't been there earlier, and in fact it must have come from the employee lunch area about ninety yards away.

Certainly, someone was out there.

I threw on a pair of jeans and boots. If there was going to be a fight, I wanted the steel toes, even though it might impair my ability to run.

My clay barrier was still in place, double-deep with approximately 3,000 pounds of porcelain, banked up with 180 pounds of chicken grit in bags. A relief. I headed back up five flights of stairs, my heart pounding, either from the surprise burst of aerobic activity or from adrenaline. Maybe I could see someone from the roof. The thought of the sniper over on the old Lutherans building worried me, but I hadn't heard gunshots for at least a month.

A month? Two months? I counted. Fourteen days. It had only been two weeks. How was this time stretching so long? It wasn't like I normally left the house, but fear and uncertainty had ratcheted every moment into an hour, every hour into a long empty road.

The air was extremely brisk on the roof. The old utility door made a tremendous rusty screech in the early morning as I closed it behind me. Keeping low, using my solar array rooftop cells as cover, I crab-walked, stopping by a vent juncture and the rooftop air conditioning unit, then peered over the edge.

South Island was mostly still, a few leaf rustles here and there, no sign of Bob, no vehicles moving. The drawbridge was still suspended up in the air.

Across the river, however, someone was lurking with purpose.

It was definitely another quarantine holdout, most likely a male, based on the gait and the clothing. The guy was checking locks at the luxury condos, checking car doors. I didn't like the looks of that, but it was across the river, and a ruined bridge stood between that guy and South Island. I counted to thirty, focusing on my own side of the river, where I had heard the noise, but there wasn't any movement. Around to the other side, the solar panels offered good cover, so I risked standing a little taller.

If people were looting, my drawbridge wouldn't hold them off for long. I had good faith in the clay box barricade on the main entrance and the fire exits, but there was also the basement access under the wet entrance, where the river ran under the building. It wasn't visible from outside the building, but if someone went snooping, like that guy across the river, they'd find the secret entrance, sure enough. It might be enough to pique their interest.

At the edge, away from the protection of the solar panels, I crouched until my hamstrings ached. I regretted not bringing gloves . . . The air was colder than I would have liked. In fact, the white cloud of my breath was probably giving away my hiding spot.

Idiot. I would make the worst sniper ever.

I risked it and leaned out over the edge of the roof. That's when it all clicked inside my stupid slow simian brain.

The Fox River lock channel had frozen over in the night.

I probably wouldn't have noticed it but for the obvious footprints crossing the ice. The footprints had a cracked aurora trail showing where the ice had wavered, but, in the end, it had held the walker across. The person crawled up the bank, cracking dried stalks and brush as they climbed.

And there was one track, meaning whoever it was left another way, maybe figured out how to lower the drawbridge, which wasn't that hard to figure out considering it took me five minutes to raise it in the first place.

Or maybe they were still on the island. Maybe they were knocking.

I crouched again. Anyone could have broken their way into any number of buildings on South Island. Before the outbreak, hundreds of people worked on the island, people who might have had keys for locks, people with intimate knowledge of food stores, possible weapons—although I couldn't imagine what kinds of weapons would be lying around a paper factory, but perhaps the crappy tavern had a few shotguns . . . or, more importantly, alcohol would be in high demand now. Self-medication. I had considered it myself and was disappointed I hadn't ventured out to check the bar for supplies already.

Supplies. Like it's Armageddon or something. But the liquor wasn't something to imbibe. It was fuel. It was combustible. It was a whole lot of angry in a pretty glass bottle.

Back down in the loft, I grabbed my gloves and a heavy flashlight. I wasn't planning to go outside, but I wanted to be prepared in case of . . . I didn't know. I hadn't been in a fight since I was fourteen, when some asshole from another school spit on me during a cross-country meet. I'd gotten my ass kicked, so my odds were poor without boots or a weapon of some sort.

I jogged back downstairs, giving the clay barricade a pat. I could reinforce it with some boards. It wouldn't take too much effort to knock over the heavy boxes. Of course, if someone were on the island, I'd be revealing the hiding spot by pounding the nails into the wall. A drill would work better. If things were fine in the basement, I could bring up some two-by-fours and get to work. Stupid of me to not even consider such important securing sooner.

Unlike the more public-facing parts of the old building, no effort had been made to make the basement look modern, so bricks and crumbling mortar columns created a labyrinthine rabbit warren of doom and spiders. The old cavernous beast was quiet, the ticking of the boiler system extra loud. I knocked some webs down with the flashlight and went straight to the river access door. Still closed, dust undisturbed. The lock was stiff with rust. I hadn't opened it in years, not since a date and I had tried to go skinny-dipping one night in the river and got freaked out by broken glass and a jumping carp.

I put my back into it and cracked the door open. The river was clear, free of ice where it ran under the building, but the banks crusted with ice along the shoreline. No visible footprints. I stepped out onto the catwalk ledge, careful to avoid the mud, peering around the corner of the building. If you knew the river well, you'd know it wasn't deep there. A pile of old four-by-four boards huddled in a corner. I could use them to span the mud to the opposite catwalk without a problem if I barricaded the main door. Which I now saw I needed to do.

It took four trips to bring eight heavy and awkward boards up the tight corners of the basement stairs.

As I turned on the power drill to anchor the boards to the wall, I wavered. This was ridiculous. I was acting like this was the end of the world or something. It wasn't. The quarantine was temporary until vaccines got made, a few weeks or maybe months, they said. This was like when a big blizzard hits the area, same precautions being taken to keep everyone safe.

So someone else was on South Island. Big fucking deal. People were on the island all the time and I didn't worry about it on an average day. Not on New Year's Eve. Not the Super Bowl, when the Green Bay Packers fans got exceptionally rowdy. Someone was on the island, like every other week, like every other day. Just because the bridges were out didn't mean the place was forbidden—simply inconvenient.

Deep inside, though, I craved being battened and hatched. It fed something lurking under my lower-level mental processes, an answer to a question that had been there for years, maybe decades. I wanted to shut everyone out, as my last girlfriend had accused me, Gemma's words now brimming to the forefront, echoing. A physical barricade was the fruition of her predictions. God damn it, Gemma was right.

I was an idiot. Physically marring this heritage masonry with a shoddy barricade certainly wouldn't do much more than slow someone down. The doors opened outward, and a patient intruder could merely disassemble the clay boxes one by one and then crawl through the boards. To make an effective barricade, the boards had to be on the OUTSIDE of the building, keeping the doors from opening, and even then, the doors were still just glass. I'd need plywood, and I'd have to stand with my back to the world and work with a loud drill—too loud to hear anyone approaching from behind.

Plus, how was I going to explain the damage to the antique brickwork next month, at the holiday studio open house? "Well, I was afraid of looters during the H3N2 thing." It seemed cowardly.

Paranoia reducing to a bare simmer, I patted the brickwork, lowered the drill, and then unplugged it from the wall.

Also, I had developed a headache. Headache. One of the symptoms. One of the symptoms. Headache. Fuck.

I would pick up the mess later. I locked the glass doors again, stacked a few boxes of clay back in place, then took the elevator to the loft. It felt better having the elevator car upstairs anyway. I grabbed two aspirin and a large glass of water and gulped. In theory, aspirin couldn't touch the impending $H_3N_2$ headaches, and the internet forums said street drugs had no real effect and might even make headaches worse. If my headache went away, then *blammo*, a headache.

I had a prescription for sleeping pills—mostly used for the few times I had flown to New Zealand and Australia, but still nice to combat the "upper" quality of my anti-anxiety meds.

From all reports, it was the relentless nervousness that people found most unsettling, the sensation that one's legs couldn't stop moving, you wanted to dance or go for a long hike at 4 a.m. There wasn't a worse fate in my opinion, as though it would become the physical manifestation of the jittery sensations I already had on a regular basis. The rancid monkey in my skull didn't need an opportunity to pull my arms and legs on marionette strings.

I popped the sleeping pills out of their individual blister packs and threw them into the garbage, covered with shaving cream and a squirt of hair gel.

It was time for my Stay Healthy regime. I imagined these words hovering in my brain, in curlicue font with beams of light shining from it. I had some Sleepytime tea and a fair number of sleep-inducing foods. Ginger was supposed to be good, and cinnamon, but I couldn't remember if it regulated blood sugar or melatonin. I thought I had a bottle of melatonin, but Gemma must have taken it with her when she left, because it wasn't with my forgotten cache of natural supplements above the fridge. "Foods to help you fall asleep" was trending on Google, and I already had most of the suggestions in the apartment: a bunch of dried Door County cherries and almonds, oatmeal and high fiber cereals—all were supposed to put you right to sleep.

In the freezer were two slightly crunchy and freezer-burned Costco-sized bags of edamame, one shelled and one unshelled, as well as a lot of miso paste to make miso soup.

Sleep diet it was. The thing I was missing, aside from the eggs, was bananas. Alas, but nine out of ten wasn't bad.

I flipped open a notebook and made bullets for the Sleep Diet regime.

8 a.m. Oatmeal with cinnamon and dried cherries, vitamins, tea
10 a.m. 10 almonds
12 p.m. Edamame and miso soup, tea
3 p.m. Hardboiled egg, 10 almonds
5 pm Fuck all this, eat a bag of Cheetos

My latest industrious attempts at maintaining the perfect body had resulted in a home bereft of any garbage calories. It was all well and good to leave a beautiful corpse, but I hadn't fully appreciated how comfortable it would be to fall into some of my old dietary habits. There was nothing like a dinner of 99-cent pizza with fake cheese to make you feel like maybe life wasn't all bad. I knew I should have picked up a few packages of Oreos or perhaps some dayglow soda pop. At least there were the Twinkies.

All this planning helped me feel like I was Doing Something. This phrase also hovered in my mind in bold block letters, written in marble. There was powerful little Doing Something that could be Helpful since the quarantine.

Was Jane thinking the same thing? She'd crave her goldfish-shaped crackers floating in soup and her disgusting waxy marshmallow cookies, which she claimed contained the secret to happiness and world peace.

Thinking of Jane was sad-making. While we were both exceptionally busy people—Jane with her life of international blogger stardom and, as she put it "tens and tens of readers," and me with my artist bullshit—it seemed silly now that we had never actually broken through our superstition. We seemed to believe our email friendship was magical, and to meet in person would render the spell completely broken. As though this knowing without knowing was the only thing keeping the illusion going. We were strangers, two ships passing in the cyber night.

I FELT like I knew her. In fact, I was pretty sure I knew her better than some of the people I considered good friends. I knew her, on some level, better than my lovers, better maybe than I'd known my mom.

Perhaps it was all another form of illusion. Jane had over 1.8M "friends" on social media. Did they feel like they knew her too? Did anyone?

I Googled "oatmeal cookie recipe" and tried not to think about my headache.

**Xi**
**@sXlilate**

Halloween used to be scary enough but now I can't imagine a more terrifying reality than hundreds of little germy hands knocking on my front door and demanding sugar.

101 2 4

**Wolf News WNBS**
**@WNBSNews**

Bishop: Wisconsin Catholics are excused from Mass http://www.bit.ly.com/catholicmass

24.5K 1.8K 5.9K

**Cosmoballiton**
**@CosmoNoFilter**

If it weren't for the headache, I could get so much shit done every night.

34 8 4

**DB Cooper**
**@DBmm**

If I were a real teacher, there would be a cafeteria to make the students' lunches and also a teacher's lounge where I could smoke and drink bourbon in peace. #quarantineschool

9 0 0

# Day 20

JANE

As I'm cleaning bird shit and dead flies off the solar panels, Patty walks up.

"Hey, you up for a little superhero stuff?" He holds up a rock-climbing harness. "Now, don't tell Rick I let you do this."

"Forgiveness is easier to get than permission."

He grins. "You're a wild woman, blog lady."

I follow him to the cliff off the shoreline, and he gestures at the harness—"May I?"—so I nod. He dresses me in the harness while I stand there, arms extended, like a child being dressed in a snowsuit. It's awkward, his arms going up and between my legs, the back of his hand brushing the zipper of my jeans. It could be a sexually charged moment, if I were not me and this were not a shit- and decay-laden landscape. Patty doesn't seem flustered, rigging and snapping the carabiner into place with the detachment of a surgeon. For the eighteenth time on this trip, I wish I had had a big brother and he was exactly like Patty. If not actually Patty. Or maybe a boyfriend like him.

He tugs the guide harness. "Come on, puppy dog." My waist obliges to his tug, and I stumble forward. He loops up the slack and hooks it over my shoulder.

He looks around to check for Rick or Pedro and picks up his radio. "Patty to house. Going down for the daily collection."

"Roger that. See you in a few." Rick's voice answers back, hollow, as though from the mainland or perhaps an echo. Once again, the feeling of this overwhelming distance, the gravity of four people on a beaten island a three-hour boat ride from the mainland.

Maybe I should ask for a radio communicator now. Would they trust me with a radio? Why has it not occurred to them to give me one? I know why—I'm not there. I'm another kelp fly to be ignored, to be swatted away from eye sockets. I glance at Great Murre Cave, the water saying *ooooh ooooh ooooh* as the waves plant a kiss on its gaping mouth.

"OK, so here's what we do. You'll go down this rope and dip the bucket into the water and then come back."

"That's it? Just dip and come back?" I take the bucket from him. It's a child's pink beach bucket with a white scalloped plastic handle. Science-y.

"Well, hang out there if you want. It's kind of cool. See the nests in the rock facing. Lots of pig gu sites. Brandt's cormorants have habitat in there."

Patty and his nests, his nicknames for things like a pigeon guillemot, a surprised-looking black dove-type bird with a white flash on the wings and bright fiery orange feet. I wish I cared about birds and nests this much. What must it be like to do the thing you wanted to do most in life? I try not to think about it too much, or the tiny ember of bile-tasting sadness will bloom and grow, heating my chest, propane and downdrafts, eventual combustion into a blustery maelstrom.

Luckily, I'll leave before getting too intimate with his joy, and before it turns any affection for him into annoyance and then resentment. I'll leave before knowing too well their satisfaction. Maintain my ember in a controlled burn, deprive it of oxygen and particles and exclamations.

He clicks the lifeline in and gives it a few good tugs. "Ready?"

"As I'll ever be. Lower me down, Captain."

He chuckles. "I think you don't understand how this is going to go. You're going to walk down. Bend over, turn away from the cliff, and walk backward."

I bend. The idea of being a superhero is less fun. "Walk backward." The birds cry and the greedy ocean slaps up against the crumbly cliff. The water might be ten feet down or fifty feet down.

"Just go down?" Something is wrong with these instructions. Something missing. After days of carefully putting my feet in specific steps, retreading the same inches, now the abandonment of rules tempts me, this freedom to allow gravity to take over. The void is calling.

"Yup. Stop when you get wet."

This is a funny joke, objectively, however not funny. Nothing will ever be funny when all my weight hangs on the rigging around my ass and hips. I'm entirely too aware of that ass, trussed like a ham, hanging in an old-time butcher shop.

"Don't drop me into the sharks! Patty! Any sharks?"

"Ah, don't worry about the sharks. If you fall, the waves will bash your head into the rocks. Sharks won't have time to kill you." He chuckles. He's trying to relax me, but the mechanism is to shame me for being afraid. This is a mechanism I'm familiar with and he has disappointed me at precisely the wrong time, making me think of my grandmother, who would also never have let me fall, but she also wouldn't have let me forget it was my fault.

I back out over the rocks, staying bent over until I'm more or less hanging rather than walking. Logically, I know I can't fall, Patty won't let me fall, but it still feels like I'll pitch over the side at any moment.

"This is nothing. Patty, I thought you had an adventure for me." I talk a big game. He rewards me with a chuckle that feels real, earnest, together, watering the seed of security that is the basis for my friendliness toward Patty. All is forgiven.

I rappel down the slick rock cliff and avoid squashing the nesting sites, crumbly with the bird shit used as glue to make homes of twigs and feathers. I'm Action Jane. Down close by the water, everything is different. On the island, it's like being on a stage. I'm so far above everything I don't get to see what's happening in the audience. But hanging so close to the water, it's more real. Seals and sea lions are hauling themselves up onto the rocks, and further out, harbor seals truck by, each honking to the other.

I have my bearings now. Now to test out some bravery, I could hang on that rope all day. The sun shines through the waves, turning them translucent. In the water, silhouettes of several sea lions race to keep pace with the tide. For a few beautiful seconds, I'm not thinking about the sharks or the inherent raw danger of the islands or the intense waves of ammonia shimmering off the nesting sites or whatever the hell is going on with what seemed to be a global death count. I'm here, soaking up some glorious autumnal sunlight and finding my place in this rough landscape.

Then I drop the bucket.

As I turn to follow a seal, the bucket slips off my hand and hits the sea with a splash. I ratchet the rope lower to try to reach it, but the bucket spins in the tide and crashes up against the rock face.

"Patty! I dropped it!"

"Well, get it back," he shouts back.

"I don't know if I can." The bucket is surging against the rock and back out again with the waves. It seems lost. *Goodbye*, it says, *I'm going on an adventure.*

"You must. We can't leave waste in the ocean."

Oh, right. My own version of the morality plays that caused the bulk of humanity to discard their waste into the ocean. Because it's a pain to pick it up, or because I might have to inconvenience myself, I might *get wet*. I'm the problem. This is how easy it becomes. *It's hard. Give up. Give in. Why try.*

I pretend I'm Catwoman with a twist, tweaking something in my lower back in the process, lean backward in the harness, then extend an arm over my head, reaching back blindly for the bucket. My fingers graze plastic but then it bobs away to the left. I spin again and stretch for it, timing my burst with the ebb of a wave, and snag the handle, lifting it up, half full of water.

"Do you need the full bucket?"

"Half is fine. I wouldn't want you to drop it again."

"OK, how do I get up? Is there an elevator?"

"Same way you got down."

"Oh, balls."

"Language, Jane, there are baby birds in those nests. You want them to hatch, don't you?"

"Oh, sorry," I apologize. Perhaps to the unhatched eggs. Perhaps to the sea. Perhaps to gravity, to my middle school gym teacher, to the years of inflexibility creating this moment.

Walking back up the vertical cliff face is surprisingly not difficult, considering I'm hauling a belching bucket of water in one hand, and I'm me, spectacularly unathletic, fabulously unfit. The rope gives me leverage to climb against, and Patty must be doing a lot of the tension work on the rope above because it feels easy. Finally, back on top, I offer him the bucket with a few inches of seawater and grainy particulate.

"They should put a rope on that thing." I swipe sweat off my forehead.

"It's never been a problem before." He looks at the water with skepticism.

"You're lying."

"OK, I dropped it a dozen times myself. Jeesh."

At the bird blind shack, where the biologists hunker down to count and observe birds without influencing bird behavior, he measures the temperature of the water along with the volume in the bucket. He explains that the data goes into decades of numbers measured in this same way, noting a complex formula, where they take the air temperature and volume of the water and can determine the rate by which the water warmed up (or cooled down) from the time it took me to get the bucket to the shack. Apparently, it took twice as long as the average temperature reading for me to get myself back up the cliff.

"We're lucky you didn't tell me you were timing me, or I would have dropped the bucket again."

"You see through my evil plan." He squints and grimaces, doing the formula, and touches his temples. I touch my own temples for a moment and then lower my hand, hoping he hasn't seen me mimicking his movements.

He snaps the notebook closed, flips his sunglasses back on, and heads out the door with a grunt.

I follow. I will always follow.

# Day 25

State of Emergency Declared, US Under Lockdown

Breaking news: The president of the United States has issued a state of emergency for the continental United States and Hawaii. All planes have been grounded for the next 24–72 hours to contain the outbreak of the H3N2 virus and sanitize all airports and vehicles. The National Guard has been activated by forty-eight state governors to maintain border patrols on state borders. Arizona is the holdout in the continental US, with Governor Louis seeking federal assistance and US troops to be deployed to maintain the US border patrol. The president will be addressing the nation tonight at 7 p.m. Eastern, 5 p.m. Mountain.

Both the NASDAQ and the New York Stock Exchange have ceased trading until Monday in response to the crisis.

**Xi**
**@sXlilate**

I can't believe these celebrities are getting tested while healthy 24-year-olds are catching H3N2 and can't sleep but must work anyway because they can't provide a positive test. Gee, I wonder why this is spreading.

24 3 5

**DB Cooper**
**@DBmm**

At least I know my kid isn't going to end up with head lice, although it's possible by the end of this pandemic, the dog will also know how to read.

412 4 12

**Wolf News WNBS**
**@WNBSNews**

Bullets to Heaven star Tom Galt has taken a leave of absence from show to focus on son Noah Galt's legal defense. Son is accused of killing 21 in high school shooting in Studio City

47K 541 3.5K

REDDIT—R/H3N2**—I GOT DA HEENIES!

-4858:3028 pm 11/01/20xx from Anthrosponder (583/12)

Check out this photo, snapped last night. Guys in hazmat suits picking up the zombie Heenies. They went all through my apartment complex, scooping them up last night. This was happening outside our neighbor's door. They knocked on our door too, and I about shit a brick, but they moved on. We're bugging out though. It was too close a call. Not infected (and God willing, never will be), but it was way too Nazi Germany for my taste.

—OP, where are you located? I'd heard the Gs were sweeping our neighborhood in East Philly, but we're still seeing lots of these sleepwalker zombie folks. Not sure if these are new Heenies though or the same ones changing clothes. LOL

—My sister-in-law sent me a photo of the same thing happening in a suburb of Indianapolis. Same uniforms, different vehicles (Pic 1) (Pic 2). The rumor is they're being treated out in this tent village set up in Monroeville (little town outside of Indy).

—(Redacted by moderator 11/02/20XX)

—(Redacted by moderator 11/02/20XX)

—Moderators, why are you deleting posts?

—Please see guidelines on this thread. (National security breaches will be deleted immediately)—mods

# Day 30

Dear Sir,

I have mailed out a change of address form, issued in triplicate and addressed to the postmaster general, but alas, it merely sits in the SEFI mailbox, a little orange postmaster flag turned upward. The gulls fight over it, as it's an ideal perch from which to remind me of everything I've done wrong in my life. You think this is me being paranoid, but you don't know how they eye me up and down, suggesting perhaps those pants don't go with that shirt. Usually, however, this is merely a distraction to give a third gull the opportunity for a stealth shit strike. Hoods, my friend. This war will be fought through the grace of excellent headgear and shit avoidance.

Go to an island in the Pacific, they said. Peace and nature, they said.

Best, Jane

Dear Ms. Jane,

Winston Churchill said, "We shall fight on the beaches, we shall fight on the landing grounds, we shall fight in the fields and in the streets, we shall fight in the hills; we shall never surrender." But I would humbly suggest we append "while wearing hoodies" to each of Sir Winston's ambitious phrases.

For my part, I took a dump while balancing myself using the front bumper of my Land Rover. I doubt the Land Rover will ever forgive me. Right by the headlights too. It couldn't even shield its eyes. I may have to rock it to sleep tonight.

Cheers, Brian

Brian,

You went out of the apartment? What happened? Did the river freeze?

Jane

Dear Jane,

Yep. So that happened.

Brian

Holy crap. Seriously. Are you OK? Is everything OK? Are you somewhere safe?

Are you still sleeping?

-J

Dear Jane,

Still nailing eight hours and every girl I see. Booyah!

As safe as I'll ever be.

Brian

**Mychelle**
**@MightyMych**

Maybe my bank's email about how they're dealing with #H3N2 is going to be the one that breaks me. Nope, it's the one from Sephora.

♡ 1.1K 27 485

**DB Cooper**
**@DBmm**

I'm starting to think this pandemic is being sponsored by homemade banana bread. I have made so many banana breads this week.

♡ 65 💬 4 ⟳ 9

**Xi**
**@sXlilate**

Holy fuck, DC now has over 20,000 confirmed cases of H3N2, and I don't even know how it's so low except nobody can get their hands on a test. STAYING INSIDE FOR LIFE = ME.

♡ 14 💬 0 ⟳ 2

**Wolf News WNBS**
**@WNBSNews**

Streaming entertainment services report record viewings of illness-themed movies such as Contagion and Outbreak
http://www.bit.ly.com/netflixnchill

♡ 3.2K 💬 165 ⟳ 905

# Ten Years Ago

Dear Brian,

Dream: I was floating down the Fox River, which is one of the few rivers flowing north (I believe the others are the Amazon and the Nile and one more) and along the side of one bank was the Kimberly-Clark plant, only it wasn't the Kimberly-Clark plant in reality. The boat I was sitting in was old, the wood burnished with patina. It had a mossy feel, as though it had been pushed up and forgotten in some boathouse someplace, by boys in knickers and leather football helmets, and it is surprising it floated at all. But it creaked. The Fox River is very wide and has rapids which are now dealt with by bridges and dams, but in the dream, there were none and instead there were these patches of low rocks, of cormorants pecking at bits of dead fish. The river was fast, and I got the impression it was an early spring day, and the river was fed by melting snow. The water was cold. I could feel the chill coming through the wood of the boat, damp achy wet cold you feel for hours later. And throughout the dream, the water smelled like Kleenex, like the fragrance they put in it. And around the shallows, there were little pastel pools, light pink, light blue, light green, where the dye had run into the water. And I remembered Kimberly-Clark was polluting the world because you told me.

Best, Jane

# Day 26

One of our biologists has come down with what we think is H3N2. Of course, we don't have access to the tests to grow a culture, but the symptoms match. I haven't been sleeping well myself, so I'm staying away from the other two biologists, who are in the other house anyway. We have been communicating via email, which is ridiculous considering the emails must traverse a satellite connection each way, using our tenuous grasp on solar power to do it, and they are literally about a hundred yards on the other side of the wall from me, but it seems like the easiest solution. Hi Rick and Pedro, I hope you guys are feeling OK.

I'd like to say I'm not scared right now, Dear Reader. We've radioed for more biologists so we can swap out our sickies, but it sounds like things are even worse on the mainland. Our volunteers have their own crises. Unfortunately, when you sign onto the island, you affirm that the agency isn't responsible for your safety. We could hire a personal craft to come out and fetch us; it has been done before, Pedro and Rick said, but it usually goes for $4,000 a trip. Doable, certainly, but right now, we can't get any takers within the network, and the one person who said he would come said it would take $10,000 and we'd have to be quarantined outside the boat for the entire trip.

I'm having a hard time sleeping, none of the fever or the headaches everyone else is reporting. Patty, however, is textbook case. I keep begging him to come back into the house, since I've probably caught it too, but he refuses and has set up a camp in the birding hut. Three times a day, I leave food and fresh water. He leaves me notes, thanking me. Even in the face of this terrible illness, these naturalists remain stoic and delightful.

## Comments (148)

Bill
Take care of yourself, Jane. I think if you had this awful crud, you'd know it. The headache is the worst thing I've ever felt in my entire life. It's like God has crushed the top of my head with his thumb.

Audrey
You don't know this monster illness welling up inside the man. It best he stays far away be safe. Sleep not come in thre3 days for this one. Head says goodbye.

Sami
Be well, Jane. Try to sleep. Do you have access to copper there? My sister's friend had a full-blown case of H3N2, and she ingested 3,000 mg of copper and sleeps like a baby now. It's out of stock at all the drugstores here but maybe you'll have some for bird purposes or something?

Joel
Sami is crazy. Copper kills in that dosage. Fucking bitch should have a license before spouting off on the internet and giving shit-for-brains medical advice.

# Day 31

Dear Sir,

I've never told you this before, but shortly after we met, I had a dream about you. It was a simple dream. We were making apple pie together in some strange kitchen that I believe in the dream was yours because I didn't know where anything was. Nothing happened, no Smurfs jumped from the pie crust, no dissertations upon whether cake or pie is the superior vessel for fat and sugar (pie, by the way, is far better. You will find no quarter here if you argue otherwise). And after all this time, I still must remind myself it was a dream, you and I have only met once on a bike patch in Crissy Field. But somehow it feels unfair that I have this memory of standing side-by-side at the sink, you fumbling with the peeler, all pomp and no circumstance. Your elbow was grazing mine, touching without comment, remaining there without pulling away. The green pectin made our hands soft. I was showing off, proud I could peel two apples in the time it took you to peel one (I'm insufferable, even in my dreams), but I slowed my pace to match yours so you wouldn't cut yourself trying to keep up. It was a good day, that day that never happened. And now it seems as though we'll never meet. This might be the end, Brian. And so, you'll forgive me for lapsing into this uncharacteristic maudlin tone and allow me to say that this little nothing does mean something. I lie in this awful house each night, listening to mice scratch out my name, and I wonder if this night will be the night I don't sleep, the beginning of one forever day that stretches for a week and then falls into nothing. I'm glad you're here, Brian. Stay safe. Sleep well.

Best, Jane

My Dear Miss Jane,

Pies. Definitely pies. Never even in question. And I'm glad you're here too. Keep passing the open windows.

Cheers, Brian

**Cosmoballiton**
**@CosmoNoFilter**

At least its almost ovr love

♡ 9.8K 💬 942 ⟳ 6.5K

**Xi**
**@sXlilate**

And now I know my first person who has died of H3N2 and soon we all will. All will know someone who was lost.

♡ 654 💬 2 ⟳ 14

**Wolf News WNBS** ✔
**@WNBSNews**

The Church of Jesus Christ of Latter-Day Saints has suspended all public gatherings around the world until further notice due to fears of H3N2 and nSFI
http://www.bit.ly.com/mormonservices

♡ 2.3K 💬 147 ⟳ 509

**DB Cooper**
**@DBmm**

Yesterday, I was completely unconcerned with my bangs, and today, they are MUCH TOO LONG AND OMG GET AWAY FROM MY FACE. How does that happen overnight? If I could sell magic overnight hair growth.

♡ 102 27 47

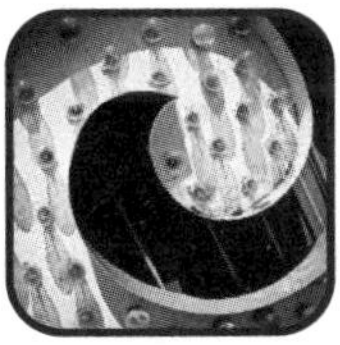

**Jane**
**@erejane**

I think I might be drunk because I kind of want to read Moby Dick for the first time in my entire life.

♡ 233 65 15

# Day 26

## Jane

I bolt straight up in bed. A noise that didn't belong. Something neither seal nor auklet, not the strange groan and creak of the wind as it whistles through the rock face of Lighthouse Hill. Boat horns? An owl smacking into the house? The air reverberates with whatever it was.

It sounds again.

Firecrackers.

No. A gunshot.

The house is quiet. Maybe Rick or Pedro will come over to check on me. Maybe it's the ghost again. A memory of the Egg Wars of the 1800s, when two men were murdered over murre eggs.

Something creaks in the house. Silent again. The auklets resume croaky lullabies.

If something bad's going on, Rick and Pedro will tell me to stay in the house. I'm worried it's Patty. Perhaps Patty found one of the guns?

The wind shakes the house, or perhaps the house answers my thoughts. I listen with my whole body. The Cassin's auklet cries transform into the singsong made-up nonsense of a melody-less tune sung by the ghost child. Its sexless high-pitched voice sings the little ditty over and over, unintelligible repeated refrains.

*No no*, I think, *you've got to go to sleep. It's late. You've got school in the morning.*

The ghost child doesn't listen and keeps keening a song in a nursery rhyme about cockleshells and elephant seal teeth and string.

I wake again, without knowing I was sleeping. The auklets are revving up, little dark bodies returning from their nocturnal open-water hunt. I flip on the light and dress. Four new mouse turds near my shoes. Then I see it. On my bedroom door, an envelope.

"Jane" it says on the front. Inside, a note and three additional envelopes, each folded.

Jane,

We're infected. Neither of us have slept for 48 hours and the headaches have become unbearable. We don't want to lose control. We're going to do it in the second house so don't touch us. We didn't want to upset you anymore than this probably already has. We regret that.

We can't say how long it will be before a boat comes for you, but when it does, here are three letters. One is for the head office, whoever is still in charge. It explains exactly what happened with Patty and must be filed as a part of SEFI history. The second letter is for Rick's wife. The third letter is for Pedro's mom.

Stay healthy if you can. Don't come into our house. Enjoy every day as we have.

Sincerely,<br>
Pedro Alejandro Muñoz<br>
Richard James Chernowski II

Do it. Do what.

Do it. It.

"PEDRO! RICK!" I tear down the stairs. "PEDRO! RICK! NO!"

From the marine terrace, a bull seal lifts his giant proboscis and honks at me for interrupting his morning bask in the weak sun. The day is gloomy, morning mist slicks everything. I rush to the second house, resting my hand on the door. There isn't a sound from inside. It feels cored—the way an empty house feels different from a house containing someone sleeping, or maybe someone sitting awake but lying still. Pedro's theory of a lizard brain and instinctual danger sensing pops into my brain. My Jane brain.

I pound the weathered wooden door. "Rick! Open this door, you fucking bastard. God damn it. God damn it!" A gull responds to the outburst, swoops in, flapping its giant wings, its pink feet splaying as it fights for its territory.

"Go away, you fucking bird."

I feel so stupid. I should have read the signs. No one kills themself without being kind of crazy, right? I've been through this before. Experienced. *Experienced. Ex Pear Eee Once Sex Peer She Chanced Hex Spear He Danced.* Behind me, the void of the dark ocean roars, licking the shoreline cliffs.

Out of the corner of my eye, a dark figure, upright: A person walks across Midland Pass.

"Rick?" It's not Rick. "Patty?"

The figure doesn't stop. It keeps moving. The Cassin's auklets, returned to their nests, sing their morning lullaby, a creepy choir of a thousand fairies in the gloom. The entire island keens. The figure hunches and lurches. It can't be Patty—his jacket has SEFI-required reflective stripes. The dark figure is the absence of light. I step off the porch and watch the figure hurry through ground studded with hidden auklet burrows. Patty knows the area is a burrow minefield, waiting to catch a foot and snap an ankle. He would be more worried about destroying a bird habitat, his own safety a distant second.

It doesn't seem wise to chase. "Patty!" I cry again. Tears run down my cheeks, or were already there, I'm not sure. The auklet colony answers back, their gasping creak a hive of crickets with bronchitis. The figure doesn't seem to hear. It dashes down to Maintop Bay, where it lingers, perhaps waiting for me to follow.

"I give up, Patty. I give up. I think Pedro and Rick are dead. I think . . . they might have killed themselves. I need your help!" I'm whispering to the figure, which can't possibly hear me.

I want to believe it's Patty. I need it to be Patty. I don't want it to not be Patty.

Then I'm in the house. I'm in my room. The Jane Fonda room. Not *my* room. I sit on the bed, the dull murmur of the auklets outside. Was the sound the ghost child? That has to have been it. I invented something to fear on this island when there are already so many terrifying things in the world. Patty demented, wandering the island, out of his mind in a mobile coma. Rick and Pedro dead. And I'm a coward for not checking on them.

What if.

What if they aren't dead? What if they're wounded? I should have checked. I never checked. *Experienced. Experiences. My fearish fences go dear good senses.*

I grab the flashlight and headlamp. It's better with the headlamp on as well as the big Maglite. The Mag is a weapon.

Downstairs, I first queue up the stereo to make myself braver. Patti LaBelle rings out, singing about a sex worker in New Orleans. This is comforting, the idea of coming back to a cheerful, well-lit house after checking that two corpses are really corpses.

The auks' nightly croaking has reduced to a low murmur, like the din of an audience right before a conductor taps his bow and the curtain rises.

Outside, I falter. I feel like I'm being watched. I look around, behind, around, up toward the hill. The ocean whispers along the shoreline. No dark figure. From the gloaming of the marine terrace, the sleeping bull seal snuffles.

"Rick and Pedro, if you're in there, I'm coming in. It's Jane. I want to check on you."

I already know I'm talking to their ghosts. I know they're no longer living, in the same way that when you look at a dead person, you know they are dead, even when they were breathing a minute before. It is an absence; a negative space has been introduced in the Coast Guard house, whether by the deaths behind the weathered beaten door or by the islands themselves. It's the same thing I feel in the Jane Fonda room every night. An emptiness. A want. Both something and nothing at once.

The door's unlocked. If they were joking about the suicide—not that anyone would ever joke about such a thing, but if it's a ruse to hide from me and Patty—then the door would certainly be locked.

"Rick and Pedro? I'm going to pop in for a second and then I'll go away and not bother you again. I want to make sure you don't need my help. I'm sorry I waited so long to check on you. I wanted to respect your wishes. My mom tried committing suicide a few times, and wrote the note and everything and the last time it didn't work, she ended up—"

I gulped. I didn't expect them to be on the sagging plaid sofa. Right there.

The headlamp illuminates their glistening, briny empty places, the shiny black wetness turning scientific and bright in the LED light, an intense tang of copper in the air.

Blur the eyes. Don't see details. I've learned how to do this before, with Mom's body. *Experiences she fears it henced.* Focus on the feet, the sanity of human feet wearing socks, looking so normal. Their house shoes are kicked nearby. Pedro lies on the couch, his shoulders and head in Rick's lap. The gun's there, touching one of the shoes. Splatter across the couch, up onto the wall, a dark grinning shadow plays tricks with my brain.

Rick. Pedro.

They're holding hands.

The room is quiet. Even the auklets have stopped.

Back out of the room. Walk sideways out the door. Shut it behind me. Enough. Done. I'm unnecessary.

An auklet runs over my foot, a soft but surprising little attack. A squeal inside my throat threatens to turn into a scream—or maybe laughter. I imagine Farallon weed growing up over the mule cart path, up over my feet, tickling my ankles and then pulling me down into the jagged terrace along with the thousand dead skeletons already crumbled into nothing. It might be a peaceful alternative. I rock, the heaviness holding me against the porch, I want to fall backward and sit against this door and never move. Allow this fearful place to take whatever it wants from me.

I'll give it gladly. Happily. Take it all.

The dark figure stands by North Landing. I stop. In the other house, Patti LaBelle has started the final chorus of her ode to Lady Marmalade. The figure turns toward the East Island.

Dullness fogs my brain. My ears are stuffed with cotton balls. The dark figure sways, maybe dancing. It might be arms and might be wings, making swoops and windmill movements. It doesn't look right, it doesn't look natural, it doesn't look sane.

I run, clutching the Maglite, acutely aware of every scuttle of stones, every rodent moving in the Farallon weed. A gull scolds me from the roof and takes a run at my face. I keep going, assuming it won't strike, but I'm wrong: It pulls some hair out as it flies off. I burst through the front door and lock it.

If the dark figure is indeed Patty, he has spent the last four days and nights outside. He can put up with being locked out. If it's not Patty, then . . . then no, it must be Patty.

I scale the stairs two at a time and burst into the Jane room, whipping off the headlamp and throwing it at Kylie's old bed. I crawl into bed, not taking off my shoes. I can't bear the sight of stocking feet. Later I'll call the mainland. When it's light and clear outside. When it's not so terrifying.

Somehow, I fall into half sleeps, minute by minute. Each time I lose the thread, dream I hear footsteps climbing the steep stairs, and bolt awake. Twice, I get up and look down the hall and see nothing. Finally, I tuck a chair under the doorknob, like they do in movies. Once more, as I'm falling asleep, the footsteps race down the stairs, pause halfway down, then continue to the bottom and stop.

In the same way a house can feel emptier than empty, the way the Coast Guard house told me Rick and Pedro were there but not there, this house feels like someone *is* there. I've gone numb. My death has already happened inside my brain, eighty times in an hour. Even a demented Patty is less frightening than what I keep seeing every time I close my eyes, the glistening, the empty places, the plaid sofa, the shoes, the socks.

The sun is coming up. Was I sleeping? Do I also have the disease? Does half asleep count when it comes to the illness? I don't know. I have a headache.

Downstairs, the stairway door hangs open. The footsteps. Everything else is exactly as I left it, outer doors locked tight. I take aspirin and start coffee.

I spend the rest of the morning trying to work the satellite phone, but no one answers. I try again. And again. I spend the entire morning drinking coffee, using the bathroom, calling, calling, calling.

**Mychelle**
**@MightyMych**

It turns out the job my boss said couldn't be done remotely when I had my surgery? Can be done remotely. Go figure.

♡ 200 12 42

**DB Cooper**
**@DBmm**

I asked my elderly neighbor if I could pick anything up for her at the grocery store and her list was literally doughnuts, vodka, and chocolate. Girl, I get you. I get you.

♡ 139 7 9

**Amy**
**@AmyBedeliaBrown**

Only after I achieved the perfect replica of the Starbucks eggnog latte at home did I remember I actually don't like Starbucks eggnog lattes.

♡ 23 💬 1 ⟳ 2

# Day 32

I have made a new friend on the island. His name is Maurice. I'm sure the biologists gave him a real name (or as real as names like Kanye Blessed and Keyser Söze can be), but since I'm not interested in digging through the island log books or determining the specific scar patterns and color variations of the various forms of seal life on the island, I'm taking a shortcut and now his full name is Maurice Ernest Gibb.

Maurice and I may get married someday. Perhaps we will go on tour. Funny Lady and her Elephant Seal! We will have grand discussions, through which I will offer insights on the plight of the planet and Maurice will bemoan the fact that he would like to move two feet over, but he is so fat. So fat!

So.

I've decided I have two possible courses of action. I can wring my hands about this scenario or I can continue the work I pledged to do for this project. I walk the island, once in the morning and then again before sunset. I record the different animals, even though my records are more like "One chirpy blue bird. Eleventy million seagulls. Two blue-footed boobies. (Heh heh . . . Boobies.)" I was all ready to rappel down and get a seawater temperature measurement from the typical place off Fisherman's Cove, but then I happened to witness (and photograph! for science!) a particularly awesome/gruesome shark predation on an elephant seal (not Maurice . . . We may all sigh in relief. His Royal Fatness continues to reign supreme for another night) right near where I would be hanging down over the water, and I decided, you know what? Temperature in Mirounga Bay is better than no temperature at all. That's what I say. Ah well, they'll probably discard my data anyway, but at least I'm trying. I logged it in the books.

I haven't seen Patty. I have a weird fantasy that a fishing boat or tourist group picked him up. Or he called one of the renegade charter services and didn't tell anyone. Then again, Patty is a man of many talents. He might have gone down into the rumored caves that twist and turn beneath Lighthouse Hill. He might be dining on sea cucumbers and urchin (the former being disgusting but nutritious and the latter costing upward of $50 a pound on the mainland) and catching fish with his shoelaces for all we know.

I miss him.

~~Sometimes I think I see him at night.~~

I spend an hour a day at the lighthouse. It's nice and warm when it's sunny outside. This has the added benefit that I show up on the camera there and watch the webcams of other cities. It looks pretty rough out there. Everyone stay safe, OK?

As for me, I have at least two more weeks of hearty eating right now—probably more like five if I ration—and Lord knows how much water. The rainy season should not be far off. And there's always fishing . . . hahaha! OK, maybe Farallon weed is delicious.

Sleep well tonight, Dear Reader.
Jane

**Mychelle**
**@MightyMych**

Advice from my choir director, a historian: Today I'm starting a handwritten journal to write about what I'm seeing in the news, how my friends are responding, what's closed. This is history.

♡ 598 3 61

**Gemma**
**@Gemma1989**

Just made friends with the neighbor who has never spoken to me or met my gaze. I've only lived here for six and a half years and we share a driveway, so that was cool.

♡ 15 2 0

# Day 34

It doesn't seem possible that just thirty miles away from where I'm tapping away at my laptop, Union Square is overrun by the sleepless. They trot up to Macy's and bang on the doors, as though late for a luncheon in the café. They murmur, having conversations with no one while ambling to and from nowhere. They lie on the street, right across the cable car rails—those are the most heartbreaking of all, as though they want to end the chaos, the smeared verse inside their brains. Maybe they like the humming, the insect metallic zither that I almost hear through the webcam.

They all wear the uniforms of sick days—yoga pants, boxer shorts, sloppy oversized concert T-shirts and droopy sweaters. Most without shoes. Those who start with shoes will kick them off in shoe piles that have formed on street corners. Do intersections inspire barefootedness? The act of pausing, perhaps, forgetting. On Mason and Turk, a snowdrift of shoddy sneakers and one perfect pair of pumps. I think a lot about the lady who left them. She must have tried so hard to be pretty, right up until the end. I wasn't on the webcam whenever she stepped out of them, but every time my mouse clicks the Mason and Turk view, there they are—those perfect bone-and-black spectator heels, resting atop the curb as though she had been waiting for her Lyft and then was lifted right out of them, pulled heavenward. As I scroll past the endless views of street cams, I can't help but wonder, *Where did you go, Miss? Is that you in the corner, cringing?* Then I click to another view.

I try not to think about specific people. My specific people especially. My Aunt Heidi. My friend Brian. Both have stopped answering my emails. They each felt like a heartbeat away, despite the continental divide between us. Then the people who matter but also, we pretend they don't. My drinking buddies. My exes. My old boss and my work wife from three jobs ago. Where are they all? Are they on those street corners, pausing, barefoot? I hope but also hope not to recognize anyone on the webcams. And you, Dear Reader. Where are you?

The worst part? Whatever they are seeing is real to them. Stuck in wakeful nightmares, a perpetual hallucination. Maybe they believe they're naked and it's final exam day. Or they're playing Little Orphan Annie melted with Scarlett O'Hara for a play they haven't rehearsed. Every day is the most amazing day of their lives and their worst day. Their mothers are still alive. Their dead relatives surround them, accusations of sins committed long ago.

I wish I could talk through the webcams. I don't know what I would say, though—it's not like I could ask someone to rescue me from this island. The people on the sidewalks are in far worse shape than me. I'd tell them to watch out behind them, assure them that it's OK, that it will be OK, everything will be OK.

Well. Not even I would believe that.

I know I'd say something nice. I'd want someone to do that for me, I think. I'd want someone to smooth my hair and be kind to me. But I suppose if I could somehow transmit my voice through the webcam, then I could also *hear* what was happening over there and I would have to hear the screamers. I know that they are screaming because they make the other sleepwalkers flinch and cringe away, pressing against buildings and corners. I usually click to a different camera when the screamers come along.

And on the Farallon webcam, you see me, sitting here with my laptop on a rock on a hillside on an island surrounded by the Pacific. If anyone is watching, that is. Hello. I'm still here, Dear Reader.

I hope that you are still there too.

I hope you are still you.

Jane

# Day 36

JANE

A smooth black body breaches the surface for a second, glossy and scarred, a dorsal fin, a flip of a jagged steak-knife tail, the hint of a white underbelly. Pretty girl. Under the water, she's safe, happy, well-fed.

At my feet, one of the thousands of gray bird carcasses, more like a feather pile than a former flying machine. Everything on the planet, every living entity becomes nutrients at the end of the long day. Nutrients in, nutrients out, and finally, nutrients for another organism to consume. Patty said that. At the time, I considered it pessimistic, but it was the secret formula, the algebraic equation. Simple. Clean. Neat. Final.

Maybe the orange inflatable boat could make it out to the container ship that lurked in the distance? How far was it, exactly? Too far, probably, and they wouldn't let anyone aboard, anyway. Plus, they'll have guns.

Rick had said the orange inflatable could have made it all the way onto the mainland if I had to. Someone had done it once. Plus, there were the original lighthouse keepers who had rowed during a foggy winter night, trying to save their child from some unknown ailment, the child screaming the entire way. They rowed for eight hours, two men taking turns against the waves, the mother clinging to the sick child and nursing another infant, whispering gentle words about warm beds and hot soup and doctors who could fix it. They couldn't fix it, they couldn't fix the child, in the end, and he had died in San Francisco, leaving his kin to row back to the island, wasted failures.

I can row. It doesn't have to be a race—I could get there when I get there, take breaks, drinks of water.

The shark surfaces again. I'm terrible at figuring out the length. Rick would know. Twenty feet? Twelve feet? I write in the logbook, "Shark, feeding, unknown size, unknown predation," and that will be good enough for future scientists.

Even as I think this, I know it isn't for them. It's for me. I was here. I saw this. *Remember me.*

**Wolf News WNBS**
**@WNBSNews**

National Guard to deploy 10,000 troops to six states in response to H3N2 and nSFI virus
http://www.bit.ly.com/natguardOctober

27K 207 5.4K

**Gemma**
**@Gemma1989**

I don't know who these superheroes are who are quarantining while wearing jeans but first, I applaud you and second, what exactly are you trying to prove?

848 16 74

**Mychelle**
**@MightyMych**

If you're lonely in lockdown and need someone to talk to, I'd love to hear from someone.

429 84 154

# Day 37

## Brian

On the news station's webcam of College Avenue, cars parked haphazardly along the side, as though parked by drunk drivers. There were a few pedestrians, but they too looked not right, stumbling and slow. Suffering.

The webcam didn't show close details, as it was mounted atop the bell tower on the Saint Phillip University campus. I flipped open a second browser and searched for other webcams in the area. I hit the first one at random. More cars parked sloppily and one person sadly banging at a store's locked door. That didn't matter to the man wearing the telltale blue polo shirt and name tag. An employee who desperately wanted to work despite the pandemic? I didn't know whether to laugh at the man or cry for him. I clicked another webcam, this one showing the riverfront, about a mile downstream from me, where the river is wide and the banks much steeper.

A girl lingered at the base of the bridge. Her feet were bare, despite the cold November sleet striking the windows of my loft. Her hair was plastered to her face and her eyes had dark circles from many missed hours of sleep. She rocked from foot to foot, as though afraid to step over the grate of the drawbridge. She was certainly awake, but even as she swayed, there was an absence about her. A man stepped into frame, walking down the centerline of the road. The familiar hump of a dead animal lay within his path, probably a raccoon. No, definitely a skunk. How could the woman stand there so close to a dead skunk?

The guy was big, unshaven, and wearing a Packers sweatshirt and no coat. He wore only socks, despite the cold rain, and was headed straight for the skunk carcass. I hoped he would avoid it, but no, he stumbled and tripped over it. He looked down, surprised, and then reared back a leg and punted the dead skunk. The body exploded on contact with his foot, splatting gore and gristle like a Rorschach inkblot. Some of the guts squirted onto the hem of the girl's dress. She didn't seem to notice. She continued swaying.

My mouth had gone dry watching this tableau. I licked my lips in disgust. Thankfully, the webcam didn't have sound. I flipped to another camera, this one the food court at Fox River Mall in the suburbs. The food stands' grates were pulled down over the counters and the neon signs were dark. The mall walkers listlessly ambled here and there, and in the center was a teenage girl curled into a fetal position, pounding on her own head. Other cams in the surrounding cities, more of the same: Catatonic walkers in varied states of agitation, few interacting with each other. They all were caught in their own dream state. Not even one wore shoes.

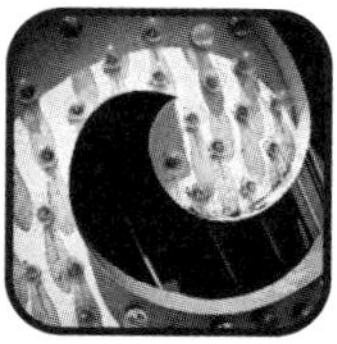

**Jane**
**@erejane**

Let's all agree that whatever we do to our own hair while we're stuck inside is no one's business. Just don't mention it. Live and let live. People got worse things going on than being judged about deciding to try pandemic bangs.

♡ 3.5K  💬 114  🔁 92

## Day 34

You swear you're awake. Like when you've shut off your alarm and you tell yourself you're going to lie there for a bit and "rest your eyes" (biggest lie in the universe) or those moments when you're thinking deep thoughts before bed and then you swear you're awake but something makes a noise and you've been half asleep the entire time.

Maybe I have the opposite of that. I worry I'm having one of those "absence seizure" things. How would I know? There's no one here to tell me.

The air feels heavier at night, even before the sun dips. This island can't wait to get the darkness started.

I lost track of time the other day and stayed up on the lighthouse too long—the camera keeps me up there. Maybe someone who loves me will see me there. A silly wish, but what else are wishes for if they can't be a little silly?

Dear Reader, I'm not afraid to be alone. I'd feel more alone with someone else here. I'd have to pretend to be brave. ~~I'd have to cheer them up. Maybe this is hermit syndrome, this conviction I'm better off alone. Maybe there's little food in the larder and with another person here, they'd have more to eat if I weren't around.~~

I'm indulging in a little maudlin-ness, mostly to distract myself from freaking out about my friends and family. You know what? There's not a damned thing I can do about it.

Once upon a time, I nestled in the warm, nice-smelling crook of a boy's neck. He was a nice boy. I liked him. He made me feel fluttery, like in high school, when my biggest crush had turned around in English class and said, "Homecoming . . . with me?" and it wasn't a joke and it wasn't because his friends dared him to do it, it was because he *liked* me. You know that feeling.

This is the feeling I'm thinking about today. A nice feeling. The moment of hope. Something amazing about to happen, like cresting to the top of a roller coaster and getting flutter tummy as the car slows and almost falls over.

That was a good feeling.

And regardless of that particular boy—wherever he is now—regardless of the fact that he cheated on me with a long willowy insect-like creature with the body composition of a nine-year-old child gymnast and a propensity to say words like "supposably." I've come to understand it wasn't about the hurt or anger I felt or Ms. Supposably. It was the memory of *that feeling*. That nestling in the underjaw, my cheek against his collarbone, the air whooshing in his lungs, his heartbeat, thrumming, his voice reverberating in his chest. A safe feeling. The moment I saw what happiness could be. The shape of the thing.

I used to think that moment helped me identify happy moments, an exemplar toward which I should be striving—like Cinderella and her glass slipper, as simple as finding the man into whose chest I could fit *just so*, my head under his jaw, my cheek resting right against the clavicle. Perhaps if I were a scientific sort, I could consider measurements, a certain number of centimeters, a standard deviation to distinguish the right physical features and discard the rest, like an NBA height chart or the arm length required to pull an Olympic-grade archery bow.

I had it all wrong, Dear Reader. I think that WAS my moment. Like a buffet, that was my scoop of perfect mashed potatoes. Not too much. Not too little. Just right. Now move on and take a scoop of cottage cheese. A little bit of pickled beets.

I'm also not relishing my reduction in diet—the pantry, as they say, is getting bare, hence the food metaphors.

It's enough to think back on that moment. That warmth. The contact, skin against skin. It's all I have, the only moment I'll get . . . and maybe that's OK. Maybe that's enough. I guess it will have to be.

Stay safe, my lovelies. Sleep well. I love you, Dear Reader.
Jane

**DB Cooper**
**@DBmm**

In the last month, we've lost my child's daycare provider, uncle, three cousins, my great-aunt, and my work wife, but since we're not allowed to gather and have funerals, it's like they're still there, not answering my emails.

♡ 3.9K 💬 142 🔁 87

**Renob**
**@renobgib**

H3N2 is the only multilevel marketing scheme that has ever been successful.

♡ 1.8K 💬 54 🔁 374

# Day 31

BRIAN

The river fully frosted over—a thin filmy glass-like layer of ice covered most of the river. Not enough to support a person, or even a large dog. Thin like the sugar coating on crème brûlée. A fat seagull waddled complacently across, nipping at bits and specks in the ice. Clouds hinted at rain or my favorite of Wisconsin meteorological conditions, wintery mix, an indescribably miserable condition, part rain, part sleet, part snow, and part tiny ice cubes stinging as the wind pelts against your cheeks. Miserable driving conditions and the kinds of precipitation that caused a sheen of pebbled ice along the roads, called black ice. Good thing no one's driving anywhere. I sipped black coffee and thought grimly about my toilet paper, slowly dwindling. Who knew that in the midst of a global emergency, the hottest, most contested item would be ass wipe? Even here in the Fox Valley, in the toilet paper capital of the world! When I eventually ran out, I would have to face the grocery store again.

I paced over to the northern window. It overlooked the little tributary lock channel along with the offshoot of the dam waters, a pleasing ripple of white caps and rapids, open flowing water.

In the shallows off the lock channel, a flash of yellow plaid shirt.

Someone was in the water.

Their arms flailed and then an open mouth gasping for air, then back under.

Bob.

I don't remember putting down my coffee cup. I don't remember leaving the loft. I remember taking the stairs three at a time, flying down, wishing I could fling myself down faster without touching a stair. Then outside and disoriented. Running toward the bank.

The clouds had the audacity to look normal, a distant smokestack chugged as though nothing were wrong.

I charged over a discarded plastic Coke bottle and waterlogged furniture padding, mildewed, then the skeleton of a carp, its dorsal fins delicately strung with residual yellowing flesh. Bob was thirty feet away. The moment my feet hit the water, the shock shock shock. Cold needles pierced my skin as thirty-two-degree water soaked into my socks. My brain screamed *this is a bad idea, very bad, very bad, so cold, call someone*. Fifteen feet away. Getting closer. It took so long to get there.

"Help!" I shouted. I roared. I was an animal. "HELP. He's drowning!"

Each step difficult, deeper, my footing more uncertain. His eyes blinked, his skin alabaster white, porcelain slip. I wanted to go back to shore, back to my apartment, a blanket, forty blankets. Coffee. Bob was drowning. A man was dying and I was thinking about coffee. Ten feet from me, eight feet, six feet.

"HELP!" I shouted again.

My fingers reached and he reached back.

I don't remember getting him up the bank. The weight of him, the surprisingly light bones and skin of him. For such a tall guy, there wasn't much to him. The water sucked back for another nibble. I was soaked and cold. Leaving the water was more painful than being in it.

Bob had no fight in him but kept himself rigid, easy to carry. He kept saying, "Ow. Ow. Ow. Fuck you. Ow."

I got him up to the building. The elevator was still upstairs, so I grabbed some of the moving blankets I used for padding and packing up larger sculptures. "Ow," he said. "Fuck off."

"You need to take those clothes off. You're going to get hypothermia." I had already kicked off my shoes and dropped my jeans.

"Ow. No. You fucking goddamned homo. I ain't gonna let you put your dick in me. I'll bite it off."

He took the blanket and wrapped it around himself, teeth chattering.

"Are you OK? What were you doing in there?" How stupid it sounded. I guess I was hoping he had slipped in, maybe he was fishing, not trying to get off the island. I had pulled up the drawbridge, leaving him no way back.

He rubbed his sternum. "My fucking chest. Hurts to breathe."

"I bet." I peeled off my sweater. The smell of river water, dank and fishy, permeated the vestibule, mixed with Bob's sour tang. "You have hypothermia, bare minimum. Get those clothes off. I'll be right back—I'm getting help." The emergency room couldn't turn away the uninsured, but I wasn't sure if anyone was even there anymore.

I huffed up the four flights of stairs and wrapped myself in a blanket while dialing 911. After a few tries, an official-sounding person answered. I gave the necessary information; paramedics were on the way, and I was to keep Bob warm. Still chilled to the bone after dressing in dry clothes, I took the rest of the pot of coffee and two mugs back down to Bob.

To my satisfaction or annoyance, Bob was still there, clutching the moving blankets, still wearing his soaked clothes.

He took the coffee from me as though he had ordered it himself, saying, "Got any sugar?"

I ignored the question. "Let's get you out of these clothes and make you more comfortable, keep from getting sick."

He eyed me sideways. "I knew you was queer."

"You can have privacy—oh fuck, shit." The drawbridge was still up. The ambulance would have no way to get onto South Island. "I'll be right back. Take off those clothes! I got to go make sure the ambulance can get in." Bob clutched the blanket tighter and gave a churlish look.

I jogged out the door before realizing I didn't have a credit card to jimmy open the lock—my wallet was upstairs. I jogged back.

"I forgot, I have to—Bob?"

He was prone on the floor, eyes closed. I knelt and turned him on his side, thinking of dry drowning social media stories. I thumped him on his back, wanting and hollow, like a rotting log. I rolled him over and began chest compressions, the muscle memory coming out of nowhere from my camp counselor Ryan's CPR lessons. *Find the sternum, buddy. Staying alive, buddy, staying alive. Count it out pinch the nose blow blow.* Bob's mouth tasted bitter.

Staying alive, staying alive, ah aah aah aah staying alive staying alive. Blow. Blow.

I don't know how long. My body ached when arms pulled me away. Paramedics took over, one inserting a plastic cup mask and shield into Bob's mouth for CPR, the other wearing a clear face protector. Both wore full PPE suits. They did chest compressions for five minutes and then loaded him onto a stretcher.

"What's the victim's name?"

"Bob. Um, I don't know his last name. He's homeless and he lives around here somewhere. I don't know. His name is Bob."

The other withdrew a bright purple wallet from Bob's pants pocket and pulled out the ID card. "Karl? Maybe Bob is a nickname?" The wallet had a unicorn on it, the kind a little girl might treasure.

My teeth chattered. "I don't know. He was in the river. I pulled him out of the river."

"Got it. OK, we'll get him to the hospital. He was in the water a long time, huh?"

Bob's slack lips were blue, his skin pale. Maybe he wasn't there anymore. It felt like he was gone, like the paramedics were saying without saying he was dead.

"Oh, wait . . . the drawbridge. I have to close the drawbridge so you can get out."

The paramedic looked at me, confused. "That little bridge over there?" He pointed to the lock channel. "It's fine. We got through fine."

How was the bridge down? How long had it been down and accessible? Did Bob lower the drawbridge himself? Did it fall? It seemed like the paramedics weren't taking much care with Bob, jostling the stretcher against the doorframe and down the single step. He was so skinny and frail. Why didn't I leave him more food? Aspirin?

The paramedics never lowered their own masks, so I couldn't read their expressions as they handed me a business card with Bob's case number scrawled on it. My jaw chittered hard against the cold air, hands shaking. Bob's bare pale feet hung off the stretcher, yellowing toenails and downy gray hairs, his toes pruned from the water.

"Bye Bob," I said to a closing door.

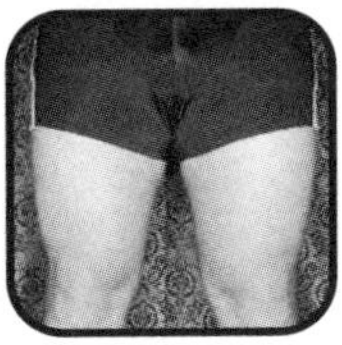

**JeSsBieU**
**@Jessbieu**

The battery on my phone is almost gone. The battery in my head is almost gone too.

♡ 5 💬 0 🔁 0

**Go To Sleep**
**@Insomnia**

We usually tweet about sleep disorders but allow me for a minute to introduce myself. Hi, I'm Karen. I have insomnia too but the anxiety kind, not the other one. 1/x

451 11 27

**Go To Sleep**
**@Insomnia**

I'm lucky enough my job allows me to stay home and work whenever. Not everyone is this lucky. We still need doctors and paramedics and cops and grocery store clerks and sanitation crews and plumbers. 2/x

607 10 4

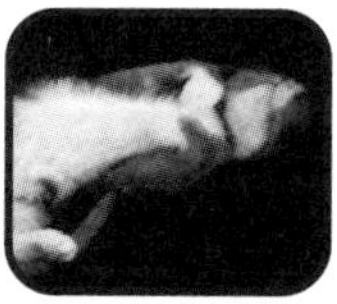

**Go To Sleep**
**@Insomnia**

And other people can't do their jobs from home and need a paycheck to eat. They can't quit and stay home. Please consider this while being patient about people outside your window. They may understand how scary it is to do what they're doing but they may not have a choice. 3/x

984 14 19

**Go To Sleep**
**@Insomnia**

Or they might be sick themselves. They may not know what they're doing and being outside is most certainly not their fault. They are not zombies. They are not going to attack your children. They are sick. This is a crisis. We need solidarity. 4/x

4.2K 45 1K

**Go To Sleep**
**@Insomnia**

How we refer to each other is foundational to building empathy, which is necessary if we're going to get through this. We can't demonize people who have the virus. They aren't Others. They are us. 5/x

3.9K 84 949

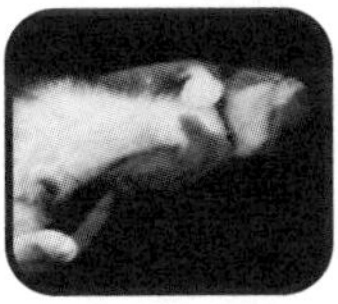

**Go To Sleep**
**@Insomnia**

Focus on small ways we can help each other. Can you spare some groceries for your neighbor? Can you check in on someone with a phone call if they live alone? People are glued to their devices right now and every update is filled with instant dread. They need distractions. We all need distractions. 6/x

6.9K 274 1.1K

**Go To Sleep**
**@Insomnia**

Our society hinges upon the decisions you make today. You learn everything about yourself during a crisis. We have to fight for each other instead of with each other. Stay safe. Take care of one another. It's all we have. 7/x

♡ 1.3K 💬 42 ⟳ 978

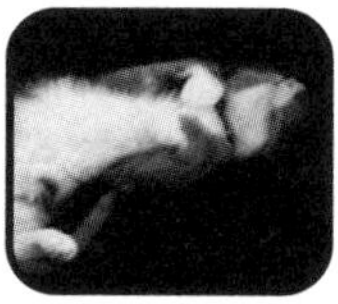

**Go To Sleep**
**@Insomnia**

Take a break. Talk to your friends over the phone. Get away from your screens. All we have is right now. Hang in there. We're in this together. Stay healthy. Stay inside. Know you're not alone. 8/8

♡ 1.9K 💬 37 ⟳ 403

# Day 35

If you're all alone on an island, how do you know if you're going crazy?

I'm kidding of course (~~or am I~~?). I have Maurice, who is not an amazing conversationalist, but he's a good listener (although downside: He has breathtaking body odor. I mean "breathtaking" as in "take my breath, please!") (/cue Rodney Dangerfield) (I may not be losing my mind, but I'm losing my funny).

There was an awe-inspiring shark attack today. (Here are photos if you click this link but it's gross because it's a shark ripping up an elephant seal, so you've been warned!) I had a box seat to the viscera and grunting and sucking. You wouldn't think sharks would be noisy eaters, but they are efficient as they bisect the torso. A lot of shaking and ripping. The birds are the loudest, though. They each egg the shark on, hoping for a tasty morsel. I love the sharks. I hate the birds. Fucking birds. "Hello, I'm a bird! Seal meat, please!" The birds never do anything for the sharks . . . It's a bullshit relationship. ~~They're like blog commenters.~~

I miss sharing these moments with Rick and Pedro. I miss being able to ask questions. I even miss Patty thinking I'm a landlubber with no fucking clue (which is true).

The sharks keep on keeping on. There are spatters of blood and blubber while they're having breakfast (or perhaps elevensies) and they don't care if they make a mess. It's all what they have to do for survival. They need to get fat to make the trek back to somewhere east of Hawaii, to that great white shark nursery where they play hide-and-seek with giant squids and have turf wars with killer whales.

~~Sometimes I think about going for a swim. I know my body wouldn't be nearly as delicious or fulfilling as an elephant seal's, and the shark might not even want to tangle with my choice bits, but it seems like a beautiful way to go.~~

Sharks keep moving. They can't swim backward. They keep going and the birds take care of their leftovers. A beautiful thing if you think about it.

Don't worry. I'm not going to go for a swim today. ~~But it's good to know there are options.~~

Stay safe out there.
Jane

**Wolf News WNBS**
**@WNBSNews**

Newborn baby tests positive for nSFI in Barcelona hospital
http://www.bit.ly.com/infantnsfi

♡ 4.8K 2.4K 9.1K

**DB Cooper**
**@DBmm**

For the first time in my entire single-mom existence, not having sex for most of this year has been a good idea and socially responsible. Look at me, being all holistic and giving back.

118 3 6

# Day 36

JANE

The internet's back again after a few hours of deadness. I make the most of it, copying and pasting the emails I've written while offline: missives to Kylie; to my former roommate and sometimes least favorite person in the world; to Brian; to my Aunt Heidi, who still hasn't been responsive; to Heidi's neighbor, asking her to call the satellite phone. I still have plenty of signal, so I copy/paste a giant list of email addresses on blind copy:

> I know everyone is dealing with the same crap—but perhaps one of you has access to a boat or a helicopter and would be willing to play superman to my damsel in distress. I'm alone on Southeast Farallon Island (link to Google Earth location) and very scared. The crew of scientists who were here with me are gone—evacuated, committed suicide, or disappeared. I have dwindling food and water supplies, but weirdly, a decent internet connection. I need help. I'm serious. **I need help.** The Coast Guard isn't risking evac for a single person who isn't dying in the next few hours—and maybe even if they are dying. I have to admit I have it better off than some. So here's the deal—I'm pretty safe on this island but I want to get off. You bring a boat and help me out and you're more than welcome to bunker down on the island until this craziness is over. Yours truly, Jane.

I reread it. How well do I know the people who will receive this? Barely. They might be more interested in this situation than my safety. It seems stupid to send it. Hope isn't a thing with feathers. It's a creature with claws. *Scrabble scrabble scrabble* inside my chest.

I click the Trash button and the draft is gone.

**Wolf News WNBS**
**@WNBSNews**

Stephen King panned for pointing out United Nations WHO H3N2/nSFI task force is 100% male and 100% white
http://www.bit.ly.com/UNtaskforce

♡ 49K 💬 1.4K ⟳ 8.7K

**DB Cooper**
**@DBmm**

You know how we're all acting like we forgot how to enjoy reading? Maybe we didn't forget—maybe the problem was society replacing connection with emphasis on work and wealth, and device screens are the result.

♡ 6 💬 2 ⟳ 0

# Day 38

JANE

Brian's emails have gone quiet. His last email was vague.

Dear Amelia Earhart—

They say that's how Ms. Earhart met her end, stranded on a deserted island with a guy who was supposed to be giving the travel authenticity—a real man's man, according to the newsreels. We all know how that ended up. Amelia would have been better off following your fine example.

I'm at my wits' end, Jane, I'm not going to lie. The river is frozen now—the sanctity of my little island has been compromised. I'm certain someone crossed the ice the other day, but so far, no sign of them. Hatches were battened, keels were hauled. Perhaps someday soon I'll load up my grease beast and make my way to San Francisco, where the two of us can hide away at the top of the Hilton or maybe that fancy Marriott in SoMA and have ourselves some nice bourbon and Brussels sprout cocktails. Or whatever the hipsters are drowning their sorrows in these days. I was never one for the hipsters—one of my better failings.

I do hope your aunt is simply at the hospital rather than out in the weather. Unfortunately, everything is so surreal you wouldn't believe it even if you could see it. Islanders as we are, we can do no better than Ms. Earhart and simply sit back and wait for someone to save us. Well, you certainly wouldn't wait. I probably shouldn't, as my island is swiftly becoming a non-island by virtue of the dropping mercury. Stupid meteorology.

Until I see you, keep passing the open windows.

-B

A bit maudlin. Typical Brian's wallowing and penchant for the melodramatic at times. But there is a detachment below the lines, the subtext of something more. He always pushes at something more, longing, lonely, and the urge feels compelling, sucks at me to fill that emptiness in his life. But in the end, I know that he is damaged, his cracks filled in with gold like a wabi-sabi kintsugi repair, beautiful but still ultimately sharp, brittle, and likely to wound. I love our friendship, but his need for me to adore him feels like a payment of sorts. He will always need it. It will always be one-sided in real life. He is only capable of reciprocity within the constraint of a tiny glowing window.

In Mirounga Bay, a seal hunts. A purple plastic Rubbermaid container floats upside down in the bay, stained. Too far to snag with the pole. Probably empty. It looks like one of Kylie's bins, but that must be a coincidence. I wish someone at the Coast Guard would answer the radio, at least to talk about Rick and Pedro.

The wind kicks up again. I check the mooring on the inflatable boat. How much gas does it have? It sounds empty. There's a full tank by the machine shed. If I can get the whaler down off the cliff and unhook it from the crane by myself. All or nothing. Certainly not worth it for a purple bin, probably empty, and certainly can't wouldn't shouldn't be Kylie's.

*And even if it's Kylie's, it's not like you can save her now.*

"Hello," I say to the purple bin, fading in and back out again with the waves, in and out, in and out. "Hello," I say to myself. "You're going to be OK."

That night, I wake with a start. There has been a voice. Or what might have been a voice—the auklets sometimes sound like words extorted. The owl grunts. A SEFI mouse for dinner. The owl sounds exactly like the neighbor, Frank McCorkle, who lived next to my grandmother's house from when I was five until twelve, until he died of a heart attack in the backyard one hot day while trying to change his pool filter. "Monica!" the owl says, like Mr. McCorkle. "Monica! Mon! Mon!"

Something sticky in the toe of my left shoe—mouse shit and piss, undoubtedly. Somewhere in the room, rasping again. The mouse—or ghost child—is back. I prefer the ghost child to the mice. The ghost is far less interested in chewing out the crotches of my underwear.

I flip on the light, but no mouse movement. That's good. The rasping continues without a hitch. "It's OK, sweetie," I murmur to the room.

The old logbooks detail the hauntings of SEFI—seeking a natural and reasonable explanation. Scientists prefer to believe in subterranean caves making low-frequency rumblings when the tide is at a certain level, the island becoming a beacon to drive us slowly crazy, rattle the fluid in our eyeballs until we start seeing ghosts out of the corners of our eyes. If impossible behemoth prehistoric sharks can patrol the late October waters like myths come to life, shouldn't I also believe in the possibility of lost souls? Or believe in a virus preventing people from falling asleep, tiny proteins in the brain nibbling their dreamworld, and then why not a lighthouse keeper's child, still bitter at being snuffed out for want of a simple bottle of penicillin?

The stairs creak.

I freeze. I wait.

Nothing.

Creep along the edges of the room, try not to hit the squeaky parts of the floor. The door is closed, but it faces the stairs. If I open it, whoever is there will be face-to-face with me, nose to nose, breathing my breath.

Wait. Heartbeat.

Breathe. Heartbeat.

Wait. Nothing.

The rasping in the room stops, replaced by the skittering of a mouse.

The air feels different again. If I open the door, there will be nothing. But moments ago, there *was* something. A something. A some and a thing. Whatever momentary magic was over. To prove it, I fling the door open wide and flip the light on with the same motion. The staircase is empty, of course.

*Of course.*

The door at the bottom is open. I closed it on the way to bed, without fail, like a paranoid spinster. I am, after all, truly a spinster with anxiety, an aging unmarried female with neuroses, with too much imagination. It's not paranoia if they're really after you.

On the marine terrace, the night is still, the ever-present mist a blanket of haze. Auklets fly back to their little burrows, tiny splashes of pepper against the moonlight. A seal vocalizes nonstop. I step out into the night, the smell of fetid seal dung wafting up from the cove. Over by the crane, a figure stands, bracing against the wind, outlined as a solid shape.

It isn't a trick—someone IS there.

"Patty!" I shout as hard as I can over the roaring waves. "Patty!" I grab some rain gear and run back. "Hey!" I shout again.

The figure is gone, disappeared in a blink. The sea churns, spitting briny spray up into my face, even though I'm fifty feet from the ledge. My sneaker slips. I slow into a careful trot. The seaside shelf is vacant, oiled in the moonlight with algae, seaweed, and bracken. Of course, no one's there.

Another trick of the light, a trick of my heart.

This entire time, I've been waiting for something. I've been waiting to be saved, for a white knight to swoop up in a yacht and carry me to safety.

I'm safe. This is safety. *This Is Your New Family, Honey.*

A lurking plan pushes forward. A boat. Survival gear. Weapons. Rations. It is maybe now or never. Maybe now? Maybe. Never.

Back in the kitchen, I set to work, making a large pot of oatmeal while whipping up some dehydrated eggs and setting them in a cake pan, where they congeal into a sulfurous rubbery mat. It will do for instant protein. In the cupboard is also some emu and elk jerky—those go into the bag, along with a small pack of peanuts and a jar of cashew butter. Finally, water—there are several water desalination kits in the storage room. Some dusty backpacks that seem shiny, like maybe they're waterproof. I stuff two desalination kits into one, think better of it, and throw a third in.

I might freeze out there and what if I got swept out to sea? I can't think about that right now, that loneliness, the legs dangling in the water, waiting for the giant shark named Roger, waiting for his sisters. I pack my clothing and gear, including my laptop and cameras and lenses, wrapping them in heavy-duty black garbage bags just in case. I distribute everything across a few different bags in case one gets lost overboard. I'm using the knowledge gained from a childhood of reading survival stories, *Julie of the Wolves*, *Island of the Blue Dolphins*, the rugby team that crashed in the Andes, even racist old Huck Finn. The utility room reveals the red headlamp Kylie used at the birding net—might use for signaling? Seems solid. I'm Action Jane.

A knock on the door.

It's an entirely benign and normal sound and without thinking of how strange it is, I jump up, as though it might be a delivery driver dropping off a package. Then I stop. I'm alone on the island. Who is knocking. It's not a question. Who. The idea of Who is an entity and I freeze. The knocking again. Who is there.

I step closer to the door and then away from it. I could hang here, caught in this moment, perhaps forever, lingering between decision and formation, the heartbeats stretching into nothing. The knock again, belying the passage of time.

Who is getting impatient.

"Jane?" shouts a voice behind the door. Who knows my name. Who is waiting there. The Who. I think about the owls—perhaps they have come to deliver messages from Elsewhere.

"Jane? Let me in." The voice is male. I should grab the large flashlight, to use perhaps as a weapon against the Who behind the door. Who is male. Who can knock.

"It's Patty," the voice says.

This breaks my trance. Patty has a voice again. I'm not alone. I peek out the window—Patty stands there, hair askew. His face is haggard, eyes sunken. I unlock the deadbolt.

"Patty," I say, not as a question or even as a fact, rather a rearranging of the reality. How many days has it been? "Where were you?"

He shakes off his wet raincoat like a dog drying off and lets it fall to his feet, then, thinking better of it, hangs it up on a peg. He grunts, kicks off his boots, socks making damp footprints.

"Hey, can we talk in a bit? I'm exhausted and I need to sleep," he says, rubbing his hands through his hair, which contains grit and small feathers. He smells of pink peppercorn and vetiver, of flannel and seaweed and leather. I want to hug him, pinch him, punch him.

"Um, sure, yeah." I say, but then add, "Where were you? Where have you been this whole time?"

He heads toward the stairs. "Rabbit Cave. No flies." This is a logical progression for Patty, a finality. Nothing has been answered, but I let him go without challenge. It will come out later.

I wasn't abandoned on this island. This story needs to be rewritten. For now, I'm not a survivor, I was an afterthought. I wasn't alone. I was never alone.

Even in my most fucked-up happenstance, I can't even manage to do that right.

Upstairs, his stompy gait, the bed creaking. Out the window, the skies rumble as a storm whips the waves into a chopping mess, flurries of white salty sprays at the cliffs. The idea of going to sleep with the door unlocked seems unappealing, but so does the idea of going to sleep with Patty in the next room. I click the deadbolt into place and turn off the outer light.

Up in my room, the ghost child sighs. Probably not actually a ghost, I think, as though the reemergence of another human has reset superstitions and gothic fantasies—particularly a nonsensical scientific human like Patty, who has a way of cutting through bullshit like no one I've ever met. Particularly my bullshit.

As if to answer my resolution about the nonexistence of spirits, the chair in the corner creaks, and then the springs on the empty bed whine as though someone has crossed the room and sat down. No depressions or dimples in the smooth woolen blanket. The coils groan again as though to say, *Yes, you heard right. I'm still here.*

Out on the marine terrace, the shape is out there in the darkness and sea spray. It's the same shape I kept thinking was Patty, but he's snoring deep and steady across the hall.

Lightning webs across the sky, and in the staccato thrums of light, the dark shape, solid but lacking definition or features, a shadow taken on corporeal form. It moves without legs, a fog or sprite or shade or—

*It's* ***your*** *shadow, dummy.* The idea rears forth as though whispered by my guardian angel. I move my arm and its arm moves. I move my head and the figure's head swells upward, growing larger and larger until it blends with the darkness.

Just a shadow.

It feels like the house has changed with Patty's return, as though the house has realized it must behave itself now that Dad is home. Even the air feels different, less volatile, more domesticated. I close the blinds and turn out the light. "Good night," I say to the room. The bed shudders in response.

I fall into a deep luxurious sleep, the kind experienced by children in the backseats of station wagons. Even the food supply doesn't bother me—Patty will have some plan of action, some way to take care of us.

In the morning, I hope the smell of coffee will rouse Patty from his intense slumber. His snores have taken on a more intentional tone, as though in warning to anyone who might think of waking him. They are serious business, these snores.

Now that Patty is back, even the coffee tastes different—it had previously tasted acrid and lonely, but now it has the convivial feel of a dark coffeehouse blend. I feel like a Valkyrie, brutal and beautiful, ready to take up arms in solidarity, and then I hate myself for having such a mindset change because a man has appeared on the horizon. I'm not Rapunzel. I didn't let down my hair, and yet it feels this way. I push these annoying thoughts away. Besides, Patty has not saved anyone. He has certainly not saved me from anything.

Wind and rain buffet the house. I note the weather conditions in the SEFI journals, write about the reappearance of master birder Patty, and omit commentary about the decibels of his snoring and the way the air smells different with him in the house.

Then the outside doorknob wiggles against its lock. I jump, hairs rising on the back of my neck. Has Patty gotten out of the house somehow? No, upstairs he gurgles and makes a large snort, partially wakened by the banging.

The banging is on the outer door. "Hello?" A woman's voice. From the kitchen window—a bulky shape, poncho hood squinched tight around the face.

"Hi Jane! I've got a bunch of action boxes here—can you get on your gear and help? Get the trash too—the boat needs to get back before curfew."

This woman knows me somehow. She sees my confusion and opens her hood more—it doesn't help. Her shiny wet red face is unfamiliar. "Jane, it's me, Liz."

"Oh!" I feel ridiculous, but I've never seen Liz without glasses. "Sorry. Hi. Hi. Yes, I'll get my stuff."

Then I remember the bodies.

"Rick and Pedro are dead."

"I know. You wrote about it on your blog. We've been calling the satellite phone repeatedly every day, but you weren't answering. It was kind of against regulations, to be honest, but we knew we needed to get out here. We're removing . . . them." Out the window, dancing flashlights in the Coast Guard house, globes flickering against the walls and windows.

I avert my eyes. I don't want to feel guilty that I didn't—couldn't—do more. At least put a sheet over them, something. What a coward.

Liz rifles through the mess in the office and finds a machine, lights blinking. She presses the button. A recording of her own voice, concerned, tinny, coming across the ether from an answering machine.

There's an answering machine?

"Jane, we saw your blog post. Please call us back as soon as possible. Is Patty there? We are gathering our crew together and it may be a while, but there are authorities who have questions." Another message, older, someone's voice: "Hello, this is Allan Berskinsky, looking for Pedro or Rick or Patty. Please radio or email the agency as soon as possible. Use the emergency channel." The messages keep coming, interspersed by beeps, each sounding more and more futile. How could I have known?

I linger in the doorway. Liz won't meet my eyes. She gathers and sorts some of the flurry of loose paperwork and tightens the stacks, tap tap tapping them on the desktop. It is something she can be doing right now, instead of talking or looking at me. "There are some authorities who will want to talk to you about Rick and Pedro—about what happened. Do you know where the gun is now?"

I shake my head. "I didn't go back over there afterward." That dark shape. "Patty is upstairs sleeping. Maybe he found it?"

Liz stops and looks directly at me. "Patty? Sleeping, you said? Rick reported him ill with the virus." Her voice lowers, worried Patty might hear. She knows the eerie way voices and sounds travel in this house, through nonphysical channels and air currents. Anything is possible. We listen to his rhythmic snores.

"See? Asleep," I say again. I'm unhelpful. I'm once again a liability.

Liz hums through her lips. "Yes. They're going to need to check each of you out, but they're dealing with the—the other house now." Her voice catches on the reference to Rick and Pedro.

"I'm sorry, Liz." I'm a pale substitute for a fresh heart; a reasonable voice is all I offer.

"Thanks." She nods, looking at the ceiling for a moment. I feel this moment, as the crescendo of tears dares to fall down her cheeks. I never grieved Pedro and Rick. I left them there. Deep shame burrows behind my sternum. This is always how it is. In the end, it's always me.

"Did he—did Rick or Pedro say anything or give any signs of, they were, they would . . . um, *that*?" She can't say the word *suicide*. No one can.

I shake my head. "Nope. No warning. They were concerned about Patty, focused on where he was or might have gone. He was hiding in Rabbit Cave, though? To try to protect us from being exposed?" I've taken on Kylie's question voice now. "Have you heard from Kylie at all?" Changing the subject feels right.

"No, not after we disembarked in Berkeley. I think she and Omar were staying with friends in South Bay. A ride picked them up. The city has been in total shelter-in-place the last two weeks, curfew, more shelter-in-place probably at least another two weeks, or, I don't know, months maybe given how the rest of the country is going. They say it will only be two weeks, but I don't know how that could even be true. Unless you're a vital worker, grocery shopping is during certain hours only, in Berkeley and Oakland. They're not allowed to be on the streets or gather, or they'll get a fine or be arrested. We left from Bodega Bay, otherwise we wouldn't have been able to even get out. I got lucky because we live near Stinson."

I nod. "Does this mean . . . I mean, I'm kind of done here, right? Do you still need me here?"

She stops, looks as though she's never noticed me. The idea they would *need* me seems absurd now that I say it out loud. "Yes," she says carefully. "We don't need you, but there's no room on this boat. Not with Rick and Pedro and the team. We didn't think Patty was going to turn up on his own—we thought we'd have to search and rescue. Maybe you didn't know where to look. Anyway, until Patty gets med checked, I'd appreciate the company. Collin's down there, planning on staying, and I think the DNR guy is staying too, but it would be good to have another face to handle the work we have in front of us. Plus, it's never nice to be the only female on the island." She winces again, looking at the ceiling.

I nod again. "The food. There's not much food." The sack of supplies sits conspicuously on the table. I was going to use it get off the island? What would that look like? Preposterous. I couldn't save myself. I overreacted. Ridiculous. I can hear my grandmother spit the words inside my brain. *Our dumpy little Jane, unable to think straight, thinking she's better than everyone while she falls on her own face.*

"We brought a core set of supplies, typical fare, two weeks' worth. No special orders, of course, but there are some fresh blackberries I managed to snag from a self-serve farm stand in Petaluma. Shouldn't be contagious but I'll wash 'em good so." My mouth waters at the thought of freshness. It feels better with Liz here, Liz and Patty. I can make this work. *This is your new family, honey.* Action Jane is instantly replaced with At Your Service Jane, a series of masks I put on, affecting even the way my muscles feel in my body. Patty is back. Patty will make things normal again.

The outer door opens and closes, and then the inner door from the fly defense station replies. Heavy footsteps—someone has neglected to remove their shoes. It feels weird to be in the house with people again, even though it hasn't been so long. Somehow the time spent alone in the house has grown, shifted inside my head and body, muscles and spine morphing into an animal protecting its burrow. Liz and Patty and these heavy footsteps, they feel like an attack.

A head pokes in, adjusting a doctor's face mask. "We're going to be awhile over there, but there's a sailboat off North Landing. Guy on it says he's looking for the blogger and is acting freaked out. We don't think he's infected because he sailed all the way here, but, you know, who knows."

They both look at me. My eyes. My blog. Someone has come for me. Someone answered.

Brian? He's my person.

Liz shrugs and says, "OK, fine, go go go." She shoos me away like she does a kelp fly.

Off the landing, two boats, one a fishing boat, blue and choppy against the waves, the other a full-scale sailboat with two gleaming masts, looking improbably chic against the waves and rough scale of Sugarloaf. They are anchored nose to nose, looking ready to throw blows, like dancing prizefighters.

A man stands by the yacht's two main sails, waving his arms. This is his moment, almost heroic, maybe. I pull out my small digital camera, thirty megapixels. Great bokeh. Photos of him standing there on the deck, Odysseus, returning from war, would be perfect. I don't know who he is, but I do know how the social media post will be worded, the hashtags, the sponsorships and affiliate links, the likes. Instead, I slip the camera back into a pocket. No one will care about this as much as I care. *No one will care as much as I care. Remember this.*

Remember this.

# Day 35

**Wolf News WNBS**
**@WNBSNews**

Will the US midterm election be canceled due to virus fears? Hear from Congresswoman Angela Stahlkoph http://www.apnews.com

16.4K 25 4.9K

**Mychelle**
**@MightyMych**

My trip to Israel is canceled. My other trip to Iceland is also canceled. One because they have too many cases of #H3N2 and the other because they aren't letting filthy foreigners into their country. Guess I'll put the money I would have spent into something else more indulgent, like food.

69 14 2

**Xi**
**@sXlilate**

There's not a lot of things I wouldn't do for a dirty martini and a long glance across a crowded room with a mysterious stranger right now. #shelterinplace #hardtimes

♡ 75 💬 2 ⟳ 0

**Wolf News WNBS**
**@WNBSNews**

Spa hostage standoff in Murray, Utah has been resolved with minimal fatalities, sheriff says. Death toll pending notification of families. Spa to reopen Friday.

♡ 17.5K 💬 1.9K ⟳ 698

**Amy**
**@AmyBedeliaBrown**

Would it be weird if I just, like, shaved my head? That would be weird, right? And yet, it's all I can think about. It's not like I'm going anywhere—this is the time to do it, right?

♡ 1.3K 💬 46 ⟳ 89

# Day 36

BRIAN

I didn't know if his number would still work, but it was worth a try.

"Taylor?"

"You have five seconds, man, or I hang up. I don't have much battery on my phone."

"It's Brian Arden. I need your help."

There was a pause. "Oh, Brian! Holy shit, man! Long time, no see. I . . . uh . . . I know it's been a while and I owe you a phone call about the . . . the loan."

"Hey, no big deal. Are you OK? Are you in a safe place?" It was all I could do to not jump up and down.

"Safe as a fucking bug in a rug, dude. I bugged out as soon as I got wind of the . . . this shit going down. Holy crap, man, are YOU OK? I mean, are you . . . are you sleeping and stuff?" The reception crackled in and out. It sounded like Taylor was on the moon, like he was answering from another place and time in history.

"Absolutely. Seriously, Taylor, it's so good to hear your voice. I can't even say how good it is. Man, I missed you. I didn't realize how much I missed you." Against my own will, I started to choke up a little. Being in a place of need was foreign. I liked even less admitting weakness to someone like Taylor.

"You too, man. You too. Thanks for calling to see if I made it out OK. It means a lot. Really a lot. You know, you're the only person who has checked up on me? That's like . . . it's huge. I mean, I know when I was using, I burned a lot of bridges. A LOT of bridges. But I've been clean for five years and even though I have a bunch of people I know from NA—people I thought were my friends and shit? They didn't even call. Not a one, man.

Not a fucking one. After the app took off, basically it's all about the money, but right now, not even the money matters."

Even clean and sober, Taylor was still worried about how people owed him. The irritation was flustering, and I fought against hanging up.

"Taylor, that's great. I'm there for you, man, you know that, right? Just like . . . like how I paid for your boat. And remember how I went up to Montecito with you? Remember that?"

"Yeah. I do remember that." Taylor's voice snapped from reminiscent to wary. He was street-smart enough to know when someone wanted something from him.

"I need a favor, man. I need the favor this time."

"Look, if it's to come and stay on the boat, I'd love to, man, but I don't have the room, OK? Or the water. It's the water. I mean, I could probably host you for a few days, considering . . . I don't know, though. The water, dude. The water is a killer for me. You can't find potable water in the Bay Area right now. I'm rationing. Also, toilet paper, if we're going to be real. You can hang your ass off the side of the boat to shit into the ocean and feed them lil fishies, but you still need to wipe with something."

"No no no, Taylor, listen, I don't need a place to stay. It's not even like that. I need a ride. A friend needs a lift. That's all. I'll even get you some more water."

Taylor brightened. "Oh, you need a lift? Well, let's go on a fucking boat trip."

What I had loved about Taylor and the thing that made me put up with him—he was always game for an adventure.

And for Jane, I would do anything.

**Doctors Without Borders**
**@drwoborders**

H3N2 appears to have been successfully contained in Yakutsk; we've concluded our emergency response.

32.3K 2.9K 20.3K

**Wolf News WNBS**
**@WNBSNews**

H3N2-inspired TikTok dance video reminds viewers to wash hands and avoid contact http://www.bit.ly.com/H3N2dance

3.3K 165 905

**DB Cooper**
**@DBmm**

I got into an argument with my mother about why she can't go out to the store and has to wait for me. Because you can't chop chicken without touching the remote with your chicken hands, Judith, how can you be trusted to leave the house in a pandemic?

39 7 9

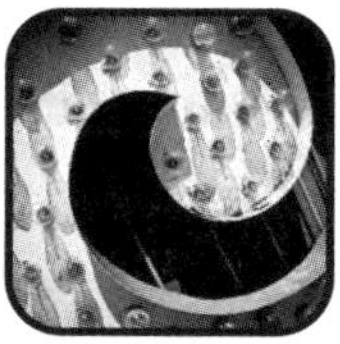

**Jane**
**@erejane**

"Stay safe" is the new "goodbye."

36.2K 842 24.5K

# Day 39

JANE

I thought it was Brian. It's not Brian.

He extends a well-manicured hand and hoists me up to the deck. His skin is chalky, pebbled, and irritated, like he's been washing with salt water.

"Hey girlie!" He smiles broadly. "I'm Taylor. Aw, you know what? You've been on an island, so you're safe to hug."

He pulls me in fast, holding me against his chest for much longer than anyone would be comfortable with. A two-second hug turns into four and then eight and then a full twenty or thirty seconds of listening to the wind and Taylor's heart beating *buboom buboom buboom*, smelling the brine and sweat on him. He releases me but grasps my shoulders, stifling a gulp of air.

One of his pupils is dilated wide, frozen from a past trauma, with a red vein snaking out to the corner of the iris.

"Jane, dude, I've been such a fan of yours for so long. You helped me get clean. Back when I was using, I was living with these guys, and they'd pass around your blog posts like they were clues to how to get laid. I remember one guy would go off about how the secret was argyle socks or something. But me, you and me are alike. It meant something, you know? One post of yours about the unlikely chance we each were born, how we were the result of a string of ancestors? It was power, man. You're power. Fucking POWER."

He pulls me close again and I don't resist. *Buboom buboom baboom.* It feels so strange to be this close to another person. It feels strange, knowing I could be infected if he's been reading the blog. He could be infected. His heart, his breathing chest. I relax and lean into it for a second and then pull back.

"Thanks, Taylor, I appreciate it. You're power too. You're a star," I say. It comes easier now, this being around people, merging the concept of Artificial Me and Now Me. Who inspired Taylor? Which one is she?

He spreads his arms wide and laughs. "Welcome to my boat, man. I can't believe Jane Fucking 'Ere is on my goddamned BOAT right now. It took a pandemic, huh? Well, another one." He laughs again.

I nod. It has taken everything. My shoes are soaked. When did my shoes get wet? They squeak against the decking.

"I want to get going, lift anchor, but walk around with me while I do stuff and I'll show you around at the same time, OK? I'm going to have to work fast since it's a one-man crew here, but we'll need to get out a bit using our engine before we lift sail."

I follow him obediently as he works through making ready, Mary's little lamb, a role I know well. So many Jane 'Ere projects require this acquiescence. He talks about spending his addiction withdrawal time sanding and rebuilding the hull. Then he stops and says, "It's OK if you want to film this. You know, for the blog readers. Might be good content."

This is always how it is with new people. They want their moment, like Tabby and Ash and Ben and Patrick and a bunch of other people I'll never let close enough to bite. My pocket camera's reassuring weight is a signal firing something in my cerebral cortex, a flip of a switch inside my personality. Once again, I'm just an eye, a conduit for the world. The responsibility for this moment is focused through the recording device. I ask him to repeat his addictions, the specific types of substances he used, because it's necessary for the audience. Context. Trigger warnings. Search engine keyword terms. Hashtags. All of this. All this.

Under the camera's eye, Taylor is even more engaged. The sunlight bounces off the waves, making his cheekbones sharp, his eyes more hazel. Instead of an unshaven jawline, the gray-and-silver beard stubble glitters in the sunlight. I should use a handheld microphone—the sound of the waves will be hell to edit against, but I move closer to him, closer, until his face fills the frame. He pauses and nods and launches into an anecdote about recovery. In this version, Taylor is his own inspiration. My blog doesn't get airtime. I don't matter. He mentions his Instagram handle, spelling it with the at sign, and then his personal website. He uses the words "marine conservation" and "nautical soul quest" and "selfie moments" and "artisanal curated Pacific experience."

I ask what advice he wants to give readers of Jane 'Ere about their own struggles. He nods and takes a breath, starts to speak but his voice catches, and then something in his face changes and he is vulnerable.

In almost a whisper, he says, "It's important to ask for help and recognize we gotta love one another. None of us can do this alone. I had a bunch of people who believed in me and supported me and I kind of shit on them for helping me, but they kept giving. They kept leaning forward and extending a hand. We gotta love one another, man, even when someone doesn't treat you right, because we got loved even when we didn't deserve it."

His voice catches again. I keep the camera steady, using my hips and a wide stance. One breath. Two breaths. He has tears in his eyes.

"My friend Brian gave me a huge monetary investment for this boat we're sitting on. I shit on him so many times. I thought he wouldn't want to speak to me. When I got to steps eight and nine and did my apologies and made amends, I skipped him. I was too ashamed. Every day is a journey and I'm working on my Brian amends right now—I'm being my friend Jane's freaking water limo right now."

He smiles, breaking the mood with his joke, coming back to me. Then he inhales deeply and exhales again. "But you know, words count. And I'm sorry, Brian. I fucked up so hard and I'm so sorry. You gave me all this and I owe you ten times what you gave me and then some. So here's to you, brother. You're my brother and you have my heart and my back, and I have yours."

He hits his chest with a fist and then wipes tears from his face. He's done. He looks into the camera, eyes blinking.

I put down the camera and rub his arm, squeezing. He puts a hand over mine and nods, understanding a message I've sent to him without words, without narration, without the reach of my voice into his ear.

His hand is rough and calloused. Then he says, "OK! Let's get this show on the road!" And the spell is broken.

As Taylor works, he talks of the restoration, the transom he had to cannibalize from another craft, the jammers he shined for hours, the special bottom paint he procured from Norway to resist marine growth. The sails cost over ten grand alone, and the work on the hull-to-deck joint took a full year. I nod appropriately, excited for Taylor the way I would be excited for new parents or first-time homebuyers. I'm so caught up in the microscopic details of the ship and how the perfection matches the cleanliness of Taylor's addicted soul that I don't notice until too late that we've left SEFI. I squint to the horizon. Taylor has been explaining how to steer using the giant Gilligan's Island steering wheel. The boat is turning a zigzag to catch the wind in her sails, but SEFI is nowhere, not port, not starboard. Not aft.

"Which way was the island? I can't see it anymore." He turns and squints behind me, over the long zipper of wake in the water. Then he consults the radar and points at the cluster of islands, barely discernible on the screen, acne, a pockmarked smudge. I stare, trying to see the clock Kylie described—Sugarloaf, Maintop Bay, North Landing, all the harsh geographic features of my last known address, my lifeline. Missing on the radar are so many things, the Great Murre Cave, the skeleton of the lady, the elephant seal and his musk harem, the lighthouse and its Fresnel lens, my lensel friend, the ghost child, Patty. *Goodbye*, I think, *goodbye goodbye goodbye.*

Taylor catches me yawning and points to a free berth. The idea of releasing control, of letting down guard around another stranger seems impossible now, after all this. I crawl in and close my eyes, focusing on the swaying of the boat, pretending I control it like a rocking chair or a porch swing, the glider on my grandmother's front porch, where I hid every day during summer, nested inside the worlds of Prince Edward Island with Anne Shirley, or creating the Honeycomb with the rabbits on *Watership Down*. Who wouldn't like a warren to dig down into, hide against the world? And really, that's exactly what I had on the island, a warren of safety and seclusion—and I'm sailing away from it toward something. What is the thing? An idea of something, then. A ghost of a past lifetime I'm destined to swim toward again and again. And Brian—did I understand? Taylor knows Brian?

I must have napped because suddenly there's a ringing bell and a marina, mostly empty. Taylor sees me. "You've been sleeping for hours, milady. I'm glad you can appreciate how gorgeous the nautical sleep is."

Taylor rubs his own eyes. How long's he been working to rescue me? "Oh my God, Taylor, I'm sorry—what an asshole I am to sleep. I should have steered or something."

"Aw, what kind of hero routine would that be if the damsel in distress had to direct the horse while Dudley Do-Right took a nap?" He wiped his hand across his face and slapped his cheek, once, twice. "But I'm gonna get you back to the marina so you can do your blog, upload those videos, huh? Then I'm going to get back to my secret sleeping cove and catch my own Z's."

A gentle bump against the pier and I'm back. A man on the other side of the dock is wearing an n95 face mask and carrying a Starbucks cup. He waves. It is painfully banal and breaks the dream of being on the island, as though none of this ever happened. Now there are boring things to think about.

"Any idea if I can get a ride share from way out here to Berkeley? I mean, I know it will cost a million dollars but still. I need to get a rental car."

"No-go, madam. No-go. Berkeley is a hot zone. You can't go back there—I doubt they'd let you in. National Guard is there to keep them in and everyone else out. Rental car places are closed anyway. You know what? Wait a second, take my car. It's over there, see it? Black one? License says EH HEE?"

I look but don't see. "No, you don't understand—I'm going to need to drive back home. I live in Wisconsin. The Midwest. Airplane travel is stopped right now, right?"

He nods. "Yeah, no planes flying. Airports are germy, I can't even imagine being stuffed in a tin tube with a screamer anyway. You drive and do it through the less populated areas. Most cities are on lockdown. Gonna take a while. I'd let you stay here with me, but . . ." He wipes his eyes again.

"Oh, you've done too much already. I mean, I don't have a good place to hunker down here in California, and I want to get back. It's a long distance."

He shrugs. "You're a FOB. Friend of Brian. I trust you with my car, hell, more than that."

"Brian. You mean Brian Arden, right?" Who else he would mean? I only know one Brian.

"Yeah. That's the Brian I was talking about. On the video. For your website." Taylor's voice is sluggish. The sun sinks in the ambiguous gray way of a Pacific sunset, a gradual reduction in light; a creeping darkness along the briny coast settles into my bones. It has become second nature. *My lesnel friends.*

"Yeah, Brian Arden. He gave me the money for this boat. He's the one who told me about your being stuck on the island. He asked me if I would mind getting you. I mean, I would have thought of it myself, I would do anything for someone down on their luck, but for Brian? I would give him the world if he asked, and all he's ever asked me for was to go and save you."

"Is he OK? He hasn't been responding to my emails."

"I talked to him last night, well, yesterday, probably around 7 p.m., so 9 or 10 p.m. Wisconsin time? He sounded fine. He told me your exact coordinates, and we talked about how far it was and how long it would take me to get there."

"Did he sound OK? What did he say?"

He rubs his eyes. "That you were all alone. He would have come if he could have but he knew it would take so long. I think he was worried about breaking some kind of rule you have? I wasn't quite clear." He yawns again. "I'm sorry, I'm exhausted. I gotta get to sleep. So, take the car. Her name is Sinead, she's a *she* like the boat. Treat her good and she'll get you back to Wisconsin. Hand her off to Brian until I come out—probably wouldn't be until the snow is gone, though. It will save me money on parking fees at the marina anyway, so you'd be doing me a favor. Would you believe these assholes are charging me for my dock fee AND for parking my car in their lot? Twenty bucks a day to park if you can believe it." He sighs and shakes his head. "I've got to get out of California. Welp, one of these days. Let me go get the keys."

When he returns, he clasps his hand over mine again, holding it there, trapping it. "Hey, other parts of the country aren't hit as bad as here—you shouldn't have a hard time getting gas and water, but maybe make sure to have extra water. Avoid Chicago too. I wouldn't stop the car within 100 miles of Chicago. Virus is so thick it's practically visible in the air."

I thank him again, then ask for a selfie with my front pocket camera. I'll regret it later if I don't get one, and the idea seems to thrill Taylor. In the frame, Taylor knits his brows together and looks off into the distance, an aging rock star making a triumphant return solo album, hugging me to his chest. I mumble something about a guest post and then disembark. He tosses down my bags, which both land on the dock with a tragic clump. The laptop is in there, cameras, the lenses. I decide it will be fine. This will be fine. I'm fine. Everything. And if not, I'll figure it out.

As I haul gear off the dock, the masked man with the Starbucks cup gives a nod and then steps back so I don't walk too close to him. Perhaps this is a new thing, a new mode of being social. Distancing. Polite nods. Taylor, perhaps, didn't get the memo.

In the parking lot, I hit unlock on the key fob and a gleaming black pearl BMW 735 hybrid sedan chirps back. The license does in fact say EH HEE. The inside is lush, sculpted and quilted.

I toss my bags into the backseat, adjust the driver's seat, and pair my phone to the car's automatic system. It says 360 miles of range and about when I'll need to stop next. I queue up the Cure's *Disintegration* on my phone, plug in the coordinates for Green Bay, and pull out of the marina.

What I don't expect is the shoes. I knew about the shoes from the webcams, from the social media feed, from everything, but it's more disconcerting to see them in person, drifts of them on corners, scattered shoes on sidewalks, missing their mates. I remember, improbably, the first shots of the sunken *Titanic* debris field, where scads of shoes rested on the ocean floor, each pointed and positioned in such a way that you couldn't help but imagine the body they'd once contained, invisible grave markers for flesh and bone long ago returned to nutrients and stardust.

Driving through Monterey, people look fine, drivers here and there, people in masks loading supplies and talking walks with strollers, swerving around piles of shoes. Asymptomatic, perhaps, or haven't gotten it yet. Or some of the lucky few who seem to be immune. I think about Taylor's phrase about the virus being visible in the air and turn on the recirculate option on the car's ventilation system. It says the HEPA filtration system is optimized, and the filter will need to be changed in 10,000 miles. There is a button to order new supplies automatically or in 5,000 miles.

Taylor? The sailboat and George Lucas pop back into clarity. Brian asked a person from his deep dark past to help. I remember the boat anecdote now, him complaining about Taylor squatting in his living room. That was so un-Brian to ask for help, to call in a favor, especially from someone he seemed to loathe. A blossom of warmth and tenderness, thinking back to how many times I might have brushed past Brian on the street without recognizing him, both in San Francisco and then later in the Fox Valley in Wisconsin. What a series of wasted opportunities. And for what exactly? For what? It seemed so silly now, these layers of protection. He cares about me. And he told Taylor about the rules of the e-lationship.

I need to see Brian. In person. I need to swallow fear and do it to thank him. Somehow, he knew what I needed without having to ask, knew someone had to break through the internet. Technically, once Liz showed up, I was saved, maybe even once Patty materialized. I wouldn't tell him.

The GPS takes me up the 101, toward San Jose, and when it gets closer to the city, it reroutes due to closures on the highway, beyond which there are National Guard trucks and blockades. I drive slowly through residential streets and see ample evidence of activity, certainly: garbage next to back doors, piled up high, showing the residents hadn't ventured much more than an outstretched hand out of the door; curtains drawn and, in some cases, front doors boarded over with rough plywood, upon which was spray-painted, "No looting. Owners have guns." In the distance, ambulance sirens, a few people shambling on the sidewalks, and I take care in case they veer onto the roads. Few are interested or concerned about the traffic. One woman passes in an SUV, wearing a surgical mask over her face and holding her phone up to her ear while driving. I honk the horn, worried she'll hit someone, but she flips the bird with her driving hand.

People who are still obviously ill loom on street corners, in doorways and under awnings. They are all sunburned and bedraggled. They look like the typical tech-boom socialites, wearing hand-loomed African prayer shawls as fashion statements, along with artisanal shoes and organic cotton T-shirts, $100 each. The kind that eschew the Gap for being corporate overlords but still shop at Whole Foods without question. I understand these types completely, their buying patterns, their click patterns, their reblogging and retweeting habits. After all, I'm their influencer.

Some of the shamblers wear similar hooded sweatshirts. In fact, many of them look like they shopped at the same store at the same moment—negating the clipped individual sameness that so many once curated within their personal brands. The women wear lavender, white, or pink hooded sweatshirts, while the men, regardless of ethnicity or other clothing, wear either navy-blue or bright-red hooded sweatshirts with Old Navy logos on them. Old Navy: The corporate sponsor of pandemics.

Ahead, a masked woman with "NOT INFECTED" scrawled on her back in black marker. She pushes a gardening cart, heaped with a pile of the same sweatshirts, bright blue, bright red, lavender, pink, and white. She coaxes the arms of a reluctant shambler into a large navy-blue hoodie. He isn't cooperating, pulls his arms up close to his chest, but she patiently guides one hand into a sleeve and then edges the jacket up behind him, her eyebrows knitting together and her mask moving as she talks to the man.

She glances up at me, paused at the stop sign, and puts a finger to her masked mouth, in a shhhhhhh movement. I wave and she nods back, zipping up the shambler with the detached maternal affect of a mother sending her toddler off on the playground. Finished, she moves on to the next person—a woman—and digs through the lighter-colored sweatshirts, her back to me.

I drive on, in the luxury automobile owned by a man I met that morning. Because Brian said I am trustworthy and need help.

After hours of driving, I rest at an observation point. It's nearly 3 a.m., although my cell phone thinks it's almost 4 a.m. and I'm not sure which time is right. After so many weeks not aware of time, it feels unimportant. My aching eyes are boss now.

Other cars do the same. I'll need gas and water tomorrow, but for now, I'm set.

*I will stay safe.* This voice repeats in my head to ward off evil.

I move Taylor's briefcase out of the backseat and pop the trunk, where I find a Tyvek suit and a respirator, along with many boxes of latex-free gloves. Taylor was prepped. The suit looks too small, but it could do if I don't close it over the boobs.

But maybe I'm infected too. I might be. I don't know.

I'll wear it for Brian, too, in case I'm one of the asymptomatic people, in case Rick and Pedro were infected. More and more I've convinced myself they weren't, that they had spiraled against each other, fueled by the knowledge of extinction events, of herd immunity, of their religion built around saving the species instead of the individual.

I slam the trunk closed, and dozens of alarmed faces pop up from the parked cars in the observation area. The car closest rolls down the driver window. "Hey, are you alone? Are you OK?" its driver asks. "We're here until 5 a.m., but I'm staying up while my wife sleeps, so I'll keep an eye open for you until we leave."

"OK, thank you," I say. "Do you guys have enough food and water?"

"Yeah, we're good. Thanks. Make sure you lock yourself in, though." The window rolls back up, and from behind it, he shows a handgun and then gives a thumbs-up sign. I hop into the backseat of Taylor's BMW and put up the sunshade along the driver's side. After pulling out my sweatshirt and jacket, I throw the gear bags into the front seat and position them like a person who might be sleeping there, then I drape another jacket over them, placing my sorority baseball cap on the top. It still has four splotches of seagull shit from the island. I think of Kylie, of Liz, of Patty. Heidi. Brian.

Wrapped in the embrace of Taylor's leather backseat, I cry and cry and cry.

In the morning, I pull into a closed truck stop and look around. The gas pumps seem viable, but I'll need more water and, quite frankly, a bathroom. The truck stop is dark, and the convenience store mostly empty of snacks. A few random things are still there—a package of Cheez-Its, a few lower-tier candy bars like Bit O'Honey and Toffifays, a bottle of Windex. The bathrooms are unlocked, but they are disgusting and the triple-blind corners make me nervous—one exit and no windows. All someone would have to do is come into the room and turn off the light and it would be all over. Instead, I kick down the toilet dispenser and grab an industrial roll of toilet paper, tucking it around my wrist like an enormous bracelet, then go behind a bush.

The highway stretches into one long gray ribbon. The billboards are a one-sided conversation about God, abortion, Election Day, and fried chicken. Driving through one area of Nebraska, I listen to a radio station host expound for hours on his theories about human vivisections and how the shamblers are all Lazarus called from the dead.

As though Christ had such an awful sense of humor.

Further east, the air gets colder, the sun more diffused. It's November, apparently? I should know that. After the sun ducks down behind some Iowa cornfields, the car's instrument panel informs it's 41 degrees Fahrenheit outside and 68 degrees inside. That night, another scenic rest stop, this one far less scenic. I join another throng of minivans and SUVs toting children. Many are single mothers in the front seat, popping straws into bags of Capri-Sun and handing them back while scanning the parking lot. I turn on the seat heater and pile everything on top of me, arranging the luggage in the passenger seat this time.

A mother in the Dodge minivan watches my preparation and doesn't nod or even react when I meet her gaze. None of the cars are running, although occasionally one starts up and runs long enough to prevent the batteries from going dead.

I set the security system, which displays an ongoing video of the area around the car. I assume this isn't draining the battery somehow, but I'm also not entirely sure how hybrids work. Even if I wanted to shut it off, I have no idea how. Having the constant visual of the area is comforting.

I tuck my head into a sweatshirt turned pillow and sleep. It feels safe. It feels like dreaming. Sometime in the night, the car's proximity sensor chirps and I open my eyes—the young boy from the SUV across the field has gotten too close to the front bumper while he pees a long fragile stream into the weeds at the edge of the parking lot, trying to knock each one down. I have one more day, a long haul but I can do it.

I push through the miles. The final stretch feels long and tiresome, Nebraska, Iowa, the Driftless Region, until finally signs count down the miles to Green Bay.

When did I become so afraid of death? I was never afraid of dying before. Now, I'm not even afraid. It's more about losing control, about having an unseemly and undignified end. Now, hell has come and gone.

Maybe I've beaten some crazy-ass bug and maybe it means something.

Nah. Like the dinosaurs, it means nothing. It is the illusion of continuity. Millennia of nothing changing and then an asteroid hit, and the next day, 99.99 percent of life on the planet was wiped out. No more, no less, the cold, unseeing eye of Mother Nature passing over without taking notice.

My phone chirps. A voicemail. I'd forgotten my phone was a phone, after so many days of nothing on the island. It's full, a cascade of voicemails. Aunt Heidi. My old college roommate. Patrick, now married, checking in to see if I need anything, saying there's room in his loft in SoMa, a pullout couch. Clients asking for new guest posts about the quarantine, one looking for a series of videos on cooking from the pantry. The amount of money she mentions is astounding, and then she adds it's just a starting point.

Then a deep baritone voice fills the car's perfectly modulated sound system.

"Hey, blogger girl, you took off before I could say bye. This is Patty—from the island. Sorry, I wanted to say sorry. Sorry I left you to deal with everything. I thought Pedro and Rick—I thought they'd—Pedro and Rick would've . . . and I wanted to know if you'll be around on the mainland. They've got to monitor me a bit more for the H3N2 thing, but things are looking good. I've been thinking about you and how you're doing. I'd like to talk a bit more, maybe get some coffee or something. Stay safe, little puppy, and call me when you have a moment." Patty gives a number and is gone.

I play it again. "Hey, blogger girl," he says. "You took off before I could say . . ."

Me. I'm blogger girl.

Patty. Instantly I'm back on the island, tethered to his gig, hanging off the shoreline while he holds me taut, in flight. I play it a third time, listening to the inflection of his voice, the way it feels bare when he says "I've been thinking about you," and there's a tiny hiccup in his voice when he says "thinking."

I dial the number. It goes to voicemail.

"Hello, this is Dr. Patagonia Brixton. From September fourteenth until November twenty-ninth, I'll be in the field studying songbird migration on the Southeast Farallon Island State Marine Reserve with limited access to a landline. You'll have better luck emailing me at pattybirbman@resources.ca.gov," then a beep.

I had planned on saying "Hey there, bird guy," but instead I blurt into the recording, "Patagonia? Your actual name is Patagonia? That is . . . that is the coolest name I never expected, and you know what? It's perfect. It's perfect, bird man. This is Jane, the blogger. Call me back. Tag, you're it, Patagonia."

And then I let go of the island and that moment.

The island will be there for me. It was real. Patty is real.

I drive east into the bright yellow of what could be a gorgeous late autumn day.

I wonder what Brian is doing.

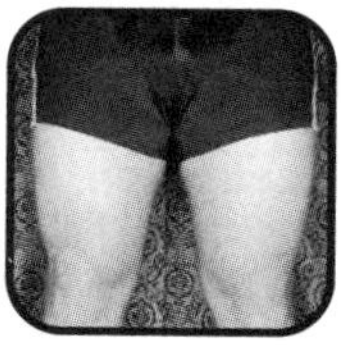

**JeSsBieU**
**@Jessbieu**

Being a part of history kind of sucks tbh.

♡ 45 💬 2 ⟳ 15

**Wolf News WNBS** ✓
**@WNBSNews**

Roseanne Barr: "Americans used to come together in times of crisis"
http://www.bit.ly.com/roseannbarr

♡ 4.2K 💬 5.8K ⟳ 661

# Day 38

## Brian

Sometimes my mother was still alive and then other times I wasn't in Chicago anymore. I dreamed I was back in the loft. On my feet were mismatched shoes. The windows were open, and snowflakes had piled up on the sills. It was freezing. I should shut the window.

Across the room, the TV flickered. It was an old episode of *The Courtship of Eddie's Father*. The show had depressed me as a child—why did that whiny little bastard get a dad, nay, *a best friend* as the song liked to remind me—while my own flesh and blood couldn't be fucked to stick around? Even the theme song gave me an icky feeling, a sense of shame. Where was my father now? What if he was out there, struggling with illness? I looked at the door—in dreams, you think of someone and they appear. The door didn't open—no father appeared. Would he be older? Would he be exactly as I had remembered him when he left, the day I couldn't recall? I could only recall the crying, the emptiness in the house, the quiet from no one shouting.

It was cold in the room. The window was open. Snow was filtering onto the floor, gently. The wind brushed the pull cord on the blinds. I rose and shut the window, but it was still cold. It would take some time to warm up the room.

I called out "Jane!" and then opened my eyes, expecting her to pop up in the dream. She was going to make soup, I seemed to think, before I went to sleep, before I drifted off. The wind blew through, rattling the blinds. I flipped the channel. I hated this show. Somewhere in the building, a door opened and closed. So, this is the dream—haunted building. Perhaps a zombie dead father. Dead Bob. Dead mother. Or dead Jane? I settled into the uncomfortable tertiary chair by the wall and waited to see who would walk through the door. I drifted off again, distracting myself. What kinds of sharks were in the water? I could remember at one time. Gummy sharks, I thought to myself. Always seemed like a good idea, except they never were. Were gummy sharks a real type of shark? A play on words I wasn't clever enough to understand.

It was still cold. The snow on the polished cement acid-washed floor looked like sifted sugar on a plate. I lowered myself down and crawled over to the snow sifting down. With my finger I drew my name, my pottery insignia. The snow was cold. I scooped some up and pushed it into my mouth, letting it melt down my throat. I was thirsty. I should go get some more snow. It smelled of winter in the apartment. The wind banged the blind against the open window. I shouldn't have touched the snow because now my hands were cold. I reached down and pulled off my socks and then stuck my hands into the socks. Better.

## Day 40

**Wolf News WNBS**
**@WNBSNews**

Scientists see correlations between gingivitis and nail biting and nSFI http://www.bit.ly.com/bloodnsfi

♡ 167K  💬 6.8K  ⟳ 84.1K

**Mychelle**
**@MightyMych**

If you had a voodoo doll of yourself, could you give yourself a good back rub? #singlegirlprobs

♡ 3  💬 2  ⟳ 0

**DB Cooper**
**@DBmm**

All I do is cook and disinfect now. That's it. That's the tweet.

♡ 7  💬 0  ⟳ 0

# Day 42

JANE

One of the many voicemails is from Aunt Heidi, who has been admitted and then released from the hospital to finish recovering at home. She's still contagious, but the hospital needed beds and oxygen tanks for more critical patients. Technically quarantined, but in good spirits and complaining about the lack of good TV during the daytime.

At the local grocery store, I find a few of Heidi's favorite sodas, six cans of tomato soup, a few frozen pizzas, and an entire bouquet of gossip tabloids.

It feels weird to see the same streets I left a handful of weeks previous.

Things are different now. It feels like an invisible snowstorm, everyone buttoned up inside, no one outside. Many front doors have quarantine signs, handmade, some with bright poster board, some written on scraps of paper. Our door has a sign too, written in Aunt Heidi's uphill script.

I haul the groceries up to the porch, knock on the door, and then scurry back to Taylor's car. Heidi pops out, looking disheveled and a little tired, but she waves brightly when she sees me. I wave back and smile. I've missed her face. Tears well in my eyes. She pulls the stuff inside and then waves again, then closes the door. Her quarantine sign has a cat smiley face on it.

I pull down the street and stop around the corner, and then, for the first time ever, I dial Brian.

This is it. The universe has finally provided me with the irrefutable reason to break the membrane of virtual connection.

His number rings. And rings. And rings.

He's always been thirty miles away from my little square room inside Aunt Heidi's house. That fact seems insulting. I've had his number for ages. I try again. Nothing still. He might be up in his studio—he once mentioned he resists bringing the phone up there with him. Why has he been silent? Maybe he's sleeping. I just drive to his address, redialing occasionally.

Highway 41 is clear of traffic—one state trooper pulled over, but otherwise freedom.

I could now consider this moment as a luxury. The world is my oyster.

I'm back home and everyone is safe. We all need to weather the cold months of winter inside, tucked away from each other, nothing more than usual for a northern climate. I can revisit my counted cross-stitch projects, abandoned somewhere in the closet. I'll read the great works, read all the Brontës once and for all.

Maybe Brian and I can do another book club together.

It takes a little over thirty-five minutes, door to door. There at the door, at Brian's door (BRIAN!), a jumbled pile of heavy boxes. Clay delivery, randomly tossed on either side of the doorway.

That feels odd. Very unlike Brian.

This is a bad feeling.

I try his phone line again. It rings and rings and bumps to his voicemail.

Reluctant to leave the cushy warm seat of Taylor's car, I PM him on our e-lationship chat.

JANEWITHAWHY: Guess where I am right now.

The little dots pop up; he is typing.

OTTERYRIDE: On an island?

I let out my breath and unclench my shoulders.

JANEWITHAWHY: Oh, so you're there?
OTTERYRIDE: I'm here. Sry, I'm sick.
JANEWITHAWHY: You're sick? Like . . . sick?
OTTERYRIDE: Prob the thing. Hypnogogic thing. The one w the most death and agony.
JANEWITHAWHY: Shit. Did you get tested?
OTTERYRIDE: No I'm spr delus, so either way the prob solves itself in a few weeks, rt?
JANEWITHAWHY: Thank you, Mister High Hopes
OTTERYRIDE: here to serve. How's island?

JaneWithAWhy: That's a funny story.

OtteryRide: I cant wait

JaneWithAWhy: Do you know a guy named Taylor?

OtteryRide: I knw many people named Taylor, varying genders, but we all know, gnder is a spectrum . . . so is being named Taylr.

JaneWithAWhy: This is a male-presenting person who also is named Taylor. Has a boat.

OtteryRide: am i being set up right now? Ill decline to answer. Ur not on island anymore?

JaneWithAWhy: I'm not on that island anymore.

OtteryRide: Well done, Wonder Woman. Onto your next adventure glad Taylor pulled through. I didn't think he wld.

JaneWithAWhy: He had a lot of amazing things to say about you.

OtteryRide: ?? prbly trying to get into uir pants.

JaneWithAWhy: I don't think so.

JaneWithAWhy: He's in recovery and he credits you for his life turnaround in this kind of reverse way.

OtteryRide: Huh.

JaneWithAWhy: You should see this boat, Brian. It gleams.

JaneWithAWhy: He sank a ton of money into it.

JaneWithAWhy: Apparently, he made a lot of money designing a bunch of mobile app games for kids.

OtteryRide: Googling.

JaneWithAWhy: I did look him up. He's one of those tech unicorns, sold big before the last crash.

OtteryRide: Damn it. That guy still owes me 10K.

JaneWithAWhy: I'm sure you'll get it back. This car has to be over 100 grand alone. It's only 18K miles.

JaneWithAWhy: It has a security video system. It's like a nightclub in here.

OtteryRide: Sounds like Taylor. Sry, I cn't stop laughing

JaneWithAWhy: I have a video of him giving you a message. He sounds like he's learned a lot and you're his Yoda.

JaneWithAWhy: Hey, have you taken a walk lately?

JaneWithAWhy: Maybe you'd feel better if you took a walk?

OtteryRide: And waste this amazing body odor I've built up?

JaneWithAWhy: I'll walk with you.

OTTERYRIDE: I cant thumb type while walking. no, I'm comfortable right here on my sofa. The light hurts my eyes outside. It started raining.

JANEWITHAWHY: Oh? Is it raining?

OTTERYRIDE: Yes, thunder and lightning.

JANEWITHAWHY: I'm sitting in your parking lot, Brian.

OTTERYRIDE: You?

JANEWITHAWHY: I am. I'm sitting here looking at your front door and your clay. It's not raining. It's sunny and crisp, a beautiful day.

I wait. No dots.

JANEWITHAWHY: Brian?

Finally, he types.

OTTERYRIDE: You broke the rules of our e-lationship.

JANEWITHAWHY: I gather there was a phone call. With you and Taylor.

OTTERYRIDE: I talk to lots of people It's foggy. possible I guess.

JANEWITHAWHY: If you recall, those were exactly the rules of our e-lationship—it had to be natural, an accident. Technically this isn't an accident—you sent Taylor, but it feels like the universe saying it was time.

JANEWITHAWHY: And it's not like you asked me to come to your loft and it's not like I wanted to swing by to say hi.

JANEWITHAWHY: He wants me to give you his car to hold for him until he comes to get it.

JANEWITHAWHY: It's swanky.

OTTERYRIDE: Taylor? That doesn't check out.

JANEWITHAWHY: He said he owes you a visit and he'll pick it up in spring, but I guess it's yours for now.

OTTERYRIDE: Keep it. Drive back to Green Bay. Or New York, isn't that where you're supposed to be next?

JANEWITHAWHY: That is postponed, like everything.

JANEWITHAWHY: Brian. Are you seriously going to be this much of a stickler about this stupid e-lationship thing?

JANEWITHAWHY: Come on, I won't bite.

JANEWITHAWHY: And if you're worried about me being contagious, I have a biohazard suit! I used it whenever I had to get out of the car. I'll stay six feet away. You'll be fine.

The dots appear and stop. Dots again, then stop. I count to sixty. Then two hundred. Then, almost at five hundred, the dots start again.

OTTERYRIDE: Jane, I'm not in the loft.
JANEWITHAWHY: Where are you?
OTTERYRIDE: I'm at the hospital, in the H3N2/nSFI quarantine. I mean, there's a chance, but it's pretty grim.
JANEWITHAWHY: Oh Brian.

Tears well up in my eyes. The bad feeling I had clears its throat and rings a little bell. I knew all this even though I didn't know all this. This is how it has always been. *Remember this.*

OTTERYRIDE: But look on the bright side, Ms. Ballsack. Think of the blog hits you're going to get off of this one.
JANEWITHAWHY: Which hospital
OTTERYRIDE: I can't have visitors
JANEWITHAWHY: Which one
OTTERYRIDE: St. Elizabeth's
JANEWITHAWHY: I'm coming
OTTERYRIDE: Dont
JANEWITHAWHY: Why
OTTERYRIDE: They won't let you in not worth the risk. quite a few of us in here thr's like a sane person group n then the people in dementia then another group 4 the people who stop talking and moving. Thyre quiet though its nice. Were across the hall from thm
JANEWITHAWHY: Oh Brian. You're making this all up.
OTTERYRIDE: I wish
JANEWITHAWHY: I'll be there soon
OTTERYRIDE: Why would you do that
JANEWITHAWHY: you would for me.
OTTERYRIDE: It's no good they won't let you in
JANEWITHAWHY: I'll sit in the visitor's lounge and talk to you.
OTTERYRIDE: I can't hear or even see visitors lnge

JaneWithAWhy: You are hearing me right now

OtteryRide: S ur going to sit in visitors lung of shoddy Catholic hspital n IM me frm across the hall?

JaneWithAWhy: You catch on quickly despite a broken brain.

OtteryRide: Touché

JaneWithAWhy: I can't believe after all this time I'm still not going to see the inside of your loft.

OtteryRide: Wait you may still get a chance yet Its not like I hv any heirs

JaneWithAWhy: I'm crying. You bastard, you fucking made me cry.

OtteryRide: I'm crying too promise me smthing

JaneWithAWhy: Anything.

OtteryRide: If you start noticing me getting wrd, tell the doctors Ill tell them ur here for me, ur my person. they can do sedation then—thts what i want bt they wont do it w/o a person who signs some forms and stuff legal shit

JaneWithAWhy: After all this time you tell me I'm your person and then you make me promise to put you into a coma?

OtteryRide: I'd do it for u n bfore they do promise me ull make one glrious last grnd jesture.

JaneWithAWhy: One grand gesture, at your service. What is it?

OtteryRide: Yell at the top of your lungs Ball sck Loud enough I cn here it so t I know its u and ure still there

JaneWithAWhy: You're the worst.

OtteryRide: Promise me ball sack

JaneWithAWhy: I'm starting the car. GPS says it's 11 minutes away.

OtteryRide: I'm not going anywhre they wn't let me

OtteryRide: So you know where I'll be.

OtteryRide: Kp passin open windows

# Day 163

If these pandemics have shown me anything, Dear Reader, it's that our sense of who we are as people is constantly evolving. My own personal mantra for life—crafted in the early days of the tech boom when I had to deal with translating coder language to marketing speak, and then translate user needs back to the ~~human automatons that tend to be fixated on pedantry at the expense of relationships and social norms~~ coders and quality check folks—used to be: "People do what works."

People do what works. That is shorthand for "People will do the thing that achieves what they need to achieve with the least amount of effort or pain."

It helped me understand the behavior of people who frustrated me. It helped me understand my own counterintuitive and often frustrating behavior. And before you rush to leave a comment that I'm not any of these self-deprecating things, hush. I am. Dear Reader, I know you have always been patient with me, more patient than I am with myself. I don't and have never deserved you.

We saw the concept of "People do what works" a lot during the early days of the war against the viruses. From the people hoarding soap and toilet paper and Pop-Tarts to the people buying up all the ammunition to the people using the crises as an excuse to live out their most violent misanthropic fantasies while still feeling like they're making the world a better place. We even saw it from the people who were infected and committed suicide in considerate ways—the people who jumped off bridges, or that entire church in Florida. They lost hope they would get better, but they all took care to prevent infection after their death for the people who had to deal with the aftermath.

It's a basic tenet, but it sums up human motivations succinctly. People do what works. The implication here is, if you want to motivate someone to do something, you must make the thing more appealing than the other thing that's easier or more satisfying, usually through reward or punishment or modifying the actual task to make it easier than the alternative. For example, if you want to prevent people from running stop signs, it's not enough to have a law saying "Don't run stop signs ~~you fucking selfish asshole~~" because for most ~~selfish assholes~~ people, the reward of running a stop sign is better than the ~~zero~~ slight sense of guilt for breaking the law. Instead, you have to put punishment into the equation—whether there's a chance an unmarked police car is around or that traffic cameras will catch you, and then also there's a fine and legal implications. You need to add the risk of a $400 traffic ticket to offset the ~~inclination to be a selfish asshole~~ tiny reward of running the stop sign—now the seven seconds or so it takes to slow down and stop seems like a good economical decision and breaking the law is less appealing ~~even for selfish assholes~~.

People do what works.

I have been ~~a selfish asshole~~ doing what worked. Until it didn't.

I've mentioned him so many times on this website. My good friend Brian Arden. My best friend Brian Arden. Brian and I have had a good and real and true friendship for more than a decade now, and one of the rules we maintained was it was only textual. No, that's not a typo—we only communicated through email, chat, and text messages.

Why? I don't know.

Now it seems so stupid.

~~It was so fucking stupid.~~

I don't know why it worked, but it really really worked, Dear Reader. I'm selfish and I didn't want to risk what we had. It was so beautiful, perfect, and amazing, a secret stash of riches to swim in in the way Scrooge McDuck swims in his vault of gold coins. His emails and chats were my own private Fort Knox of delight.

He saved me when I was stuck on SEFI in the early days of the outbreaks, during the first wave. He sent ~~Taylor Hummel—yes THAT GUY one of the Forbes 40 Under 40 Tech Tycoons, inventor of Sail Lyfe, Boat Lyfe, All Lyfe apps, the guy who did that viral Ted Talk~~ such a caring and thoughtful person to pick me up on his yacht. Brian called Taylor while he was waiting for the ambulance. His nurse told me later he had on a Tyvek suit and a ventilator when the ambulance got there. He was so nervous about contaminating them that he waited for them outside on the cold ground, shivering.

We've all lost our people in this thing. We're feeling all the feelings. The death counts seem meaningless. As of this morning, more than fifty-one million people have left us, a sixth of the US population, each of them beautiful and important, each with dreams and their people. It's impossible to believe. We've all seen the semitrailers; we've all seen the mass cremation piles. And then there's the millions with post-viral encephalitis syndromes.

Like Aunt Heidi, Brian has other complications. Unlike my aunt, he's got many challenges. Even before this happened, he would have reminded me, he was so broken. As are we all. Each one of us.

But he's still in there. Aunt Heidi understands him better than I do. He can type on a tablet, and he's working clay balls to increase his hand-eye coordination. He'll get better. We have faith. His neurologist told us to be prepared that he may never regain his speech, but he can type once he gets more control of his fingers. It uses a different part of the brain. On hearing that, Brian had nodded enthusiastically and made a happy sound. It reminded me of the email where he said he hated small talk and preferred email anyway.

People do what works.

Aunt Heidi, conveniently, is his live-in nurse and physical therapist. Thankfully Brian has incredible medical insurance and long-term disability insurance that's covering all of it. Who would have thought that the highest-paying career would be nursing? At least the baby boomers left us something after they absconded this mortal coil—a glut of nurses out of work, just in time for a mass debilitation event that ensured job security for the rest of their lives. The universe abhors a vacuum.

The thing about being broken is this: It doesn't have a demographic. It doesn't make any fucking sense. It is. Like a kidney stone or a torn Achilles tendon or a brain that doesn't let you fall asleep anymore until that's all you think about and all you tell yourself. This new world order has sent us all into our safe places and it's slightly smarter than us because it knows our weaknesses and it knows exactly how to hit us where it hurts. Right in our sad lonely heads. It's easier to avoid talking about it or going outside or connecting in person because it's less scary and it's safer and people do what works.

People do what works.

My Gentleman Caller, as it turns out, has made a point of taking a six-month assignment here to study Midwestern herons and egrets. When I questioned him about it, about the longevity of his intentions with us, me and him, he shrugged and chucked me under the chin and said, "Tag, you're it." He, more than me, knows exactly what it takes to recover. He's lucky to not have any lingering effects from his own infection. He helped us bring Brian home from the hospital, back to Brian's loft. Now Brian can gaze out at the river and sometimes make pinch pots when he's feeling up to it. Birb Guy and Brian hang out together sometimes, quietly. Brian seems to like him too. It's hard not to like Birb Guy. He knows how to exist among the fragile.

While in the hospital, Brian designated me as his guardian ad litem. Between that and Heidi living as his caregiver, we all hang out at Brian's most of the time. It's a handy home base for Birb Guy because there are so many water birds for him to study, right out the door. And it's nice to be close together. We all have meals together, like relatives who have always known each other.

That's what we've become. A kind of family. I have developed a new mantra since the pandemics changed everything: Kindness is never wasted.

We need to take big risks. We need to be vulnerable. We need to live knowing that this morning might have been the last moment we had a moment of sleep because the alternative is we are never actually awake. And if something bad happens? Something bad happens. But at the end of everything, something bad always happens, so wouldn't it have been better to know you were kind? To know you never wasted a moment to share a friendship with a connected heart? To know you went after lost causes because it was never a lost cause, we're all lost until we're not.

We're all in this together, friends, and life is so incredibly short even without a pandemic trying to replicate over and over. This is our new normal. Every face-to-face encounter is a risk. We might catch something. We might get hurt. We might have to rely on the kindness of almost-strangers. We've got to figure out how to do what works. Because kindness is never wasted.

In Brian's studio, there are currently seventy-eight bone china vases, all in varying shades of pink. I brought one to him and asked, are they for an order? *No*, he typed out on his tablet, *for Jane. Not pink enough yet. Will keep passing the open windows until it's right.*

For me.

I thought he was selfish in not making me the Barbie-pink vase I requested, but he was trying to get the glaze just so. It looks like a sunrise.

Each of them is as empty as my broken heart. When I pick one up and hold it against my chest, pressing its heavy hollow form against my sternum, the vessel is warm, and faintly, I hear my own heart beating in return.

Xoxo,
Jane

**DB Cooper**
**@DBmm**

Asked funeral director for Wi-Fi password. He looked pained for a moment behind his mask and then literally said "um . . . try Death1." I gawked at him and he said, "Capital D in death, then the number one." If you put that in a movie, someone would say you made it up. I did not make that up. Will he be offended if that's my Google review title of this funeral home? Capital D in death!

♡ 9.1K 💬 288 🔁 65

**Go To Sleep**
**@Insomnia**

Another one from the Germans: Kummerspeck! Describes emotional eating/weight gain, but its literal translation is "grief bacon." GRIEF BACON!

♡ 54.1K 💬 32 🔁 1.8K

**Julie Mons**
**@monsjul**

On this special day of remembrance, let us all have a moment of silence for all the people still wearing Crocs. #forthecure #yesallcrocs

♡ 987 💬 24 🔁 84

**Cosmoballiton**
**@CosmoNoFilter**

I will never be able to cope with artificial intelligence. My robot vacuum floats around cluelessly with a Post-it note stuck to it and I'm so ashamed for it. It probably looks at my wheelchair and is ashamed that I'm not also vacuuming while flailing my way through the loft to empty my cath bag.

♡ 685 💬 45 ⟳ 15

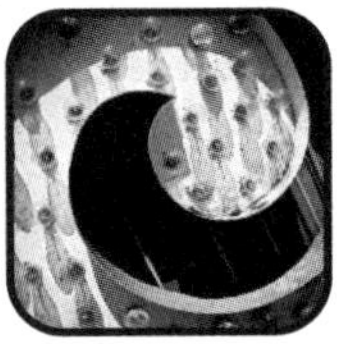

**Jane**
**@erejane**

is thinking about throwing her laptop out the window into a snowbank. Stupid supply chain. Stupid viruses. Stupid future. But my Gentleman Caller would go get it because electronic waste is terrible for the environment, and then he'd figure out a way to make it work. No one tells you that relationships make it difficult to have a bad day.

♡ 13.3K 💬 17 ⟳ 45

# Day 258

JANE

Patty kicks off his boots outside the door, nodding to Aunt Heidi and Brian, who are deep into their lunch ritual, Brian with his PICC line and tablet, Aunt Heidi with her avocado toast, logic puzzle, and a cup of Diet Coke.

"When you're ready, down to the studio?" Patty says to Brian. Brian squinches his face and makes a negative sound, then motions to a waxy ball of clay sitting in a Tupperware bowl, covered with a sheet of plastic.

Heidi shakes her head. "You must have your artist time too. I'm fine down there, I have my book and my chair by the window." Brian rolls his eyes at her and blushes. He may be unable to talk, but he's still working on being reliant on her. They have an interesting relationship—before this, I had rarely seen Heidi in nurse mode, the efficient way she moves through spaces, chucking tubes out of the way with a woosh of her hip, hefting a man half again her size out of his chair. She's so respectful of Brian's privacy and dignity, holding up sheets like curtains, showing him how to hold a spoon in his stiff grasp while talking about something benign and maybe almost flirty? As fucked-up as it seems, Heidi needs someone to need her, and Brian needs someone who can manage it without feeling like he's a chore or a child.

"Let me know," Patty says to Brian, and Brian nods. They have an interesting friendship, too—Patty's natural reticence and Brian's aphasia work well together in a way that my instinct to fill the silence with explanations and summaries and inanities does not.

Patty pads over to me. He is the only person who could walk silently over the creaky century-old floorboards. How someone that large could be so light-footed makes him seem magical.

"You should have been a dancer," I say, peering over my laptop.

He leans over and whispers into my ear, "You've said. I think you want to see my legs in tights?" I blush and peek at Heidi and Brian, who either haven't heard or are pretending not to.

Patty sits next to me on Brian's down-filled sofa, sinking his weight into the cushions. He picks up his bird journal and flips it open, pulling a short pencil out of his pocket.

It's the same pencil I used when helping him log birds on the Farallones, so many months ago. "You kept it?" I say.

He stops and looks at it, then at me, a shiver of a smile in the corner of his mouth. "Of course. That was the day I met my personal unicorn."

*Get a room you too*, a notification from Brian pops up into my chat window. I peer over at him and he gives me a sarcastic *kiss kiss* face, then sticks out his tongue.

I reach for Patty's large hand and he takes mine and gives it a squeeze.

*Remember this.*

# *Acknowledgments*

It's nearly impossible and very daunting to recognize everyone who contributes to the undertaking of a novel. This novel was inspired by a shark cage diving trip on the coast of the Farallon Islands in fall 2008. It took about ten years to complete, and I finished writing in the fall of 2019. I wrote and rewrote it probably four times, changing points of view, removing entire subplots due to length (Brian originally had a very acerbic art agent and was poised to take over care of her dog Moribund when she came down with the illness), consulting with several doctors on prion diseases, researching heavily the ways that pandemics spread, going deep into the annals of the 1918 Spanish flu pandemic (and the lesser-known 1968 influenza A pandemic), and spending hundreds of hours researching the history and geography of the Farallon Islands, which have their own history of contagions and grief. We all know what happened in the spring of 2020. That set back the publication of this novel until we all got our heads (mostly) around what was happening. Everyone who had read portions of this novel in advance decided that I could see the future. No, just the past.

Early readers of this novel (either in full or parts) include Michael Moore, Amy Fleming, Eric Fleming, Jake Kenny, Monique van den Berg, Molly Ann Magestro, June Schuchart, Maile Chapman, Doug Unger, Kelly Mays, S.L. Wilton, Kara Fortuna, Eileen Snider, Sarah Patrick, Mary Schreiner, M.A. Hurley, Alycia Calvert, Chelsi Hicks, Mary Kate DeJardin, Meghan Bonikowski, Adria Cruz Tabor, Sam Goodman, Robert Ren, Joe Milan Jr., Oscar Oswald, Lindsay Rhean Griffin, Tonya Todd, Ilanit Moskul, Amanda Skenandore, Oksana Marafioti, Alex Galt, Naomi Moes, Alexandra Murphy, Dayneé Alejandra Rosales, Flavia Stefani Resende, Dylan Fisher, Chantelle Mitchell, Susana Ferreira, Jordan Sutlive, Cody Gambino, Sara Tausenfreund, Z Wilson, Sam Smith, Carrieann Cahall, Al Hastings, Roy Johnson, Brian

Lin, Susan Joslyn, Megan Vos, Charlie Stephens, Alexander Chee, Wendy Mitzel, Catherine Niu, Rhoda Berlin, Sarah Fuchs, Gerardo Lamadrid Castillo, Randall Van Nostrand, Soni Brown, Michelle Sleater, Sara Stewart, Danielle Blue, Lisa Houlihan, and other people I'm definitely forgetting because long COVID brain fog, but know that I love you very much.

Writing is very much a lonely business, and it would be so sad without the support of so many amazing people. Writers are so amazing at lifting each other up and I must thank the wonderful Dan Chaon, Christina Clancy, Lori Rader-Day, Kate Harding, Jennette Fulda, Melissa Gorzelancyzk, Elizabeth McCracken, Margaret Atwood, Christopher Moore, Jean Thompson, Steve Almond, RL Stine, Robert Olen Butler, Kristen Arnett, Tayari Jones, Rebecca Makkai, Jane Hamilton, Maggie Ginsberg, Danez Smith, Eric Duran-Valle, Deesha Philyaw, Denise Sweet, Wendy McClure, Andrew Bourelle, Liam Callanan, Thomas Williams, Dave Housley, Joe Killiany, Patricia Skalka, Melissa Westemeier, and my beloved community of Wisconsin writers. In addition, I have received countless blessings in the form of Amy Mazzariello, Jessica Teague, Anne Stevens, Ellen Rosewall, Sarah Sudgen, Brian Simons, Kaitlin Clinnin, NPR's Doug Gordon, Tim Erwin, Peter Allen, Elizabeth Sachs, Beverly Rogers, John Hay, Karen Meisner, Doug Julien, Christine Stroud, Samantha Jacquest, Abigail Parins Reynolds, Linda House, Caide Jackson, Kellan Braddock, Kymm Zuckert, Fred Green, Steven Schuchart Sr, Kelley Quakelaar, Jess Krcmar (who took my author photos and is an enchanted princess with the camera), Melissa Kuypers, and you, gentle reader, who deserve additional praise for reading through this enormous paragraph of names.

Early forms of this novel contained images of friends who had given their permission to be used in the social media feed. Unfortunately, many of the illustrations were unsuitable due to the rigors of publishing (not to mention file size requirements), but my gratitude to Julie Blutstein, Suzy Pietras-Smith, Selilia Xi, John Texiera, Rachael Barry, and others previously mentioned for offering their photography. Thank you to Karen Meisner, who photographed Selilia Xi and replaced Selila's original photo she provided for this project before her death. Thanks, Selila and Karen; you're both the best.

And without a doubt, I'm most grateful to my ever-steady Gentleman Caller, Steven J. Schuchart Jr., who delivers hot coffee to my writing desk, keeps the dogs from being Velcro chaos demons, makes the most delicious chocolate chip cookies and fantastic ratatouille and other things he doesn't even like but makes them anyway, and drove me across the country and back on the *Entry Level* book tour when my long COVID ME/CFS prohibited air travel, and without whom this novel literally would not exist if he hadn't goaded me into starting it in 2009. Yes, dear reader, he used my own competitive nature against me and without it, I would never have had the faith and perseverance to unpick the snarls of this tangled story. My favorite person. Always. Forever.